P9-EFI-219

She's going to love him with every breath she takes, even if it was never meant to last....

PRAISE FOR
SILVER THAW

"Master storyteller Anderson has skillfully penned the heart-wrenching story of domestic abuse and its aftermath . . . compelling."   —*Booklist* (starred review)

"The stuff romances are made of."
—Heroes and Heartbreakers

"I'd recommend *Silver Thaw* to contemporary romance readers who like to go deep into a novel that explores many emotions."   —Harlequin Junkie

"I am totally hooked. . . . Thank you, Catherine Anderson, for this wonderful story."   —The Reading Cafe

"Romance veteran Anderson is a pro at making readers weep."   —*Publishers Weekly*

"Sweet and inspirational."   —Smitten by Books

"Mystic Creek was a close-knit, loving community that made you feel warmth and a giving human spirit . . . [a] heartwarming romance."   —The Reader's Den

"A good winter read in which love heals the worst wounds."
—The Romance Dish

"Heartwarming and heart-wrenching."
—Open Book Society

continued . . .

PRAISE FOR THE ROMANCES
OF CATHERINE ANDERSON

"Clever, emotional, and totally entertaining."
—Fresh Fiction

"Uplifting and emotionally riveting. . . . Get ready for one magically heartwarming experience!"
—*RT Book Reviews* (top pick)

"This is a story not to be missed . . . delivers on all levels and is a fantastic read that will touch readers at the very core of their being." —The Romance Readers Connection

"This smart, wholesome tale should appeal to any fan of traditional romance." —*Publishers Weekly*

"The kind of book that will snare you so completely, you'll not want to put it down. It engages the intellect and emotions; it'll make you care. It will also make you smile . . . a lot. And that's a guarantee." —Romance Reviews Today

"Readers may need to wipe away tears . . . since few will be able to resist the power of this beautifully emotional, wonderfully romantic love story." —*Booklist*

"Emotionally involving, family-centered, and relationship oriented, this story is a rewarding read."
—*Library Journal*

OTHER NOVELS BY CATHERINE ANDERSON

Mystic Creek Novels
Silver Thaw

"Harrigan Family" Novels
Morning Light
Star Bright
Here to Stay
Perfect Timing

Contemporary "Coulter Family" Novels
Phantom Waltz
Sweet Nothings
Blue Skies
Bright Eyes
My Sunshine
Sun Kissed and *Sun Kissed Bonus Book*

Historical "Coulter Family" Novels
Summer Breeze
Early Dawn
Lucky Penny

Historical "Valance Family" Novels
Walking on Air

The Comanche Series
Comanche Moon
Comanche Heart
Indigo Blue
Comanche Magic

Other Signet Books
Always in My Heart
Only by Your Touch
Coming Up Roses
Cheyenne Amber

NEW LEAF

A MYSTIC CREEK NOVEL

Catherine Anderson

A SIGNET BOOK

SIGNET
Published by New American Library,
an imprint of Penguin Random House LLC
375 Hudson Street, New York, New York 10014

This book is an original publication of New American Library.

First Printing, January 2016

Copyright © Adeline Catherine Anderson, 2016
Excerpt from *Silver Thaw* copyright © Adeline Catherine Anderson, 2015
Penguin Random House supports copyright. Copyright fuels creativity,
encourages diverse voices, promotes free speech, and creates a vibrant culture.
Thank you for buying an authorized edition of this book and for complying with
copyright laws by not reproducing, scanning, or distributing any part of it in any
form without permission. You are supporting writers and allowing
Penguin Random House to continue to publish books for every reader.

Signet and the Signet colophon are registered trademarks of
Penguin Random House LLC.

For more information about Penguin Random House, visit penguin.com.

ISBN 978-0-451-41835-7

Printed in the United States of America
10 9 8 7 6 5 4 3 2 1

PUBLISHER'S NOTE
This is a work of fiction. Names, characters, places, and incidents either are
the product of the author's imagination or are used fictitiously, and any resemblance
to actual persons, living or dead, business establishments, events, or locales
is entirely coincidental.

If you purchased this book without a cover you should be aware that this book is
stolen property. It was reported as "unsold and destroyed" to the publisher and neither
the author nor the publisher has received any payment for this "stripped book."

Penguin
Random
House

In Loving Memory
This book is dedicated to my husband,
Sid Anderson, the love of my life.

Chapter One

April 2015

The headlights of the county-owned crew-cab truck cut through drifting snowflakes to bathe quaint storefronts in flashes of gold as Barney Sterling circled the town center of Mystic Creek and then turned right onto East Main. Paul Kutz, better known as Pop, the proprietor of Antiquarian Books in the Mystic Creek Menagerie, had just called in a complaint about loud music keeping him and his new roommate, Ray Burke, awake. It wasn't yet nine, but Barney guessed that people on the high side of eighty went to bed early.

Reaching across the console, he crumpled the top of a white paper bag that held what remained of his night-shift meal, fresh from the ovens at the Jake 'n' Bake. He'd ordered three Italian panzarotti, small closed pizzas filled with tomato, mozzarella, and sausage. Now a dusting of confectioner's sugar clung to his fingers from the warm cream horns he'd been · about to devour for dessert. The interior of the cab smelled of vanilla filling, yeast bread, peppers, and cheese, with a touch of his Polo cologne underscoring the lot.

A woman's voice came over the radio. "You gotten there yet, Barney?"

Doreen, a plump redhead and newly hired dispatcher, hadn't memorized any police codes yet. Nearly everyone at the sheriff's department was willing to bet that she'd still be yacking over the airwaves in plain English come next Christmas. It had become a sore point with most of the officers. Doreen used the names of individuals in town, gave details about complaints over the air, and pretty much broke all the FCC regulations in every other way as well. Barney knew that the sheriff had been in a pinch for a new dispatcher when he hired Doreen, and the man had probably anticipated that she'd apply herself to learning how to do her job, but so far she just wasn't getting it.

In such a small town, certain informalities over the radio did occur, but Doreen carried informality to a whole new level. Anyone out there with a police scanner could listen and learn particulars about other townspeople that they had no business knowing.

"You'd better get your only bullet out of your pocket and load your weapon, Deputy," she said with a laugh. "This might get sticky. Kutz just called again, madder than a wet hen. He says that Taffeta Brown's music is turned up so loud that it's vibrating his walls clear across the street and Ray is about to go ballistic."

Barney didn't care for Doreen, partly because she didn't know much of anything about being a dispatcher and also because she kept a wad of bubble gum wedged between her teeth and cheek. But the biggest thing about her that ticked him off was that she wouldn't stop razzing him with Deputy Barney Fife jokes. He'd heard enough of those by the time he was on the force for only a week.

What was her deal? Barney disliked his first name, but it was the handle his mother, Kate, had given him, and he didn't want to hurt her feelings by changing it. Besides, it wasn't his mom's fault that he had gone into law enforcement and become a deputy. If he'd had any sense, he would have been Barnabas the dentist, or Barney the builder. Anything but a deputy.

Deciding to let Doreen's wisecracks pass, Barney asked, "Is the complainant certain it's the accused's music?"

"The *what* and the *what*?"

Barney bit down hard on his molars. "The complainant—the individual who called in the complaint. The person being complained about is the accused." He keyed his mike again to add, "It's difficult for me to believe that loud music is coming from the indicated location."

Barney had good reason to wonder if the information was accurate. Paul Kutz was deaf as a post, and Ms. Brown had never struck Barney as being the loud or rowdy type. In fact, he reflected, the woman hadn't made much of an impression at all. Ms. Brown had opened a health store on East Main nearly a year ago, and on the few occasions that Barney had gone in there, she'd defined the word *mousy*, both in demeanor and appearance. Not that Barney visited her shop often enough to have a clear memory of what she looked like. A vague image of drab clothing, dark hair, blue eyes, and an unremarkable face entered his mind. Maybe at night her wild side came out.

Doreen snapped her gum. The sound grated on his nerves like a fingernail scraping a blackboard. Enunciating carefully around the sticky mass, Doreen informed him, "Paul says he can see Taffeta Brown dancing in her apartment over the shop. So far as I know, his eyesight's still fine."

"You're not supposed to reveal too much information over the air, such as people's names or what they're doing."

"Well, how will you know who's doing what, then?"

Barney sighed. As far as he was concerned, Doreen's lack of knowledge about appropriate dispatching exchanges was the sheriff's problem to rectify. He wasn't about to spend his whole shift trying to teach her how to properly convey information over the radio.

On occasions like this, Barney wondered why he'd given up being a state policeman to become a small-town cop. His hometown was mostly crime free, and unless he maintained a keen sense of humor, keeping the peace could get downright boring. There were occasional incidents of domestic violence to keep him on his toes, and barroom brawls occurred once in a blue moon. Sometimes a group of teenagers would get up to no good, and they'd had a few burglaries last year. But overall, Barney spent more time climbing trees to rescue cats than he did enforcing the law.

Yesterday afternoon while cruising the streets, he had been over on Elderberry Lane trying to settle a quarrel between Christopher Doyle and Edna Slash, both older than Methuselah. The garbage company had just picked up the trash, and the two geriatrics had been nose-to-nose over their empty aluminum cans, arguing about whose was whose. When Barney pointed out that both containers were exactly alike, they'd started berating *him*.

He eased the county truck up to the curb in front of Paul Kutz's upstairs apartment. The old man had sold his house after his wife passed away and now lived above Creative Jewelry Designs, run by a young woman named Marjorie Brogan. Barney suspected Kutz's move had been prompted, at least in part, by the apartment's proximity to several local eateries. Paul wasn't exactly handy in the kitchen.

"Why didn't you just tell Pop to turn off his hearing aids?" Barney winced at the slip. Doreen could blab people's identities to the world if she wanted, but he didn't like doing it. Then he decided to hell with using codes since the damage was already done. "That'd be an instant fix, and I wouldn't have to slosh around in the snow for no good reason."

"Cranky, cranky. You there yet? Old Man Kutz is calling again. He probably hasn't had this much excitement since the last Veterans Day parade."

"Tell him to keep his shirt on. I'm here. Ten-four clear." Barney cut the truck engine and licked the sugar from his fingertips before reaching for his dark brown Stetson, which rode shotgun on the passenger seat beside him. Because of his height, he couldn't wear it inside the vehicle without crushing the crown. The smell of the cream horns still tickled his nose and titillated his taste buds. *Warm vanilla filling.* He would have loved to sink his teeth into the pastries before they grew cold. Fat chance of that. Communicating with Paul Kutz took forever because he could barely hear a word that was said to him.

A loud popping sound came over the radio as he pushed open the driver's door. He realized that the dispatcher was still on the channel. He grabbed the mike and clicked it several times to cause burps of static at her end so she would get her finger off the microphone button. "Dammit, Doreen. You can chew gum on the job and get away with it, but blowing bubbles over the airways may get you fired."

"Oops! Sorry," she said in a tone from which regret was successfully banished. "I thought you'd signed off. And I'm not blowing bubbles. That takes no skill at all. You have no clue how long I practiced before I learned how to snap my gum."

And he wanted to remain blissfully ignorant. "Ten-four clear. That means I'm finished talking, in case you don't know. And one other thing, Doreen. If you have your mike on, how in Hades do you think I can radio in if there's an emergency?"

"You said you were finished talking."

Barney squeezed his eyes shut and took a fortifying breath of icy air. "Never mind that. How is anyone supposed to radio in if you're attempting to eavesdrop?"

"I just wanted to listen for a minute. Maybe it'll get exciting!" she said with an eager chirp in her tone.

"You can't hear anything at my end until I turn my mike on."

I'm dealing with an imbecile, he thought, wondering if Sheriff Adams had hired Doreen when he was drunk. *Nah.* Blake seldom imbibed and never while on duty. Well, not normally, anyway.

Barney exited the vehicle and pushed the door closed with his hip. A few lights illuminated second-story living quarters along the street. The faint smell of fried chicken wafted to him on the breeze. The smell failed to entice him, partly because it was probably the main dish of a frozen dinner, which he hated, and also because he'd already eaten. All he wanted now was his dessert.

To his surprise, music did indeed thrum in the air, and when he glanced up, he saw a shadow dance playing out on Taffeta Brown's window curtains. He froze and then found he couldn't look away. His eyes widened. The sleek yet curvaceous silhouette of a woman gyrating her pelvis to the lively beat of "(I Can't Get No) Satisfaction" was an unexpected highlight of his evening. Watching slender hands slide provocatively over ample breasts and rotating hips might have given him an instant hard-on if snow hadn't been pelting him in the face. Come to think about it, the snow stinging his cheeks wasn't offering much competition to the tingling sensation that he felt in another location.

Shit. Barney clamped the Stetson on his head and strode across the icy street to reach the opposite parking curb where a glowing light post stood sentinel in a swirl of breeze-tossed snowflakes. No wonder Paul and Ray were in such a dither. What man this side of heaven could sleep when a performance like that was going on?

As Barney gained the sidewalk, he searched his memory again for a clear image of Taffeta, wondering if his male radar had malfunctioned the few times that he'd entered her shop. Normally when he came across a sexy woman, he at least noticed her. About all he really recalled about the Brown woman was that she seemed to blend into the woodwork.

He decided the oversight might be due to his habit of ignoring single local women. When Sheriff Adams retired, Barney intended to run for the office. He wouldn't get many men to vote for him if he hit on their female relatives.

Barney drew a flashlight from his belt and flicked it on. The beam reflected off the display window of Healthful Possibilities. He had to step close to see inside. His gaze landed first on a bottle of berries sporting a label that read LOSE WEIGHT FAST. A sign over a collection of boxed items promised FIVE SUPPLEMENTS TO CURE ERECTILE DYSFUNCTION. Barney blinked and read the advertisement again. He couldn't imagine any male in Mystic Creek, no matter how desperate, walking into Taffeta Brown's shop and having the nerve to take one of those boxes up to the cash register.

Darting his light beyond the pills, Barney peered into the bowels of the shop, which was closed for the night. With her music turned up so loud, Ms. Brown with the mind-blowing dance movements wouldn't hear him knock. She probably wouldn't hear him if he attacked her door with a chain saw.

Sighing, he left the window to play his light over the

clapboard siding near the door. When he saw a buzzer button, he pressed it with his thumb, hoping the sound would peal through the upstairs flat and get the lady's attention. If not, he could try pounding on the door, and if that failed, he carried a master key to all the businesses along Main in case of an emergency. Somehow he didn't think a woman dancing in the privacy of her own home qualified—unless her sexy shadow play sent Paul Kutz or his roommate into cardiac arrest. Barney grinned. It might. Men that old probably hadn't seen anything to equal this in over sixty years.

Actually, he realized, he had seldom seen anything to equal this, either, and he didn't exactly live like a monk. Being a small-town deputy complicated his love life. Gossip traveled through Mystic Creek faster than beer down a parched throat. Barney drove to nearby Crystal Falls when he got a hankering for female company. In civilian clothes, he could blend in with the crowd, have fun, and not worry about tarnishing his reputation. Or, God help him, having to endure scathing sidelong glances and a pungent comment or two from his mother if she ever heard of his exploits. Kate Sterling wasn't very broad-minded when it came to sex outside of marriage.

The frigid night air had already chilled Barney's hands, and as he tapped his knuckles against the wooden door, pain shot from the impact points to his elbow. The music upstairs continued to reverberate off the winter landscape. It wasn't over-the-top loud, but in the quiet of Mystic Creek on a weeknight, every note seemed invasive. Paul definitely had a legitimate noise complaint. Barney decided that he was down to his last resort, the master key.

He drew the large ring from his belt and fanned the pieces of metal. An instant later, he was inside the store. He used his flashlight to avoid tripping over obstacles. When he reached the old wooden stairs, he tromped up the risers, hoping Ms. Brown might finally hear him. He didn't want to scare the woman half to death.

No such luck. Now, instead of fried chicken, he smelled tomato soup and grilled cheese sandwiches, which once again spurred his memory of his canceled date with warm cream horns. It was a curse to have such a sensitive nose. His whole family teased him about his overdeveloped smeller, saying he could detect food at five hundred feet. Once on the creaky landing, he saw a glimmer of gold seeping out beneath the door. He hoped the sudden noise wouldn't frighten Ms. Brown when he knocked. Assuming she heard him at all, that is.

Taffeta was in the middle of a waking dream starring the handsome Mystic Creek deputy, Barney Sterling, as her male lead and dance partner. As silly as it was when she analyzed it, she had developed a huge crush on him the instant she first saw him. But it was an attraction she'd never act on. A relationship with a man, no matter how good-looking, wasn't on her present agenda.

She jumped with a start when a loud knock jolted

her back to reality. She clamped a hand over her heart. No way could she answer the door looking like this. It would blow her cover. And who was it, anyway, a polite burglar? Trying to twist her hair back into a knot and feeling as if she'd grown ten extra fingers, she started toward her bedroom to get her robe. Then she switched directions and hurried into the kitchen to find a skillet she could use to defend herself. Her shop was locked up tight. Whoever stood on her landing must have broken in.

Pulse pounding, she approached the door with the frying pan held high. "Who is it?" she called shakily.

A deep, masculine voice replied, "Deputy Sterling."

Taffeta blinked. Once. Twice. Coincidences like this didn't happen in real life. *"Who?"* she asked again.

"Ma'am, can you please turn your music down and open the door?"

It *was* him. She recognized the voice, an unforgettable, honeyed baritone that she'd heard only a few times. Taffeta ran over to the stereo and hit the OFF button. Panic buffeted her. *Oh God.* She was wearing makeup and very little else, only a dark blue satin chemise that ended well above her knees. Letting go of the skillet for a second, she twisted her hair into a tighter knot at the back of her head. The chain guard on the door was engaged. She could look out at him through the crack without him seeing anything but her face. Just in case it wasn't Barney Sterling, she snatched up the skillet. If whoever it was tried to shoulder his way in, she'd bean him.

Giving the knob a twist, she opened the door and

angled her body to peer out. The beam of a flash-light got her right in the eyes, and for a second, she went as blind as Helen Keller.

"Oops, sorry," he said. "It's pitch-dark out here."

Blinking away big white spots, Taffeta saw the beam go out, which left him standing in blackness except for the elongated rectangle of illumination coming from her apartment. She glimpsed a brown bomber jacket, a V of khaki shirt, part of a star-shaped badge, and a holstered gun riding his hip. Definitely it was the deputy. Only what had she done to bring a cop to her door? A shudder ripped through her body. According to the law, she'd already done plenty.

"Can you open up, Ms. Brown, and turn on the landing light so you can see me properly?"

Taffeta was far more concerned about him seeing her. "No! I'm not dressed for company."

"Can you grab a robe?"

Taffeta had a fleece robe in the bedroom, but in order to fetch it she'd have to cross the living area where he'd be able to see her. "Uh . . . no. Well, only if you turn your head."

She thought she heard him chuckle. "No problem."

She sprinted to the bedroom door, dived into the room, and pulled on her robe, tying the sash before she emerged. Then, trying her best to look calm and collected, she retraced her steps. *Why is he here? Did he run a background check on me?*

She disengaged the chain and opened the door for him. Then she flipped on the landing light. Barney Sterling had been in her shop three times and each occasion was indelibly etched into her gray matter.

He had come once to get vitamins for his mom, another time to buy ibuprofen for himself, and during the last visit, he'd purchased protein shake powder. Watching him stride up and down the aisles had given her a pleasant buzz, but being the sole focus of his attention now was downright unnerving, especially in a bathrobe. He was tall and slender, with shoulders as wide as a gladiator's.

His chiseled face, burnished by the sun, reminded her of carved and seasoned oak. He had tawny hair, mostly covered by his Stetson, but a shank swept over his forehead to gleam beneath the brim. His hazel eyes had gold flecks in them, making them shimmer like sun-shot tequila. No wonder she fantasized about dancing with him—and more sometimes. It got her through the long, lonely nights when she missed her little girl so badly that she ached.

She found the presence of mind to ask, "What do you want? Have I done something wrong?"

He inclined his head at her stereo. "Your music was loud. Paul Kutz, across the street, called in a complaint."

Relief flooded through Taffeta. *Nothing serious.* He still knew very little about her. As long as he didn't recognize her from the pictures that had been splashed all over the front pages of every newspaper in the state nearly two years ago, she was home free. "I'm sorry. I didn't think I had the volume up that far."

His firm lips tipped into a grin that showed off his strong white teeth. "Well, it *was* loud, but not really that loud. I think Mr. Kutz—or possibly his roommate, Ray Burke—was more disturbed by your dance performance. With the light behind you, your silhouette showed through the curtains."

Silhouette? Taffeta stared at him, her cheeks on fire with embarrassment. If Paul Kutz had seen her dancing, then so had Deputy Sterling. She wasn't an exhibitionist, and making a public spectacle of herself was humiliating. About a month ago, the relentless loneliness of her life had gotten to her, and she'd decided to allow herself one night a week to wear makeup, shake her hair loose from its clip, and dress sexy. She saw no harm in doing that in the privacy of her own apartment. Only apparently it wasn't all that private.

Just then the hastily secured knot in her hair came loose, and her heavy tresses spilled down over her shoulders. *Crap.* Since moving to Mystic Creek and starting her business, she had tried so hard never to draw attention to herself. Now she'd entertained two old men across the street and this lawman with a dirty dancing performance. What must he think? Hopefully he'd just pegged her as being a little nuts.

He glanced at the skillet that she'd dropped on the mauve carpet. His eyebrow quirked. "Were you planning to hit me with that?" Another grin touched his mouth, and he didn't wait for her answer. "I'm glad I knocked."

"My shop was locked. I thought you might be a polite burglar."

"I pounded on the street door and leaned on the buzzer."

"The buzzer is broken."

"Oh. Well, anyway, you didn't hear me, so I used the master key to get inside."

"Master key?"

"A key that fits all the shop doors along East and West Main," he expounded. "In emergencies, we can use it to get inside."

Until now, Taffeta had felt safe behind her locked doors. It was unsettling to know that the deputies of Mystic Creek could get in whenever they wanted. She hugged her waist before forcing herself to formulate a response.

"In the future, I'll keep my music turned down," she assured him. "And I'll also order a window blind for under my curtains."

"Good idea." He flipped his flashlight back on but kept it directed at the floor this time. "Have a great evening. I'll lock the shop door as I leave. There's no need for you to follow me down."

Taffeta grasped the doorknob but remained in the opening to watch him descend the stairs. For such a large, muscular man, he moved with catlike grace. When she heard the shop door close behind him, she retreated into her apartment and leaned her back against the wall. She wished that he—oh, she didn't know *what* she wished. Barney Sterling had made a fabulous imaginary boyfriend. In her fantasies, he said what she wanted to hear and made all the right moves. But in the flesh, he was a whole different kettle of fish. Her weekly dance night was over. She'd had enough of Barney Sterling to last her for another month, possibly even longer.

She looked down at her discarded frying pan, thankful that she hadn't brained him with it. She was already on probation. If she added assaulting a police officer to her record, she'd be in big trouble.

Again.

As Barney walked back across the street to speak with Paul Kutz and hopefully settle him down, he kept glancing over his shoulder at Taffeta's window. She'd dimmed her lights, and her shadow had vanished. *Hot damn.* The drab gray mouse could transform herself into one of the most striking women he'd ever clapped eyes on. He remembered something his mother had once said about still waters.

Barney's chat with Pop and Ray Burke started off badly.

"Ms. Brown has turned her stereo down," Barney said. "You fellows should have no trouble sleeping now."

"Come again?" Ray inclined his ear toward Barney. Rumor had it that he and Paul had once been college buddies, and after losing his spouse, Ray had moved here to help Paul in the bookstore. "I'm a little hard of hearing."

"He's deaf, son," Paul inserted, clearly suffering from the same complaint himself, since he hadn't heard Ray just explain that.

Barney stifled a sigh, increased his volume, and repeated himself, thinking that the two old men looked like mismatched bookends, Paul tall and thin, Ray short and plump.

"What do you mean, she turned me down?" Ray asked. "I barely know the woman, and I sure as sand never asked her to sleep with me." The old boy actually winked at Barney. "She interested, young fella?"

By the time Barney got back to the department truck, he was stifling laughter. Those old guys probably hadn't had this much excitement in ages. Removing his Stetson, Barney slid behind the steering wheel and closed the driver door. *Ah well, maybe it will put a bounce back in their steps for the next few days.*

Doreen's energetic masticating crackled over the airway when Barney called in to report back. "What happened?" she asked

Staring through the windshield at Ms. Brown's now dark window, Barney shook his head, still feeling incredulous. "The music was a little loud, but it definitely wasn't enough to vibrate walls or wake snakes in five counties. The accused was very cooperative about rectifying the situation and apologized. I got the complainants settled down. Now I'm heading back out to cruise the roads."

"That'll be exciting with all the hardened criminals out there bent on committing murder and mayhem. You might even find a homicidal squirrel."

Barney decided that Doreen might start to grow on him in time. At least she had a sense of humor, offbeat though it might be. "I'll call in for backup if I encounter anything I can't handle alone."

She replied, "Be safe, Matt."

Barney frowned. Who was Matt? Oh yeah, Matt Dillon in *Gunsmoke*. Kitty, the saloon owner, used to say that to him before he left on a dangerous mission. "I've got your number now, Doreen. You're an old television series buff."

She laughed. "Yep. Be safe, cowboy."

"Ten-four clear," Barney said with a smile.

When the radio went silent, he resumed his study of Ms. Brown's window while he wolfed down the cold cream horns. He couldn't help wondering about the secret life of the quiet shopkeeper. During the day, she was so colorless and unassuming. It just didn't tabulate for him that a gal would hide all those sexy curves under bulky sweaters and loose slacks. The women he knew wanted to show them off, not pretend they didn't exist.

What else was she hiding, and why?

Barney shoved the last half of a congealed cream horn into his mouth and chewed vigorously. *Turn loose of it,* he admonished himself. The lawman in him was coming out, and he was smelling trouble where there wasn't any. What people did behind closed doors was none of his business as long as it harmed no one else. Granted, Taffeta might have caused one of those old men to have a heart attack, but that hadn't happened. It was time for him to get on with his shift.

Barney pulled away from the curb and drove west. He passed an oncoming Cadillac that went so slow the driver could have jumped out and had time to watch the car slide off the road. *Must be slick.* He decided to drive out to Seven Curves Road. It was a hot spot for wrecks when the asphalt got icy. As a teenager, Barney had wrapped his first pickup around a tree out that way. Those turns were so sharp a car could kiss its own back bumper as it rounded a curve.

An image of Taffeta Brown's mouth, shimmery with kissable gloss, flitted through his mind while he drove. She intrigued him. She was new to Mystic Creek and had no family here so far as he knew. That meant he could ask her out without any backlash.

Only something told Barney that she might be a lot more complicated than she seemed.

Chapter Two

Two hours before his shift began the next day, Barney drove toward town, going over his mental to-do list. He needed feed for his hens, a new sprinkler and some three-inch PVC for his irrigation system, and some vitamins for his cow, which he hoped was pregnant. Intending to get a cup of java and then stop at the feedstore, he was surprised to find his truck heading for Healthful Possibilities instead. He was so curious to learn whether Ms. Taffeta Brown had undergone a permanent transformation last night—for the better, in his opinion—that he even postponed his trip to the local coffee kiosk. What would he find? Miss Mousy and Meek, or a woman who radiated sex appeal?

The instant he stepped through the doorway of the shop, he had his answer. The only colorful thing about Ms. Brown, who stood behind the cash register, was the bright red blush that whipped into her cheeks when she saw him. Her overlarge shirt, in a color that reminded him of the brown baby poop he'd seen in his nephew Jeremiah's diaper, completely hid the lush curves he now knew lurked beneath it. Her hair, still damp from the shower, was pulled back from her oval face and caught in one of those curly-toothed clips that a lot of women wore before or after exercising. Only Taffeta wasn't in workout mode.

The faint, yeasty scent of toasted bread drifted on the air. He pictured her descending the stairs from her flat, balancing breakfast-to-go in one hand. Barney stepped into the herbal supplement aisle, pretending that he was looking for something. She hesitated, but when he didn't immediately make a selection, she approached him. Stopping more than an arm's length away, she asked, "Can I help you find something?"

Knowing that he shouldn't tease her but unable to resist the urge, he glanced up. "Do you carry anything that might help an old fellow with heart palpitations?"

She took the bait and came to join him in the aisle. That gave him a look at the rest of her. Faded blue jeans completed the picture the shirt had hinted at. They were baggy enough that they were swimming on her. An expression of concern had replaced the flush of embarrassment on her cheeks. That told him she had a caring heart. He liked the dark blue of her eyes. Black outlined the irises, enhancing their color.

"Has he seen a physician?" she asked. "That would be my first recommendation. If he hasn't, he should do that right away. Heart problems are nothing to fool around with."

"He hasn't had time," Barney replied. He noted that the top of her head reached to just above his shoulder, making her about five foot seven. That was tallish for a woman, but she still seemed petite next to him. "The irregular heartbeat didn't start until last night."

Her gaze sharpened on his, and a flare of anger sparkled in her eyes as she realized that he was referring to either Paul Kutz or his roommate, who had witnessed her seductive dance performance. *Quick-witted*, he decided. He felt almost disappointed that she'd caught on so fast. Then again, maybe he'd stuck his foot in his mouth a lot further than he had intended. The look she gave him wasn't hostile, exactly, but it wasn't friendly, either.

Her face went pink again, but her tone was controlled. A little too controlled. He'd ticked her off, all right. "I assured you that I'll keep the volume on my stereo down, and I've already ordered a window blind to block the light at night." Fire still lingered in her eyes. "Now, Deputy Sterling, if you're quite finished having me on, is there anything legitimate that I can help you with?"

He winked at her. He wasn't sure why. He only knew that there was a whole lot more to Taffeta Brown than she revealed to her customers. She glared up at him just long enough to allow him a close study of her face. She did indeed have the bone structure to be a total knockout if she wore a touch of makeup and did something pretty with her hair. Hell, even without cosmetics, she looked damned good. He smiled.

"You intrigue me, Taffeta Brown." He hoped for a reciprocal grin. What he got instead was a quick flash of what he was willing to swear was alarm. What the hell? Was the woman leery of men?

"There's nothing intriguing about me," she snapped. "What you see is what you get."

Not even close, lady. Barney had glimpsed enough of her from the neck down last night to know for dead certain what that baggy outfit concealed. He felt like a kid tempted to snatch goodies from the cookie jar. This time using both hands.

She spun away, stopping to straighten merchandise on the white shelving as she returned to the checkout stand. Each time she bent over, Barney's attention centered on her upturned posterior. What the Sam Hill had gotten into him? Normally he didn't ogle women. Well, he looked sometimes, but he tried never to stare.

"Have a great morning," he called over his shoulder as he left the shop. "And stay warm. The weather report predicts more snow."

Out on the icy sidewalk, Barney took a deep breath of the crisp air. *I don't mess with local women,* he reminded himself. But even as the warning slithered through his brain, a little voice of temptation whispered that Taffeta Brown had no relatives living in town. That made her someone he could date without worrying about complications.

Or did it? As Barney cut across the street toward his blue Dodge Ram, he had a nagging feeling that Ms. Brown might be one of the most dangerous ladies he'd ever come across. Something about her got to him in a way that few women ever had. He wanted to get to know her better. *Hell, who am I kidding?* What he'd really like was to be in her apartment when she was dancing. He recalled the song playing on her stereo, "(I Can't Get No) Satisfaction." He'd jump at the chance to give her some.

Damn that man. An hour after Barney Sterling left her shop, Taffeta still felt so distracted that she'd shelved a carton of gummy vitamin supplements with the protein powder. As she was angrily moving the vitamins, the door opened and a woman entered, carrying a dark-haired little girl on her hip. A rush of icy air accompanied her arrival. Looking at the child made Taffeta's heart pang, for she greatly resembled her daughter, Sarah.

"Good morning," Taffeta called. She straightened from her task. "May I help you?"

"Oh, I hope so," the woman said with a roll of her green eyes. "Leg pain." She jostled the girl, who looked about four. "It was horrid. She cried half the night, and I couldn't make the cramps stop."

Sarah had suffered with leg cramps after she turned three. "Growing pains," Taffeta replied. "Lots of kids between three and twelve get them. A recent study revealed that a large percentage of children who get leg pain at night are deficient in vitamin D."

"Really? I had no idea. How would you suggest I increase her vitamin D levels?"

"The natural way, exposing the skin to safe amounts of sunlight, is always best." Taffeta pointed toward the window. "But at this time of year, that can be challenging. It's too cold to bare very much skin."

A flash of Barney's burnished face shot through her mind. He definitely didn't have a vitamin D deficiency. His left cheek creased when he smiled, making her wonder if he'd once had a dimple that deepened over time from sun exposure. She forced her attention back to her customer. "My first recommendation would be that you take your daughter to a pediatrician and get her checked over. If she's vitamin D deficient, the doctor can advise you on how many IUs of vitamin D to give her each day, and he can do follow-ups to be sure her levels don't get too high."

"Can it build up in her system, or something?" the woman asked.

"Yes, so throwing supplements at her could cause vitamin D toxicity. The safest thing is seeing a doctor."

Pushing a wisp of coppery hair from her cheek, the woman glanced at her child. "I'm wary of supplements."

Taffeta knew about feeling wary. Right now she felt wary of a certain deputy. *"You intrigue me, Taffeta Brown."* She didn't want any man to be intrigued by her, especially not someone involved with law enforcement. She hoped he never came into her store again. When he smiled, flashing those strong white teeth, her knees went weak and her brain went on vacation.

Forget about him. She had a customer to deal with. "It's good to be cautious with supplements. Toxicity can be dangerous, but so can a deficiency. As parents, we need to know what we're doing before we throw vitamins at a problem. If you can afford to take your daughter in to be checked, that's the wisest course of action."

"I can afford it. I just had no idea the leg pain might be caused by a vitamin D deficiency. I hoped you might have something over-the-counter for muscle cramps." The redhead rolled her eyes again. "I don't know if I can survive another night of her screaming, and heaven only knows how soon a doctor can see her."

"Does she like dill pickles?" Taffeta asked.

"She loves them."

"Well, until you can get her in to see a pediatrician, give her a dill pickle at bedtime. If she gets cramps during the night, give her another one. The white vinegar in the pickling brine often helps ease leg cramps, and in small doses like that, it should be safe."

After the mother and child left, the shop went quiet. Taffeta could only shake her head because she'd talked herself out of another sale. Oh well. She felt obligated to give her customers the very best advice she could.

By this time of morning, Taffeta was usually busy. She suspected the lack of customers was due to icy streets and sidewalks. Just what she needed, a lull in business. It gave her too much time to think.

She threw herself into the task of cleaning shelves and merchandise, but even when she started to break a sweat, she still couldn't evict thoughts of Barney Sterling from her mind. One look from him had made her skin tingle from head to toe. She wondered how it would feel if he kissed her—or touched her. *Where did that thought come from?* Irked with herself, she rearranged her display window, refusing to let herself watch the East Main traffic for a white truck with COUNTY SHERIFF'S DEPARTMENT emblazoned on the side. Then she caught herself freezing in midmotion when a white vehicle turned the corner.

Mary Alice Thomas burst into the shop just then, stomping her fur-lined snow boots on the entry mat. "Brrr, it's brutal out there today."

Taffeta always enjoyed this woman's visits. Most people in town called her Ma, which Mary Alice claimed was due to the beginning letters of her first and middle names, but Taffeta suspected it was because the older woman seemed so motherly and sweet. A little on the plump side, she had perfectly coiffed gray hair and looked darling in a bright red wool jacket over slate gray slacks. Her wide smile creased both cheeks, which were apple pink from the cold, and her eyes twinkled with a zest for life.

"Trust me to go shopping on a day like this!" She drew off suede gloves that matched her footwear and tucked them in a pocket. "I had no choice, though. When you run out of things, you're out and have to get more."

"Well, you're in luck," Taffeta assured her. "Your special vitamins came in yesterday afternoon. I intended to call you in a few minutes." *Liar, liar.* Taffeta had completely forgotten. "I got sidetracked rearranging my display." *You got sidetracked by lusting after a dangerously handsome deputy.* "Just a sec, and I'll get them for you."

Mary Alice chattered as merrily as a bird greeting

the new day as Taffeta ran her credit card. She owned Simply Sensational and Beyond, and a potpourri of perfumed scents emanated from her clothing. Taffeta was left feeling lonely when the woman departed. Ma Thomas filled a room with warmth.

The rest of the day dragged by. Taffeta spent hours removing merchandise from shelves to give them a good scrub. When she glanced at the clock and saw that it was only a half hour until closing time, she sighed with relief. She'd managed to twiddle her way through one of the deadest days since she'd opened her business. Exactly five customers had come in, if she didn't count the deputy, who hadn't bought anything anyhow.

Well, at least the lack of customers meant she could get an early jump on her closing routine. It was unlikely that she'd get any more business. This beastly weather had people diving for cover. Luckily for her, she lived over her shop and didn't have to face the icy roads and treacherous driving conditions. Taffeta stepped behind the counter to count down her till.

As she opened the cash drawer and lifted out the tray, she glimpsed a flash of khaki tan outside the window. *Barney?* Her fingers lost their grip on the metal. The till plummeted to the floor. Coins exploded in all directions. Taffeta bit back a swearword. A second glance at the dismal street revealed that there was no deputy in a khaki uniform on the sidewalk outside of her shop. Thank heaven for small miracles. All she needed was to be caught crawling around on the floor to recover money from a dropped till.

What is wrong with me? she wondered, grabbing

two bills that had landed beside the wastebasket. *I'm behaving like a dimwit. What is it about that man?* Had she learned nothing from her marriage to Phillip? *Instant attraction* was just another term for chemistry, and it fizzled out quickly. She couldn't allow herself to feel this way about anyone, especially not a lawman.

Deputy Barney Sterling had access to information that most people didn't. If he got curious enough, he could run a background check on her. Taffeta shivered. If word got out about who she was and what she'd been accused of doing, she'd probably have to leave town. All her efforts to build a life here for herself, and hopefully someday for Sarah, would be down the drain.

She was happy in Mystic Creek. Well, as happy as she'd ever be without her daughter, anyway. *I'm just lonely.* She hadn't had sex in—God, she couldn't remember the last time Phillip had turned toward her in bed for a quickie that had left her staring at the ceiling, wanting to feel what she'd heard other women did, yet relieved that it was over. *Phillip.* Anger burned through Taffeta. She pitied his second wife, Melanie, a buxom blonde who dressed like a hooker. No woman deserved to be nothing more than an ornament on a man's arm, not even a bimbo.

Taffeta slumped back on her heels to stare at nothing. She would never be so stupid with men again. The next time she fell for a guy, if she ever did, she'd be sure he was as stable as a pillar set in concrete. But for now she had other important goals: building her business, getting some more education under her belt, and making a life for herself and her daughter. She could fantasize about Barney Sterling all she liked at night when darkness blanketed the town and held reality at bay. But during business hours, she would be a rational, mature, and responsible woman who understood that her reaction to the lawman was caused by nothing more than physical need, overactive hormones, and loneliness. Fantasizing was safe. Involvement wasn't.

Her till was four dollars and sixty-four cents off even though she'd picked up every coin she saw. She released a weary sigh as she locked the shop door and flipped over the CLOSED sign. A long, hot bath sounded fabulous. Then she'd have soup and half a sandwich for dinner while she watched a program on her boxy old television. No foolish dreams for her tonight, and definitely no dancing, not until her new blind arrived. She couldn't afford to attract attention. Once was enough.

The next morning, Taffeta got up early. It was stock-ordering day, and if she wanted to be focused on that, she needed to get it done before the shop got busy. Normally things were fairly quiet until mid-morning.

Taffeta yawned as she fired up the store computer to get on the Internet. She'd tossed and turned nearly half the night, and had once even gotten up to prowl the darkened rooms. She refused to acknowledge, even to herself, about whom she'd been thinking as sleep eluded her.

As if her thoughts conjured him up, Barney Sterling

opened the front door, juggling two capped cups that bore the Jake 'n' Bake logo. He balanced the cardboard carrying tray on the palm of one hand, holding the door back with his opposite elbow to make it over the threshold without jostling the drinks.

"Good morning! I bring coffee!" he announced.

With an attractive shift of his slender hips, he strode to the counter. She tried not to notice the length of his strong legs or the easy way he moved. His boots made sharp raps on the planked wooden floor. Taffeta felt sure she could close her eyes and still tell that the footsteps belonged to a man. *What*, she wondered, *do I find so sexy about that?*

He set the tray on her counter and rested his folded arms on the edge. His dark brown jacket had a thick lining that added breadth to his already impressive shoulders. With a nudge of one knuckle, he indicated which cup was hers.

"I wasn't sure how you like yours, so I went for French vanilla, a shot of caramel, and lots of sugar." He curled the long, sturdy fingers of his right hand around the other cup. His amber-flecked gaze settled on her face. "You look tired. Have a sip. It'll perk you up."

It miffed her that he'd somehow guessed how she loved her coffee. She didn't often indulge herself with creamers and sugar because she didn't need the extra calories. She decided to make an exception this morning, though, not because she yearned for caffeine, but because opening the cup would give her something to do with her hands. *No fidgeting allowed*.

He pushed up the brim of his Stetson and treated

her to one of those devastating crooked grins. When that crease appeared in his lean cheek, every rational thought in her head leaked out her ears. She pried the lid from the cup, hoping her fingers wouldn't tremble. *Why is he here? What does he want?* She glanced up at his burnished features. A friendly twinkle danced in his eyes, and she felt sure that if he knew what she had supposedly done, he'd be grim-faced and glaring at her. And he wouldn't be here with coffee in the first place.

She hadn't been born yesterday, and when a man came sniffing around, it normally indicated that he was interested in a woman. She assumed that he had found her attractive when he caught her dancing, and he was back again to check her out a bit more. God help her, knowing that made her pulse quicken. It also scared the crap out of her because he was a law enforcement official.

Feeling off balance, she groped for something to say. "Thank you for the coffee." *That was brilliant.* She took a careful sip because heat swirled up from the toffee-brown liquid. "Mm. Just the way I like it."

Still bent at the waist, he shifted his weight from one booted foot to the other. "Tell me something, Taffeta Brown. Do you enjoy reading?"

Taffeta blinked. She had no idea where that had come from, but she didn't want to piss him off by refusing to answer. "As a matter of fact, I do." She didn't ask whether he did. She didn't want to encourage the man. He was already as bold as brass.

His mouth curved slowly into a grin. "What are your favorite novels of all time?" He took a sip of coffee and whistled away the burn. "I've reread *To Kill a Mockingbird* and *The Catcher in the Rye* so many times I've lost count."

Those two titles ranked at the top of her favorites list. So far as Taffeta knew, her ex-husband, Phillip, had never read a single book from cover to cover. "Every time I read *To Kill a Mockingbird*, I'm captivated all over again by the characters."

"Who is your favorite?"

"Scout," she replied without hesitation. "I can totally associate with her."

"Ah, a tomboy, were you?"

Without weighing her words, Taffeta said, "A very angry and resentful tomboy."

Why had she told him that? Her childhood was not up for scrutiny. Her memories were too painful to share with a man she barely knew.

As if he sensed that she regretted speaking so honestly, he said, "I liked all the characters, but I found Boo to be most intriguing. An air of mystery always captures my interest."

Yesterday, he'd told her that he found her intriguing. Was that because he thought she was mysterious? *Careful, Taffeta.* He had a talent for prying information out of her, and that made him treacherous. She lifted her cup, forgot that the coffee was steaming hot, and burned her lips when she took a quick sip. *Ouch.*

Mouth still stinging, she asked, "Where do you like to read?"

He turned his cup with a deft twist of his fingers. "Mostly in my recliner by the fire. The flames give me something to stare at while I try to picture a scene in my mind. For me, reading is like watching a film, only I have to work harder to see everything. Scout in a ham costume. Jem breaking his arm when Bob Ewell attacks them on their way home. I could almost feel the chicken wire in Scout's ham outfit prickling my skin when Ewell grabbed her. And I wanted to see more of Boo coming to their rescue, but Scout's vision was partly blocked." He had a distant expression in his eyes, but then he came back to the moment and smiled sheepishly at her. "Sorry. I tend to get carried away. Where do you like to read?"

Again, he lured her into blurting out the truth without thinking. "In the bathtub. For me, nothing quite compares to a long soak in a hot bath with a fabulous book in my hands."

He grinned, and she felt herself redden. *What* had made her say *that*? He was probably picturing her naked in water up to her breastbone. She wanted to zip her mouth shut. The sooner she got him out of here, the better.

"How do you pull that off without getting the pages wet when you turn them?"

"I'm very careful."

He chuckled. "Does the air turn blue if you lose your grip and drop a book in the water?"

A chill of wariness slid over her skin. "I can't say, because I've never dropped a book in the tub. To me, books are treasures."

"Uh-oh. You one of those people who would never dream of turning down a page corner to mark your place?"

To Taffeta, books were like old friends, and the more dog-eared they got, the more she valued them. "I'm not quite that bad. I prefer to use bookmarks, but I almost always lose them."

With the same suddenness with which he'd picked reading as a topic of conversation, he switched to music. "After hearing '(I Can't Get No) Satisfaction' blaring on your stereo last night, I know you like the Rolling Stones. What other groups appeal to you?"

She glanced with yearning at the shop door, willing a customer, any customer, to come in. But it was early yet and wouldn't get busy for another hour, weather providing. She had a hunch that Deputy Sterling knew that. A lawman kept his fingertips on the pulse of a town and knew its changing rhythms. She was stuck with Mr. Charisma for a while, and he was worming personal information out of her with frightening ease.

She settled for saying, "I'm not big on particular groups or singers. If I hear a song I like, I'm sold."

He nodded. "I'm the same. I may love one song a band records and dislike everything else they put out." He gave her another of those unnerving studies, making her feel as if he saw straight into her heart. "So, pardon me for asking, but have you ever been married?" Humor crinkled the corners of his eyes. "Just curious. So far, I've evaded capture, just in case you'd like to know."

Red alert. Taffeta didn't want to lie. She hated lying. But she didn't want this man to learn too much about her, either. She considered saying that it was none of his business—which it wasn't. In the end, though, she decided that refusing to answer might deepen his curiosity about her. She felt sure that one's marital history was a fairly common topic to arise when two people were getting to know each other. "I'm divorced."

"Ah. Any kids?"

Taffeta's mouth went dry. "A little girl. My ex-husband has temporary custody."

The twinkle in his eyes dimmed and blinked out. "That must be really hard. Do you get frequent visitation?"

Taffeta couldn't do this. If she told him that she no longer exercised her visitation rights, he'd only fire more questions at her. Clamping a hand to the crown of her head, she cried, "Oh my gosh, I don't know what I've been thinking. I'm sorry to be rude, but I forgot to do something very important."

She hurried into the back room and then stood there holding her breath, listening for him to leave. She had to let her lungs expand again and concentrated on her breathing for several minutes before she finally heard his boots ring out on the wooden floor, followed by the overhead bell and a thump of the shop door closing. She went limp against a storage shelf. *Good riddance, and don't come back.*

If he did, no matter how charming and friendly he was, she'd give him the cold shoulder. No more Q&A

sessions. No more friendly chats over coffee. She couldn't believe that she'd told him she liked to read in the bathtub. What had she been thinking? If he felt physically attracted to her, her saying that had been the equivalent of waving a red cape in front of a bull.

Chapter Three

Barney drove his beat, which he normally enjoyed, on autopilot for the rest of the morning. Most times, he'd see people he knew and stop to talk, partly because it kept him in the know about what was happening in town, but also because he liked to check on folks. Mystic Creek was a close-knit community. People watched out for one another. Barney found it rewarding to lend a hand when needed. Sometimes he'd give a lift to someone who'd gone shopping and was trudging home with an armload of groceries. Cars with flat tires on the shoulder of a road always brought him to a rolling stop. He saw his share of dogs that had gotten out of their yards as well, and he had gotten to know the habitual runners almost as well as he did their masters.

Today he had blinders on, and barely noticed the faces of those he saw in other vehicles or walking along a road. His conversation with Taffeta had left him even more curious about her than he'd been before. He couldn't shake the feeling that she'd invented an important task she needed to do in order to end their chat. Maybe talking about her child was too painful. That made sense, he guessed. She seemed like a nice woman. He couldn't imagine a court refusing to grant her a generous visitation plan. That said, though, it wasn't often that the father of a young child, especially a girl, was given custody. It was a commonly held belief that young kids needed the gentle nurturing that only a mother could provide.

Barney didn't necessarily agree with that. His dad, Jeremiah, had been a wonderful parent, a firm disciplinarian only when required, and all about making his children feel loved the rest of the time. It was a toss-up which of his parents had read to him more, and unless his memory failed him, he'd fallen asleep in his father's arms as often as he had in his mother's. Men could be just as gentle and nurturing as women.

Barney sighed. What was it about Taffeta Brown that kept him so focused on her? He had enjoyed talking with her. It wasn't very often that he met a gal who'd enjoyed reading *The Catcher in the Rye* or *To Kill a Mockingbird*. Not that he normally asked a woman what she liked to read. His mind usually wasn't on novels when he was surfing the nightspots of Crystal Falls, and truth be told, he had little interest in getting to know most of the gals he met that well.

Suddenly he felt shallow. Was he becoming an opportunist, a man who cruised the honky-tonks as if they were meat markets to find a choice cut? He was fast approaching thirty. Wasn't it about time he took women more seriously and found out what was between their ears instead of what they had to offer from the neck down?

He headed over to his brother Jeb's place during his lunch break. Huckleberry Road still wore a blanket of snow that glistened as if it were sprinkled with diamonds. He started to park in front of the large post-and-timber home, then changed his mind. *No point in walking out back to the shop when I can drive.*

He circled the house and cut the engine of the Dodge just outside the cavernous building. Smoke trailed from the stovepipe chimney, a sure sign that Jeb labored inside on a woodworking project. He made fine furniture and cabinetry, a career that had started as a hobby years ago. Now Jeb worked at it full-time and made good money doing what he loved.

As Barney swung out of the truck, he heard a rhythmic swishing coming from inside the shop. He'd been around Jeb while he worked enough times to recognize the sound and knew his brother was patiently sanding one of his creations. His boots crunched on the frozen snow as he strode to the front personnel door. He took an appreciative sniff of the wood smoke that canted in the breeze and rekindled old memories of his dad's shop fires on cold winter days. The frosty doorknob chilled his palm as he turned it and stepped inside.

"Yo, bro!" Jeb flashed a broad grin. "What brings you out this way?"

After closing the door behind him with a bump of his hip, Barney chafed his hands as he circled piles of scrap to reach the woodstove. The musty smell of sawdust enveloped him. "It's colder than a well digger's ass out there. April in Mystic Creek. You gotta love it."

Aside from being older, Jeb looked enough like Barney to be his twin, same hair, same eyes, same build. It had always bewildered Barney that he and his brothers could look so much alike and have such different personalities. Jeb worked with wood. Ben, the next oldest, raised, trained, and leased out rodeo livestock. Barney loved law enforcement, and Jonas, the youngest, was studying psychology. His sisters, Sarah and Adriel, had taken after their mother, Kate, all three of them petite dynamos with expressive brown eyes. The only trait they had inherited from their father was the color of their hair.

Jeb ran a palm over a beautifully carved cabinet door to test for smoothness and then resumed making passes with the fine-grain sandpaper. "Coffee's on. Help yourself."

Barney knew from experience that Jeb started the shop coffeepot at around five in the morning, and by early afternoon, the brew had turned to sludge. In fact, he caught the scorched stench even over the smokiness emanating from the stove. "No, thanks. I've had my coffee for the day." Turning from the heat, he walked through another obstacle course to where Jeb labored. He sat on a nearby stool, which his sister-in-law Amanda often occupied. A playpen for their son sat off to the right. "Maybe that's why I've got the jitters and all-over itches . . . too much caffeine."

Jeb glanced up to study Barney's face. "Uh-oh. That doesn't sound good." He cocked an eyebrow. "I know that look. You're ruminating on something. What's up?"

Barney shrugged, fiddled with his hat before set-tling it back on his head, and then sighed. "I'm not sure what's up with me. You ever met Taffeta Brown, the lady who opened the health store over on East Main?"

Jeb nodded. "I can't say I've met her, exactly, but I've been in the shop. Why?"

Quickly recounting the shadow dance story, Bar-ney said, "I never paid her much mind. But now she's like a chigger that's gotten under my skin."

"She got your attention, did she?"

"Boy, howdy, did she ever! I took two coffees to her shop this morning and stayed to chat. There's something about her that has me interested in get-ting to know her better." Barney hooked a boot heel over the top stool rung to rest his arms over his bent knee. "It's completely out of character for me. I don't do local gals. How does a guy feel when he finally meets Miss Right?"

Jeb chuckled. "There's no easy way to describe how a man feels, and I'm not sure all of us feel the same way." Lowering his voice, he added, "I felt befuddled, a little scared, and a whole lot reluctant. Mandy gave me no signals at first that I stood a chance with her, and I didn't want to get my heart broken. But even though my rational side told me to run the other direc-tion, I couldn't do it." He gave Barney a wink. "When it's the real deal, a man just knows."

Barney shook his head. "Taffeta Brown is totally not my type."

Jeb barked with laughter. "It's entirely possible that you won't know what your type is until you meet her."

Barney heard the door open behind him just then, and Amanda's musical voice rang out. "What's so funny?"

Barney sent Jeb a charged look and then turned to greet his sister-in-law. She wore a parka and snow boots, and in her gloved hands, she held a tray covered with aluminum foil. Below the fur-lined hood of her jacket, her large dark eyes gleamed with curiosity. As he often had, Barney noted her resemblance to their mom.

"I've been entertaining him with crazy cop stories," he said, which wasn't really a lie. He'd told Jeb about the shadow dance.

"Ah." Amanda toed a piece of wood out of her way and brought the tray to Jeb's workbench. "Well, I saw you pull up, so I made extra sandwiches. Couldn't juggle drinks. You guys will have to make do with that mud Jeb calls coffee."

Barney laughed and peeked under the foil. "Yum. Those look fabulous. How'd you know I'm starving?"

Amanda's cheek dimpled in a smile. "You're *always* hungry. I wish I could stay and eat with you, but little Jeremiah is taking a nap. Bozo is babysitting." Bozo was Jeb's dog, a mottled brown-and-gold mastiff nearly as big as a horse. "Needless to say, I have to race right back."

She pushed off her hood, revealing a thick mane of dark brown hair, and stepped around to hug her husband. Jeb bent his head to plant a kiss on her cheek. Barney was glad that his brother had finally found someone wonderful. He had contentment written all over him.

Barney's thoughts drifted to Taffeta again. Maybe Jeb was right, and a man didn't know what kind of woman suited him until he met her.

Taffeta had only just flipped over the OPEN sign the following morning when Barney Sterling shouldered open the front door. *Again.* This time he carried a bag of pastry along with two coffees, and her heart skittered as she watched him balance the load. For so big and muscular a man, he moved with a precise economy of motion.

Give him no encouragement, she reminded herself. *Chase him off with frigid indifference.* Only with the rush of cold air that came inside with him, she caught the scent of his cologne and something else exclusively his own. Saliva pooled under her tongue, and she knew it wasn't the delicious aroma of coffee and warm cinnamon rolls that had her responding to his presence.

This man made her yearn for everything she'd never experienced—things it seemed many other women took for granted. To be held in strong arms. To have someone treat her as though she was special. Oh, and feeling sexually satisfied just once in her life wouldn't be hard to tolerate, either. Somehow she knew instinctively that Barney would eclipse Phillip in the bedroom.

Except she couldn't let herself go there. *So what if he's cute? So what if he makes your knees feel weak?*

So what if he loves To Kill a Mockingbird *and can talk in depth about the scenes? Or that he looks irresistible in his uniform?* She had never understood women who drooled over men in uniforms. Now she finally got it. His badge winked at her from under the front edge of his brown jacket. Her gaze dived from there to his belt buckle. When she realized where she was staring, she jerked her focus back to his face. He gave her a knowing look and treated her to a grin that made her blood go molten. Not good.

Panic electrified her nerve endings. He needed to back off. She had no business even looking at a man. Yet Barney, with his sexy grin and charismatic personality, was to her the equivalent of chocolate to a dieter. Tempting, oh, so very tempting. But she would risk more than a few ounces of weight gain if she dared to take a bite.

"Good morning," he said, his deep voice curling around her like tendrils of warm, spun sugar. "I brought pastry to go with our coffee this morning. Not even a reluctant lady can say no to that."

Taffeta couldn't help smiling. "I have work to do, you know. Running a store isn't as easy as it looks."

"Which means you need nutritional fuel. A piece of toast for breakfast isn't enough to last you. By noon you'll be running on empty, and you don't take a break for lunch."

"How do you know I have toast for breakfast?"

He placed his offerings on the counter between them and assumed the same position as yesterday, his folded arms resting on the Formica's edge. It was as if he'd never left. With a touch of one fingertip, he pushed the brim of his hat back so she could better see his face.

"I'm psychic." The crease that might once have been a boyish dimple flashed in his cheek. "Actually I smelled the toast yesterday. And as for your not eating lunch, I used a lawman's amazing talent for investigative deduction. You never close the shop during the day to take a break."

Taffeta knew she should shut him down, but a part of her rebelled at the thought. They were only talking, after all. It was no different from when she chatted with other customers. *Yeah, right. Next you'll be selling yourself the Brooklyn Bridge.*

"How do you know I don't run upstairs for something and eat while I wait on people? You're also forgetting that a few restaurant owners come into the shops and take orders. Hunter Chase from Chopstick Suey offers a mean lunch menu, and Joe from the taco joint delivers as well. So does Sissy Sue over at the Cauldron."

"Not your style, ordering in," he observed. "You wouldn't want a customer to catch you with your mouth full."

Taffeta had a sudden feeling that he knew her habits almost as well as she did. He opened the pastry sack and laid out white paper napkins. "Cinnamon roll or a cream horn?"

The last thing she wanted was to eat with him. It seemed too intimate, somehow. "Neither. I try to avoid sweets."

"Ah, come on. We all have to sin a little sometimes." He drew out a roll and a cream horn, placing both on her napkin. "Enjoy. If you gain a single pound, I'll take you jogging to work it off as soon as the snow melts."

Why couldn't the man take a hint and go away? "I don't need to jog. I do a lot of heavy lifting, bending, and running in this shop."

"So eat," he volleyed back.

Taffeta found cinnamon rolls almost irresistible, and this one looked amazing with a thick drizzle of glaze on top. She picked it up, stared at Barney accusingly, and then took a bite of his offering. As the taste slid over her tongue, she nearly moaned with pleasure.

"You see?" He drew out a cream horn for himself. When his teeth sank into the pastry, a dab of white filling oozed out and stuck to the corner of his mouth. "Never giving in to temptation is bad for the soul."

Without thinking it through, Taffeta reached out to wipe the cream from his lip, much as she once had done when her daughter had something on her face. As she started to withdraw her hand, he grasped her wrist and drew her cream-smeared fingertip into his mouth. Silky heat. She'd never felt anything so amazing—or sensual. The muscles in her lower belly snapped taut. Even her toes curled. Her cinnamon roll slipped from the suddenly rigid fingers of her other hand. When he finally let go of her arm, she couldn't think what to say or do.

"Don't make off with any of my cream," he said with a laugh. "It's my favorite part."

Taffeta retrieved her pastry, which had landed on her napkin. This man surprised her at every turn. She couldn't help wondering what he might do next. Even so, she wasn't sure she wanted to find out.

"Relax," he urged. "Enjoy the sweets, drink your coffee, and talk to me."

"About what?"

"Tell me your favorite scene in *The Catcher in the Rye*."

Talking about books seemed a lot safer than having cream suckled from her fingertip. He wasn't a child who needed his mouth wiped. Why had she done that? He rattled her, she decided.

In answer to his question, she said, "When Sunny's pimp beats Holden up to make him pay her more money."

"Ouch. You're a wicked lady, Taffeta Brown." He took a sip of his coffee, making even that ordinary gesture seem sexy. "Have you read *Robinson Crusoe*?" he asked.

"Who hasn't?"

"You'd be surprised how many people never read the classics nowadays. They're all into popular fiction or movies, mostly movies because they can go almost brain-dead while watching them."

The next thing she knew, they were deep in a conversation about the story and nearly an hour passed without her realizing it. If her coffee hadn't gone cold, she might not have noticed the time lapse even then. Barney Sterling stimulated her intellectually, not to mention in a variety of other ways.

Startled by how much time she'd wasted, she said,

"I truly do have work to do. It'll get busy here soon, and I won't have my till set up."

"You don't set it up before you open?"

"No. I rarely get a customer in here before nine, or later. I open and then set up while it's still slow."

He began gathering their used napkins to put them in the now empty sack. As he put the lids back on the coffee cups, he said, "I'll see you tomorrow, same time."

This was taking entirely too much for granted, Taffeta decided. Did he expect this to be a regular thing? "I'm not sure that's a good idea," she retorted.

If she'd hoped to faze him, she was totally unsuccessful. "Sure it is. We're partners in sin. It's a great way to start the day. Do you have a favorite pastry? Jake has a fabulous selection."

All Taffeta really wanted was a taste of him, and that thought alarmed her. "Don't you ever work?"

"My shift doesn't start until ten and ends at six. You should try it. It could be argued that opening every morning at eight is a waste of your time because you get no business for over an hour. Don't you ever want to stay up late and sleep in?"

"I utilize the time for filling out orders and cleaning shelves. It works for me."

He touched the brim of his hat. "Good-bye, Taffeta. Try not to do anything too wild or impulsive for the rest of the day."

She nearly said she'd already made that mistake by talking with him, but she managed to choke back the words. He left as suddenly as he'd come, and the quietness of her store closed in around her again.

* * *

Barney visited her shop for three mornings running, arriving shortly after eight and leaving at a quarter after nine, which put her in a pinch for time before customers started coming in. Yet Taffeta found herself looking forward to their talks. He kept the conversations impersonal for the most part. She wondered if he realized that all his questions the first morning had made her uncomfortable.

Right before he left on Thursday, he asked, "What do you have planned for Saturday night?"

Taffeta realized that he was about to invite her out on a date. And, oh, how she yearned to accept. When in his company, she didn't think of Sarah constantly or dwell as much on the past. He also made her laugh, something she hadn't done spontaneously in a long time.

"It's my night to relax, watch a movie or read until late, and sleep in the next morning."

"Can we change it up this week? How about going out to dinner with me? I'll let you pick the restaurant."

Taffeta squared her shoulders. "I'm sorry, Barney, but I'm not in the market for a relationship."

He chuckled. "I'm not asking for a relationship. I'm just asking you out on a date. Big difference."

Taffeta shook her head, determined to get rid of him before she did something she'd regret. Building a life here so she might one day get Sarah back was all that she should focus on. "I have a no-dating rule, and I never make exceptions."

He cocked his head to study her. She had the eerie feeling that he saw far more in her eyes than she wished to reveal. "Is it too soon after your divorce?"

Taffeta nearly grimaced. Her marriage to Phillip had been a disaster from start to finish. Even so, she grabbed at the excuse the way a rock climber might a well-anchored rope. "Yes, that's exactly it. It was a messy ending, and I'm still packing a lot of baggage."

He shrugged and smiled, taking the rejection with good grace. Then he stepped over to jot something down on the notepad by the register. "My cell number," he said. "If you ever change your mind about the no-dating rule, give me a call."

She stared after him as he exited her shop. When he reached the sidewalk, which was finally free of ice, she feasted her eyes on him, admiring the fluid strength of his body, the sure way he stepped, and the rhythmic swing of his arms. She wanted to run outside and call him back. Everything about him felt so right, so absolutely *right*.

Depression dogged Taffeta all that day and into the lonely evening. Would he take no as truly meaning no, and not return? Did she even want him to return? Well, okay, she wanted him to, but only if he discussed impersonal subjects and didn't ask her out. She found herself blinking back unwanted tears. Would she never have a normal life? She'd been deprived of that during her childhood, and then, during her marriage, things had gone from bad to much worse.

Later that night, Taffeta lay in bed with her light on so she could fall asleep staring at her daughter's photograph. What a sweet and beautiful little face. Sarah had Phillip's brown eyes and Taffeta's thick dark hair.

The little girl's image blurred as Taffeta lost her battle against tears. She wrapped her arms around herself. Normally she tried never to cry. But, as Barney said, everyone had to sin a little sometimes. She wept until she fell into an exhausted sleep.

Barney didn't usually drink alone, but that night he indulged in three beers, guzzling one right after another. He couldn't get Taffeta Brown off his mind. He felt as if he'd had something possibly wonderful right at his fingertips, and then she had put the kibosh on it. All the signals from her had been promising. She'd been hesitant and wary at first, but then she'd started to relax, allowing him glimpses of who she really was. He'd seen nothing about her that he didn't like—a *lot*. He didn't get why she wasn't at least willing to explore the possibilities with him. He sensed that she felt the incredibly special connection building between them. Why did she insist on turning her back on it?

Barney didn't count himself as being one of the handsomest guys around, but he wasn't homely, either. He had a respectable job. Taffeta didn't know that he owned a home, which was also a plus for most women. He had everything lined out to step up to the plate when the right lady came along.

Too soon, she'd said. With a sigh, he finished off his last beer and made himself accept that she had issues. He knew enough about women to understand that recovering from a divorce wasn't something you could hurry along. Maybe after a few months, she'd be ready to leave the past behind and move ahead with something new. Until then, he had to shrug it off. He'd taken his best shot. *No big deal*. She wasn't even that pretty.

Only Barney knew that she hid her natural beauty. In different clothing, with a touch of makeup and her hair loose, she'd been gorgeous. Why was she so determined to hide her light under a bushel? It made no sense to him.

At least, he consoled himself, she wasn't dating anyone else, even if she didn't want to date him.

Taffeta awakened the next morning with the awful feeling that something was wrong. She leaped from bed, her first thought being that something had happened to Sarah. *Ridiculous*. She was just in a sad mood. That was all.

After staggering sleepily to the bathroom, she stared at her puffy eyelids and red nose. Some women looked beautiful after a good cry. Taffeta wasn't one of them. And, along with a ravaged face, she always had a headache the next morning. She knew from experience that she wouldn't look normal again until late in the afternoon. Thank goodness Barney wouldn't drop by her store today. He'd instantly know she'd been weeping. He wasn't a man who missed much. She couldn't withstand a barrage of questions right now. She might lose it and answer them honestly.

After a quick shower, Taffeta put ice on her swollen eyes. She didn't want all her customers to see her like this. Sitting at the table with a cup of bitter black coffee, she held the pack against each eye socket until her brow and cheekbones throbbed.

She was on her way back to the bathroom to check her face when her cell phone rang. She dashed back to the tiny kitchen to collect it from the table. With a glance at the caller ID panel, she saw that it was Bud Pierce, the private investigator she'd hired in Erickson, Oregon, to give her weekly reports on Sarah's well-being.

"Hello," she said.

"I've got disturbing news, Ms. Brown, and I'll apologize in advance for failing to tell you sooner."

"Is Sarah all right?" Taffeta heard the panic in her voice. "Please tell me she's okay."

"She's fine for the moment, but the situation isn't good."

Taffeta sank onto a chair. What the investigator told her next knocked her orderly little world clear off its axis.

Barney's personal cell phone seldom rang while he was working. Mostly only his family members had his number, and they knew not to bother him unless it was an emergency. He drew the communication device from his jacket pocket and took his gaze off the road just long enough to see who was calling. *Taffeta?* He answered on the second ring.

"Hello?" The truck bounced over a rut as he pulled over onto the shoulder of the road. "Sorry about the noise. You caught me driving. What's up?"

"I, um, was wondering if you'd meet me tonight for dinner in Crystal Falls."

Her voice sounded shaky. Barney decided it must be due to a bad connection. "I thought you had a no-dating rule."

"I do," she replied. "Or at least I did. Please don't say no. I have a proposition for you."

A proposition? What the hell did that mean? "Where do you want to eat?"

She gave him the name of a little out-of-the-way Italian place. He knew of several establishments that served much better food and at least offered decent ambience. Maybe she wasn't familiar with Crystal Falls. Or maybe she didn't wish to be seen with him. And why the sudden about-face? Yesterday, she'd given him the boot. Now she was asking him out on a date?

Hell. Why not? "Sure," he agreed. "What time works for you?"

"Seven is good."

He wondered why she wanted to take separate cars. It made more sense to take one vehicle. Maybe she was just extra cautious. Whatever the reason, he wasn't going to pass on this unexpected opportunity to see her again. "Seven it is. It'll be tight timing for me, but I can make it."

"Thank you, Barney. It means the world to me. I'll see you at seven."

When the call ended, Barney stared through the windshield, going back over the conversation. It meant the world to her? Pretty strong language for a first date. A proposition? Some kind of business opportunity, maybe? He wouldn't let himself hope for anything personal. She'd made it pretty clear that any kind of relationship was out of the question for her right now.

"It means the world to me." She'd meant that. The words echoed in his ears with the sound of her emotion-laden voice.

He couldn't put his finger on the reason why, but he had a bad feeling about this.

Chapter Four

Once his shift ended at six, Barney got into his blue Dodge Ram and raced for home. He had no time for a shower. After throwing on civilian clothes, he grabbed a quick shave, slapped on aftershave, and then added a splash of cologne. His horses would get fed a little late tonight, but it wouldn't harm them. Depending on the road conditions, the drive to Crystal Falls took anywhere from a half hour to forty-five minutes. He didn't want to be late.

The dumpy little Italian place was even worse than Barney remembered. The gravel parking lot had iced-over mud holes deep enough to bury a Volkswagen Bug. The pale blue clapboard siding of the building needed paint, the windows looked cloudy with grime, and when he ascended the steps to the entrance, he felt the wooden planks give a little under his weight.

The interior wasn't much better. The stench of rancid oil blasted him. Pots of fake green ivy sat on dividing walls that formed eating areas, and the leaves looked coated with dust. The red-checkered table-cloths were plastic. The flatware sat on paper napkins.

He saw only two couples in the dining room and a handful of people at the bar in the back. Taffeta sure knew how to pick them.

Glancing around, Barney didn't see her. He concluded that she hadn't arrived yet. When an older woman came to seat him, Barney held up two fingers and said, "Do you have a secluded table where I can watch the entrance? My date isn't here yet."

The waitress pulled two plastic-covered menus from a rack and led him to a bistro table tucked into a corner near the bar. Barney took one of the two stools and watched the front door through a tangle of gray-green ivy leaves.

His breath hitched in his throat when Taffeta finally walked in. She wore a pink, figure-hugging knit top, a tight black skirt that reached to just above her knees, and sassy strapped heels the same color as the skirt. Boy, oh, boy, did the girl ever have legs! To hell with dinner. He wanted to go straight for dessert, which, if he had his druthers, would be her.

He waved so she would see him. She nodded and moved toward him with purposeful strides and a seductive swing of her hips. *Holy crap.* He'd known Taffeta could be a knockout. Kissable pink gloss shimmered on her lips again. Her eyes, deftly enhanced with shadow, seemed to dominate her face. Not that he could stay focused on her face for very long. She was dressed to kill, and she was stunning enough to knock a man on his ass from fifty feet away. This was a hell of a turnaround from a woman who came to work disguised as the local bag lady and had told him point-blank that she didn't date.

With an upward twist of one hip, she perched on the tallish stool across from him.

"Thank you so much for meeting me," she said.

The shakiness he'd heard in her voice earlier hadn't been due to a bad phone connection, after all. With visibly trembling hands, she toyed with her flatware. Under the blush that she had applied to her cheeks, her skin was drained of color. She was one very upset lady.

"Taffeta, what's wrong?" he asked.

She finally met his gaze. "Can I trust you with a secret that may destroy my life in Mystic Creek?"

That wasn't at all what Barney had expected to hear. He searched her eyes and saw both fear and panic in their blue depths. "Taffeta, I'm a county deputy. I can't give you a blanket promise like that. What if you've done something illegal?"

She rushed to assure him, "I haven't! Not really, anyway. And I'm paying my debt to society."

His stomach lurched. "You're *what*?"

"I'm on probation," she blurted. Then she stared at him, looking on the verge of tears, with her bottom lip caught between her teeth. "Please don't tell anyone, Barney. I've invested a lot of time and money to build a life for myself in Mystic Creek. I don't want to start over again somewhere else."

"Did you say probation?" He could scarcely believe his ears. Taffeta didn't strike him as the criminal type, and he prided himself on being an excellent judge of character. "What did you do wrong?"

"Nothing!"

He shook his head. "A person isn't put on probation for doing nothing."

She inhaled a shaky breath and lifted her gaze to the ceiling. "I was wrongly convicted of child abuse. I didn't do anything of the sort, I swear. My husband lied about me in court to discredit me so he could get a divorce without making his father mad."

As a lawman, Barney had heard way too many I-didn't-do-it stories, and so far, hers wasn't very convincing. "He accused you of child abuse in order to get a divorce? That doesn't ring true, Taffeta. Why would a grown man go to such lengths, if he simply wasn't happy and wanted out of the marriage?"

She rested an elbow on the table and cupped a hand over her eyes. "Barney, I swear to you that it's the truth." Then she locked gazes with him before she continued speaking. "Phillip is an immature, selfish man who lives way beyond his means. He loves fancy clothes, racy new cars, and young women. Prior to our marriage, he wheedled money out of his wealthy parents to maintain his lifestyle. When he was almost thirty, his father finally got tired of it and gave him one year to grow up, get married, and act responsibly. Phillip decided to create the illusion of what his dad wanted to see, and he started hunting for a wife."

The waitress came to take their orders. Barney signaled that they weren't ready with a slight shake of his head. When she walked away, he said to Taffeta, "And he found you?"

"Yes," she answered with a nod. "I worked in a sports bar to put myself through college. I'd paid a pretty price for a fake ID and wasn't yet twenty when we met. Phillip decided that I would be the perfect stage prop. His father is a high-end attorney at a fancy law firm. Phillip is, or was, a junior partner. I had just enough education not to be an embarrassment to him. I was young and easily impressed. Phillip charmed my socks off." She gestured helplessly with her hands. "I thought he was wonderful."

"But he wasn't," Barney guessed.

"No, definitely not. The ink was barely dry on our marriage license when he stopped bothering to be charming. He was far too immature and self-serving to have children. I would eventually have ended up leaving him, I'm sure, but I accidentally got pregnant. I was on the Pill, got a bad case of strep throat, and the antibiotics rendered the contraceptive ineffective."

Barney vaguely remembered reading somewhere that antibiotics had the potential to decrease the effectiveness of birth-control pills, so at least this part of her story rang true to him. He just wasn't sure why she was telling him all this. He sensed that she wanted something from him, but he couldn't imagine what.

"Phillip was furious," she said shakily. "He demanded that I get an abortion. I flatly refused, and our marriage, already on the rocks, completely fell apart. He stopped coming home except for when his parents came to visit. No matter what, he had to keep his dad convinced that he was a loving husband and an eager father-to-be." Her eyes swam with tears, and she avoided meeting Barney's gaze. He got the impression she didn't often cry and felt embarrassed for letting him see her on the verge.

"When our daughter, Sarah, was born, his parents fell completely in love with her. Phillip pretended to love her, too, whenever his parents were around, but in between those visits, he barely came home often enough for Sarah to know him as daddy. He only showed up when his folks would be around, and then he played his role as a devoted family man to the hilt."

"Where are you going with this, Taffeta?"

She gave him a pleading look. "I know it's a long story, Barney, but please, *please* hear me out."

Nodding reluctantly, Barney said, "Go for it. The evening's still young. But I think we should order some food."

Since his date didn't seem interested in the menu, Barney perused the selections and ordered spaghetti and meatballs for them both. He ignored the wine selection and settled for drinking water. They both had to drive home, and the way this conversation was going so far, he'd need the clearest possible head. When the waitress left, Taffeta resumed telling her tale.

"I never lied to you, Barney. I'm divorced. I have a little girl. Phillip was granted custody. It was my plan to get Sarah back as soon as I could."

He took a sip of water. As he set down his glass, he said, "So you were convicted of abusing your child." It was a statement, not a question, and Barney felt sick to his stomach. He had been attracted to this gal, *deeply* attracted.

"Yes," she confessed, "but I'm not guilty."

That was what they all said, and Barney had been around that block too many times to fall for it. He kept his expression neutral.

"During my pregnancy, Phillip stopped bothering to hide his infidelities. He knew I wanted to provide stability for our daughter and wouldn't leave him. I had no money of my own. I hadn't finished my education. I couldn't properly raise a child while waiting tables at a sports bar. And I honestly no longer cared who my husband slept with. I contented myself with being a homemaker and a mother. I figured I could stay in the marriage for Sarah's sake.

"What I didn't count on was Phillip developing an attachment to another woman. She was a blonde named Melanie who looked— Well, I know it sounds judgmental, but she looked like a hooker. I guess Phillip found her a lot more exciting than me, because he wanted out so he could marry her. Only that was sticky because he knew his father would stop cutting him big checks if he divorced me. Both his dad and mom liked me. In order to get out without pissing off his father, Phillip needed an inarguable reason."

"I see," Barney said, but in truth, he didn't see anything clearly and felt as confused as hell.

"One night when Sarah was three, she got up after I'd put her down for the night, unfastened the safety gate on the upstairs landing, and fell down the condo stairs. She was bruised up and had a gash on her head that bled like anything. I was terrified. Ambulance response took fifteen to twenty minutes. I didn't know scalp wounds often look worse than they actually are, and I knew she needed medical attention. I bundled her in a blanket and drove her to the hospital myself.

"I was frantic to get in touch with Phillip. I didn't phone him often, but even so, he seldom answered my calls. He was always too busy bonking other women. Finally an ER receptionist called his cell number, and he answered when he saw the name of the hospital on the caller ID."

She glanced away and saw the waitress coming with their food. She wiped under her eyes with her napkin and sat straighter on her stool. After their laden plates were placed on the table, Barney stared at his dinner, feeling as if he had swallowed a toddler's building block that had stuck at the base of his throat. He wouldn't be able to eat a bite.

When the waitress was once again out of earshot, Taffeta said, "I remember being so relieved that Phillip was coming. But when he entered the emergency treatment room, he took one look at Sarah and started yelling that I'd gone too far this time. I didn't get what he meant. I thought he was mad because he'd gotten pulled away from whatever he was doing at the time. I don't think I totally realized what he was capable of until the cops came and physically removed me from my daughter's bedside. They charged me with child abuse, I was put in jail, and because I had no money to hire a good attorney, the court appointed a public defender for me."

"There must have been evidence against you, Taffeta. You were convicted of the crime."

"Phillip lied," she said, her voice trembling. "He was still being discreet at that time about his unsavory nightlife. On the surface, he was a successful young lawyer and family man. His father was a greatly respected person in Erickson. Who was the jury going to believe, Phillip, from a well-known local family, who was so suave and convincing, or me? After we got married, I lost touch with my friends at college. The only social contacts I had were with friends of Phillip's or his parents' friends. I had no one I could ask to be a character witness for me."

"Couldn't you have asked members of your family?" Barney inserted.

"I have no family."

Barney gave her an incredulous look. "No family? How did that happen?"

"My birth mother gave me up as an infant for adoption, I wasn't adopted, and I grew up in foster homes." She sighed and passed a hand over her brow. "Back to my trial. I was out on bail by then, but all my things were still at the condo and Phillip wouldn't let me in to get my clothes. I had little money, no decent clothing, no hair tools. I was a mess compared to Phillip in his expensive suit. He got on the stand and testified that I had abused Sarah countless times. He said he'd hoped that it would stop happening, but instead it only got worse. Then he said I went too far. He even sobbed and wept, as if what had happened to Sarah completely broke his heart. He claimed that he could no longer pretend or keep my behavior a secret. Next time I might kill our daughter."

"And the judge believed him? You were convicted of abusing your daughter on his testimony alone?"

"Yes. Mostly, anyway. Sarah did have cuts and bruises from the fall. And she had been taken to the ER twice before for treatment after she'd had accidents, once at a playground and once by the condo kiddy pool. Phillip swore that even those injuries had been inflicted on his daughter by me. The hospital records were inconclusive and looked bad for me, especially when Phillip's attorney put his own spin on them." She lifted her hands in a helpless gesture. "When those two earlier incidents occurred, I didn't think I'd ever need witnesses to testify that I didn't cause my child's injuries, and by the time of my trial, I couldn't recall the names of the people who'd seen what happened."

Barney knew that eyewitness testimony was sometimes enough to get someone convicted of a crime, but normally the court also wanted at least some physical evidence. "Did your daughter's cuts and bruises look like injuries she might have gotten from a beating?"

"The ER doctor said that they could have been inflicted by a fall down the stairs or by a beating. He couldn't be sure which. But he also said that to his knowledge he'd never had a person falsely accuse a spouse of abusing a child. What reason would Phillip have to tell such a horrible lie?"

Barney sat back in his chair to study her. Now that he'd heard the whole story, he supposed that she could be telling the truth. He just wasn't sure why she was involving him.

"The judge was lenient with me," she went on. "I guess they often are with first-time offenders. I got five years of probation plus mandatory attendance at anger management counseling bimonthly. Phillip immediately started brainwashing Sarah to be terrified of me. I was granted monthly court-supervised visitations with my daughter, but with each visit she was so increasingly traumatized by seeing me that I finally decided I was doing more harm than good. It was the hardest choice I've ever made, but I had to think of what was best for my little girl. People in Erickson thought I was guilty. They hated me. I couldn't even go to a grocery store without something unpleasant happening. When a man spat at my feet and an older woman on a sidewalk called me a monster, I petitioned the court for permission to relocate. Permission was granted, and I was appointed a probation officer and counselor in Crystal Falls. That's when I came to Mystic Creek. I used a small divorce settlement from Phillip, which he gave me only to make himself look good, to lease my shop and start my business."

Barney forked up a bite of spaghetti. It tasted like cardboard with a drizzle of grease on top. Offhand, he couldn't remember when he'd pegged somebody so wrong. "I'm sorry you've had such a rotten time of it," Barney offered. "But I still don't see how I can possibly help."

She leaned closer. "I hired a private investigator to keep me updated on Sarah's well-being. He called me this morning. I knew Phillip had divorced Melanie, but I had no idea that his father had finally gotten fed up and stopped giving him money. I also didn't know that Phillip's mom, Grace, is gravely ill and unable to care for Sarah. They've been taking care of Sarah for Phillip since his divorce. His dad is, of course, distraught over his wife's health. Phillip had no choice but to step in and provide care for his daughter. But he's doing a horrible job of it, leaving Sarah with one strange woman after another. My investigator says rumor has it that Phillip is maintaining his fancy lifestyle by dealing in drugs now that his dad won't cough up any more cash. I suspected Phillip dabbled in rec-reational drugs during our marriage, but this is even lower than I would have thought he would stoop.

"Sarah—she's only five, Barney. The girlfriends who are taking care of her may be using drugs while she's with them. Sarah is missing a lot of preschool because Phillip can't be bothered with taking her to class every morning. Her teacher says she isn't getting along well with other kids. She's acting out and dress-ing inappropriately, whatever that means. In short, my little girl is in a very perilous situation, and no matter what it takes, I have to try to get her out of there."

Barney turned his glass, staring into the remain-ing water. "How do you think I can help?" he asked. He'd known from the start of this conversation that she wanted something. Now maybe she'd spit it out. "Shoot."

"You're a deputy."

He sighed and gave his glass another turn. "Being a law officer doesn't empower me to cure all the prob-lems of the world. I can't bust Phillip for using and sell-ing drugs unless I catch him in the act, and Erickson is way out of my jurisdiction."

Her gaze clung to his. "You don't understand, Bar-ney. I don't want you to bust Phillip. You're a respected man in Mystic Creek. If you and I were together, it would make me look more squared away and respect-able. I might have a chance of getting custody with you standing beside me. I'm not talking about a real marriage, at least not a permanent commitment. It would be only temporary, and of course I would grant you conjugal rights for the duration. Once I get Sarah, we can get a quiet divorce."

Somewhere in the middle of this announcement, Barney knew his jaw had dropped open. Of all the things he might have expected her to say, this wasn't it. Now he was glad they had come in separate cars, because all he wanted was to get the hell away from her and her wild stories and even wilder ideas.

A pretend marriage? Was she out of her mind? He believed in the sanctity of matrimony. For him, it was a forever deal. On top of that, his parents frowned upon divorce unless it was absolutely unavoidable. They would be extremely upset if he married a woman and then divorced her a year or so later. In fact, he reflected rapidly, *upset* didn't describe it by half. If his mother thought he was at fault, she would shorten him by a head, deputy or no deputy.

"A marriage with benefits?" Barney heard the outrage that rang in his voice, but for the life of him, staying calm was impossible. "I'm sorry, lady, but what the hell makes you think I'm that hard up?" He pushed off the stool. "My answer is no. Not now, not ever."

"Please, Barney, don't go. At least think about it before you turn me down. My little girl is in danger!"

Barney grabbed his jacket and shoved his arms into the sleeves with a lot more force than was necessary. "And I'm really sad to know that. But bottom line is, she's not my problem. When you said you had a proposition for me, I never for an instant suspected that it would be something this crazy." He turned for the door, stopping only long enough to drop a couple of twenties on the table. Over his shoulder, he said, "You've got to be kidding."

* * *

Taffeta was shaking so violently after Barney stormed out that she knew she shouldn't drive. She sat alone at the table, staring at the grease bleeding off her untouched meatballs and spaghetti. The smell alone made her want to gag. She felt so stupid, not to mention frightened, rejected, and totally humiliated. Barney Sterling now had it within his power to destroy her future in Mystic Creek, and she had handed over the information to him on a silver platter. What had she been thinking?

Taffeta's only excuse was that she felt completely and utterly desperate. Stepping back from her daughter's life was one thing when she thought it was the only option for her daughter's well-being. But she'd missed her terribly every day they'd been apart and now Sarah needed her. Asking Barney to pretend they were in a serious relationship had seemed like her only hope. Taffeta could think of no other way she might stand a chance of contesting Phillip's custody. As Barney's wife, she might have had a shot. She certainly wouldn't have a prayer if she filed for custody as a single mother who had already been convicted on one count of child abuse.

Taffeta recalled all the lonely nights that she had endured during her marriage to Phillip. Now he was abandoning Sarah in the same way. Even worse, he was leaving her with strangers who were possibly abusing drugs. Had she failed to drive that point home to Barney? She hadn't offered him sex because she thought he was hard up for it. She had offered it as a way of paying him back if he helped her.

Her heart sank when she thought of what her little girl might be witnessing right now. *Oh, Sarah.* She was a confused little girl who couldn't possibly begin to comprehend why her daddy didn't love her and resented being around her. And what line of bull was Phillip feeding the women he was using to watch his kid? Taffeta could almost hear him. *"The firm is litigating an important lawsuit. My mom is gravely ill. My dad's falling apart. While I burn the midnight oil to do all the casework, I need someone to look after my child."* How would those girlfriends react toward Sarah when they discovered Phillip wasn't working, but was instead having a fine time with some other woman? Taffeta was particularly worried about Sarah's caregivers being under the influence. They could be violent. It was a bad situation for Sarah all the way around.

Taffeta finally composed herself enough to feel safe behind the wheel. As she drove back to Mystic Creek, her mind kept circling one question over and over.

What would Barney do with all the information that she'd given him? He had never promised that he would keep what she told him a secret.

If he chose, Barney Sterling could destroy the solid reputation she was trying so hard to rebuild.

Chapter Five

Barney fumed half the way home, until he realized he was doing fifteen miles an hour over the speed limit. He jammed his foot on the brake, pulled over briefly, and smacked his free hand against the dashboard. A speeding ticket would look just great in the personnel file of a county deputy, and he'd be damned if he'd give Miss Taffeta Brown the satisfaction of being responsible for a mark against his character.

He rolled down his window and took several head-cleansing gulps of cold air before he calmed down enough to think straight. He had heard some tall tales in his time. Either the Brown woman had an unrivaled imagination or she was—just possibly—leveling with him. Not that it would make much difference, either way, but at least then he wouldn't feel so repulsed by her that he couldn't be her friend.

When he reached the outskirts of Mystic Creek, he took a right off North Huckleberry onto Creek Crossing Road to stop by the department headquarters. Before he ran home to feed his horses and fell exhausted into bed, he intended to do a little research on Taffeta Brown.

When Barney entered the building, Doreen glanced up over a bank of monitors, momentarily ignoring the voice of Serena Paul, another deputy, that came over the radio. She smiled at him, and snapped her bubble gum. Her curly red hair gleamed in the fluorescent lights that hummed softly above her. "Hey there, Deputy Barney. Have you taken time to polish that bullet in your pocket today?"

Barney walked straight past the woman without speaking. Myriad smells drifted through the rear desk area when he stepped inside. Someone had ordered in pizza from Wood Fyre Delights, a parlor a little west of there. He saw the crumpled box stuffed in a trash can. The unmistakable aroma of a hamburger and fries also assaulted his nostrils. His empty stomach snarled in response.

Sheriff Adams, an older man who had developed a paunch, emerged from his office preceded by his belt buckle. His thinning brown hair, now threaded with silver, sported a circular indentation from the Stetson he normally wore. "What are you doing here, Sterling?"

"I'd like to use one of the department computers for a while if that's all right."

Adams arched a grizzled eyebrow, and his intense brown eyes filled with question. "Personal or department related?"

"Personal. I have two systems at home, but the Internet speed here is faster."

Adams stepped over to the coffee machine, presenting his back to Barney. "Help yourself. Just don't lose sleep and be an asshole tomorrow."

Barney grinned. "Speaking of which, you're here mighty late. Did something come up?"

"Nah. The wife is out of town visiting her sister, so I went to the Cauldron for supper." Marietta, Blake Adams's spouse, was a plump blonde with a smile that could melt ice and a personality to match. Barney imagined that the sheriff felt lost without her. "On the way home, I decided to stop in here and check on things. Nothing to do at the house but eat chips and watch TV."

Barney moved deeper into the room, which accommodated six metal desks. The deputies in Mystic Creek shared the office furniture and equipment. Because they rotated in and out, doing desk duty only when they weren't working in the field, six computers facilitated everyone. Barney waved at a couple of buddies and then got on a computer toward the back of the room where no one would see what came up on the screen.

Barney knew the newspaper in Erickson, Oregon, was named the *Sentinel Guard* because the publication was sold at newsstands in Mystic Creek. When he ran a search on Taffeta Brown in the online archives, he came up with nothing. He decided she might be using her maiden name now, so he ran a search on attorneys in Erickson with the first name Phillip. He found several, but he was able to rule out over half of them because they looked too old in their photographs to have been her husband. He began pairing Taffeta with the remaining surnames as he searched the newspaper archives.

Bingo. Her last name had been Gentry.

The story she had told Barney at the restaurant pretty much matched what he read in the news articles. It still troubled Barney that she'd been found guilty if she actually wasn't, though. He believed in the court system. He understood that sometimes people were wrongly convicted of crimes, but he liked to think it didn't happen often. It looked as though she'd been convicted more on testimony than actual evidence, but he couldn't be certain.

Barney wished he could review the court documents, but though he had spearheaded many investigations during his career, he had never had reason to peruse old trial records. Luckily he had a friend who might be able to tell him how to do it.

Finished with his mission, Barney stopped by Sheriff Adams's office to say good night and thank him for the use of the computer. He told Doreen to stop popping her gum as he passed her station. Ignoring her irked look, he left the building. The air outside smelled like smoke. He remembered that a low-pressure system had moved in, suppressing the drift from people's chimneys. When that happened, the whole town smelled like a damp campfire.

Once in his Ram, he called an old classmate of his from the University of Oregon who now practiced law in nearby Erickson. His name was Bryan Vorch, which had always made Barney think of some character in

Star Wars. He supposed that a lot of people had reason to dislike their names. Jokesters like Doreen made him detest his more with each passing day.

"Hey, Barney!" Bryan said when he answered the call. "Good to hear from you!"

"We need to do a better job of keeping in touch," Barney replied. "I think of you a lot, but I'm so busy that I never get around to contacting you. We burned a lot of midnight oil together studying for finals."

"And guzzled so much coffee that I'm surprised my eyes didn't turn brown."

They shot the bull for a minute before Barney told him why he had called. "I want to review a court case," he said, "and I don't have a clue where to start."

"Court proceedings are public records and available to almost everyone," Bryan told him. "Normally a person has to fill out a form and sometimes pay a small fee to review public records, but I do it so much in my line of work that I pay an annual fee for almost instant access. I could pull the docs up and e-mail them to you. Or, if you'd like to cut me a check for the cost, I can send you a download for the recorded version."

"I'll take the files, thanks." Barney had to watch his budget. "And it's great of you to offer to do this, Bryan. There's only one wrinkle. The lady who stood trial is a friend of mine, and I don't want word to get out here in Mystic Creek that she was convicted of a crime."

"I'm your man, then. You're the only person in Mystic Creek that I know."

Barney laughed and gave him Taffeta's married name. "She was convicted of abusing her little girl."

"Oh, shit, I remember the trial," Bryan said. "It

dominated the front page of the *Sentinel Guard* for over a week. She was married to that dickhead Phillip Gentry." Bryan whistled. "He's bad news, dude. I'll be happy to e-mail you the files. I still have your e-mail address unless you changed it."

"I haven't. I have enough trouble trying to remember my current one," Barney said with a chuckle. "I really appreciate this, Bryan. I owe you one."

Barney had just pulled up in front of his house when his phone pinged to notify him of an incoming e-mail. *Hopefully from Bryan,* he thought.

Normally Barney went to bed fairly early unless he went to Crystal Falls for an evening on the town. But despite his former weariness, now he suddenly felt wired. He got that way whenever something intrigued him, and Taffeta Brown sure as heck did, even though he'd been thrown by her crazy proposition.

He fed his two geldings and Mary Lou, the cow, before he went inside, cursing when bits of hay got under the collar of his shirt. He usually wore a wool jacket with the collar turned up when he tended to his animals. He'd filled the chicken feeder that morning, so the hens needed no attention.

He flipped on a light as he stepped through the back door into the kitchen. His brother Jeb had helped with the remodeling, designing banks of new cabinets that looked nearly as old as the ones they had replaced. True to the character of the structure, he'd said, and Barney liked the results, which were countrified, warm, and perfect for an old farmhouse. He opened the stainless steel fridge to get the fixings for a sandwich and grabbed a can of soda to wash it down. Minutes later, he had a fire snapping and popping in the hearth, and he sat in his burgundy recliner to open his laptop. The flames cast an amber glow over the room, highlighting the rustic barn-plank flooring, which had taken a year of his savings to install. Sitting there reminded him of when he'd told Taffeta where he most enjoyed reading. The memory made him sad. She had seemed so right for him when they were discussing favorite books. Oh well, he guessed that every guy got bamboozled by a female at least once.

He spent the remainder of the evening reading about Taffeta's trial. Barney was no attorney, but it appeared to him that there had been little, if any, solid evidence presented by the prosecutor to prove that Taffeta had purposefully harmed her daughter. Just as she'd said at the restaurant, she had wrapped the child in a blanket and driven her to the hospital. Nowhere did Barney read that police officers had visited the house to examine the accident scene. *Accident?* Was he starting to believe her claims, after all? He guessed maybe so. It looked to Barney as if she had been convicted mostly on the strength of her husband's testimony.

It had grown too late to call Bryan Vorch back to ask his opinion, so Barney sent his old friend an e-mail, asking him if he'd be willing to review the case and share his thoughts on the apparent lack of physical evidence. Would Bryan feel that Taffeta had gotten a fair shake?

Saturday morning dawned bright and sunny, and while Barney drank his wake-up coffee, he stared out his kitchen window, wishing he could spend the day behind the wheel of a county truck, driving the streets and roads of Mystic Creek. Count on it to be a lovely day when he'd be stuck inside. Desk duty had never appealed to him. He hated all the paperwork, and when calls were directed to him by the dispatcher, he yearned to be out in the field talking in person to the individual. It was connecting with people that made him love law enforcement. If and when he became the sheriff, he would pawn the paperwork off on subordinates as much as possible and work the streets. Until then, he had to climb the ladder.

Anne Warf, a well-seasoned dispatcher, greeted Barney with a halfhearted smile when he arrived for work at ten. A slender woman with dark eyes, black hair, and eyebrows that looked as if they'd been drawn on with a felt pen, she had celebrated her forty-fourth birthday last month, and in June she would mark her twenty-fifth anniversary with the department. Most of the time, her seniority afforded her the privilege of working weekdays, but every once in a while, she got stuck working Saturday and Sunday to give someone else time off.

"Don't tell me what a beautiful day it is," she warned. "I'll say I'm sick and go home."

Barney couldn't help laughing. He poured her a cup of coffee and brought it back out to her. "Maybe this will cheer you up," he said as he set it on her desk.

"Nothing will cheer me up. It's the first real day of spring, and I'm stuck at this stupid station fielding calls that make me grind my teeth! Christopher Doyle called in to say that Edna Slash is parading around on her porch half-naked, and he wants her arrested for indecent exposure."

Barney nearly choked on a laugh. "Those two are always bickering about something, Anne. I think it's the geriatric version of flirting with each other."

"They're a pain in my arse," she shot back. "It's the first real day of spring, I'm telling you."

That made him laugh again. "Anne, you've lived here too long to believe that this break in the weather means anything. Mother Nature loves to play games with us in April and sometimes even in May. The second we start to believe spring has finally arrived, she dumps a foot of snow on us."

"My crocuses are blooming. My daffodils are poking their heads up. That's a sure sign."

"You say that every year." As Barney walked back toward the desk area, he said over his shoulder, "I detest desk duty, you know. We can grouse about having to be here all day, or we can make the best of it."

Garrett Jones, one of Barney's fellow deputies, gave him a mock salute from a corner desk. His dark brown hair looked as if he'd been thrusting his fingers through it, and he had circles under his blue eyes.

"Late night partying?" Barney asked.

Garrett ignored the dig. "You ever wonder what the fricking hell everyone else does when they have desk duty? It sure as hell isn't paperwork."

Studying the piles of stuff in front of him, Barney saw Garrett's point. "Maybe they play games on their phones."

"There's an idea, only I hate playing games. And Sheriff Adams has the computers locked down so tight that you can't do much of anything on the Net except research. Facebook is blocked. Blogs are blocked. It's a boring pain in the ass."

Barney had never tried to go online except for department business. He'd been taught good work ethics by his parents, and fooling around when he was being paid to do a job didn't occur to him. He blocked out Garrett's whining and started sorting through the backlog of reports.

By noon, Anne had patched in only two calls on his phone line to break the monotony. Marjorie Jane Roberts, who lived on Bearberry Loop overlooking the golf course, wanted to know if it was too close to fire season for her husband, Pete, to use their burning barrel. Devon Penny called to ask if Barney had any work on his property that Devon could do for ten dollars an hour. Barney felt badly for saying no, especially when the boy dickered with him on the wage, dropping it to eight an hour. Devon was a nice kid with a single mom who struggled to make ends meet. But on a deputy's salary, Barney couldn't afford hired help. He suggested that Devon call his brother Jeb, who often brought in kids to help him out.

By two, Barney's stomach felt as empty as a beggar's pocket. He was just tidying up his desk before going out for lunch when his personal cell phone rang. *Bryan Vorch.* Barney signaled to Garrett that he was leaving for his break and answered the call as he passed Anne's station.

"Hey, Bryan. I didn't expect to hear back from you this soon."

Bryan chuckled. "My wife took my little girl shopping in Eugene, so I found myself spending Saturday alone. It's raining like a son of a bitch over here in the valley, so I can't get in a game of golf. And it's too damned wet to do any yard work, thank God. Reading about Taffeta Gentry's trial was a lot more interesting than raking up rotten leaves that I missed last fall."

Barney crossed the parking lot to sit in his truck, where no one would overhear his side of the conversation. "You've already gone over the file?"

"Oh yeah," Bryan confirmed. "And you're right on target, Barney. There was no concrete evidence to convict this lady. The prosecutor's case rested mainly on Phillip Gentry's testimony. The little girl's physical injuries *could* have been sustained from a beating, but they also could have happened during a fall down a flight of stairs. You have to remember that Phillip swore on the stand that Taffeta had abused the child countless times. The hospital records of the two earlier accidents that Sarah had were ambiguous, allowing Phillip's attorney to imply that the injuries could have been inflicted on the child by her mother."

"How can someone be convicted on testimony alone?"

"It happens," Bryan assured him. "And Phillip Gentry wasn't just any witness. He was Taffeta's husband. At the time of the trial, Phillip's father, Cameron Gentry, had been pulling strings to cover up his son's unsavory behavior, so Phillip appeared to be a credible witness—a charming, successful young attorney with a brilliant future. Why would a judge think that he'd tell such outlandish lies about his own wife?"

Barney had no answer. "So you think Gentry lied?"

"I didn't at the time, but I sure do now. Cameron Gentry can no longer cover up Phillip's reckless lifestyle, so Phillip's credibility is down the drain."

"Exactly what do you mean by reckless lifestyle?" Barney asked.

"Phillip is a complete jerk, Barney. He can't even be faithful to a mistress, let alone a wife. He's got a reputation for barhopping and hitting on young women—*really* young women. Not long ago, he was charged with statutory rape because a girl he bedded was under eighteen. He got off only because she used a fake ID to get into the drinking establishment. Phillip's attorney argued that even the doorman believed she was twenty-one." With a snort, Bryan added, "When I see a young girl slathered with makeup and dressed to seduce, I can usually tell, if I look closely, that she isn't of age. And while having sex with her, Phillip had to have gotten a really close look unless he was too drunk or tweaked to see straight."

"Tweaked?"

"He's into meth. In fact, rumor has it that he's dealing now that his father has washed his hands of him. Without Daddy's money, Phillip has to bring in cash somehow to maintain his playboy lifestyle. If he doesn't get a brand-new Corvette every year, he thinks it's the end of the world."

Barney stared blindly ahead. "So Taffeta told me the God's honest truth last night."

"Yes, and in answer to your e-mail question, I don't believe she got a fair shake during the trial. Cameron Gentry, her former father-in-law, is a great attorney, a decent person, and he's devoted to the law. But his son? He's a complete prick, and now just about everyone in Erickson knows it. I'd bet my bankroll that the bastard lied on the stand."

"According to Taffeta, he wanted out of the marriage when she got pregnant and refused to get an abortion. He didn't want kids."

"He's too immature and selfish to want kids," Bryan said. "Think about it. It's expensive to raise a child, and Phillip probably didn't want big chunks of his allowance from Daddy to be wasted on a brat. As for divorce? Hell, no. Taffeta would have gotten custody, and Phillip would have been ordered to pay child support. Even worse, Cameron Gentry would not have approved if Phillip ended the marriage without good reason, and he might have stopped giving Phillip money. Phillip's a player, Barney. He pretends he's still in his early twenties. Having a family would screw with his image and cramp his style. The guy still drives to Eugene and hangs out on the U of O campus, preying on young girls."

Barney didn't get how anyone could be so selfish that he never wanted children because of money. Sure, raising a family was costly, but kids brought people joy and gave them a reason for being.

"You should have seen his second wife," Bryan went on. "A sleazy blonde with a bad boob job. I'm talking huge knockers, man. They looked like overblown balloons. She was twenty, and she danced in strip clubs. A few months ago, she left Phillip and filed for divorce because he couldn't keep his fly zipped."

"So you really believe Taffeta is innocent." Barney felt nauseated. He had been downright rude to her last night. She'd left herself wide-open to rejection and humiliation, and he'd delivered on both counts.

"I do," Bryan replied without hesitation. "At the time of her trial, I have to admit that I thought she was guilty, just like everyone else in town did. Phillip appeared to be a squared-away guy back then. But now the truth is out. He's a scum ball, and I wouldn't put anything past him."

"Does Taffeta have any recourse?" Barney asked.

Silence came over the line. Bryan finally replied, "She should file for an appeal to get the conviction overturned. I happen to know a halfway decent attorney who'd do that for her at a discounted rate."

Barney smiled. "That's really generous, Bryan."

"Lawyers like Phillip Gentry give the rest of us a bad name. I'd love to peel his hide off in court."

"It won't ever come to that, will it?"

"It will if I can get Taffeta's conviction overturned. That opens the door for me to file charges against Phillip for perjury."

Barney heard what sounded like water running at Bryan's end.

"That kid is in a bad situation. Getting a hearing set up in appellate court will take time. If there's any way that Taffeta can get the little girl back before this goes into the appeal stage, she should go for it. Trust me, Phillip Gentry is not the fatherly type. I wouldn't put it past him to dump the child on any woman who'll watch her, and with drugs involved, his taste in females has deteriorated. The gals he hangs out with now are screwed up. They shouldn't be in the same room with the child, let alone be watching her. It's a sad mess."

Barney felt a bitch of a headache taking up residence behind his eyes. "How can Taffeta possibly get her daughter back with a conviction of child abuse still hanging over her head?"

"Here's my thought," Bryan answered. "According to the scuttle, both of Phillip's parents once thought highly of Taffeta. They changed their minds about her when they thought she'd beaten their grandchild. But at this point, with their son being such a loser and humiliating them in public at every turn, isn't it possible that they're wondering now if Taffeta was actually innocent?"

"It's possible," Barney conceded. "Parents can only lie to themselves about their offspring for so long."

"Exactly, and now he's dragging their granddaughter from one pesthole to the next to avoid having to take care of her. If Cameron Gentry would support Taffeta's petition for a reversal of the custody ruling, she might have a shot, especially if it's already on record that she has filed for an appeal. Any judge in Ash County has to know by now that Phillip is a scumbag. His testimony against Taffeta should definitely be in question, and if Phillip's own parents turn against him—well, you get the picture. A judge will hopefully at least give Taffeta an audience and keep an open mind."

Barney rubbed his temple. He reluctantly asked, "If Taffeta were married to a sheriff's deputy with a flawless reputation, would that increase her chances of getting the child back?"

Another long silence followed. "Are you shittin' me, Barney? You're thinking about marrying her to help her get the kid back?"

Barney felt as if an ice pick stabbed into both his pupils. He fumbled to open the console compartment of his pickup, where he kept a bottle of ibuprofen. Tucking the cell phone under his chin, he shook out four coated tablets, tossed them into his mouth, and swallowed them without water. "I'm just asking, Bryan. Would it look better for her if she were married to me?"

Bryan guffawed. "Dude, that's like asking me, 'Do bears shit in the woods?' Of *course* it would look better for her. I mean, I can't say it'd be a guarantee she'd get custody, but being married to someone like you certainly couldn't hurt. I, um—well, I didn't realize last night when you contacted me that you were hung up on this gal. I thought it was a professional inquiry, a lawman doing some digging to help out a friend."

"I'm not hung up on her, and I can't believe you still say 'dude.' You're dating yourself, bro. Move into the twenty-first century."

Bryan guffawed. "Some things never change. When you get irked, you still bare your teeth."

Ignoring that analysis, Barney asked, "Are you serious about giving Taffeta a discount if you take her case?"

"Hell, I'd be tempted to do it pro bono. It'd be a public service to put Phillip Gentry behind bars for a while."

"I'll tell her about your offer," Barney said. "She runs a little health store, and I doubt she's rolling in dough."

He could almost hear Bryan smiling. "All the more reason for me to help her out."

Chapter Six

When Barney got off work at six, he headed straight for his parents' house. As a formality he rapped on the door of their ranch-style home even as he stepped into the entryway. His mother, who still didn't look a day over fifty with her mane of dark hair and beautiful brown eyes, appeared in the family room and smiled when she saw him.

"Ah. My baby finally shows up to visit me."

Barney gathered her in his arms for a hug. A fabulous smell wafted on the air. "You've been baking horse cookies."

"Yes," she confessed. "And you stay out of them."

He laughed. As a kid, he'd loved stealing a few of the horse treats while they were still warm from the oven. Now, even though they contained only human-grade ingredients, he steered clear of them. He'd learned the hard way that they were hard enough to break his teeth.

"Jeremiah!" Kate called. "Look who's here!"

Barney followed her into the kitchen. His father sat at the table where Barney had once wolfed down breakfast every morning with his siblings. Fond memories spiraled through his mind.

"Mind your manners and take off your hat," Kate instructed as Barney walked toward his dad. "People will think you were raised in a barn."

Barney laughed and laid his Stetson on the island bar. Soft stereo music played somewhere in the house, making Barney appreciate his dad's reluctance to become a couch potato who sat glued to the television all evening. Jeremiah held up his mug. "We've got a pot of decaf on. You want a cup?"

"I'd love one." Barney grinned at his dad. There had always been a deep and quiet affection between them. In coloring and build, Barney and his brothers had taken after Jeremiah. Barney could only hope he aged as well as his dad. Jeremiah had been a farmer all his life, and the hard work had kept him fit. Now that he was older, he'd slacked off a little, but not much. "Don't get up," Barney said. "I'll serve myself."

Kate resumed her seat beside her husband. Armed with a cup of hot coffee, Barney sat across from them. They studied him with expectant expressions. He decided that he needed to visit more often because they clearly didn't think this was only a social call.

Barney wasn't sure where to start this conversation. He only knew that the outcome would determine whether or not he helped Taffeta Brown.

His mother gave him a lead-in. She could read him like a book. "What's going on?" she asked.

"What I'm about to tell you must never be shared with anyone," he warned them. "A very nice woman's future in Mystic Creek depends upon absolute discretion."

Kate reached over to pat Barney's hand. "You know you can trust both of us, darling. What's troubling you?"

"I've got a dilemma," he said, and the rest of the story spilled from his mouth like water from a spout.

Kate's eyes had gone dark with sadness by the time he finished. "You say the little girl's name is Sarah?"

Barney gave his mom a sharp look. Surely she wasn't tapping into this merely because Taffeta's child bore Barney's sister's name. Jeremiah's jaw muscle started a tic.

Barney didn't hold much hope that his parents would approve of the short-term marriage idea. They were both romantics at heart, and the muscle that bunched rhythmically in his dad's cheek didn't bode well.

"What do you think you should do, son?" Jeremiah asked.

Barney had been mentally circling that question ever since he talked with Bryan, but he was still taken off guard by his father saying it aloud. He had expected Jeremiah to protest that this was the craziest idea he'd ever heard. "Well, I'd like to help the lady if I can."

"So why are you here, talking with us?" Jeremiah demanded.

Barney replied, "Because you and Mom are old-fashioned and don't approve of divorce unless there's no way around it. If I help Taffeta Brown, our marriage

won't be a forever kind of deal. Once she gets custody—
if she gets custody—we'll dissolve the marital union."

"And you're worried that we'll be disappointed in
you," Kate inserted.

Jeremiah glanced at Kate. Then he met Barney's
gaze. "You know how much your mother and I love
children. If what you've said is true, that little girl is in
a really nasty situation. Did I raise you to be a man
who can turn his back on a child in jeopardy?"

Barney couldn't quite believe his ears. His mother's
old teapot clock ticked loudly on the kitchen wall. The
sound, something he normally barely noticed, seemed
suddenly deafening even with music in the background.
"Mom?" he said. "Are you with Dad on this?"

Kate's eyes sparkled with unshed tears. "I'm behind *you*, Barney. Marriage is a big decision, and I
certainly won't blame you if you choose not to do it.
But if you do, I'll feel nothing but proud."

"It's a long shot that her being married to me will
help," Barney warned.

Jeremiah piped in. "The hell it won't. You were a
state patrolman, and now you're a deputy here. There
isn't a single black mark on your record. No judge in
his or her right mind would think for an instant that a
child might be abused under your watch. I agree with
your mother. I won't blame you if you don't do it, but
if you do, we'll both be prouder than punch."

Kate sighed. "It's not healthy for a child to be left
with one stranger after another, especially when drugs
may be involved. The girl might even be physically
harmed. And I think Bryan Vorch nailed it on the head.

Grace and Cameron Gentry must realize that their son is heading down a slippery slope. If they once liked and admired Taffeta, it's entirely possible that they now regret supporting Phillip and turning against their daughter-in-law."

As Barney walked back out to his truck a few minutes later, he felt a bit dazed. He'd come here thinking that he knew both his parents, inside and out, and could predict how they might react in any given situation. He'd expected—well, he didn't really know what he'd expected. Doubts, at the very least. But instead they had surprised the heck out of him. They not only seemed ready and willing to temporarily welcome Taffeta Brown into their family, but also gave him the impression that they might be disappointed in him if he didn't help her. That was—well, mind-boggling.

He swung by his place to feed and water his critters. Then, without bothering to change out of his uniform, he hopped back in his Dodge and drove into town. There was a pretty brunette on East Main to whom he owed an apology.

Taffeta had just cleaned up her dinner mess in the tiny kitchen and settled on her sofa to watch some television for an hour, hoping it would take her mind off Sarah and stop her from thinking about her meeting with Barney last night. She hadn't thought about much else for the past twenty-four hours, and her mind felt as if it had been caught in an out-of-control eggbeater.

She nearly parted company with the couch cushion

when someone rapped on her apartment door. She could tell by the emphatic thumps that it was a man's knuckles connecting with the wood. Since her shop was closed for the evening, she suspected that her caller was a certain deputy with a master key to the downstairs door. If so, he was the last person in town whom she wanted to see.

She sprang to her feet. "Who is it?"

"It's Barney Sterling," he replied, his deep voice as clear to her ears as if no door separated them. "Can you let me in, Taffeta? I need to talk with you."

Taffeta's cheeks burned as she disengaged the door chain and dead bolt. Barney stood with a shoulder against the doorframe, and for an instant, his chest seemed at least a yard wide. She forced herself to meet his gaze. His hazel eyes and firm mouth glimmered in the light coming from her living room. His burnished face, partially cast in darkness by his hat, looked tense.

"I know you're probably pissed at me," he said. "And for the record, I don't blame you. But I hope you'll hear me out."

Taffeta stepped back to let him in. He dwarfed the tiny living area. The enticing scent of his cologne teased her nostrils. To her surprise, he immediately removed his hat.

With a sheepish grin, he said, "I just left my parents' house, and my mom climbed all over me about minding my manners."

Taffeta wanted to smile back at him, but her face felt as if it were covered in a dried face mask. "Please, have a seat." She gestured at the living room. "Pardon the shabby chic. When I moved here, I spent most of my money on opening the store. Furnishings for the apartment took a backseat."

He moved his gaze slowly over the room. "It doesn't look shabby to me. It's cute and cozy."

He bent his long legs to sit on the sofa, rested his Stetson on the cushion beside him, and shed his jacket. She lowered herself onto the old easy chair across from him.

"The Stetson is part of my uniform," he explained. "I rarely remove it while I'm working, except for inside the patrol truck because I'm too tall, and I crush the crown. Otherwise it stays glued to my head, and then I forget to take it off when I should."

His lengthy explanation about the hat told her that he was tense and uncertain about what he wanted to say next. "It's fine," she said. "I don't care if you don't take off your hat."

He puffed air into his cheeks and rubbed his palms together, another indication that he was nervous. That made two of them.

"About last night," they both said at once. Taffeta gestured at him. "You can go first. I'm in no hurry."

"I owe you an apology for the way I acted at the restaurant," he said.

Taffeta held up a hand. "I blindsided you with a crazy story and an even crazier request. I should never have put you on the spot that way." She shrugged and sighed. "I've wished all day that I'd never called you. I don't know what on earth I was thinking."

He studied her, his gaze so intent on her face that her skin burned. "You were thinking about your daughter,

Taffeta. And you took a huge risk by telling me everything that you did. I realize that now, but last night—well, I've been in law enforcement too long, I guess. You learn after a while that practically all criminals say that they're innocent. Most of them have sob stories, but at least they're believable. Your story sounded like—well, a not very convincing tale."

Taffeta stiffened. "What are you doing here, then?"

"I deserve that," he said. "In fact, I'm probably lucky you even let me in the door." He raked his fingers through his hair. "I had a chance to think about it. You could have made the story easier for me to swallow with a few lies tossed in, but you didn't do that. Sometimes, Taffeta, the truth sounds more incredible than a whopper."

"Are you saying you believe me now?"

He nodded. "I'd like to say that I just took it on faith, but the truth is, I did some investigating and called an old friend who's now a lawyer to help me get my hands on the trial records. So yes, I believe you now, not because I'm a good guy with a kind streak, but because the files back up your story. I saw not a lick of solid evidence against you. The prosecutor's whole case rested on Phillip's testimony. The cops didn't even go to the condo to examine the crime scene—or should I say *accident* scene? To be sure I wasn't missing something, I asked my lawyer friend, Bryan Vorch, to review the case.

"He completely agrees with me, and to say that he has a low opinion of Phillip Gentry would be an understatement. He backed up everything you told me about your ex-husband, he doesn't believe you're guilty, and he has offered to file an appeal for you at a discounted rate."

He lifted his hat and ran the brim through his hands. "I'm very sorry that I so quickly discounted everything you told me, Taffeta. And I'm sorry I refused to help you without at least giving it some thought. My parents raised me to believe in the sanctity of marriage. They're wonderful people, but they're old-fashioned and frown upon divorce unless there's no way to avoid it. I couldn't enter into a short-term marriage and then blindside them with a dissolution."

"You don't need to explain yourself, Barney. I should never have asked that of you. After I heard from my investigator about Sarah's plight, I went into desperate mode. I'm glad you believe me now, though."

"What you shifted into was protective mode. Your little girl is in a precarious situation, and her father is an irresponsible jerk. Bryan Vorch says Phillip is keeping company with women who are meth heads, and he's leaving Sarah with them so he can party. If there's any way possible for you to get your daughter away from him, you need to do it."

Taffeta's heart twisted. Barney had said nothing that she hadn't thought herself. "The deck is stacked against me."

"Bryan feels that you'll possibly have a better shot if you're married . . . to me."

Taffeta stared at him, uncertain what to say. That had been her idea, but he hadn't reacted favorably last night when she broached the subject.

"I talked with my folks," he went on. "They're both

very concerned about Sarah. They adore kids. When I told them your story, they both gave me their blessing to marry you. They understand it will be temporary, but in this case, they're okay with that."

Taffeta blinked. "What are you saying, Barney?"

"That I'll help you," he replied. "But it won't be a marriage with benefits, with you giving me sex in exchange for my support. That isn't how I operate."

Her heart started to pound. "But what will be in it for you, then?"

He tossed his hat back onto the cushion. "Knowing that I've done my damnedest to help a little girl will be a nice perk, and that's nothing to sneeze at."

Taffeta placed a hand over her heart. It felt as if it might pound through her rib cage. "Last night when I suggested marriage, it sounded like a good idea to me, but now—well, it just sounds nuts."

A twinkle started to dance in his eyes.

"We barely know each other," she added. "We've talked over coffee a few mornings. Otherwise we're practically strangers."

He leaned slightly closer to search her gaze. "What more would you like to know about me?"

The air in her apartment felt suddenly thin. "Barney, you've knocked the breath right out of me. I haven't a clue."

He laughed. "I hate my first name. Let's start with that. Do you have any idea how many times I've had to endure Deputy Barney Fife jokes?"

She gave a startled laugh. Then she confessed, "I hate my first name, too. I've never met my mother. She gave me up for adoption right after I was born, but if I ever do meet the woman, the first thing I'll ask her is why she gave me such an awful name."

"I think Taffeta is a fine name."

She shook her head. "When I was a kid, being bounced from one foster home to another, everyone called me Taffy. At school, the boys called me Daffy or Daffy Duck. When I got emancipated at seventeen and started college, I went by Taffeta and jumped down people's throats if they dared to call me by that nickname."

"I like Taffy," he argued. "It suits you."

"Don't even *think* about it," she warned, which made him laugh again.

He bent his head. When he looked back up at her, the humor had vanished from his expression. "I'm sorry I was so self-righteous last night. I could have at least shown some concern."

"You reacted like almost anyone would," she assured him. "And, honestly, I can scarcely believe you're willing to help me now."

"There's no guarantee that my badge will tip the scales in your favor," he warned, "but I can't see how it can hurt your case."

She hugged her waist, her whole body going suddenly tense.

"Where do you think we should live?" he asked. "At my place or here?" He glanced around. "I vote for my place. It's nothing elegant, just a renovated old farmhouse on an acreage, but it's got four bedrooms and three baths. Your flat is cozy, but it's small and isn't really a home. There isn't even a second bedroom for Sarah, and judges take things like that into account when they consider a child's future welfare. I also have livestock to care for, and it's safer for them if someone is in the house at night. If a predator starts pestering the animals, I'll hear the ruckus. You can drive from my place to the shop each morning. It's not that far away."

She nodded in agreement. He smiled and asked, "Are you still worried that we don't know each other well enough to do this?"

"Sort of. It'd be scary even if we'd known each other for a year."

He settled back on the sofa. "Where did you attend college?"

"The University of Oregon. Erickson is only a hop away from Eugene."

He snapped his fingers. "I went to the U of O, too. You see, we have something in common besides hating our first names."

Taffeta said, "I wanted to become a pharmacist. Then Phillip came along and asked me to marry him. Like an idiot, I said yes."

"I took criminal justice courses before entering the police academy," he said. "I wanted to be a state cop and specialize in criminal investigation. That requires more education."

"So how did you end up here, being a deputy?" she asked, sincerely curious.

He grinned and shook his head. "You won't laugh?"

"Of course not."

"I didn't like being a state cop up north. Bigger towns, more people, and crime out the yang. Bottom line, I got homesick for Mystic Creek and my family."

He shrugged. "When you grow up in a town like this where everyone knows practically everyone else, you miss it. My family is also pretty close-knit. It felt as if a huge chunk of who I was had gone missing."

"Why would I laugh about that?"

"Well, some people might think I'm a mama's boy."

She did laugh then. "Do you hang out with your mom a lot?"

"No, not half as much as I should. Tonight when I dropped by, she was surprised to see me, and I think she knew right away that I had a reason for being there. That bothered me. She is a fabulous mother. My dad is the salt of the earth. They provided me with a wonderful childhood, and I know they'd like to see more of me."

Taffeta thought of her own childhood. "You are so very lucky. As an infant, I got sick. Some kind of weird anemia, and at first the doctors thought it might be leukemia. I was taken off the adoption market for the first year of my life, and by the time I was well, I was over a year old. Young couples prefer to adopt newborns. Nobody stepped forward to take me."

His usually bright gaze darkened. "I'm so sorry."

She scrunched her shoulders. "Lots of kids grow up in foster care. When I was five, a couple almost took me. I got to meet them and grew excited, thinking I might finally have a real mom and dad. That didn't happen. Later a set of foster parents considered adopting me, but in the end, they decided against it. As I grew older, I learned not to get my heart set on anything. Now I'm alone in the world except for Sarah. I have no idea who my mother and father are."

"You could probably track them down."

"I have no desire to find them, Barney. If they were interested, they'd be trying to locate me, not the other way around. When you grow up like I did, you learn to be alone and feel okay about it. Sometimes it bugs me, like when I visit a doctor and need to fill out my family history. Does ovarian cancer run in my family? Do relatives of mine have early onset diabetes? I have no idea. My genetics are a complete mystery. It's a concern now that I have a daughter."

"I can't imagine not having my family," he said. "When one of us needs help, everyone circles the wagons. It's a good feeling to know you can count on people to be there."

He told her about his brother Jeb's wife and how Jeb had rescued her and her daughter during a horrific ice storm. "She was on the run from a crazy husband who had abused her and her little girl. While she was staying with Jeb, the bastard tracked her down. It was a life-threatening situation, and at times Jeb needed help protecting her and the child. All of us boys had his back, and so did our dad. I don't think Jeb or Amanda will ever forget that."

"Phillip isn't physically violent, thank goodness." Taffeta smiled. "He's self-centered and careless with people's feelings, but he's too involved in his own gratification to be focused on deliberately harming anyone."

"He sure as hell harmed you, not with his fists, but with vicious lies."

She nodded. "Yes, but there again, Phillip was thinking about himself, not me. To understand him, you have to know him. He never actively wanted to hurt me. I stood in his way, plain and simple."

"You're very forgiving."

"Actually I hate his guts," she confessed with a laugh. "But I also know it was never his sole aim to ruin my life. He doesn't think about the other side of the coin. Phillip is all about Phillip. His wants, his needs, his happiness. When he lied about me on the stand, I doubt he spared a second thought for what it would do to me. He wanted out of the marriage, and Sarah's accident gave him a window of opportunity to divorce me without incurring his father's wrath."

"How could any man fail to understand what such lies would do to the mother of his child?"

"Barney, he just doesn't care—about me or about Sarah. She's a nuisance to him, something to be displayed when it makes him look good and ignored the rest of the time, just like I was. I was only ever a stage prop, the crowbar Phillip needed to pry money out of his dad." Taffeta got up and moved toward the kitchen. "Your stomach is growling. I have a feeling you haven't eaten."

He placed a broad hand over his abdomen. "I'm sorry. I was so intent on what you were saying, I didn't notice. Truth is, I spent my lunch hour talking with Bryan Vorch, and I went straight to my parents' place after work to get their take on a temporary marriage. After that, I went home to feed my animals before coming here, but I didn't think about feeding myself."

"Well, I can whip you up a grilled cheese with a side of tomato soup," she offered. "That's what I fall back on when I'm tired and don't want to walk over to

Flagg's Market. I don't have much food storage in this dinky place. I can offer you a beer, though. I enjoy one every now and again."

"You don't have to feed me."

Taffeta motioned him toward the kitchen. "It's not like I'm offering you haute cuisine."

"Do you have enough bread for two grilled cheese?"

She grinned, glad that he had agreed to eat there. "Two sandwiches, coming right up." She flashed him a look over her shoulder as she grabbed the skillet she'd used earlier from the dish drainer. "You went without lunch and dinner for me. It's the least I can do."

While she sliced cheese and spread mayo over the pieces of bread, Barney fished two longnecks out of her fridge and popped the caps with an opener he found in a drawer. He liked that her refrigerator looked tidy and the drawer was well organized. He wouldn't be sharing his house with a slob.

He set her beer on the counter near where she worked, and then turned one of the two dinette chairs around backward so that he could straddle the seat. She glanced over her shoulder and dimpled a cheek at him. "That is such a guy thing, sitting on a chair that way."

Until that moment, he hadn't realized that she had dimples. That sent him down memory lane, trying to remember if he'd ever seen her smile during their chats over morning coffee. She had laughed. He distinctly remembered that. But he guessed she'd never smiled broadly enough to make the indentation appear. Tonight she seemed more relaxed. Perhaps it was because for the first time in a long while she had a plan to clear her name after her ex-husband's false accusations.

"It's comfortable, sitting this way," he said. "I can use the chair back as an armrest."

She gave her head a shake. "I use the table."

"That's bad manners when you're eating. This way, I can brace my arms while I eat, and my mother can't give me an ass chewing."

She giggled. "Your mom sounds wonderful. Does she really jump all over you about your manners?"

"And about my language," he revealed. "Jeb and Amanda have given her two grandkids, and no foul language is allowed now, period. To this day I'm wary if she threatens to wash my mouth out with soap. She wouldn't hesitate to do it."

Taffeta turned a questioning gaze on him. "How big is she?"

"Physically no bigger than a minute, but she makes up for her lack of bulk with attitude." He took a swallow of beer, pleased that she liked Indian pale ale. "We need a courtship plan, you know. We can't just get married and hotfoot it to Erickson to see a judge. We have to establish that we met, fell in love, have been dating for months, and are as happy as clams. You never know when the court will check us out, maybe send a PI over here to ask around. We want people to say that we're the perfect couple."

Taffeta turned a questioning gaze on him. "How in the world will we accomplish that? How long are you thinking before I can hotfoot it to Erickson? My little girl needs me *now*."

"A month." Barney saw no point in breaking that to her gently. "We need to set the stage, Taffeta. It's crucial to your chances."

The sizzle of butter popped in the hot skillet. His mouth began to water as she put the sandwiches on to brown. He wasn't sure which struck him as being more delicious, the food or the woman. *Not good.* He'd only just told her he didn't expect sex to be a part of this arrangement. And he'd meant it. But that didn't mean he didn't *want* to have sex with her.

The problem was that he found her so damned attractive. Even dressed in her plain Jane outfit, she looked good enough to devour, and now that he felt certain beyond a reasonable doubt that she hadn't harmed her daughter, his hormones had gone into overdrive again.

But he still wasn't going to collect that way for helping her out, no matter how many cold showers he had to take.

Chapter Seven

While Barney ate the grilled cheese sandwiches and soup, he sipped on his beer. He and Taffeta shared stories of campus life at the U of O. He confessed that he'd blown off studying the first few months and had only started cracking the books when his dad laid down the law. She confided that she'd seen excelling at academics as her only way to rise above being a foster kid with no family and no money to back her. She needed to maintain her scholarships and financial aid. No adult praised her when she graduated with honors from high school at only seventeen. No one encouraged her when she worked nights to pay her own way and pulled a 4.0 GPA by studying until the wee hours of the morning.

They laughed a little, and then Barney steered the conversation to more practical matters. "It'll look strange to people in Mystic Creek if we suddenly get married, but if we mean to help Sarah any time soon, we can't waste time pretending to date and fall slowly in love. I suggest that we drive to Reno this coming Saturday and get hitched in one of those chapels that offer quick weddings. Then we'll tell people that we've been dating on the sly in Crystal Falls since shortly after you moved here."

Barney could tell by Taffeta's troubled expression that her thoughts had turned to Sarah's welfare. "That's a whole week away. Who's watching my little girl tonight? Are the adults around her under the influence, not only of alcohol, but maybe drugs? That thought alone breaks my heart and terrifies me. I'm tempted to go to Erickson and kidnap her."

"You can't do that. If you were caught—and you *would* be caught—you'd end up doing hard time, and where would Sarah be then? It's better to work within the legal system. It's going to take some time," he warned. "We have to spread our story around and appear together in town, pretending to be madly in love. It'll be crucial that people here are convinced that we're the perfect couple in case the Erickson judge has us investigated."

Even though Barney saw concern etched all over her face, she nodded. "Do you think people will believe we've been secretly dating all this time?"

Barney considered the question. "I hung around mornings in your store nearly every day this last week. Trust me, in Mystic Creek, people notice things like that. I think they'll buy it, especially if we make a show of being lovey-dovey in public after we're married."

"The question is, will Sarah survive the situation she's in for a whole month? And maybe even much longer!"

Barney didn't know how to reassure her. "You can

only hope that God is watching over her. Let's pray her babysitters are women with good hearts who don't grow angry and violent when they're high."

"Or when they go through the initial crash, when using more meth has no effect. I've seen people act crazy then."

Barney's attention sharpened on her face. "You know a little about meth addiction, I take it?"

She shrugged. "In college I knew some kids who got messed up. If you're asking if I ever experimented, no. I did try pot a couple of times, but I hated the way it made me feel. Meth is something that I never touched." She flashed her pearly whites in a forced smile. "I'd like to keep my teeth."

Barney took a swig of his beer. "Me, too. And I also want to keep a clear head. Like you, I tried pot a couple of times. But I didn't care for it, either, and I knew my folks wouldn't approve. I'll have a few beers now and again, or mixed drinks at a special celebration, but I've never liked to feel out of control." He winked at her. "Will you marry me next Saturday in Reno, Ms. Brown?"

Her expression didn't brighten. "Of course. I'll do anything to help me get Sarah back."

"Ouch."

She giggled, but the laugh sounded forced. "I didn't mean it *that* way. I'm extremely grateful that you've agreed to do this, Barney. All indications are that you're a fine man with a caring heart. I'm just worried about Sarah being left in that mess for so long."

"I know." A heavy, tight feeling filled his chest. "It's only a little over a month, though, with added time for all the red tape we may face afterward in Erickson. Think you can handle snuggling up to me and swapping a little slobber in public? We'll have to put on a show all over town."

That turned her strained giggle into a mirthful chortle. Her cheeks went pink as well. "That depends. Are you a good kisser?"

It was his turn to laugh. "I've never gotten any complaints." Barney tried never to lie and held up a hand. "Well, actually, I did get one when I was a teenager and experimenting with chewing tobacco. I forgot to rinse my mouth before I laid one on a girl."

Taffeta's delicate nose wrinkled and she said, "Ick! That's nasty."

He chuckled. "Well, the girl sure thought so. Now I brush my teeth and rinse with mouthwash before a date—and I never chew anymore."

"Good, because if you dare to lock lips with me when you have anything horrible in your mouth, I'll punch you."

Barney caught himself staring at her soft mouth. How would he get through kissing her, even if it was only for show in public, without having a physical reaction? He decided that he would cross that bridge when he got to it.

Taffeta felt as if she'd climbed on a runaway bus as she escorted Barney to the door to see him out. Everything from here forward would happen quickly. Not fast enough to suit her because of her concerns about

Sarah, and yet too fast for her peace of mind. On Saturday morning, she'd be leaving for Reno to marry this man, and when they got back, she would be the equivalent of an actress on a stage, pretending to be wildly in love with him.

"I'm not a very accomplished liar," she admitted as he settled his Stetson on his head and adjusted it to just the right angle. "I don't know if people will believe me when I say I've been dating you in secret."

"That's good to know." He opened the door and turned to look down at her. "That you're not an accomplished liar, I mean. Normally I don't lie, either." He curled a finger under her chin. "Relax, Taffy. My family will help spread the word. Even if none of us lies very convincingly, we'll carry it off with strength in numbers."

"All of your family is going to know?"

"They'll have to. I can't let them think it's a real marriage. And they're a great bunch. For Sarah, they'll happily climb on board with us."

"You just called me Taffy."

He laughed and stepped out onto the landing. "It has such a nice ring to it." He leaned back in to grin at her as he drew on his jacket. "And now I'll say good night—Taffy."

After he started down the stairs, she kept the door ajar to listen to the masculine thud of his boots. Her hated nickname sounded like an endearment when he said it. Raising her voice to be heard, she yelled, "If you ever call me Daffy, I'll brain you with my skillet!"

She heard him chuckle. Then the downstairs door

rattled open. "If you ever ask if I've polished the single bullet in my pocket today, I'll divorce you!"

To cover for a sick deputy, Barney worked the night shift three times running the following week, going in at six and getting off at four in the morning. Despite the lack of sleep, he appeared at Taffeta's shop right after she opened at eight each morning, bringing coffee, pastry, and a devastating grin that still made her nerve endings trill. Only now he stayed until ten so customers would see him, and he made sure that it looked as if he were flirting with her over the checkout counter.

"All this caffeine is going to keep you awake," Taffeta worried aloud on Monday as he sipped his java. "You'll be so exhausted tonight that you'll fall asleep behind the wheel when you're driving around town."

He toasted her with his Jake 'n' Bake cup. "Decaf, darlin'. I'll hit the sack at eleven and sleep like a baby."

"But you have to start work at six tonight. You'll only get about six hours of sleep."

"I've managed plenty of times on far less, and it's important for people to see me in here."

"I feel bad about you losing rest."

His white teeth flashed in a grin. "You're starting to sound very wifely already."

Taffeta wrinkled her nose, and he chuckled.

Minutes later, Joe Paisley, owner of Taco Joe's, entered the shop. He stopped dead when he saw Barney and Taffeta nearly nose-to-nose over the counter. About six feet tall with deep brown hair and brown eyes, he looked to be about thirty and—at the moment—surprised and uncertain what to say.

"Excuse me. I didn't mean to interrupt."

Barney's mouth was so close to Taffeta's that she could feel his breath on her lips. He grinned and straightened away from her. "No worries, Joe. I've just been asking this lady to marry me, and she keeps breaking my heart by saying no."

Joe glanced at Taffeta. "Oh. I, um, didn't realize you two were seeing each other."

Barney, the very picture of nonchalance, shifted his weight to turn toward the restaurateur. "She's shy about it, so we've been hooking up in Crystal Falls. You know how it goes in Mystic Creek. One whisper of gossip, and the next thing you know, it's all over town."

Joe inclined his dark head. "I'll keep it under wraps, then." He smiled at Taffeta. "I know you never order, but I stopped in to see if you'd like something hot for lunch today. I'm running a special: two tacos and a medium soft drink for a buck fifty."

Taffeta shook her head and returned his smile. "That's a great deal, but I'm watching my calories. Thanks for thinking to stop in and ask, though."

Joe stuffed his order tablet back in his jacket pocket and reopened the door. On his way out, he said over his shoulder, "Barney's a great guy. Half the single gals in town are head over heels. You should take him on faith and say yes."

When they were alone again, Barney gifted Taffeta with a teasing look. "How the hell does he make a profit with prices that low?"

"I think he knows I pinch my pennies and offers me special deals. And your evasion tactics won't work. You gave me no warning that you were going to mention marriage, absolutely *none*. I could have gotten flustered and blown it."

He chuckled and tweaked her nose. "But you didn't. And you have to be ready to play this off the cuff, following my lead."

"Maybe I'll want to take the lead sometimes."

A glint crept into his eyes. "Fine by me. I love it when a lady takes the lead." Then, as if he had said nothing untoward, he glanced at the wall clock. "It's nearly ten. Our mission for the day is accomplished. A lot of people go into Joe's joint for lunch. Word will be out in no time."

Taffeta frowned. "But Joe said he'd keep it under wraps."

Barney threw back his head and laughed so hard that his Stetson was nearly unseated. "You haven't lived in Mystic Creek long enough. Joe is a good guy, and he won't mean any harm, but he'll blab it to someone. Human nature always prevails." He straightened his hat. "Not much happens in this town, Taffy. People love to gossip."

He moved away from the counter.

"You're leaving?"

He winked over his shoulder at her. "I can grab a few extra minutes of sleep. Have a great day, and I'll see you again tomorrow morning."

Biting the inside of her cheek, Taffeta watched him depart, wondering how she would ever get through this. Barney clearly didn't want anything intimate to happen between them. It had been hard enough for her to keep a clear head around him before this play-acting thing had started. Now, with him pretending to be in love with her, she was challenged to keep reality and make-believe separated.

True to his word, Barney reappeared in Taffeta's shop at shortly after eight the next morning. By now, she'd grown accustomed to enjoying pastry and sipping coffee with him. He assumed his usual stance across the counter from her. She noted that the lack of sleep was starting to show on his tanned face, and her heart panged with sympathy.

"You have shadows under your eyes."

He smiled and shrugged one shoulder. "I'm on day shift Thursday and Friday, so I can rest up before we take off for Reno on Saturday morning. You have all your clothes packed yet?"

"For the trip?"

"No, to move in at my place."

Taffeta toyed with her napkin. "I'm working on it. I'm trying to decide what to take over there. I have a lot of clothes, some that I haven't worn since moving here."

He took a bite of cream horn. "Oh yeah, I forgot. You're the lady with two lives, one wearing a killer outfit and heels, the other draping herself in loose clothing the color of baby poop."

In Taffeta's experience, baby poop could be bright green if an infant drank grape juice. "Which outfit are you referring to?"

"That icky brown shirt that billows around you

like a tent." He arched a tawny eyebrow. "Bring some of your Erickson clothing to my place." He glanced down at her baggy, olive green sweater. "When we go out on the town after we get back from Reno, it'll be easier to pretend you knock my socks off if you look fabulous."

Taffeta plucked at the pilled yarn. "Are you saying I'm not attractive dressed this way?" To not stand out had been her goal since coming to Mystic Creek, but now her feelings were a little hurt. She knew it made no sense, but she was a female, after all. How she felt didn't always have to be understandable to a member of the opposite sex. "Ouch."

He grinned. "I'm learning to look beyond the drab colors, Taffy. You're a beautiful woman, no matter what you're wearing, and I think you're well aware of it. But a little more flash won't hurt when I'm pretending to salivate over you for the next month."

Pretending. Taffeta didn't like the sound of that and realized she had waded neck deep into pure trouble. When she was around Barney Sterling with those twinkling amber eyes and all that raw masculinity emanating from the pores of his skin, her saliva glands overreacted, and no pretense was involved.

"Hey," he said softly. "What's up? I didn't mean to offend you."

Taffeta jerked her chin up. "You didn't offend me. I'm just worried that you're one of those husbands who'll expect me to crawl out of bed every morning looking all made up and perfect."

He gave a slow shake of his head. "If I were your

husband—for real, I mean—I'd expect you to crawl out of bed looking mussed and sleep-deprived because I'd be making love to you half the night."

He turned to leave her shop. Taffeta knotted one fist. "You're going to say something like that to me and then just walk out?"

Challenge glinted in his eyes as he opened the door and turned to look at her. "It's all pretend. Right?" He peeled back his jacket cuff and glanced down at his oversize gold wristwatch. Most young guys wore leather bands nowadays, but Barney seemed to prefer shiny metal. Taffeta scolded herself for it, but she liked that little bit of shimmer on him. "And it's ten o'clock," he added. "My bed is calling my name."

He walked out. She stared after him. Was he attracted to her, or not? Taffeta huffed and vented her irritation by kicking at the cushioned rubber mat on the floor behind the register. Her toe glanced off the edge and caught the small plastic trash receptacle she used for debris. Crumpled paper fanned across the floor.

Dammit. She swore under her breath as she bent to pick up the wads. *This whole situation is driving me over the edge already, and we've barely started our campaign yet.* She felt for the cell phone in her jeans pocket, tempted to call Barney and tell him her old shirt was *not* baby poop brown. It was camel colored. *Men.* They were horrible at naming colors. Barney would probably call mauve something dumb, like wilted rose pink.

* * *

By week's end, Barney dreaded the trip to Reno. What was it about Taffeta Brown that rattled his chain every time he was near her? *Shit*. He had tried his best all week to play his role, allowing customers to see them cozied up to each other, but whenever he reminded himself that he and Taffeta were only play-acting, her face fell as if he'd just kicked her. Did she want the attraction between them to be real? If so, why the hell didn't she just say so? He was ready. All she had to do was press his "go" button.

Only that wasn't really true. No matter how much she turned him on, he couldn't, in good conscience, make love to her, even if she asked him to. She had only ever offered him sex in the first place as a lure to get him to help her regain custody of her daughter, and now she undoubtedly felt obligated to him because he had agreed to marry her. He'd be taking advantage of the situation if he took her to bed, and he wasn't that kind of man.

As Saturday swiftly approached, Taffeta concluded that in the end her acting ability might not be put to a test when she and Barney returned from Reno as a married couple. Barney had been in her store every morning and spent the entire two hours of his stay doing everything possible to behave like a man who was deeply in love. Any pedestrian on either side of the street could look in the front windows and see them. Any customer who entered the shop also saw them. Barney made sure that he put on a show for everyone. For that reason alone, she had already lost a big piece of her heart to him, and heaven help her, fondness wasn't the only emotion that he elicited from within her. With increasing frequency, he still played a starring role in her lonely-night fantasies.

She had to remember that reality seldom measured up to a dream, and she should remind herself countless times a day that Barney probably wouldn't—or couldn't—compare to her imaginary, perfect man. So why did she allow a mere glance from him to make her ache with yearning? It was a question for which she had no answer, and that made no sense at all. She had been disappointed once before by a man, deeply disappointed and betrayed. Had she learned nothing from that experience?

She needed to remain focused on her daughter. Barney said that as soon as they established themselves as a blissfully happy couple in Mystic Creek, they could turn their attention to getting Sarah back. His attorney friend was in the process of compiling the paperwork to file Taffeta's appeal, and he had mentioned to Barney that he intended to represent Taffeta for only a nominal fee. Taffeta could scarcely believe that a successful lawyer would be so generous, but Barney claimed that Vorch wanted a chance to annihilate Phillip later on charges of perjury. Apparently Phillip's shady behavior had earned him many enemies in the legal community of Erickson.

On Friday while Taffeta and Barney shared a cream horn in her shop, Barney lifted his coffee cup to her and said, "Tomorrow's the big day. I'd like to hit the road by about five in the morning so we won't be rushing to find a chapel after we reach Reno."

"Would it be safer to make reservations at a chapel now?"

"I called around to see how far out most wedding venues are booked, and I was told that last-minute arrangements can be made at almost all of them. It sounds like marriage at a drive-up window. That being the case, I thought I should wait to choose a chapel with you after we get there. Despite it not being a real marriage, I still thought the chapel should at least appeal to both of us."

Taffeta appreciated his thoughtfulness. Where they got married didn't matter in any practical way, but she didn't want to look back someday and have awful memories of the place. "I'm an early riser. Being ready to leave at five won't be a problem for me."

"I talked with Bryan as I drove over here," he said. "He says it's important to file the appeal as soon as possible. The process can take some time. Just getting all his ducks in a row to file involves a lot of red tape, but once your case is reviewed and deemed worthy of a hearing, he feels almost certain that he can get the conviction overturned. Phillip's testimony was the only damaging evidence the prosecuting attorney had, and once a judge starts to question whether or not Phillip was telling the truth, he or she will have no choice but to wipe your record clean. To convict, the evidence must show that a person is guilty beyond a reasonable doubt. If Phillip's testimony is discredited, the physical evidence, of which there is little, won't hold up in court."

Barney made it all sound so simple that Taffeta couldn't help getting her hopes up—to be proven innocent was something she hadn't even let herself hope for. She would always remember how devastating it had been when the judge dropped the gavel and delivered the verdict against her.

Chapter Eight

As if Barney sensed Taffeta's soaring hopefulness, he made a soft sound deep in his throat and trailed a fingertip along her cheekbone. "It won't all be easy," he reminded her.

She rushed to assure him, "I know," loving the way his touch made her feel. "Nothing worth having comes easily."

He nodded. "Meeting with your former parents-in-law to ask for their support when you petition the court for a reversal of the custody order may be one of the most difficult things you've ever done."

Taffeta's heart sank. "Meet with them? Oh, Barney, I'm not sure—"

He cut in with "Grace and Cameron Gentry once liked you, honey. The three of you had a good relationship until Phillip destroyed it. Now that he's messing up so badly, don't you think his parents are smart enough to figure out that he probably lied about you?"

Taffeta still dreaded having to meet with the Gentrys. At one time, she had loved them as if they were her own parents, and she believed that they had loved her in return. The fact that they could believe Phillip's lies about her still hurt her deeply. "What if they still hate me?"

He leaned in closer. "If it gets ugly, you'll have me there to run interference."

"You'll go with me?"

"Of course. For moral support if nothing else."

A burning sensation stung Taffeta's eyes. In all her life, she'd never had anyone who stood beside her. *Never.* "You're a very special man, Barney Sterling." Even to her ears, her voice sounded thick. "I'm very lucky to have you as my friend."

The moment she said those words, Taffeta wished that they could be more than friends. Dumb, dumb, dumb. If she didn't tread carefully, she was going to get her heart broken, and it wouldn't be Barney's fault. He'd made her no promises. Never once had he hinted that their forthcoming marriage would be anything more than a sham to strengthen her chances of getting Sarah back.

She glanced at the wall clock behind him and saw that it was nearly ten, time for him to leave for work. A disturbing thought struck her. "Barney, I thought you said that your day shifts start at ten. Are your visits here this week making you late for work?"

He popped the last bit of his cream horn into his mouth. After swallowing, he said, "Only about five minutes. It's a short drive to the department from here. No big deal."

"You've been late just to be here so customers might see you? Doesn't your boss get mad?"

"Blake? Nah. I work extra shifts anytime he needs me to cover for someone." He drank what remained of his coffee and put the empty container into the pastry bag. "He knows that he can count on me, so he cuts me some slack when I need some leeway here and there."

The anxiety that had welled so suddenly within Taffeta began to abate slowly. "So you haven't gotten in trouble, then."

"Heck, no. It isn't like most jobs, where you clock in and out, working an exact number of hours. I practically always work over. At the end of a shift, I have to update the deputy taking over, and then I have to do my shift report. That can take a half hour sometimes. The way I think Blake sees it is that it all evens out."

Taffeta sighed. "I just don't want you to jeopardize your job for me."

"I won't, so stop fretting about it." He crumpled a soiled napkin in his hand and hoop-shot it into the sack. "I still haven't lost my touch."

"You must have played basketball," she observed.

"Oh yeah. Football and wrestling, too. My dad believes in encouraging teenage boys to stay busy to keep them out of trouble. With sports and horses, I was a pretty active kid."

Taffeta looked at the clock again and knew he needed to leave. She didn't want their time together to end. "Were you good? At sports, I mean?"

"Honestly?" His lips tipped into a sheepish grin. "I was barely good enough at basketball to make the team, and I totally bombed at football, mostly because colliding with guys on a field never made sense to me. But I kicked ass in wrestling. Placed second in the state my senior year of high school. I hoped to wrestle in college and did for a couple of years until the wrestling program was cut."

"Second in state? You must have been something!"

"I still am. Knowing how to take a man down and pin him is helpful in my line of work. I practice with my little brother Jonas whenever he's home. He's better on the mat than I am, but I still hold my own." He pushed back his hat, leaned forward, and startled her with a quick kiss on her cheek. "I'll show you some of my best moves sometime."

Taffeta's heart was still racing as he strode out the door. She rested her fingertips over the spot where his lips had touched.

Five o'clock on Saturday morning came early for Taffeta. She dozed through her alarm, and when Barney rapped on her apartment door, she still had sleep in her eyes and was washed but not dressed. She threw on her robe to let him in, and when he saw her, he rocked back on his heels, grinned, and touched the brim of his hat.

"Top of the morning to you," he said with a fair rendition of an Irish brogue. "I thought you were an early riser."

"I normally am, but I had trouble sleeping and then didn't hear my alarm."

"Troubling thoughts? That's usually what keeps me awake."

Taffeta had been thinking about Barney showing her some of his best moves, but never in a million years would she tell him that. "I normally stay open on Saturday, and I got to worrying about being closed today." She hurried back to her room. Two stuffed suitcases and a large box sat at the foot of her bed. They held clothing she intended to take with her to Barney's house. She bypassed the containers and went to stand in front of her closet again. What did a bride wear to a Reno chapel wedding? "Oh *God*," she muttered. "This is going to be a disaster."

"What is?"

Barney's voice came from the doorway behind her and startled her half out of her wits. "Excuse me," she said with strained patience, "but I'm about to dress."

"The latch didn't catch, so the door swung back open." He leaned a shoulder against the jamb. "I have two sisters. When a female stands in front of her closet, whispering about disaster, it normally means she doesn't know what the hell to wear."

Taffeta folded her arms at her waist and turned to face him. "It's not just any old day. Even if it's only for show, we're getting married. I've never had to pick a proper outfit for a wedding."

"What did you wear the first time, nothing?"

Taffeta realized that he was enjoying her discomfiture. "My mother-in-law and a dressmaker chose everything I wore. In Erickson, Phillip's marriage was a big event."

"Ah, well, think along more casual lines than that. Look at me. I'm not dressed up. It'll be a Reno wedding. People gamble in a casino, suddenly decide to tie the knot, and go get married. I don't think there's a dress code."

She took in his attire. He wore a tan Stetson instead of the usual chocolate brown one, and he looked wonderful in fresh Wrangler jeans that skimmed his muscular legs, polished brown riding boots, and a blue western-cut shirt with pearled snaps instead of buttons.

She resumed staring helplessly at the few remaining clothes that hung on the rod. "Nothing I haven't packed is appropriate."

He chuckled, and she felt the vibrations of his footfalls crossing the ratty old carpet. He stood behind her, bent his knees to be at her eye level, and said, "The brown shirt is definitely out. What's that flowery thing, a sundress? That won't work. You'll freeze your ass off." He reached past her to finger the pink knit top she'd worn to the dumpy Italian restaurant. "This will work. It looks awesome on you, especially with that itty-bitty black skirt you paired with it."

"The skirt is packed to go to your house."

"Oh. Well, do you have a pair of jeans that fit?"

"Of course. I wear jeans a lot down in the shop."

"No, I don't mean denim tents. I mean jeans that actually *fit*."

She gnawed the inside of her cheek. "Tight ones, you mean?"

"Not *tight*, just snug."

"I have a few pairs that I wore in Erickson. They were snug at the time, but I've gained a little weight since moving here. They may be skintight now."

"Perfect," he said. "Squeeze into them, add the top, find some sensible walking shoes, and meet me in the kitchen. I'll have coffee waiting." He moved toward the door. Before exiting into the living room, he added, "And today, can you ditch the schoolmarm hairdo? Pretty please, with sugar on top? Wear it down, or I'll be afraid to say *ain't* all the way to Reno in case you reprimand me for poor grammar."

"In all the times we've talked, I've never once heard you say that word." She cast him a blistering glance. "You're telling me how to dress, and we're not even married yet."

"Oops. Can I deduce from the resentment I hear in your voice that Phillip told you how to dress?"

Taffeta stiffened her shoulders, unwilling to answer that question. He might never understand the pressure that she'd been under during her marriage to measure up to the standards set for her. The wives of the attorneys in such a classy law firm dressed to the nines, and Taffeta hadn't known what to wear then, either. Phillip never hesitated to criticize when her choice in attire failed to please him. "Out. I can't squeeze into jeans with you watching."

He left and closed the door. She had showered already, so all she had to do was dress, wash her face, and brush her hair. *Easy,* she assured herself. Only when she stood in front of the dresser mirror, she didn't like what she saw and spent twenty minutes with makeup and a curling iron.

When she appeared in the front room, Barney rewarded her with an appreciative whistle.

* * *

Barney had gotten coffees and pastry to go from the Jake 'n' Bake. Jake hit the deck early every morning to make pastries, and he'd opened up for Barney as a special favor. Taffeta sipped from her sugar-enriched java as Barney's truck rumbled from Mystic Creek on an eastward highway. Her jeans hugged her belly and thighs like a girdle and were so tight around her waist that she could barely take a deep breath. All she could think about as she consumed more calories was how much weight she'd gained since moving to Mystic Creek. *Too much comfort food.* All those grilled cheese sandwiches for dinner had taken a toll.

Needing to fill the silence between herself and her soon-to-be husband because she felt unaccountably nervous, Taffeta asked, "Was it a hassle getting the weekend off?"

He chuckled. "Adams looked shocked, not because I ask all the time, but because I seldom do. I'm a believer in building up my sick days and vacation so I can have important times of the year off to spend them with my family. I work a lot of weekends, covering for people who want off, to add to my cache." He lifted his hands briefly from the steering wheel to shrug. "Why not cover for them? I've got no family, so it works for me."

"Having long stretches off, even if you had a family, might be lovely," she suggested. "Trips to Disneyland or somewhere else would be nice for a wife and kids."

"Careful, there. Trips to Disneyland are expensive, and I'm existing on a deputy's wages."

"Don't you get paid by the hour and make more money for the extra time you put in?"

"Nope. I get a salary. But when I work an extra shift, I earn another vacation day, and saving them up is, in my opinion, better than putting money in the bank. I enjoy doing simple things that don't cost very much—long horseback rides into wilderness areas to camp at high-mountain lakes to fish. I also like to work on my house. It was dilapidated when I bought it. I save up to make improvements and then try to do most of the work myself when I take vacation."

Taffeta relaxed in the bucket seat, trying to picture Barney's life. She decided that she was much like him. Expensive vacations didn't matter to her. She would have loved to have a family like his, large and close-knit, and to know that they loved her enough to always be there. Barney might not make a lot of money being a deputy, but he loved his work, he owned a house, and, far more important, he could spend time with people he loved whenever he wanted. On Sundays, Taffeta watched television, read, or studied online to become a licensed herbalist. She missed having human contact and could barely wait for Monday morning.

As if Barney sensed that the silence between them made her edgy, he turned on the stereo and tuned in to a station that featured a variety of music genres. The instant that Tony Bennett's voice filled the cab, crooning about San Francisco, Barney started singing along.

He had a deep, rich voice, and he could carry a tune, which was more than Taffeta could boast.

He glanced over at her. "Come *on*. Get into it with me."

"I can't sing," she confessed. "I sound like a bullfrog and only do it in the shower."

He leaned his head back and laughed. Then he turned the music up. "*Sing!* Who cares if you sound like a bullfrog? With it this loud, who'll hear you?"

Taffeta tentatively joined in, and when he didn't cringe, she raised her voice. Soon she was belting out lyrics as if she were a rock star, with Barney harmonizing with her. Or at least trying. She wasn't very good at carrying a tune. He didn't seem to care.

Then, to her mortification, the Rolling Stones came over the airway, and she was confronted with "(I Can't Get No) Satisfaction." Barney winked at her. Then he started shouting the lyrics.

She couldn't help laughing because if any man on earth could find satisfaction, it had to be this incredibly handsome deputy with those seductive and intoxicating amber eyes.

She couldn't resist joining in, yelling the words at the top of her lungs. Pretty soon they were laughing so hard that they had beads of sweat on their foreheads. And then "She Loves You" by the Beatles burst from the speakers. Who could resist that?

They sang for over an hour. Taffeta was slightly hoarse when Barney turned off the stereo so they could talk. He told her funny stories about his childhood. She particularly loved the one about him and his brothers painting their black Lab yellow. Taffeta had no funny tales to tell about her childhood. Maybe lots of kids had good experiences in foster homes, but she hadn't been so lucky.

Barney said he didn't care whether her stories made him laugh. He just wanted to know her better. Taffeta relented and discovered she did have some funny stories, after all. She recounted the time her foster brother put baby powder in a hair dryer and laughed until he wet his pants when their snotty foster sister came out of the bathroom screaming. The boy got in trouble and had to clean the bathroom, but that didn't stop him from sealing the top of the commode with plastic wrap the following week. Their foster father went in to use the toilet and splattered urine everywhere.

Barney laughed and sent her a warm look. "I'll bet that incited his wrath."

"He threw Rodney against the wall. He had a bad temper, and his wife never tried to stop him when he got mean."

Keeping his gaze on the road, Barney said, "You must have had at least one nice foster parent."

Taffeta's heart twisted. "Once there was an old lady. She'd been taking in foster kids for years with her husband. They'd never been able to have children. When he died, she was going to quit taking in kids, but she made an exception for me." Taffeta glanced over at him. "I felt like she really cared about me. When she got the monthly checks, she gave me a portion of the money to spend however I wanted. I didn't feel as if I was a meal ticket. Her name was Mrs. Brassfield, but she let me call her Emma. One Saturday a month, she drove me to the mall. While I shopped, she sat in a mall café sipping tea, and she seemed really glad when I found something special to buy."

"Uh-oh. You've got the Sarah look in your eyes."

Taffeta questioned him with her gaze. "What is the Sarah look?"

"Sad. I see pain in your expression. Something bad happened to Mrs. Brassfield."

"She died," Taffeta pushed out. "We were doing dishes together. She seemed perfectly fine, and suddenly she hit the floor. I didn't know what to do. I tried to wake her up. Then I called for an ambulance, but it took forever to get there. For a while, I could still feel her pulse, but then it just stopped."

"My God. How old were you, Taffy?"

"Thirteen."

"Now I better understand why you bundled Sarah in a blanket and drove her to the emergency room yourself."

Her chest ached as the memories moved through her mind. "You never forget watching somebody die, especially when it's a person you care about."

"No, I don't think you do," he agreed. "I'm sorry you lost her that way. A kid shouldn't have to witness something like that. But as badly as it ended, I'm glad you got to be with someone who cared about you for a while."

Taffeta nodded. "She taught me how to love." A

smile curved her mouth, and she glanced sideways at Barney. "Emma would approve of you."

"Oh yeah? What would she like about me?"

"She spent most of her adult life trying to help kids who were in bad situations. She would admire you because you're so willing to go the extra mile to help a little girl you don't even know."

Barney drove through the outskirts of Reno, trying to imagine Taffeta's life as a kid, and it was beyond him. He'd grown up with so much love surrounding him, and all she'd ever had as far as positive memories of her childhood went was a short stint with a caring old lady.

He used the navigation application on his phone to find the casino hotel where he had booked two rooms last week. The place had looked halfway decent online, but the instant they walked through the revolving glass door, he knew he'd made a mistake. The place reeked of cigarette smoke and vomit. *Never believe what you see in pictures,* he decided. "We can't stay here. This is awful!"

Taffeta giggled. "And I'll bet you paid in advance."

"Yes."

She bumped his arm with her shoulder. "It'll be better upstairs. Casino floors always stink of cigarettes and stuff. People get sick from consuming too many free drinks."

Barney couldn't wait to check in and find an elevator. On the way upstairs, he said, "I hope the rooms don't stink."

As he got Taffeta settled in her suite, which was next to his, he thanked God that he'd asked for smoke-free accommodations. Unfortunately the room wasn't much better than downstairs.

"This whole place is a dive," he said. "I'm sorry."

Taffeta ran her fingertips over a battered dresser. "It's fine, Barney. We're only staying one night." She turned to smile up at him. "I'd like to reimburse you for the rooms. You're doing this for me and Sarah. That only seems right."

"I've got it covered," he said.

"But you can't afford this. You're a deputy."

Barney laughed. "I can afford it. I'm not poor, Taffy. I make a decent wage."

"Which you like to spend on your house. Please, let me cover the cost of this."

He shook his head and turned for the door. Then he hesitated. He didn't want her to feel guilty because he was paying for everything. He swung around to look at her. "If you really feel obligated to—"

"I *do*!" she interjected.

"Okay, fine. I'll keep all the receipts, and when we get home, we'll split the cost down the middle. Does that sound fair?"

"No. You wouldn't be here if it weren't for Sarah."

Thinking fast, Barney shot back, "That is so not true. You see before you a man who loves to gamble. Once we tie the knot, I plan to have one hell of a good time at the blackjack tables. If I don't pay for half of the rooms and food, I'll feel guilty and won't enjoy myself as much."

She studied him dubiously. "Okay, we split it down the middle for the rooms and food. But I'm covering the wedding costs, no arguments."

Barney didn't like the idea of allowing her to pay for anything. She had lawyer fees lying ahead of her. Even though Bryan planned to give her a break, the hit might still hurt her financially. "I will pay for half of the chapel costs, too."

"No," she said with adamant firmness. "A bride's family traditionally pays for the wedding. It's *my* bill."

Barney couldn't argue the point. He decided to let her pay for their wedding. Later when she felt the pinch, he'd help her out.

"Fine, then. You pay." He flashed her a grin. "But don't think for a minute that you're going to cover my gambling costs. After we're hitched, we'll sniff our way back to find a casino that doesn't stink."

Considering his poor choice of hotels, he was glad he'd waited to choose a chapel with Taffeta. After getting settled in his suite, he rang her on her cell and asked if he could bring his laptop to her room. Minutes later, she opened the door and let him in. They sat on the stained and worn sofa to peruse the places where they could be married. He half expected Taffeta to say it didn't matter where they tied the knot, just as long as they tied it. He sure as heck didn't care. It wasn't as if the nuptials would mean anything.

But Taffeta took this seriously. She discarded one place because it looked tacky. The next one looked tacky to her as well.

Barney said, "Taffy, I'm afraid a lot of them are cheesy. It's Reno!"

"Still." She wrinkled her nose. "I really don't want

to have a Johnny Depp impersonator officiate at our wedding. Even worse, a fat Johnny impersonator."

A horrible thought suddenly struck Barney. "Shit," he interjected. "I just realized we don't have a marriage license. How the hell can we get one on a Saturday?"

Chapter Nine

A panicked look spread over Taffeta's face. She jerked the laptop from Barney's hands and started typing in another search term with fingers that danced over the keyboard with far more speed than his own.

"Oh God, oh God. I never even thought of a marriage license." She glanced up at him with eyes as round as nickels. "After all the hours it took to get here and all the expense for everything, we can't let this be a wasted trip. What if we can't get married?"

Barney had no answers, but he strove to reassure her. "People elope in Reno all the time. In the movies, couples get roaring drunk, decide to get married, and wake up in the morning wondering how it happened. Somehow they all got marriage licenses."

The rigidity left Taffeta's shoulders as she read what she'd found on the Net. "We're good," she said with noticeable relief. "We have to go to the Marriage License Bureau. There are directions. It's open seven days a week, according to this, from eight in the morning until midnight."

"Only in a city like Reno is a municipal office open until midnight," he said with a laugh. "Not that I'm complaining."

Next, Taffeta selected a chapel that she felt was the least tacky of the lot. Barney called to book a time slot, and then they drove to the Marriage License Bureau, which took forever because of road construction and detours. After procuring the license, they went directly to the chapel. Barney was surprised that it was so pretty, a small white house that had been tastefully converted into a wedding venue. Taffeta chose the least expensive marriage package, a basic civil ceremony for seventy-five dollars. Considering that the license had cost only sixty, Barney felt relieved. At least getting married wasn't costing her a fortune.

Then, of course, they had to buy rings. She picked out the least costly band in the display case for herself and offered up her finger for a quick sizing. Barney followed suit and beat her to the punch by handing over his credit card to the cashier before Taffeta could get hers out of her purse.

"This is supposed to be on my dime," she protested.

Barney winked at her. "We never discussed the rings." In truth, he'd forgotten that they'd need them. "Besides, I'll want to keep mine as a souvenir of my first marriage."

Taffeta's first wedding had been picture-perfect. By comparison, the chapel ceremony seemed superficial. But, for reasons beyond her, it meant more to her than it should have, far more. As they exchanged vows, Barney turned toward her and grasped both her hands. The honeyed timbre of his voice curled around her. Warmth radiated from his well-toned body. His scent titillated her nostrils. The expression on his face looked solemn, sincere, and sweet.

The JP had the ceremony memorized, but he tried to make it special with the vows. As Barney promised to care for her and cherish her, he gazed straight into her eyes as if he meant every word with all his heart. When it came her turn, she couldn't look away from him.

With graceful ease, he slipped the smaller band onto her left ring finger. She nearly dropped the larger one and then struggled to get it on him. The crease flashed in his cheek.

After they were pronounced man and wife, the JP told Barney that he could now kiss his bride. Taffeta hadn't anticipated this part of the ceremony, although why not, she hadn't a clue. The groom always kissed the bride.

Barney winked at her as he bent his head and touched his lips to hers. It was a sweet, tentative kiss, the press of his lips as light and airy as gossamer, but even so, Taffeta's pulse quickened and her breathing hitched. She could only hope that Barney didn't notice.

When they got back inside his truck a few minutes later, Taffeta grumped, "Why do they so often pronounce newly married people as man and wife?" She prayed that her miffed tone would conceal her reaction to his kiss. Her hands were still shaking. "Why not call us man and woman? Or husband and wife?"

He grinned as he accelerated the Dodge and

turned out onto the street. "Does it really matter? We accomplished our mission. We're married. That's all that counts." He missed the first detour, swore, and circled the block. "And we can forget the lovey-dovey act here in Reno. Nobody knows us."

None of this was real, Taffeta reminded herself. Only when Barney had gazed into her eyes as he professed his vows, she believed for a moment that he sincerely meant the promises he was making to her. Even worse, she wished that she could honor her vows to him for the rest of her life. Loving him, caring about him, being loyal to him. She could make that commitment to him so easily. Whenever she considered the magnitude of what he'd done for her—and also for Sarah—she couldn't help feeling halfway in love with him already, and she knew that she could take the remainder of the leap without any hesitation at all.

Barney found a parking spot along the Strip, and they walked the brightly lighted sidewalk to check out the casinos. All of them stank of cigarette smoke, but they finally found one that was classier and less offensive to their noses.

"Dinner first, and then I'll teach you how to play blackjack," he said.

Taffeta hadn't realized she was hungry until he mentioned food. They took an elevator upstairs to eat at a tower restaurant that sported tables draped in white linen and centerpieces with flickering candles.

"I'm not dressed for this," she whispered as the maître d' led them to their seats.

"You look fabulous," he whispered back. "I love that top on you."

Taffeta cringed when she saw the prices on her menu. "Barney," she said in a hushed voice, "we can't afford this!"

He smiled. In the candlelight, his hazel eyes shimmered as if they'd been sprinkled with gold dust. "Regardless of the circumstances, this is our wedding night, and I'll be damned if I mark the evening by eating crap from that downstairs buffet. Ignore the cost. Order your dream meal. Once we decide, we can select a wine."

The price of a bottle of wine would have covered a third of Taffeta's monthly car payment. Despite what he'd said, she chose the cheapest entrée, a chicken cordon bleu dish. He ordered shrimp scampi. They savored a lovely white wine as they ate. Neither of them had room for dessert.

Barney paid the tab. She covered the tip.

Back downstairs, they scouted the tables until Barney found one that allowed one-dollar bets, and even that filled Taffeta with trepidation because she'd never played blackjack and didn't wish to lose a lot of—or even a little—money.

Barney seated her beside him. Then, bending his head toward hers, he explained the rules and playing strategies. "I'll help you with your hands for a while," he said. "Players can get prickly if a newbie screws up the flow of cards by taking stupid hits."

"What's a hit?" she asked. "That sounds violent."

He laughed. "Watch and learn."

Taffeta found herself enjoying every moment of the remainder of the evening. Barney was handsome, thoughtful, patient, and one of the most genuine people she'd ever met. He also had an uncanny way of making her laugh, and it felt divine. The time she spent in his company was the happiest she could remember feeling in years. Not allowing herself to fall in love with him would be a challenge, and she already feared that she was losing the battle.

In clothing that revealed her curvaceous figure and with her glossy dark hair flowing like silk around her slender shoulders, Taffeta was a knockout. Barney wrestled with his own demons and tried to tamp down his attraction to her. With touches of makeup to accentuate her eyes and lush mouth, she could have made a guy swallow his tongue without half trying. *Amazing.* She hadn't had a chance to freshen up before they left their hotel, but she still looked fabulous.

Thank God I booked separate rooms. He wasn't sure that he could keep his hands off her if she slept only a few feet away from him, his for the asking.

She wouldn't say no. Hell, she'd put that offer on the table from the start, and he'd been the one who turned it down. Now he almost regretted his noble inclinations. How would he manage to keep his pants zipped when they got back to Mystic Creek and started living together?

Barney had no answers. When he leaned close to look over her arm at her cards, he had to school his gaze so he wouldn't gape at her cleavage, modestly revealed by the scoop neck of the clingy top.

Throat tight, he said, "You've got twenty-one, honey. Lay your cards faceup on the table."

"Is twenty-one good?"

God, he wanted to kiss her again. That fleeting taste of her mouth at the chapel had whetted his appetite for more. He'd made it a quick, friendly brush of his lips over hers, and he hadn't expected the zing of electricity that jolted through him. The lady packed one hell of a punch.

"It can't get better," he explained. "If the dealer also gets twenty-one, it'll be a push, and you won't lose your bet. If the dealer doesn't get a blackjack or goes bust, you'll double your money."

She shifted on the stool. "Really? Oh, Barney, I never thought I'd like gambling, but this is *fun*."

Her enthusiasm warmed him. Okay, everything about her had his body humming. The only way he could keep his word to her about the no-sex arrangement was to stay in the bedroom at the back corner of his house. Then he'd pray that Taffeta didn't parade around in front of him half-dressed.

When they cashed in their chips, Taffeta was fifty dollars ahead, and he was twenty in the hole. "Beginner's luck," he said.

She grinned. "You're just jealous." She crumpled the bills in her fingers. "I could stay up all night playing that game! I truly could. It's a shame we have to head out in the morning."

"We'll come back soon," he said, "and spend a whole weekend gambling and staying up till the crack of dawn."

Where had that come from? Barney wanted to stuff a sock in his mouth. He'd forgotten for a moment that theirs wasn't a real marriage. They didn't have a future lying ahead of them. In a matter of mere months, they would get a divorce and move on with their separate lives.

While driving back to the stinky casino and ratty rooms, Barney almost ran a red light, and some cranky bastard leaned on his horn to complain about the sudden stop. *What the hell's wrong with me?* Barney had slept with a lot of women, and he had been plenty turned on during the flirtation stage of an evening. But never had he gotten so rattled that he drove like a maniac.

Once in the hotel elevator, he tried to get his head on straight. Taffeta stood across from him, digging in her purse to find her room key. She looked so damned sweet, not to mention delicious. He wished he could scoop her up in his arms and carry her over the threshold as a real groom might. Then he would slowly undress her, tasting every inch of her skin as he bared it. And when he got her into bed, he'd make damned sure she got some satisfaction. He'd make her come until she screamed.

As he guided her from the lift into the hallway, he felt as if he had a log in the crotch of his jeans. Holding her arm, he hurried toward their rooms, not wanting her to see that he had an erection.

"Is this the right way?" She glanced at her key card. "I think the arrows pointed the other direction."

Barney braked so suddenly that he damned near dislocated her shoulder. She threw him a startled look.

"Arrows?" he echoed, knowing he sounded dumber than a rock.

She glanced down to where his fingers were clenched

just above her elbow. "Barney, you're, um, pressing too hard."

Barney had never in his life hurt a woman, not even as a kid when his little sisters had gone into brat mode. He let go of Taffeta's arm so fast that she lost her balance, prompting him to grab her again to steady her. "I'm sorry. My mind was on other things. Are you all right?" He pushed at the knit sleeve of her top to bare her skin, only not in the same way that he had imagined doing. "Did I bruise you? God. I'm so sorry."

She searched his gaze with those incredibly blue eyes. "I'm fine, Barney." She stilled his hands with a cupped palm over his fingers. "You only gripped me a little too hard. What were you thinking about that upset you so much?"

Barney had been upset, all right, but not in the way she meant. His heart was pounding, and the blood rushed through his veins, making a swishing sound in his ears. He thought fast.

"I wasted that twenty bucks," he blurted. "I love to gamble, but I always get pissed when I lose."

"Uh-oh." The dimple in her cheek winked at him as she smiled. "A gambler who's only happy if he wins. How does that work out for you?"

"Not well, I guess." Barney drove all thoughts of her naked body from his mind, gained control of his physical response to her, and guided her along beside him as he retraced their steps. This time he paid attention to the damned arrows and delivered her to her room. "I hope you sleep well," he offered. "It's been a long day."

She nodded and flipped her key card back and

forth between her nimble fingers. He wondered for a moment if she hoped for a good night kiss. *Stop it.* He slammed down hard on the thought. Then she smiled and turned to slip the card into the slot.

"It truly has been a long day," she agreed. "What time should we ask for a wake-up call?"

"Six?" he suggested. "It's over five hours to drive home. And we have to move your stuff to my place once we get there. We should head out early."

"So, when will we leave? Around seven?"

"Sounds good to me."

She nodded, treating him to another long study with those blue eyes. He'd heard of men feeling as if they might drown in the depths of a woman's eyes, but Barney had never experienced the sensation— until now. Even worse, he feared that once he dived in, he'd never want to surface for air.

"Good night," he said, his voice twanging in his ears like an overly tight guitar string.

Long after she closed the door behind her, he stood in the hall staring at her room. *What are you hoping might happen?* he wondered. *Do you think the door will reopen if you wait here long enough? Get a grip, Sterling.*

Chapter Ten

Taffeta enjoyed the long drive home, which became even longer because of road construction. Barney set the heater at full blast to keep the cab toasty warm, allowing both of them to shed their coats. On the outskirts of Reno, he had stopped at a convenience store for drinks and snacks, which they munched on when lunchtime rolled around.

The drone of the studded tires lulled her to sleep for a short nap. When she awakened, the first thing she smelled was the faint but enticing scent of him, a blend of freshly laundered clothing, shaving cologne, bath soap, shampoo, and a lingering trace of outdoor aromas, which she guessed clung to his discarded jacket draped over the console between them. Why she found the latter intoxicating was a mystery to her. She supposed it was the essence of Barney that held such strong appeal. Somewhere she'd read that one's sense of smell played a huge role in physical attraction. Oh, how she wished it were so simple. To get over him, she could just stuff cotton balls in her nose.

"Hey, sleepyhead." He flashed her a grin. "It's about time you returned to the land of the living. I was getting bored." His smile broadened. "How about another sing-along?"

Taffeta laughed. "If your ears can stand it, I'm game."

After they had sung until she was almost hoarse, he suggested that they play a travel game called "I see." It was at times frustrating but also entertaining, and keeping their minds occupied seemed to make the time pass quicker. Taffeta couldn't help thinking that Barney would make a fabulous father, at least on road trips. Instead of asking, "Are we almost there?" his kids would be too busy enjoying themselves to worry about it.

When they stopped at a rest area along the way, Barney couldn't get his truck to restart. After messing around under the raised hood, he told Taffeta that he'd seen nothing abnormal and believed it was a blown starter fuse, which would only take minutes to fix if there were an auto parts store nearby. But, of course, there wasn't. A temporary repair of the fuse could sometimes be done with a bit of foil, he'd told Taffeta, and they'd begun searching his vehicle for something that might work.

Finally they gave up on that idea, and Barney tried to call out on his cell phone to get help. He grimly related to Taffeta that his phone said it was searching for service. They were in a dead zone. Typically of Barney, he kept Taffeta smiling with silly jokes and stories as they sat in the pickup, hoping someone with a piece of foil might pull into the rest area for a break. None of the individuals Barney approached had anything in their cars made of foil.

Finally after being trapped there for three hours, a man driving a pickup that was the same model as Barney's pulled in and parked beside them. When Barney exited his vehicle to ask if the guy had any foil, he hit pay dirt. The stranger kept extra starter fuses in his glove box and gave one to Barney for free.

"Always carry extra starter fuses," the fellow said. "This model blows them out a lot. I learned that the hard way."

They were about fifty miles from the Mystic Creek city limits when Barney's cell rang. He glanced down at the screen, immediately started pulling over, and muttered under his breath that he should have paid for hands-free calling when he ordered his truck. Taffeta saw his point, but he had his cell phone for navigation and probably didn't have to pull over to talk all that often.

"Hi, Mom. What's up?" he said after answering the call.

Taffeta couldn't hear his mother's side of the conversation, and Barney's made little sense.

"I'm sorry. It's over a five-hour drive, not counting stops, and we ran into road construction that cost us about two hours in delays. Plus, my starter fuse blew out, costing us another three hours. We didn't get out of Reno until after nine. It took forever to get our breakfast order, and the hotel checkout line was horrific. Some kind of convention in town." And, "You did what?" Then, "Mom, she hasn't even met any of you yet. That's going to be pretty overwhelming for her."

When Taffeta's curiosity was piqued to almost torturous levels, Barney ended the call and pulled back out onto the highway. "That was my mother, if you didn't already guess. She and my sisters got the harebrained idea to book Dizzy's Roundtable Restaurant for a wedding reception this evening. It starts at four thirty. Mom has invited half of Mystic Creek, and we, of course, are the guests of honor and absolutely *must* show up."

Taffeta gulped. "Half the town will be there?"

Barney rolled his eyes in her direction, his expression sulky. "Well, she said she invited all of her and dad's friends, and Mom is friendly with practically everyone." He sighed. "She means well. And, according to her, there's no better way to launch this fake marriage thing than to do it with a bang. She and my sisters have probably worked their asses off, trying to throw a big party on such short notice. My whole family plans to be there to lend us moral support and spread our story—that we've been dating on the sly for months. We should be grateful. Right?"

Taffeta had a perverse urge to laugh despite her discomfort. She had avoided crowds ever since she was found guilty of child abuse. The thought of attending a large party rattled her nerves. But Barney looked even more reluctant than she felt. "Any kind of social gathering requires a lot of work, so yes, I think we'd better be appreciative."

He nodded. "You'll love my mother. *Everyone* loves

my mother, including me. But she's got a surplus of energy and an impulsive streak. I can never remember exactly how long she and Dad have been married, but he's been trying to bridle her for years. She balks like a mule."

"I can't believe you just likened your beloved mother to a mule."

"Actually there isn't a mule alive that can compare to her." His expression relaxed, and the ghost of a smile touched his mouth. "I can't believe she went to all this trouble. She knows the marriage is all for show, and so do my sisters. That's why none of them came to Reno for the nuptials. If it had been a real marriage, I would have had to beat them away with a ball bat to find any time alone with you."

Taffeta's throat tightened. While in Barney's company, she was finding it increasingly difficult to remember that this union wasn't meant to last. She forced herself to focus on the party. Despite her weariness—which she suspected was caused more by emotional stress than anything else—she would put on a happy face and exclaim over how lovely the reception was. Barney's family wasn't doing this for him; they were doing it for *her*. Kate Sterling might be an impulsive woman and headstrong, but she definitely had a big heart.

Barney and Taffeta reached Mystic Creek at a little after five o'clock, allowing them no time to stop at their respective homes to change clothes and freshen up. The reception had started at four thirty, and Kate

Sterling was undoubtedly fretting because the bride and groom were late.

Barney was exhausted by the time he and Taffeta entered the Mystic Creek Menagerie, an old, cavernous, round building that had once been a lumber mill. Several years ago it had been converted into a mall with shops encircling a gigantic round table that served as a dining area for Dizzy's. For special events, Tony Chavez, the restaurant owner, moved all the tables and chairs off to the sides to create a revolving dance floor. Barney liked Tony. Almost everyone in town did. He was a generous guy with a keen sense of humor. Along with the specials that he ran every week, he also offered a Joke of the Day, an off-color version for men who came in alone and another version suitable for mixed company.

"Holy hell," Barney muttered when he saw the size of the crowd.

Everyone seemed to be dressed in ultracasual clothing. Barney suspected that was his mother's doing. She hadn't wanted Taffeta, still rumpled from a road trip, to feel out of place. Not that Taffeta looked rumpled in snug jeans and a long-sleeved red T-shirt, but she would have felt conspicuous if everyone else had been dressed up.

After they shed their jackets and hung them on wall hooks just inside the door, Barney curled an arm around Taffeta's shoulders. Her soft curves molded against his harder angles. She glanced up at him, her expression one of barely suppressed panic.

"It's going to be fine," he assured her.

"Not if someone recognizes me," she reminded him. "My trial was big news, and my face was plastered on the front pages of newspapers all over the state."

Fear shadowed her eyes, and seeing it made Barney's heart catch. For appearances' sake, he forced himself to grin. "If anyone recognizes you, just say you're innocent and that you've filed for an appeal to prove it."

She pasted a smile on her face. "People are staring at me."

"Only because you're so beautiful, Taffy, not because they recognize you from old newspaper stories."

She took a deep breath and released it. "Oh, Barney, would you just look at all that food?"

Barney took stock of the laden tables on the left side of the mall. From the corner of his eye, he saw people glance their way and then do double takes when they noticed how different Taffeta looked. Music streamed through the building from ceiling speakers. Some guests had already sat down at the empty tables to eat. Others stood in small groups, nibbling from white plates and sipping wine or beer.

Off to his left, Barney saw Garrett Jones and Sheriff Adams chatting with each other. Marietta Adams stood beside her husband, her plate heaped with a variety of appetizers that she was probably sharing with Blake.

To Taffeta, Barney said, "I wonder how much of the cooking my mom and sisters did. A spread like this would cost a small fortune if Tony did all the preparation."

Just then, Barney saw his mother slipping through the throngs of people to reach them. Kate's dark hair, loose around her shoulders, shone like satin in the overhead lighting. She normally dressed up for parties, but tonight she wore a blue blouse, faded jeans, and well-used riding boots. Barney made a mental note to thank her later for being so thoughtful of Taffeta's feelings.

Trailing behind his petite wife, Jeremiah took one step for every two of Kate's. He grinned at Barney over the top of her head.

"You're late!" Kate exclaimed when she reached them. "Everyone else has already started eating appetizers."

"It's a long drive, Mom, and we ran into delays. We got here as fast as we could."

Acting as if they were good friends, Kate hugged Taffeta. In a voice that Barney could barely hear, she said, "I'm Kate, Barney's mother." Clasping Taffeta's shoulders, she stepped back, gave her a measuring look, and added, "You're absolutely lovely."

Barney embraced his mom. Jeremiah curled an arm around Taffeta, giving her a friendly jostle as he quietly introduced himself. Without taking his eyes off her, he said, "See that long center table with all the food? Barney's brothers and sisters are standing there. The girls are Sarah and Adriel. The boys are named Jeb, Ben, and Jonas. You'll get them sorted out when you actually meet them."

Barney could tell that Taffeta felt overwhelmed, but he doubted anyone else would notice. She was doing a pretty good job of appearing to be relaxed and smiled up at her father-in-law as if what he said was amusing.

Barney had always appreciated the loyalty of his family, but never more so than now. His mom and dad acted as if Taffeta were actually their new daughter-in-law, not a temporary stand-in, and they did such a good job of carrying it off that Barney was half convinced of it himself.

"Come on," Jeremiah said as he drew Taffeta into a walk. "I want to show off my new daughter."

Barney tensed. He wanted to stay close to his wife in case she needed moral support. But Jeremiah was having none of that.

"Quit frowning," Kate scolded. "Your dad will take good care of her, and this is supposed to be one of the happiest moments of your life."

He forced his lips into a smile. "She's scared, Mom. This is the first time she's been seen in public looking like her real self. What if someone recognizes her? It could get ugly, and I'd like to be with her, just in case." Barney gazed after Taffeta. "Besides, isn't it customary for the bride and groom to stay together at a wedding reception?"

"We aren't following any particular protocol," Kate replied. "For one thing, we didn't have time to plan anything. And there was no wedding here in town, which would have given us a starting point." She saw Barney glance at Taffeta again. "Sweetheart, relax. Your dad will take good care of her, and if someone recognizes her, he'll handle the situation." She took Barney's arm. "Let's circulate, and then we'll join your father and Taffeta to eat. The way I see it, announcing your marriage at a huge party will help circumvent any gossip. Jeremiah will act as if he knows Taffeta quite well, and people will be more likely to believe that the two of you have been dating for a while."

Barney couldn't argue with that. "Did you and the girls make all the food?"

"A lot of it. Tony supplied the rest without any markup on price. It's his wedding gift to you guys."

Barney winced. "Damn, Mom. I hate that he did that. We may be getting a divorce before the ink is dry on our marriage certificate."

"Hush. Someone may hear you."

Kate led him toward Garrett and Sheriff Adams. "Marietta," she cried. "I'm so glad you got home in time for the party!"

Marietta tipped her blond head and offered a bright smile. "I headed back the moment Blake called me. I wouldn't have missed this for the world."

"You sneaky son of a gun," Sheriff Adams said, clamping a beefy hand over Barney's shoulder. "When you asked for the weekend off, you didn't so much as hint that you were going off to get married."

Barney laughed. "Taffeta took some convincing. I didn't want to make a big deal out of it and have her get cold feet."

Blake glanced across the room to where Taffeta stood with Jeremiah, talking to Crystal Malloy, a woman in her late twenties who owned and operated Silver Beach, Mystic Creek's version of a high-end salon. The woman's long hair was bright red with neon blue streaks today. Tomorrow, it might be apple green. Crystal enjoyed advertising her hair products. "Apparently you're good for Taffeta, Barney. I barely recognized her when she walked in."

Barney had no idea how to explain Taffeta's change in appearance, so he let Blake's comment pass.

Garrett broke in with "I didn't recognize her, either. When I went into her shop, she never looked that hot."

Blake gave his deputy a warning look. "Careful, Garrett. That's Barney's wife you're talking about."

When Barney and Kate moved away to circulate, Barney said, "Taffeta needs to eat, Mom. All she's had since breakfast were a few snacks. I intended to stop somewhere this afternoon, but we got held up by roadwork and a blown starter fuse, and then you called, so there wasn't time."

"Oh my. I had no idea. Let's round her and your father up. Tony designated one of the larger tables for our family. She can meet the rest of us while we eat."

Minutes later, Barney's brothers were ribbing him and stealing kisses from his bride. His sisters flanked Taffeta, pretending that the three of them were good friends. Townspeople came and went, all of them hearing the story of how Barney and Taffeta had been dating on the sly for several months. To Barney's relief, everyone had the story down pat.

Jeremiah worked the crowd, playing the part of a proud father-in-law as the family filled their plates and went to sit together at a table. Taffeta leaned in close to Barney and said, "Your family is incredible."

Barney swallowed a bite of pulled barbecue pork. "Aren't they just?" He bent his head to kiss her on the cheek. "And you're pretty amazing, too. I know this has to be even more overwhelming for you than it is for me."

"It was hard at first, but I'm starting to relax now. Your dad didn't give me a chance to get the jitters."

"Man, this food is fabulous," he said. "Talk about a perfectly orchestrated reception! We need to thank Tony. He supplied a lot of the food with no markup on the price. It's his wedding gift to us."

Much as Barney had, Taffeta winced. He knew exactly how she felt, but before he could commiserate aloud with her, Chris and Kim Peck, the owners of Peck's Red Rooster Restaurant, appeared at the table. Barney wasn't sure how old they were, but he'd heard that Chris was around thirty, Kim a couple of years his junior. They were young to be so successful. Their restaurant offered fine dining, a novelty in Mystic Creek. Most of the eating establishments were less formal or downright casual.

"Congratulations to both of you!" Kim beamed a smile. A natural blonde with gray eyes, she looked tiny beside Chris, a tall, slender guy with wavy black hair, a friendly blue gaze, and a neatly trimmed mustache. "What a wonderful surprise."

Chris grinned. "We didn't have enough warning to get you a wedding gift, so Kim and I want to wine and dine you at the restaurant instead."

"You don't need to do that," Barney replied. "Having you here at the party is all the gift we need."

"For once, it was easy for Kim and me to take a night off. All of our regular customers are feasting over here."

Kate glanced at the milling crowd. "Oh dear. We didn't mean to lure all your business away."

Chris chuckled. "Hey, we're enjoying the night off. I cranked out a limited menu, and Darina is holding down the fort. She's turning out to be a pretty good cook, not to mention the best waitress we've ever had."

Darina Penny was a single parent who worked as many shifts as she could and rode herd on Devon, her teenage son. Barney respected the woman. Raising a kid alone had to be difficult.

When the Pecks drifted away, Barney and Taffeta finished their meals and then went to find their host, Tony Chavez. He was in the kitchen, positioned at the rear of the restaurant behind the cashier's stand. Black hair gleaming in the overhead lights, he was busy washing off counters.

"Hey, Tony!" Barney called out. "Taffeta and I want to thank you for the great food. What a wonderful wedding present!"

Tony tossed down a white towel and turned to greet them with a smile. His teeth looked whiter than white in contrast to his dark skin. He wore a chef's coat that was spotted with the ingredients of the dishes that he had prepared. "It is my pleasure." He winked at Taffeta. "I have selected special music for the two of you." His brown eyes twinkled with good humor when he locked gazes with Barney. "It's time for you to dance with your bride."

"Dance?" Barney repeated.

"It's customary for a newly married couple to start off the dancing with a solo performance." Tony laughed. "It will be your first dance as a married couple! You can't chicken out on me. Everyone is waiting."

The next thing Barney knew, he was leading Taffeta onto the revolving dance floor. As he took her into his arms, he said, "This could be tricky. I've never waltzed on a moving surface. Have you?"

Taffeta grinned up at him. "We'll manage well enough as long as you don't step on my toes."

Just then Garth Brooks's voice resounded through the building, singing "If Tomorrow Never Comes." It was one of Barney's favorites. Tightening his arm around his wife, he executed the first step. He expected her to be nervous, stiff, and halting in her movements, but instead she flowed with him in perfect harmony. It was as if they had danced together countless times. Her full breasts grazed his lower chest. He tucked her in close as he executed the swirls, acutely aware that his thigh pressed against the apex of hers. Gazing down into her lovely blue eyes, Barney wondered if they'd move together this well in bed.

Shit. I'm in trouble here. He had to be a man of his word. *No sex, not even if it kills me.* He was doing this to hopefully help a little girl, no paybacks expected.

When the song ended, everyone applauded, and then Jeremiah came onto the round table to dance with his new daughter-in-law. Barney started to leave the floor, but his mother mounted the steps just as Tony got the regular music going again, all romantic songs suitable for a wedding party. Kate held out her hand, Barney took hold of it, and they moved into another waltz.

He had no idea how long he danced. Both of his

sisters got their turns, and a couple of women from town cut in. Then, of course, Barney danced several times with Taffeta again, which was physically torturous for him. Weary from the long drive, Barney just wanted to go home. But all the guests seemed to be having fun, and he hated to slip out with Taffeta for fear it would seem rude. Besides, his bride was still dancing, and she seemed to be enjoying herself.

Barney finally escaped into the crowd and found his brothers. Ben, dressed casually in jeans and a western shirt, handed him a beer. Jonas laughed when Barney took a swig and moaned in appreciation.

"Long weekend?" he asked.

After leaving the party, Barney walked Taffeta to her apartment. She ached with exhaustion, but she still felt on edge about the rest of the evening. In reality, she and Barney were newly acquainted, and now she was about to move in with him. She felt edgy and wasn't sure what to say or do next.

He'd parked his truck in front of her shop. She unlocked the street door and led the way upstairs. Barney went directly to her bedroom, grabbing the heavy box first. Carrying one of the suitcases, she followed him back down to the truck. He put the carton on the backseat and the suitcase on the floorboard.

They reentered the flat moments later. Barney fetched the second piece of luggage and carried it out for her. Taffeta started to follow him, but she paused in the doorway first to look at her living quarters. She had called this tiny flat home since moving to Mystic Creek, and she'd tried her best to be happy here, but the early days had been unpleasant considering she had just recently lost custody of her little girl. She'd felt so lost, alone, and angry. How many nights had she been unable to sleep? Her only escape from the depression had been to throw herself into building her business and indulging herself once a week with dressing normally to dance and dream about a sexy lawman. She'd clung to the hope that if she made a home here in this town, she might someday have Sarah with her again.

Now Barney had entered her life, and for the first time, her wishful thinking seemed like a real possibility. Tears stung her eyes.

She jumped with a start when his warm, heavy hand curled over her shoulder. "What's wrong, Taffy? You having second thoughts?"

Taffeta swallowed hard and blinked. "Nothing's wrong." She sighed and turned to look up at him. "I'm just so grateful to you for supporting me this way. Whether you realize it or not, you've given me a precious gift, a real hope that I may be able to get my little girl back."

Barney drew her into his arms and rested his lean cheek against her hair. "I can't promise you anything. But Bryan Vorch is a good lawyer, and if he thinks you have a fighting chance, then you have a fighting chance. You need to hold that thought close while we ride this out."

"I wonder how long that may take. I'm so worried about Sarah. Heaven only knows who Phillip left her with tonight."

He smoothed her hair. "We made good headway at

the reception," he assured her. "You have to be patient." He set her gently away from him. "We're going to be out in public every damned night, whispering to each other, gazing into each other's eyes, and smooching up a storm. Give it a month, Taffy, and then we'll head for Erickson. It'd be better if we had a year of marriage under our belts, but we don't. We can only hope that a judge doesn't get hung up on details."

Taffeta nodded and closed the apartment door. Side by side, they descended the stairs. When they reached the bottom step, she couldn't help wishing that their marriage were the forever kind and that tonight was the beginning of the rest of their lives.

Chapter Eleven

Barney's house sat in a grove of pine trees. In the wash of the truck's headlights, Taffeta saw that it was a large one-level structure, painted smoke blue with white trim. A charming wraparound veranda sported Adirondack chairs and hanging flowerpots that would be empty until the weather warmed. It was a home that greeted you with a friendly welcome and made you yearn to go inside. She envisioned herself and Barney lounging on the porch on summer evenings to watch the sunset, chat, and gaze off at nothing.

"Oh, Barney, your place is darling."

"When I first got it, it was a mess. I've done a lot of work on it." He opened the driver door and exited the truck. Taffeta got out and circled the pickup bed to help carry her things inside. "I can get this," he said. "Go on in. The door isn't locked."

She shook her head. "I can help. I'm not that tired." With a questioning look, she added, "A lawman who doesn't lock his house. Surely that isn't wise, Barney, not even in Mystic Creek."

"We have very little hard-core crime in this town,"

he assured her. "I think that's because everybody knows everybody else. It's one thing to damage or steal a stranger's property, and it's quite another to wrong a friend. Besides, a determined burglar will get in, one way or another. Locked doors get kicked out of their framework. Unlocked doors sustain no damage."

He carried the box. Taffeta grabbed a suitcase. Following him through the darkness toward the house, she said, "You could come home sometime and surprise an intruder."

He laughed as they climbed the veranda steps. "In which case, I'll do my damnedest to kick some ass. But I don't really worry about it. I'm a lawman here, remember. Over the last month, the most exciting thing I had to investigate was a complaint that a pretty lady was entertaining her East Main neighbors with a sexy shadow dance."

"Will you *ever* let me live that down?"

"Probably not," he confessed.

She followed him inside. When he flipped on an overhead light, she took an appreciative breath of surprise. She'd been expecting a typical bachelor pad, but instead she saw country charm. An old brick fireplace held court along the far wall of the living room, which had been done in a sunny yellow, perfect for a farmhouse. He had paired the brick with beautiful, barn-plank flooring. Above the mantel hung a gorgeous painting of a tree-lined mountain stream. Burgundy throw pillows on the brown sofa matched the recliner near the hearth. She instantly pictured Barney sitting there to read.

"The bedrooms are all in back," he said.

Taffeta followed him through the dining room. A western-style table, easily big enough to accommodate a large family, and matching chairs, carved along the edges to resemble rope, sat in front of a complementary hutch filled with red Fiesta dinnerware. The table centerpiece, unlike any she'd ever seen, consisted of an old riding boot, painted with clear satin varnish and filled with greenery. It sat at the center of a horseshoe wreath.

"I had no idea you were so clever at decorating," she exclaimed. "Where did you get the idea to weld horseshoes together?"

He paused in an archway to grin at her. "My mom designed it, and I did the torch work. And for the record, I didn't do the decorating. She and my sisters did."

After moving through the archway into the kitchen, he turned right into a long, wide hallway. Taffeta trailed behind him, trying to feast her eyes on the interior of the house, but he covered ground too quickly for her to see much more than a blur. The faint scent of what smelled like homemade bread and oranges wafted around her. In the hallway, she smelled the delicate essence of spring wildflowers, which hinted that he used plug-in deodorizers in the bedrooms paralleling sunny yellow walls with white trim. A group of framed family photos graced one section of wall, but she had no time to study any of the images.

"Supposedly they decorated to reflect my personality," he said over his shoulder. "I guess that means I'm a horsey, countrified, doggy kind of guy who likes my family, guns, lassos, equine tack, and antiques. All the antiques are replicas. I can't afford any real ones. My sister Adriel found a genuine antique coat tree, the kind built like a chair with a mirrored back, but it cost eleven hundred! She said it was a steal, and I retorted that it definitely was highway robbery, straight out of my wallet. I sent it back and got a refund." He veered left into a spacious bedroom. "This one has an adjoining bath. The other two spare rooms don't. People who overnight in them have to use the main bath—or the *guest* bath and *powder* room, as my mom calls it."

Taffeta couldn't help grinning. Barney didn't put on airs. With only a few words, he'd let her know that his discretionary funds were limited and that he wasn't keen on fancy terms for ordinary things. As she set down the suitcase, she trailed her fingertips over a colorful wedding ring quilt.

"No," he said with a laugh, "I didn't make it."

"Your mom again?"

"She's a lady with many talents. My idea of decorating is to hang my hats on nails. I might even tack up a calendar. That said, I like the look that they came up with. The house is a lot homier than it would have been if left up to me." He stepped over to the doorway. "Go ahead and start getting settled in. I'll bring in the other suitcase."

After he left, she heard a horse whinny somewhere outside. The sound startled her. She'd never been around many animals. She opened the top drawer of an old oak dresser and found it empty. The closet stood empty as well. She would have plenty of room to put her things away, although she doubted that she'd do anything tonight. She would just unearth her pajamas. Her toiletries would be easy to find. They were in the small bag that she'd taken to Reno and forgotten in the pickup.

When she stepped out into the hall to go get it, she saw Barney round the corner, carrying the bag in one hand and her second suitcase in the other. He deposited both in her room at the foot of the bed.

As he emerged into the hallway again, he gave her an apologetic look. "I have to go feed the animals. My poor horses are telling me that they're starving."

"I heard one of them a minute ago. Please, Barney, don't worry about me. I'll be fine."

He started to walk around her and then stopped. "Would you like to bundle up and go out with me? I can turn the yard light on so you can see my quarter horses. It's too late for you to meet my other critters."

Taffeta was tired, but not so drained of energy that she could pass on an invitation like that. All her life, she'd yearned for a pet. Horses were a bit large to qualify, but she'd always been fascinated by them. "I'd love to see them."

He led the way to the kitchen. Gleaming granite counters topped distressed cabinets that had been stained a dark honey and then washed in black to highlight the imperfections. A huge stainless steel side-by-side refrigerator and freezer had been built in along the left wall. Over the kitchen sink, also stainless steel, a window draped in tied-back tiers of white eyelet displayed knickknacks on the sill. *White eyelet?* Barney wasn't a frilly sort, so she assumed his mother had been in charge of the curtains.

He stepped over to a coat tree in one corner of the room and handed her a slick nylon parka. "You don't want to wear your own jacket," he said. "It'll never be the same."

He grabbed the ugliest, most hay-covered wool coat that she'd ever seen and shrugged into it. Under all the hay, it was a red-and-black plaid. "Hay sticks to wool," he explained. "That's why I wear this. I get less junk under my collar."

Taffeta changed jackets and followed him outside. Crisp cold air greeted them. On the breeze, she caught whiffs of horse odors—manure, alfalfa, and a sweet smell that she suspected came from grain. She found it an oddly pleasant blend of scents.

As they crossed the backyard to reach the barn, he said, "I hired Devon Penny to feed for me mornings and evenings while I was gone, but tonight, dinner is all on me. I feel bad for letting them go this long without eating."

He stepped over to a post, and light suddenly bathed the area. Taffeta saw two horses standing on the opposite side of a rail fence. One was a palomino. Even she knew that much. The other one was a reddish brown fellow with a blondish mane. "Oh, Barney, they're gorgeous."

"I got them in Montana. They're heritage quarter horses. That essentially means that the breeder's remuda must consist of registered quarter horses that have been used mostly for working ranch cattle, and the rancher must have been in operation for at least ten years. Well, I think it's ten years. These boys have good heads on their shoulders and are rock-solid for trail riding. Not much startles them. They're both seven and got trained doing all manner of ranch work."

Taffeta could hear in his voice that he was very proud of the geldings. "I know next to nothing about horses—or any other kind of animal. As a kid, I never had pets."

"Uh-oh," he said. "Is that resentment I detect in your voice again?"

"I always wanted a dog, but it wasn't allowed because I might not have been able to take it with me to the next foster home. I've seen horses only from afar. I've always thought they are beautiful, though."

"Well, now you can get up close."

He reached in his pocket and drew out several molasses-brown cookies. "Horse treats. My mom makes them. Would you like to give them to my fellas?" He stepped close to the fence and started petting the thick, arched neck of the palomino. "This is Beau. The red roan is Shiner."

Taffeta stepped up beside Barney. "Will he bite?"

Barney laughed. "They're both perfect gentlemen. They might bite accidentally when you're feeding them from your hand, but they'd never do it intentionally."

"I'll pass on giving them the cookies, then."

His next laugh rang deep and rich. "There's a trick to it, Taffy. I won't let you do anything that might get you hurt. Cup your hands."

With the palms of her hands, she made a bowl, and Barney dumped the cookies into it. "Slip all but two in your pocket."

She did as he told her. Then Barney grasped her right wrist. Her skin tingled where his fingers pressed. "Okay, flatten your hand out and set a cookie on it." When she'd done that, he lifted her palm toward Beau's nose. "Keep your fingers straight. It's important. He won't accidentally bite you that way."

Taffeta's pulse kicked as Beau took the cookie with a tickling flutter of his lips. An instant later, she heard his powerful jaws and teeth crunching the treat. "He really likes them."

"Oh yeah." Barney released his grip on her arm. "Now pet him. It goes with the treats, the petting. I always like to scratch them behind the ears. Someone eared both of them pretty hard before I bought them. I want them to know it'll never happen to them here."

"Eared? What's that mean?" Taffeta reached up to scratch behind the horse's ear. He threw his head high and snorted, startling her. "He doesn't want me to touch him."

"What he wants is another cookie, but he knows the drill. His payback for the cookie is to let me scratch behind his ears. Once I start, he likes it. You just need to take a slower approach." Barney ran a hand under the horse's mane at the arch of its neck and began scratching as he moved upward to give Beau a brisk ear rub. "See there? His bottom lip is relaxed, and look at his eyes. You see no white around the irises. You can tell a horse's mood by looking at him." He ran his hand along the ridge of the animal's neck and gave it a massage. "See how loose his poll is? That's another sign of a relaxed horse."

Shiner bumped Taffeta's shoulder with his nose and chuffed at her. She nearly lost her balance. She laughed and put a cookie on her flattened hand. "Here's yours, Shiner." The horse grabbed the treat. She stroked the arch of his neck and then reached up to scratch behind his ear while he chewed. "I did it!" she exclaimed. "You still haven't told me what 'eared' means."

"To control a horse, some people grab its ears and twist them. It hurts like the very devil and can make horses head-shy. I don't like to hurt my animals, so I don't approve of the tactic. I also want to halter my horses without a big to-do, and a head-shy horse can make haltering difficult. That's why I make a point of the ear scratching a couple of times a day."

"Why would anyone want to twist on their ears? How mean."

"They're huge, powerful animals, and sometimes that's the only way someone can control them."

Taffeta gave the horses what remained of the treats and rewarded them with ear scratches after each serving.

"Look at you. You're a natural." Barney hooked up a hose to a faucet that stood two feet up from the ground on a vertical water pipe.

"Why is the pipe so tall?" she asked.

"It's a frost-free faucet. I think most of them are tall."

He lifted the lever handle and poked the hose between the fence rails into a black, rubbery-looking trough. "I need to get more hay out of the barn," he said. "I'll be right back. If you pet them now, make sure they see that your hands are empty."

Taffeta had heard the crunching power of the horses' jaws and decided to err on the side of caution. She wrapped her arms around her waist. Barney returned, hefting a huge bale of green stuff. It was bound together with bright blue nylon twine. He found another length of twine on the ground, slipped it under the binding, and pulled back and forth until the friction cut through the braid. He tossed two sections of hay over the fence for each gelding. Then he carried more beyond the reach of the light to feed an animal she couldn't see.

"Those are called flakes," he told her when he returned, inclining his head at the sections of hay his horses were eating.

Taffeta nodded. He rested one arm on the top rail of the fence while they waited for the trough to fill.

"You do this morning and night?"

"Yep. Usually like clockwork. They aren't accustomed to getting fed late. That's why I wanted to leave Reno fairly early this morning."

He turned off the water, disconnected the hose, and then walked with it draped over his shoulder to drain out the water. "Sorry. In this country, the hoses can freeze if you leave water in them. I've forgotten a few times. Worst-case scenario, the hose ruptures. Pain-in-the-ass scenario, no water passes through the next day because the hose is plugged with ice."

On the way back to the house, Barney turned off the yard light. Taffeta leaned back her head.

"Would you look at that sky? The stars never seem so bright in town," she said.

"Out here, it's darker because there's not as much artificial lighting."

"What road is your house on? I didn't think to look at the sign as we drove here."

"Sugar Pine. My folks live farther east, closer to Mystic Creek Elementary School. Jeb lives on Huckleberry. Ben's place is out on Natural Bridge Road. My sisters rent a house together on the south side of Mystic Creek across from the cemetery."

"Spooky."

"Nah. Dead people are perfect neighbors. They never bother you, and they don't throw wild parties late at night."

Taffeta took Barney's lead and scraped the soles of her shoes clean on the bristly outdoor mat before following him into the kitchen. It seemed gigantic to her after making do with a cooking area not much larger than a closet.

She couldn't resist asking, "Did someone make you some homemade bread?"

"Yep. Me." He gave her a wink. "Are you hungry? I can slather some softened butter on a slice."

Taffeta still felt full from dinner. "Oh no, thank you." Then, unable to conceal her surprise, she added, "You actually make your own bread? Let me guess; you use a bread machine and mixes."

He settled his hands on his hips. "No, I make it from scratch. My dad doesn't believe in raising sons who can't cook. Or do other domestic things. Even in the age of permanent press, I had to learn to iron. At twelve, I felt abused because he made me do *girl* stuff.

Now I realize that there's no such thing as girl stuff. It's all *necessary* stuff, and I'm darned glad he made me learn. If I eat out of a can, it's because I choose to, not because I can't put a great meal together."

"Do you enjoy it? Cooking and baking, I mean."

"I do. When I have the time, anyway. At first, I stuck with the basics. Now I like to watch cooking shows and be a little more adventurous. Right now I'm trying to perfect homemade sourdough."

Taffeta tried to picture him cooking. He emanated strength and masculinity, and in her experience, big, strong men didn't often stand over a stove. For lack of anything better to say, she observed, "Your barn-plank floors are gorgeous."

He doffed the hay-covered jacket and hung the one he'd lent Taffeta beside it on the coat tree. "I almost went on the cheap and got a look-alike laminate, but Jeb pitched a fit. He does fine woodworking for a living, and to him, nothing compares to the real thing. These planks cost me a small fortune."

"Reclaimed wood isn't cheap," she agreed. "But it is beautiful."

He stepped to the stainless steel side-by-side. "Want a beer?"

"Why not? Maybe it'll help me fall asleep."

They sat across from each other at the small kitchen table. It was round and looked like oak. As she sipped the ale, she searched for something to say. Nothing came to mind, and Barney didn't broach a subject, either. *Silence.* For a moment, Taffeta had an urge to fill the air between them with nervous chatter, but then she decided that she had spent enough time with Barney to feel comfortable with a lull in conversation.

The beer relaxed her. Barney put her empty in a recycling tub in the pantry and walked with her to the bedroom to make sure she had fresh towels and washcloths in the bath.

After seeing to her needs and bidding her good night, he lingered in the doorway for a moment. She could have sworn that electricity snapped in the air between them. His gaze locked with hers, and she sensed that he wanted to say something. But he spun away without speaking. Listening to the sound of his footsteps recede to the far end of the hall, she closed the door and prepared for bed.

Once she had snuggled down under the quilt and an underlying fleece blanket, she stared into the darkness. Sleep eluded her. She wondered if Barney had already nodded off, but somehow she doubted it. Had she imagined that a strong attraction sizzled between them?

She finally drifted to sleep, remembering how wonderful it had felt to be in his arms on the dance floor. *Perfect* was the only word she could think of to describe it, and she wished that the next time he held her like that, he wouldn't do it only because they were dancing.

Chapter Twelve

The next morning came early for Taffeta. She dug in the cardboard box for her robe, quickly ran a brush through her hair, and walked to the kitchen, where she found Barney standing at the sink and wearing only sweatpants. Bare from the waist up, he was putting on a pot of coffee, and his tawny hair stood up in tufts atop his head.

"Oops," he said. "You caught me. I wanted to get the java on for you before I showered."

Taffeta's tongue felt as if it had stuck to the roof of her mouth. She'd thought that the burnished tone of his face had come from exposure to sunlight, but his upper body was the same color, reminding her of melted caramel. She'd known he was muscular. Even when he was fully clothed, she had seen evidence of that in his shoulders and arms. But the picture that had formed in her mind of his bare torso didn't compare to the reality.

He flipped on the coffee machine and turned to catch her staring. Taffeta couldn't look away. His broad chest sported a furring of golden hair that tapered to his waist like an arrow, drawing her gaze to his well-defined abdominal muscles. He was, without a doubt, the most sculptured specimen of manhood that she'd ever seen.

"Sorry," he said, his voice sounding oddly thick. "I, um—I'll go shower and get dressed."

Taffeta didn't allow herself to watch him leave the room. She'd come in for a drink of water. After this, she'd keep a glass in the bath that adjoined her room so she wouldn't catch him by surprise again. Seeing him half-dressed had left her feeling breathless and a little dizzy. *Not good.* She had gaped at him. *Gaped.* She wasn't a teenage girl, so why on earth had she behaved like one?

Barney stepped into the shower, letting the stream of warm water pour over him. He leaned his forehead against the tiled wall, squeezed his eyes closed, and cursed. *No sex.* Why had he ever suggested such a stupid arrangement? She was hot for him. He'd seen it in her eyes. And, dammit, he was equally attracted to her. How in the hell could they live together without acting upon that desire?

Barney had no idea. He remembered hoping that she would never parade around in front of him half-dressed. And then what had he done but do it himself the very first morning? *Great move, Sterling.*

After exiting the shower, he dried off and put on his uniform. Taffeta hadn't driven her car out here last night, so he'd have to take her to the shop. He saw no point in wearing civilian clothes into town and then coming all the way back home to dress for work.

He found Taffeta at the kitchen table having a cup of coffee. She had skimmed her wet hair back into a knot again. She wore not a trace of makeup. And, to top it off, she had thrown on a drab green blouse that was at least two sizes too large for her. He had to bite his tongue to keep from saying anything.

"I'm more comfortable dressed this way," she said, as if he'd criticized her choice of attire out loud.

Barney almost told her that the plain Jane look wouldn't work when he took her out on the town that evening, but he decided to address that problem when he got to it. Instead he poured himself a cup of coffee. As he took his first sip, he gazed out the window over the sink at his horses. Sunlight pooled on their backs. It promised to be a nice day, not summertime warm, for sure, but pleasant. He wondered if Anne would be in a foul mood because she'd be trapped inside until six and miss most of the springlike weather.

He glanced at his watch and turned from the sink. "If I'm going to get you to the shop by eight, we'd better get cracking."

She pushed up from the chair and moved past him to rinse out her cup. She smelled faintly of roses, and he wanted to lean in closer to get a stronger whiff.

"Thanks for making the coffee," she said as she put her mug in the dishwasher. "I had time to drink more than you did."

He almost said that she cleaned up faster than any female he'd ever known, but he swallowed back the comment. It wouldn't have been intended as a compliment, and he didn't want to start the day by taking shots at her.

*   *   *

Taffeta expected Barney to just drop her off at the store, but he parked out front and walked down the street to the Jake 'n' Bake. When he returned minutes later with flavored coffees and pastry, she couldn't help laughing.

"I'll grow as big as a barn if I do this with you every morning," she said.

"Nah. With the weather turning, we'll exercise any extra pounds off you. Riding horses will be a good workout. And if you don't like to jog, there are plenty of places to walk at my place."

He came behind the counter with her. "How do I set up your till?" he asked.

Taffeta opened the safe and got out the money bag she'd prepared on Friday at closing. She showed him where the bill denominations went and then how to sort the change. "You'll be working your own shift today, Barney. You needn't stay here to help me."

"We're newlyweds. I think a man who's head over heels in love with his wife would stay with her as long as possible. Besides, I like learning new things. As a teenager and then later in college, I worked for my dad, no money tills involved. I've only seen you work with customers a few times, but I noticed that you count back the change. With digital registers that tell you how much money to hand back, that has become a lost art. Can you teach me how?"

"It's very easy," she said. "Let's say someone buys something for three dollars and sixty-six cents, and he hands you a ten. You count in your head from three sixty-six up to four dollars as you take out the change, and then you count from there up to ten with bills." She watched as he lifted the money from the till, and then she held out her hand. "Now, starting at three sixty-six, count it back to me."

It made her feel good to be showing Barney how to do something. Unlike her, he had finished his education at the university, and he had acquired a wealth of job experience as well. She doubted that there were many things he didn't know how to do.

"Ten," he said as he placed a five on her palm. Then he grinned, looking proud of himself. "I did it!"

"And very well," she assured him.

With Barney helping, Taffeta was ready for customers in no time. They took up their usual positions at the counter to enjoy the coffee and baked goods. She frowned when the sunlight outside blinked out.

"Oh no. I think our pretty day just went on vacation," she said.

He turned to look out at the street. "Damn, it's trying to snow. That's Mystic Creek weather for you."

"I didn't move here in time to experience a whole spring last year."

"Welcome to my world. Do you have studded tires on your car?"

"No. I seldom needed traction tires in Erickson."

"Well, if the road conditions get nasty, wait here for me to pick you up." He glanced at the street again. "I don't want you to go off in a ditch between here and my place."

Taffeta agreed to do that.

"Where's your car parked?" he asked.

"Out back." She gestured with her thumb toward the back room. "There's a little carport out there."

The snow began to come down heavier. Being in the warm shop with Barney felt cozy, and she wished, not for the first time, that he didn't have to leave. They chatted for a while about a mystery novel that he'd been reading. Before she knew it, the wall clock read five minutes until ten, and he had to go. He leaned in close, his eyes twinkling with mischief. "A brand-new husband should get a good-bye kiss from his wife."

"There's nobody watching," she pointed out.

"To be convincing when someone *is* watching, we both need the practice," he retorted. "And someone across the way could be spying on us. Come on. Lay one on me."

Taffeta wasn't sure this was a good idea. She tipped her head one way, started to press her mouth to his, and then backed off. He smiled, cupped a palm over the back of her neck, and drew her in, taking control. His mouth, still sweet from the coffee, covered hers. He touched the tip of his tongue to her lips, asking her to open them. Her heart caught. Her senses reeled. And then he was tasting the inside of her mouth.

When he lifted his head, Taffeta blinked. He lightly tweaked the end of her nose. "Not bad for a real first kiss, not bad at all."

Feeling dazed, she could only stare after him silently as he left her shop. He seemed unaffected by the kiss, but she had found it incredible.

* * *

The snow backed off and melted by late afternoon, allowing Taffeta to drive back to Barney's in her own car, a tiny, older-model Honda that she'd bought secondhand after the divorce. It was fifteen minutes after six when she pulled up in Barney's graveled driveway. She cut the engine and stared at the dark windows of the house. It was still light out, but knowing that the doors of the home had been left unlocked sort of spooked her. Maybe Barney could kick some ass if he surprised an intruder, but Taffeta needed a skillet as an equalizer.

It felt silly to sit in her car, though. He'd think she was a big chicken. She decided to walk out back and visit his horses. He'd probably get home at any minute, and that way he wouldn't know that she was nervous about entering the house.

As she expected, she'd barely told the horses hello when she heard his truck pull up out front. She retraced her steps to meet him in front of the veranda. He studied her with the sharp gaze that always made her feel as if he missed nothing. A tawny eyebrow arched over one of his gold-flecked hazel eyes.

"Taffy, you aren't nervous about going inside alone, are you?"

She almost denied it, but she tried never to lie. "It's unlocked," she reminded him. "Someone could be in there, and there'd be no evidence of a break-in to warn me."

He sighed and led the way up the steps. "All right. For as long as you're living with me, I'll lock up when we leave. I don't want you to feel nervous if you get home before I do."

"You think I'm being silly."

He flashed her a grin. "Not at all. My mom insists on locking their house. When Amanda's ex-husband was threatening her and Chloe's safety, they even put in a security system."

"But you never lock your doors."

He opened the front portal and stood back to let her go in first. When she hesitated, he chuckled and said, "I'll be right behind you. And I'll lock them from now on—just for you."

They had no sooner gained the living room than Barney said, "Go slick up, Taffy. I'd like to take you out for dinner."

Taffeta had known all day that their campaign to convince the people of Mystic Creek that they were madly in love had to continue. She hurried along the hall to her room, wishing now that she had unpacked all her clothing last night. She'd have to dig for something suitable to put on.

"If there's a burglar back here, come if you hear me scream!" she yelled.

After entering her room, she piled most of her clothing on her bed and then stood back to stare at the mess. She'd worn loose, drab garments and drawn her hair back into an unattractive twist for so long that it had become second nature. Dressing to look good didn't come easily to her now.

Barney tapped on her closed door. "You need help deciding what to wear?"

Taffeta called, "You can come in. I'm still decent."

Barney poked his head into the room, saw the heap of clothing, and said, "Uh-oh. No wonder you're having trouble. What a mess."

"I was tired last night and didn't unpack."

He drew up beside the bed and homed in on a sassy black dress that she hadn't worn in ages. "This will work. Where are those heels you wore that night at the restaurant?"

"In the unopened suitcase. I used it mostly for shoes."

"Perfect." He started from the room and paused in the doorway to look at her. "I hope you'll wear your hair down. Aim for sexy and beautiful. Don't worry about someone recognizing you. Half the town saw you last night, so I don't think it's going to happen. But if it does—and it may, sooner or later—we'll face it together. You're no longer in hiding. Before long, you'll be trying to get Sarah back. The moment word of that gets out, gossip will run rampant. I wouldn't be surprised to see your face plastered on the front page of Erickson's *Sentinel Guard* again."

At the thought, Taffeta's stomach clenched.

"I'm sorry. I can tell by the look on your face that you hadn't thought about that."

"I don't think I can live through it again," she said shakily.

"We'll live through it together," he promised her.

"People can be vicious to a convicted child abuser."

"We'll get through it, and I honestly don't think anyone in Mystic Creek will act that way."

"Why? Do you think that people here are some-how more tolerant than those in Erickson?"

Barney grinned. "No. But in Erickson, you weren't married to a well-respected deputy who'll shove it back down someone's throat if a mean word is said to you. And in Erickson, you didn't have parents-in-law who would jump in to defend you if they heard a slight against you. It'll be different here. Who in this town would ever believe that I'd hook up with a child abuser?"

Taffeta searched his expression and knew, beyond any doubt, that Barney truly would shove unkind words back down someone's throat. Though theirs had not been a long acquaintance, she had learned that he was a man of his word.

When she stepped out into the living room a half hour later, Barney rewarded her with an appreciative whistle. "You are a knockout in that dress!"

Heat crept up Taffeta's neck. They weren't out in public yet, so surely he wasn't playacting. Did this mean that he still found her attractive? She recalled the electricity that had snapped between them when he was visiting her shop and flirting with her—and then again last night. Then she gave herself a silent scold. *That was then, and this is now.* If she allowed herself to believe any of this was real, she would regret it.

She bent her head to smooth the silky material. "The dress looks better now, but at first it was pretty wrinkled."

"Well, you're perfect now from the top of your head to the tips of your toes."

Taffeta took in his outfit. He wore jeans and a western shirt about the same color as her eyes. He had accessorized with a black western jacket, a bolo tie, and gleaming black boots. "You're not half-bad, either," she said.

"Sweetheart, together we're gonna knock the ball clear out of the park."

When they left the house, Barney surprised her by stopping to lock the front door. "I already got the back one from inside. I ran the dead bolt home after I fed my horses."

"Thank you, Barney." Phillip would have snarled and told her to get over it. "It's sweet of you to change your habits for me."

"I think that's what married people are supposed to do. At least my folks talk about it being a fifty-fifty compromise. Actually they say they always try to give in sixty percent of the time. If they both do that, it ends up being a relationship that always accommodates both parties."

Taffeta could only imagine being in a marriage like that.

She'd draped a black wool shawl over her scantily clad shoulders, but it wasn't thick enough to completely protect her from the chill evening air. The sun wouldn't officially set until about a quarter to eight, but Mystic Creek rested in a mountain-encircled bowl, and the warmth of the sunlight had already vanished behind the peaks. Barney got a firm grip on her arm in case she lost her balance in her high-heeled shoes as she crossed the uneven ground to his truck.

"I'd happily take you out in your car," he said,

"but I tried to drive one of those roller skates once, and no way could I fit. My head poked into the ceiling, and I had a crick in my neck for days."

"I'm happy to go in your pickup. I didn't think I would, but I like big, rumbly vehicles."

Taffeta had reason to regret those words a moment later. Climbing into the Dodge proved to be difficult. Her skirt was too tight to lift her foot to the running board.

From behind her, Barney laughed. "Brace yourself, gorgeous. This calls for a cowboy lift." Taking her off guard, he scooped her up into his arms and gently deposited her on the seat. Then he leaned in to fasten her seat belt, lightly grazing the tips of her breasts with the side of his hand as he pulled the nylon strap over her chest. Taffeta's breath snagged in her throat.

As if he hadn't noticed, he said, "You like big and rumbly, do you? Someday I'll take you for a ride in my John Deere tractor, just like in the song."

Taffeta had heard that song. She'd also heard one about a cowboy who took a woman into the woods for a walk and then told her he needed to check her for ticks. If given her druthers, she'd take the second scenario.

Dusk blanketed Mystic Creek by the time Barney turned onto the lane that encircled the town center. Taffeta had often walked on the cobbled pedestrian path, but never just before dark, with upper-story apartment windows glowing gold and streetlights starting to come on, their globes haloed in the frozen, sparkly air. It reminded her of a Christmas card scene, with quaint, old-fashioned buildings looming.

He took her to dine at the fanciest restaurant in town, Peck's Red Rooster. The dining area was large and attractively appointed with rustic barn-plank walls and tables draped with white linen and sporting contrasting barn red napkins folded to resemble roosters. Half partitions separated some of the eating areas for those seeking solitude while they ate, but the nooks didn't infringe upon the large windows at the opposite end of the room, which offered a spectacular view of Mystic Creek and the natural bridge.

Chris Peck must have spotted them as they entered, because he emerged from the kitchen off to the right to greet them. "So the newlyweds have come to receive their wedding present," he said with a pleased grin. "I'm delighted to see both of you."

Barney looked startled and then chagrined. "Oh, man, I totally forgot about that, Chris. I only want to wine and dine my bride—on my own dime."

Chris shook his head. "Wine and dine her, then, but Kim and I will be very disappointed if you don't accept this evening as our gift to you."

As he led them to a table for two near the windows, Taffeta glimpsed a display of children's drawings. "Are those from the elementary school?" she asked.

Chris smiled. "No. On Saturdays I host an art hour for any local kids who like to draw. I'm supposed to pick out the best drawing and give that child a free ice cream." He winked at Taffeta. "I can never choose the best artwork, though, so they're all judged to be the winner, and everyone gets free ice cream. It's a hoot."

"That's so kind of you."

"Aw, well, possibly. On the other hand, maybe I'm just trying to lure parents in to eat."

He drew out Taffeta's chair. When both she and Barney were seated, he said, "I hope you enjoy your meal and will humor us by not worrying about the tab."

Taffeta watched Barney's warring expressions and knew the precise moment when he realized it would be rude to refuse. With a chuckle, he said, "Okay, you win, but we'll bear in mind that someone else is paying for our orders."

Chris left briefly and returned with a pitcher to fill their crystal water goblets. Then he disappeared again, only to reappear with an uncorked bottle of wine in one hand and two wide-mouth wineglasses in the other. A crisp white linen towel was draped over his right arm. "I've been saving this for just the right occasion, and this is the night," he said, holding up the bottle. "It's a Blue-Gold award winner, bottled in 2006, a great pinot noir that I'm sure has grown better with age."

Taffeta sent Barney a look that she hoped didn't convey her dismay to their host. An award-winning wine? What was Chris thinking? He was treating them like royalty.

"You *do* imbibe, don't you?" Chris asked her.

"Oh yes. *Yes!* It's just that—well, it's beyond generous, Mr. Peck, and I feel guilty about accepting."

Chris shrugged. "We don't stand on ceremony.

Please call me Chris and don't for a moment feel guilty. Everyone in town has been hoping that Barney would meet the right lady, and this is a joyous occasion to celebrate. As for this being a red, it's only a starter to set the mood. If you choose chicken, fish, or seafood, I have some fine white wines in mind for you."

He set a goblet by each of their place settings, then expertly poured both Taffeta and Barney a small amount for taste testing. Barney swirled the glass to study the wine's legs. Then he sniffed its bouquet and drew in a small amount to roll it over his tongue. With a nod, he said to Chris, "It's fabulous, Chris. Thank you so much."

Taffeta nodded in agreement. "It's delicious. I detect a hint of oak, and the tannins are in perfect balance."

With a wink, Barney smiled broadly at the restaurateur. "Just don't let me leave here intoxicated. I'd have to give myself my first DUI."

Chris barked with laughter and put a generous measure of wine in each of their glasses. "We have a chauffeur who happily drives intoxicated diners home and then brings them back the next morning to get their vehicles. Her name is Kim. So enjoy. I'll bring your menus in just a moment." He glanced at the bottle after he set it on the table. "I read the reviews, but it's been a while. As I recall, it has a hint of clove and is sweet with plum."

Taffeta took another sip of wine. "It's awesome, Chris. I definitely taste a hint of clove. Very vibrant with a savory scent and fruity on the tongue."

As Chris walked away, Barney leaned closer to the candlelight that flickered between them. "What I know about wine fits in a thimble. I've read enough about tasting to pretend I know what I'm doing, but I honestly don't. Do you really detect clove?"

Taffeta leaned closer as well. "I attended the wine-tasting school of hard knocks," she whispered. "When you hang around with the upper class for three years, you learn to fake it."

Barney burst out laughing, and then he tasted his wine again. "It's really good. Better than the mediocre stuff I normally buy. I look for bottles that are eight bucks or less."

It was Taffeta's turn to chuckle. "I hear you. Only my budget dictates six dollars or less. The last I saw on the Net, now I have to brand-shop my cheap wines because several have been fingered for containing arsenic."

They slipped easily into a conversation about wine and the professionals who graded them, Barney stating that he didn't know how people trained their taste buds to detect the many flavors that could be present in different fermentations.

"I can pick up on some things," Taffeta said. "But mostly I wing it. To say you detect a hint of oak is usually a safe bet because most good wines are aged in oak barrels. And the tannins are normally present because they're used to clarify wine. Tannins can be bitter and overwhelming in some wines. If you aren't overwhelmed by any bitter taste, you can say that the tannins are perfectly balanced."

"I should hang out with you more often. I may not

know my wine, but with those tips, I can at least pretend I do." He took another sip of the pinot. "I don't detect a noticeable bitter taste in this."

"Which is why I mentioned the perfect balance," Taffeta said. "It isn't that I wanted to impress Chris. I only wanted him to believe we have the trained palates necessary to appreciate his gift. I've been served much older award-winning wines, which probably cost a small fortune, but this is a nice, upper-scale wine, possibly around fifty dollars per bottle originally and now worth more because it has aged."

Barney's eyebrows arched. "Shit. He should have just bought us a toaster."

For some reason, his comment struck both of them as being hilariously funny, and they laughed until they almost cried. Taffeta was the first to collect herself, not because she no longer found it amusing, but because tears would smear her makeup. She wanted to look as good as she could for this man.

Barney sobered and lifted his glass. Gazing deeply into her eyes, he gently tapped his goblet against hers. "To us," he said. "And to our success. Maybe one day soon, we'll have your little girl here to go out to eat with us."

Taffeta's heart clutched. Was he real, this man? He cared—he truly *cared*—about a child that he'd never met. Sarah's father had never once shown as much concern for her as Barney was. And how could Taffeta resist him, knowing that? He was the perfect blend of rugged masculinity and compassion.

With the flicker of amber flame dancing over his chiseled features, he was, without question, one of the handsomest men Taffeta had ever met. The sharp planes and strong angles of his features would, she felt sure, tempt any artist to capture his face on canvas. And, she realized with dismay, she would probably empty her meager savings account to possess the painting. He fascinated her so that she could have studied his countenance for hours without growing bored.

He gazed back at her as if he found her to be equally attractive. An act? Taffeta didn't know, but the intimate setting and the charming ambience of the restaurant—elegant, yet welcoming—lured her into relaxed enjoyment of the moment, which was so seductive that she couldn't determine what was real or what wasn't—and she didn't really care.

Chapter Thirteen

Chris delivered embossed leather menus to their table, and after he left, Taffeta perused the entrée choices. This was her first visit to Peck's Red Rooster. Compared to the prices she had once encountered in Erickson, she felt that these were more than fair, which, in her opinion, explained why this establishment drew so many customers. The Pecks offered fine food that even a working stiff could afford occasionally.

Vaguely aware that the dining room was crammed with people, Taffeta listened to the drone of conversation all around her, but she couldn't make out any of the words. She guessed that the Pecks must have consulted with acoustic experts before designing the building. She'd eaten at too many restaurants where the sound of voices was almost deafening. No matter how nice the surroundings, she found it difficult to enjoy a dining experience when she couldn't hear what others at her table were saying.

Bearing in mind that her meal would be on the house, Taffeta decided on the least expensive entrée she saw, chicken cacciatore with roasted garlic and lemon asparagus. Just as she set her menu aside, Darina Penny delivered small tasting platters of appetizers to their table.

A slender woman, she wore a uniform shirt and slacks that matched the table napkins, but that didn't prevent her from looking classy. She appeared to be in her early thirties and wore her blond-streaked hair pulled up into a spiky but attractive topknot. Carefully applied cosmetics accentuated her delicate features and twinkling brown eyes. She flashed a bright smile.

"Compliments of Chris and Kim," she said cheerfully. "Not every appetizer that they feature is present, but this will give you a fair idea of Chris's talent in the kitchen."

"Oh, how lovely," Taffeta replied.

The waitress held out her hand. As Taffeta grasped her outstretched fingers, the other woman said, "I've been in your shop, Taffeta, but it was always so busy that I never introduced myself. My name is Darina."

"I know your name," Taffeta said with a laugh. "In a town this size, where everyone knows almost everyone else, I guess introductions aren't necessary. It's great to actually meet you, though."

Barney inserted, "Darina's son, Devon, fed my animals while we were in Reno."

"And loved getting the work!" Darina fixed her warm gaze on Taffeta again. "A teenage boy with a single mom is always trying to earn money for something. Thanks to Chris and Kim, I make a nice income here—enough to support us, anyway—but it often doesn't stretch far enough for the special things he wants."

As Darina turned her attention to the appetizer platters, Taffeta wondered why she was single. In her opinion, Darina was very appealing.

With a flutter of her graceful fingers, she said, "A bit of fresh fruit, orange supreme." She rolled her eyes. "Chris is always after me to pronounce it orange sooh-prem, but it seems to stick on my tongue. Then we have sautéed oyster and button mushrooms, with thinly sliced lemons, lemon essence, and scallions, cooked to delicate perfection in extra-virgin olive oil, butter, and dry white wine." She grinned. "Next up, stuffed fingerling potatoes. I don't know how he makes them taste so good, but I can never eat only one. And I know you'll enjoy the Gruyère puffs. He seasons them with special herbs."

"Wow," Barney said. "I could make a meal with only the appetizers."

"Oh, Chris and Kim will never let you get away that easy," Darina assured them. "Have you each selected an entrée yet?"

Taffeta said that she had decided on the cacciatore, which made Barney laugh because he'd meant to order the same thing. Darina convinced both of them to try the filet mignon instead, despite their unspoken concurrence to order on the cheap.

After the waitress left to place their orders, Taffeta took a small serving from each appetizer platter, as did Barney, and they conversed over the offerings like two people who were completely absorbed in each other. Even discussing how Chris and Kim folded the napkins to resemble roosters seemed intimate.

Barney occasionally reached over to touch her cheek or hold her hand. He told her the legend of Mystic Creek and how, supposedly, two people who met on the bridge or along the stream were destined to fall in love. Taffeta had heard different versions of the tale from her customers, all with the same theme. Her favorite was that any lonely stranger who stood along the stream would fall in love with someone and live happily ever after. When she first moved here, she'd stood on the bank of the creek, wishing the legend were true, even though she'd long since decided that she would never be lucky in romantic relationships.

"Do you really believe that there's something magical about the creek?" she asked him.

Barney smiled. "My parents met by the creek—or on the bridge. I can't remember for sure—but they got married shortly thereafter, and to this day, the one thing they argue most vehemently about is whether Dad got her to the altar in only three weeks or if my mom held out for at least a month."

Taffeta laughed. "And I take it that they've been blissfully happy?"

"Very." He shrugged. "And then my brother met Amanda here, and they're happy as clams. He loves her little girl, Chloe, as much as if she were his own. So I guess it's possible that magic is at work here in Mystic Creek. We have a lot of couples who met each other here and appear to have solid marriages."

Taffeta could only wish that fate might one day lead her there—and, if possible, with this man.

After enjoying a superb meal, Barney escorted Taffeta out onto the deck. The air was crisp, and the water-kissed breeze cut through her shawl to make her shiver. She whimsically wondered if their standing together over the water might mean they were going to find love to last a lifetime.

"Ah, honey, you're cold." Barney looped an arm around her and drew her in close to share his heat. Gazing down into her eyes, he bent his head. Taffeta knew that he intended to kiss her. She also knew that he was only playing a role for the audience of diners inside and the gesture would mean nothing.

Only when their lips met, her head swirled and desire flared low in her belly. His mouth felt silken and tasted heady from the wine. The light release of his breath feathered over her face. He demanded nothing, but he was a master at inviting her to offer him more. And she was helpless to resist, going limp as he turned to embrace her with both arms. She wasn't a petite woman, but he seemed to tower over her. He felt so warm and sturdy, every line of his body steely with muscle. He ran a big hand into her loose hair to caress the nape of her neck as he deepened the kiss, delving deep to taste her mouth. Her breathing hitched and then grew rapid and uneven.

When he finally lifted his head and broke the contact, she could barely stand without support. As if he sensed that, he grasped her arm to hold her steady. When they reached his truck minutes later, she couldn't remember walking to it. Had they taken the outdoor path to the front parking lot, or had he guided her back through the restaurant? She'd lost her mind. That had to be it. This was nothing more than an act to him, and she could no more resist him than a fruit fly could the sweet smell of a ripe banana.

After getting Taffeta settled inside the Dodge, Barney paused at the tailgate as he circled the truck, trying to collect his composure with little success. He'd kissed plenty of women and slept with a number of them. The foreplay had always aroused him. The sex had been satisfying as well. But never in his life had he been bowled over by his attraction to anyone. With only a touch of her mouth on his, Taffeta drugged his senses, making him forget who he was and where he was.

All his good intentions to be an honorable man were in grave danger of flying out the proverbial window. He wanted this woman in a way that he had never wanted anyone. He didn't know how she felt, but for him, that kiss on the deck had been pure dynamite.

He sucked in a deep breath and slowly released it, trying to regain control of his physical reaction to her. Fat chance. He could stand at the back of his rig half the night, and his blood would still be running hot.

When he finally climbed inside the vehicle and twisted the key in the ignition, he was acutely aware of her sitting across from him. Her scent, which always reminded him of roses, curled around him. Darkness had fallen while they dined, but the glow of the dash lights faintly illuminated the cab. Even as he pretended to be focused on only the road, he took in her legs, which were bare from the hem of her skirt down to those sexy heels she wore. He salivated over the graceful curves of her calves and the dainty turn of her ankles. How would it feel to have those gorgeous legs locked around his hips as he drove his throbbing manhood deep into the hot, moist core of her?

He'd never know, he thought dismally, because he'd been taught by his father that his word was his honor. Maybe after she got her daughter back—maybe when they got a divorce—he could convince her to be with him in a real, meaningful way. Not within the lockdown of marriage, but as two consenting adults who found each other physically attractive. Some of the pressure eased from his chest. The hardness that throbbed against the fly of his jeans softened. *Yeah.* By holding on to that plan, maybe he could get through this without breaking his promise to her.

When they got home from the restaurant, Taffeta was as jumpy as a water droplet on a red-hot skillet. She had dressed seductively, per his request, and now she felt self-conscious. Eager to ditch the sexy black dress and heels, she hurried toward her bedroom and collided with Barney, who reached the dining room archway just as she did. The impact nearly knocked her down. The spiked heels gave her no edge on keeping her balance. Barney caught her arm to keep her from falling. She looked up, and their gazes locked. He grasped her shoulders and turned her toward him. A whooshing pressure throbbed against her eardrums, similar to when she cracked a window in her car while driving at high speeds and the interior of the vehicle formed a vacuum—only this wasn't a result of that. She *wanted* him. She *ached* to feel his arms around her. She fleetingly considered locking her own arms around his neck and kissing him until he lost control.

Only he never gave her a chance. He cursed under his breath. Then he angled his head and brought his mouth down on hers, and the next thing she knew, she was sandwiched between his big, hard body and the dining room wall. His large hands clamped over her hips and moved swiftly upward, his fingers skimming, probing, and lightly caressing her, seemingly everywhere at once. She could barely breathe, and every rational thought in her head vanished. *Barney.* She felt him grappling with the hem of her dress. Then his fingertips delved between her thighs, rasping against her sensitive skin.

"Oh *yes*," she pushed out, her voice thick and husky. She wanted him to touch her, to feel her wetness. She wanted the dress and her underthings gone so she could feel the hot, silky pull of his mouth on her nipples. "Oh *yes*."

He drew away from her and deprived her of his support so fast that she slid a bit down the wall before she could lock her knees to remain standing. She blinked to bring him into focus. He stood two feet away, thrusting a hand through his hair. Eyes glassy with desire, he avoided looking at her.

"Wait—we have to figure this out." His voice grated like a well-honed knife over sandpaper. Grabbing his Stetson from where it had fallen to the floor, he circled the long table, jerked back a chair, and sank onto the seat as if his legs felt as weak as hers did. "Take a load off." He gestured for her to sit across from him. "We need some ground rules, or I'm not going to be able to do this."

Taffeta moved carefully forward. Legs that had turned to jelly didn't operate well when one was wearing three-inch heels. She took a seat across from him. He braced both elbows on the table, rubbed his face with one hand, and then set the hat back on his head. Still feeling dizzy, she wondered if he needed the Stetson for strength. She definitely needed something.

He puffed air into his cheeks and released it in a rush. His gaze locked on hers. He looked so handsome in the black jacket that she wanted to crawl across the table to steal another taste of his mouth. But to say that he looked unreceptive to an advance would have been an understatement.

He cleared his throat. "We, um, have no choice but to put on a show in town," he said, his voice strained. "But from now on when we get home, I'll need some recovery time." He stared out the paned window at the end of the room. It was dark outside, so she guessed that he simply didn't wish to look at her as he spoke. "I—well, I'm a guy, you know? Certain parts of my anatomy don't recognize playacting from the real thing. I apologize for jumping you like that. It was inexcusable. I gave you my word that I wouldn't ask you for sex, and then—" He broke off and shrugged. "It won't happen again, not if we both agree to some preventive measures."

"But I—"

He held up a hand to cut her off. "Tomorrow night, if you'd go directly to your room and change into something less—well, that dress you're wearing is fabulous for in town, but maybe I'll be less inclined to repeat what just happened if you hurry to put on something less enticing right away. I'll hang back in the living room until you holler, and then I'll go change." A wry smile touched his mouth. "During the evenings, your icky brown shirt, or something like it, would be better."

Taffeta gathered her courage. She'd never said anything like this to a man. "Barney, I *wanted* you to grab me."

He blew out another breath. "Of *course* you'd say that. You need my help to get Sarah back. But let's be honest, Taffy. You didn't ask me to marry you because you had the hots for me. You were desperate to rescue your child from a bad mess."

"True, that's true," she confessed. "But I also had a thing for you." Heat crawled up her neck. "A crush, I guess you'd call it, and I fantasized about you from the moment I first saw you."

He rolled his eyes. "Out of all the guys in Mystic Creek, I'm the one who caught your eye? Come on, Taffy. Off the top of my head, I can think of a dozen young men in town who outclass me in the looks department, nine ways to hell. You don't need to do this. Just because my hormones are playing hell with my good intentions, you don't have to flatter me. I'm not going to back out on our plan."

"But, Barney, I—"

"Enough." Anger edged his voice. "I didn't agree to this deal for sex. The whole thought of that—well, it's sleazy. And that isn't who I am."

Taffeta realized that Barney honestly didn't know how devastatingly handsome he was. How could he possibly rank himself low on the charts in the looks department in any town, let alone one as small as Mystic Creek? Did he focus on tiny facial flaws or what he felt were his physical shortcomings when he looked in a mirror? She only knew that he wasn't seeing the man she saw who moved with easy, masculine grace and flashed a grin that made her bones go limp. And didn't he understand that a man's magnetism had little to do with looks and nearly everything to do with who he was as a person and how he projected himself to others?

She saw a man who was a curious blend of steely strength and gentleness, a man with a caring heart, a captivating sense of humor, a sharp wit, and a rare honesty about who and what he really was. No pretense. No trying to impress people. And yet, with the exception that he rarely remembered to remove his hat when mannerly conduct dictated that he should, he could mix easily with individuals from all walks of life. He was well educated and loved to read. His tastes in music ran to down-home country, but he also appreciated classical, jazz, and blues. He was—*oh, man, I'm in love with him. No maybe to it. No trying to stop myself from taking the leap. I'm totally head over heels.*

"Are y-you saying that being with me would be sleazy?" she asked, hating that her voice trembled.

"*No!*" He jerked his hat off and slapped it on the table, sat back in the chair, closed his eyes briefly, and then gave her a burning look. "There's nothing sleazy about you. You're beautiful, classy, sweet, and—" He shot up from his seat and lifted his hands, as if he was at a loss for words. "It's just—it's this whole marriage thing that's hog-tying me. Under any other circumstances, I'd hit on you and hope you said yes. I'm attracted to you, *very* attracted, and I can tell that you're attracted to me. But it just can't happen right now."

"Why?" she demanded. "We're both adults and—"

"And you have too much at stake to tell me no," he finished for her.

Taffeta couldn't deny that. When she'd asked him to marry her, she offered him conjugal rights to sweeten the deal. Now, looking at that from his viewpoint, she felt embarrassed—and ashamed. In order to save her daughter, she'd been willing to prostitute herself. And he was right. Even if she hadn't wanted to make love with him tonight, she would still pretend that she did. When it came to ensuring her daughter's safety, she would do anything.

"I'm sorry," she said. "I've put you in a horrible situation."

He sighed and ran a hand over his hair. "You're the one in a horrible situation, not me. All I can do is try my damnedest not to take advantage of it. I didn't mean to let things get out of control a few minutes ago, but I did." He stripped off the jacket and tossed it over a chairback. "I will need your cooperation so it won't happen again. When I kissed you outside the restaurant—well, for me it was pretty spectacular."

"For me, too." She gnawed her bottom lip, trying to choose her words carefully. "I need you to know that it's a first for me, Barney. I was so focused on getting good grades in high school that I had only one boyfriend and lost my virginity to him in the backseat of his father's car. It was awful. Well, not *awful*, really. It was his first time, too, and for me, it was an awkward incident that ended up with me crying, not only because it hurt, but also because I got scared when I saw blood. *Mine*, of course. He was turned off. I was turned off. He took me home. I was determined never to go out with him again, and he never asked me, so I guess the feeling was mutual."

"And then?" he asked.

"I focused on academics so I could go to the university. Then I met Phillip. He courted me, dazzled me with his charming lines, his sophistication, and his family." Her cheeks burned. "I liked it okay when he kissed me." With a shrug, she added, "At least he knew *how*. When we finally had sex, it was—well, not great, but at least it didn't hurt, and he wasn't awkward."

Barney arched an eyebrow. "Why are you telling me this?"

"Because I need you to know that I don't normally offer my body to men, that when I approached you it was totally out of character for me. I don't sleep around. I've never slept around."

The glints of gold left his eyes, making them look dark with shadows. "I never for a second thought otherwise," he said softly. "If I somehow made you feel that I did, I'm sorry. You've never come across that way, Taffy—just the opposite in fact."

He rested his hips against the china hutch behind him and folded his arms. "We have a common goal, getting Sarah out of Erickson and here with you. I'm in for the duration. I just need some help with keeping my hands off you."

Taffeta wanted so badly to tell him that she didn't want him to keep his hands off her, but she refrained, not because it wasn't true, but because she didn't want him to think she was lying out of desperation to save her daughter.

She settled for saying, "I'll do everything I can. Can you give me some suggestions?"

The twinkles of gold finally returned to his eyes. "If there were such a thing as an ugly pill, I'd ask you to take one morning, noon, and night." His mouth twitched at the corners. "Unfortunately I'm not sure even that would help. It's not only that I like the way you look. I like *you*, the person you are. Everything about you is attractive to me."

Tears burned in Taffeta's eyes. She blinked to hold them back. "That's a lovely compliment, and I feel the same way about you."

"Don't tell me that, or we'll end up in bed, and I'll hate myself in the morning."

Taffeta knew he meant for her to laugh, but she couldn't dredge up any humor. Instead she pushed herself to her feet. "I guess I'd better go change into something less . . . dressy."

"How about a pair of those baggy jeans and a shirt that hangs on you like a tent?" he said with a chuckle.

She hurried to her bedroom, kicked off the heels, and peeled off the dress. Then she went in search of the ugliest, baggiest clothing she could find. Once dressed, she cleansed all traces of cosmetics from her face and skimmed her hair back in a tight knot at the back of her head, secured with a clip.

When she returned to the living area of the house, she found Barney in the kitchen measuring flour into the silver bowl of his stand-up mixer. He glanced over his shoulder at her, studied her for what felt like several seconds, and then said, "Thank God I decided to try my hand at another batch of sourdough bread. You still look good enough to eat. This will keep me preoccupied."

In her opinion, he was the one who looked delicious, but she was coming to accept that he wasn't hers to taste—and probably never would be. "Do you find sourdough difficult to make?" she asked.

He had changed into faded jeans and a white T-shirt that skimmed his upper body like a second skin, showcasing a fascinating play of muscles every time he moved. "Yes," he replied. "I've decided it's an art, and I'll either master it or die trying. Every loaf I've ever made refused to rise and was so dense with such a thick crust I could use it as a weapon to coldcock someone."

She forced her gaze away from him to look at the stove clock. "Isn't it a little late to be starting bread?"

He laughed and winked at her. "The way I see it, I won't be able to go to sleep anyway."

"Because of me?"

His grin broadened. "Taffy, it isn't your fault. Okay? When you're dying to eat a piece of chocolate, do you blame the chocolate?"

"Yes, because it's there to tempt me."

He chuckled again. "Well, I'm not of that mindset. For me, you're the chocolate, and I just have to use my willpower to resist you." He scooped a cup and a half of gooey-looking stuff from a glass crock into the mixing bowl. Then he gestured with his head at a rack of wine bottles at the end of the counter. "Crack open a bottle, why don't you? Maybe a couple more glasses will mellow me out."

Taking care to cut a wide circle around him, Taffeta walked over to the wine. After studying the labels, she asked, "Which kind would you like?"

"I'm not particular, but if you see one called Limp Dick, I'll drink the whole bottle."

Caught by surprise, Taffeta chortled. "Sorry. You're out of luck." She selected a merlot, searched through the drawers for the corkscrew, and seconds later set a filled wineglass next to him on the counter. "Mind if I join you?"

"Hell, no. We're not driving anywhere. Maybe we'll get drunk, have mind-blowing sex, and I can blame it on the alcohol in the morning."

Taffeta could think of no response to that. In her experience, a lot of men went to bed with women and never gave it a second thought. She suspected that Barney had traveled that path more than a few times with other women, but because he believed that she felt obligated to him, he refused to go there with her.

She didn't know whether to laugh or cry. For the first time in her life, she really, *really* wanted a man to make love to her, and he was too honorable to accommodate her.

She was a grown woman. If she wanted to have sex with him, why couldn't he accept that it was her decision to make?

Other women made love with men they desired all the time, and Taffeta had never once been afforded that experience. It didn't seem fair. In fact, the more she thought about it, the more irked she became. She understood Barney's reluctance to take advantage of a woman who felt obligated to him, but where did *her* wants, needs, and, most important, her right to make choices for herself, factor into the equation? Studying Barney from the corner of her eye, Taffeta wondered what would happen if she tried to seduce him. She had zero experience at seduction, but if Barney was truly attracted to her, and apparently he was, maybe it wouldn't be all that hard.

Chapter Fourteen

Over the next week, Barney and Taffeta went out on the town every night, pretending to be wildly in love with each other. Barney called it "Doing the hootchy-kootchy act." Only Taffeta no longer wanted it to be only an act, so she did everything she possibly could, and at every opportunity, to turn him on.

At Dizzy's Roundtable, Barney ordered bread pudding with bourbon sauce for dessert. Recalling the morning that he'd sucked cream horn filling from her finger and how sexy that had been, Taffeta decided to try that tactic herself. She eyed his plate, deliberately dimpled a cheek, and asked, "May I have a tiny taste of the bourbon sauce? I've never tried it."

Barney started to reach for her spoon, but Taffeta forestalled him with "No, no. Give me a taste with your finger." Lowering her voice, she added, "It'll look so much more convincing that way. Don't you think?"

He shrugged and dipped his forefinger in the sauce. "You better hope my hands are clean."

Taffeta giggled. "What are a few germs between lovers?" She leaned across the small table for two, clasped his broad wrist, and guided his fingertip to her mouth. No way was she going to just suck the sauce off. Oh no. She was going to lick it off, and then she'd suck his skin clean. *Oh yeah.* If he already wanted her, that would send his blood pressure rocketing clear off the chart. "Oo-oo-oh. Mmm-mm-mm." She daintily circled his fingertip with her tongue. "That is *so* good it's almost orgasmic."

She felt his arm tense. "Taffy, people are staring."

She winked at him. "That's the whole idea, isn't it? To convince them we're madly in love?" She licked his finger again and moaned. "Oh my God. How fabulous can it get?" She met his startled and suddenly glassy gaze. "How am I doing with the act?" she whispered.

"Pretty damned good." His voice had gone gravelly and thick. "But I—"

Taffeta interrupted him with "Oh, that's a relief. I'm such a lousy actress."

When she released her hold on Barney's wrist, he looked as if he'd just been shocked with high-voltage electricity.

"That bread pudding and sauce is so divine. The next time we come here, to heck with having plain old cheesecake for dessert."

Taffeta picked up her linen napkin, but instead of dabbing her mouth with it, she used the tip of her tongue to clean her lips, even though absolutely none of the sauce still clung to them. She glanced up to find Barney's gaze riveted to her mouth. She'd gotten to him, big-time. She just *knew* she had, and she'd only just started to play this game. Before much longer, she would have this man in her bed, making passionate love to her. She *would*. He could stuff his blasted honorable streak under a pillow.

My turn, she thought. It wasn't that she didn't admire Barney for sticking to his principles. Of course she did. But how could she be sure she'd ever again meet another man who appealed to her in all the same ways that he did?

When they got home, Barney didn't wait for her to change into loose, ugly clothing. He sped past her with long, purposeful strides and called over his shoulder, "G'night, Taffy. Sleep well. I'm totally beat."

Taffeta looked down at her dress, a strappy, red knit shift that clung to her body like a second skin. She'd worn it for a charity event while still married to Phillip. Most of the fund-raisers had called for more subdued outfits, but that particular event had been a rare glitzy affair. She'd worn silver spike heels, lots of matching bangles, and a choker. Tonight she wore her black heels and no jewelry, except for her cheap wedding band, but a dress like this didn't need any flash. It made its own statement.

She lifted her arms and twirled in the living room, gyrating her hips and softly singing, "I *can* get some satisfaction." *Yes.* She doubled her fist, raised it high, and brought her elbow down in a sharp dive.

Still shivering from the cold shower he'd just taken, Barney lay on his bed and stared blindly at the ceiling. He had a hard-on that tented the quilt he'd drawn over himself, and he had a bad feeling that he'd be in this condition all night.

He felt pissed at Taffeta for doing this to him, but

a stab of guilt quickly drove the spurt of anger away. She'd been with only an inexperienced jock in high school and her ex-husband, who'd been too selfish to bother with making her happy in bed, so she couldn't have very much experience with men. It followed that he couldn't, in good conscience, be mad at her for turning him on. She'd put on a great show at the restaurant to convince onlookers that they were deeply in love, and it wasn't her fault that he'd had a physical reaction. Bottom line, she hadn't deliberately pushed all his buttons, and she was probably sound asleep by now, blissfully unaware that she had subjected him to an entire night of pure misery.

At her shop the following day, Taffeta tried to think of some way she could turn Barney on again that night. She couldn't ask for a taste of his food again. That would be too obvious, and he would realize what she was up to. So what *could* she do? Per Barney's request, she was already dressing sexy when they went out, but that alone didn't work because she had to change as soon as they got home.

I'm up against a brick wall, she thought dismally. *I'm a total bomb at seduction.* She sorely wished she had a girlfriend who might give her some ideas, but relationships like that took time to build.

To cheer herself up, Taffeta turned on the radio behind the counter, selected a popular country station, and began restocking her shelves from boxes that had been delivered that morning. The song about a guy giving a girl a ride on his John Deere tractor came over the air, reminding Taffeta of Barney saying that he'd give her a ride on his tractor someday. Her first thought had been that she'd prefer it if he took her out into the woods and checked her for ticks.

Do they even have ticks in Mystic Creek? Taffeta didn't know, so that plan was out. A few minutes later, Crystal Malloy, who owned Silver Beach, came into the shop. Today her waist-length, wavy hair was its natural red. She wore calf-hugging black boots and a green knit dress that showcased her figure.

"You look fabulous," Taffeta said, and sincerely meant it. The Crystal Malloys of the world could seduce men without half trying. "I love the natural color of your hair."

Crystal laughed. "Thank you. I decided to be me today. I get tired of advertising my rinse-away dyes by using them myself. Sometimes it's scary when I look in a mirror because I forget what wild colors I chose for the day."

She pushed up the sleeve of her dress. "Do you have *anything* for a nasty spider bite?"

Taffeta gasped when she saw the huge red lump on the beautician's forearm. "Oh, ick. That really is nasty. It must hurt like the dickens."

"I'm sensitive to spider bites," Crystal said. "Otherwise I'd be racing over to Mystic Creek Urgent Care on Red Barn Road, convinced a recluse bit me."

"Do we have brown recluse spiders here?" Taffeta shuddered at the thought. "I've been terrified of spiders since early childhood. Why, I don't know. But all kinds send me running in the opposite direction."

"I'm with you on the terror," Crystal replied. "And yes, we do have the brown recluse. I don't think they're indigenous to our area. From what I've heard, they come in on trucks in boxes, get loose inside buildings, and set up camp. I called a bug control place in Crystal Falls this morning. They're coming tomorrow to spray my shop and apartment." She turned her arm to look at the bite. "I can't quite afford it, but this convinced me I can't afford not to have it done."

Taffeta led the way to her first-aid aisle. "This will help," she said, lifting a box from the shelf. "It'll stave off infection, and it has a numbing agent in it to ease the tenderness." She handed Crystal the ointment. "But, in all honesty, I'd use a baking-soda poultice on the bite first. I know it's an old home remedy, but I think it actually works. I've used it on bee stings and other bites. I swear, you can see it draw out the poison sometimes."

Crystal kept the ointment and questioned Taffeta with her gaze. "How do I make a baking soda poultice? I've never heard of it."

Taffeta gave her instructions. "Leave it on the bite until it dries and starts to flake off. Then wash the area, dab it dry with sterile gauze, and apply the ointment."

Crystal left moments later with the ointment and a package of gauze. Taffeta stood behind the cash register, staring at nothing. *Mystic Creek has brown recluse spiders.* Her mouth quirked as she suppressed a grin. Crystal didn't know it, but she'd just given Taffeta an idea how to seduce Barney tonight.

* * *

Taffeta dressed for dinner in skintight jeans and the pink knit top that Barney loved. She also followed Crystal's lead and wore her high-heeled black boots, which hugged her legs to the knee like the skin on an onion. She could hardly wait to get home after dinner, because she had a fabulous seduction plan cooked up. Even better, she felt confident that she could pull it off. Just thinking about spiders made her feel panicky, so playing her role wouldn't require much acting ability.

After they left the house, Barney was quiet as he navigated his truck along the country roads toward Mystic Creek. Taffeta sensed that something was bothering him, but she didn't know what. Concern edged away her excitement about her seduction scheme.

"What's bothering you, Barney? You're very quiet."

He sighed. "I hate having to say this, Taffy. But as a deputy, I really can't afford to pay for fine dining every evening, so some nights we're going to have to slum it. I'm thinking about doing dinner at Taco Joe's tonight. Just as many people will see us together. You like tacos?"

Taffeta's heart caught. Of *course* he couldn't afford all this eating out. Where had her head been, in the sand? "Oh, Barney, I'm sorry. From now on, I'll pay for our meals. We're eating out because of Sarah. It's not your expense to pay."

He executed a curve and then threw her a perturbed look. "You can't do that. We're married, remember? In this little town, onlookers would notice you paying for our meals and wonder what the hell is going on. Normally the husband pays."

Taffeta thought that was a bit archaic. Nowadays many wives were professionals who earned good incomes. But this *was* Mystic Creek, a quaint, old-fashioned little town populated by people who thought differently about many things. "You've definitely got a point," she conceded. "So I'll settle up with you at home and pay for our meals."

"Do you have a problem with slumming it?" He gave her a questioning look. "Just curious, because after I divorce you, I might like to date you, and I can't afford high-maintenance women."

She laughed. "I happen to like tacos—and hamburgers. Sissy Sue, the little gal who runs the Cauldron, makes my mouth water when she comes in around lunchtime, offering franks simmered in sauerkraut, hot corn dogs with the house dip, freshly made chili, and the most fabulous fries!"

"She's new in town," Barney said, "a relative of the old lady who once owned the place and passed away. Sissy inherited the business. I don't know her life story, but I have a feeling she grew up without much and feels like she just hit the jackpot."

"A foster kid, maybe, just like me? Hello, I didn't grow up enjoying gourmet cooking. Mostly I got hamburger goulash or beans with ham, only I went blind looking for the ham. Maybe I should get to know Sissy Sue. We might have a lot in common."

His shoulders relaxed. "Well, I'm sorry you grew up that way, and I'm sorry if she did. My mother managed to serve fabulous meals, even during the lean years. We raised so much of what we ate that us kids never felt the pinch."

Taffeta had only good feelings about Kate Sterling. She radiated warmth. What a joy it must have been for Barney and his siblings to have her as their mother. And Jeremiah? He reminded her strongly of Barney, tall, handsome, and powerfully built, yet gentle and caring.

"Let's do Taco Joe's tonight, and tomorrow night, I'd dearly love to try the Cauldron," she said.

He nodded. "Maybe we can get to know Sissy a little better." He winked at her. "I think she's younger than you, but it would be good for you to have a best friend." The crease in his cheek flashed as he grinned. "A best friend besides me, I mean."

Taffeta didn't correct his assumption that he'd become her best friend. Despite the sexual tension that came to a high boil between them at night, Barney *had* become her buddy. Why not? If she couldn't have him as her lover, she needed some kind of connection with him that meant something.

"Yep," she agreed. "You're, hands down, the best friend I've ever had."

"Don't get mushy on me," he ordered as he muscled the huge truck into a parking place on West Main in front of Taco Joe's. "Otherwise, wearing those damned tight jeans, you'll end up being a flattened decoration on my dining room wall later tonight."

Taffeta choked back a giggle. She would have loved to hang on his wall again—if he was holding her up.

Joe yelled hello when they entered his eatery. Like

every business in Mystic Creek, his place was quaint with gnarled myrtle wood tables in the booths, old pictures of Mystic Creek lining the walls, and a rack of forgotten ball caps that Joe had turned into a conversation piece. After she and Barney placed their orders, Taffeta couldn't resist studying the collection. Barney joined her, probably not because he'd never seen all the hat logos, but because he wanted to play glued-to-his-bride. One caption read SCREW MY BRAINS OUT. I DON'T GOT NONE, ANYHOW. Another one read MY WIFE THINKS I'M FISHIN'. Taffeta particularly liked the one that said I'M THE CAPTAIN OF THIS BOAT. MY WIFE SAYS SO.

Barney let Taffeta look at every cap. Joe hollered from the kitchen pass-through that men had started leaving their hats behind on purpose, and he named off a few of the owners who had wanted their headgear to be mounted on the Wall of Fame.

Taffeta and Barney wandered to look at old photos of Mystic Creek that peppered the other walls. Both of them greeted fellow patrons and fielded questions about how they were liking married life. Taffeta found a dated picture of East Main more fascinating than all the others. Her shop had once housed a saddle and tack store, and next door there had been a soda fountain.

"I loved going there," Barney said, pointing to the fountain. "An old man named Mac owned it, and after Friday night games I used to take my girlfriends in there for a root beer float, hoping to score."

Taffeta gave him an inquiring look.

He chuckled and said, "Sweetheart, back then,

scoring meant a girl liked me enough to share the same straw."

After enjoying tacos for dinner, they took a stroll to the town center. Barney kept one arm loosely curled around her shoulders. At the water feature, a spewing fountain that emptied into a small pond, they each tossed in a penny and made a wish. Taffeta hoped that Barney would fall in love with her. She had no idea what he wished for, but given the constant sexual frustration, she suspected that he wanted this fake marriage to be over with quickly.

When they got back to his house, Taffeta hurried into the dining room as if she meant to race to her bedroom and change into baggy clothing. But as she came abreast of the table, she executed her next seduction plan.

"Oh *God*, oh *God*!" She peeked down the scoop neckline of her top and shrieked. Then she started slapping her breasts. "Help me! *Help* me! There's a spider in my bra!"

Barney recognized true panic when he saw it, and Taffeta was in the throes of a full-blown attack. He leaped into action, afraid she might bruise herself with all the blows she was dealing to her chest.

"Taffy, *stop*! It's only a spider. I'll get it off you. Just calm down."

"Recluse," she cried. "It's a recluse! I saw the fiddle shape on it!"

Before Barney could reach her, she grabbed the hem of her top and skimmed it off over the top of her head. He'd seen plenty of women in underclothes, but

Taffeta had an ampler bosom than most, and she had on a lacy pink half-cup bra. His eyes nearly popped out of their sockets. With her bouncing around and shrieking like this, he half expected her breasts to spill out. And God help him, he thought, *Bring it on, baby.*

He grabbed her wrists and tried his damnedest to banish all lustful urges from his mind. "It's okay. Trust me. I'll catch it and smash it."

She squeezed her eyes closed. "It's in my bra! I can feel it crawling! Get it! Get it! Off me, *off* me!"

"Be still," he ordered. "A recluse bites when it gets startled. They're aggressive little buggers."

Barney felt sweat bead on his forehead as he dipped his fingertips under the pink lace to peek inside her bra. Her warm, silken skin grazed his knuckles. *Oh, man.* He forced himself to focus on only the task at hand and peered inside one lace cup and then the other. He saw a dark brown splotch next to her left nipple.

"Don't move," he whispered. Barney had seen pictures of recluse bites, and they were horrible. People's flesh sloughed off, leaving disfiguring holes. Just the thought of that beautiful breast being destroyed made him feel half sick. "I see it," he said softly. "I'm going to grab it really fast and smash it between my fingers."

Her eyes went wide, and all the color drained from her face. "You *see* it?" Her body stiffened. "Oh God, a spider's in my bra?"

Before Barney could reply, Taffeta freaked out even more. She jerked from his grasp, unfastened the front catch of her undergarment, and the most beautiful breasts he'd ever seen burst free from the lace confines.

She spun in circles, brushing frantically at her skin. "Where is it? Oh God, get it off me!"

Barney grabbed her by the shoulders. "I'm sure you've knocked it off by now." He glanced down. The brown splotch by her nipple was still there. *A mole.* "Wait. It's not a spider. It's a blemish."

She stopped wiggling in his grasp. "A blemish?"

"Yeah, a mole, not a spider. I caught a glimpse of it, and I thought it was a recluse."

I can't do this, he thought. If he stayed in this room one second longer, he'd lose it and make her forget all about spiders.

"Maybe it fell on the floor," he suggested, trying to regain control of himself. "I'm certain it can't still be on you." He thought he saw it on the speckled barn planks. "*There* it is." He bent over, studied the spot, and added, "Nope. It's just a splash of old brown paint."

He'd never known anyone so terrified of spiders. Later, when he felt it was okay to have sex with her, he'd know how to get her to shuck her clothes nice and fast. All he'd have to do was yell, "Spider!" God, she was beautiful, and not in a plastic, artificial way, but just naturally lovely. Her heavy breasts drooped just a bit. If they had been completely perky, he would have been turned off. He liked soft, plump breasts, not hard balloons created by a surgeon's knife and bags of saline.

"I don't know where it went," he said, "but I can guarantee that it isn't on you."

She glanced down, and her cheeks flamed pink, the color a perfect match for her nipples. Barney almost lost it then. He wanted her so much, and the sight of all that gloriously naked skin tested his will-power nearly beyond endurance.

"I'm going to bed," he said. "There's no spider, and if I stay here, things will happen between us that we'll both regret tomorrow."

He released his hold on her, circled her to escape through the kitchen archway, and then strode down the hallway, his body on fire with need.

It was one of the longest walks of his life.

When he got inside his bedroom, he sat on the bed and cradled his head in his hands. This was a night-mare. He nearly groaned aloud. *And I created it.*

Taffeta hugged her pillow and stared at the shifting patterns of moonlight that played over the window glass in her bedroom. Lingering embarrassment still warmed her face. She hadn't intended to take off her bra, only she had panicked when Barney said he saw a spider inside one of the cups. At that moment, all rational thought had sped from her mind, and she'd gone on autopilot.

What must Barney think?

Her plan had been to remove only her top. Strip-ping down to one's bra wasn't really that risqué. Nowadays, bikini tops revealed just as much as a bra did, if not more. But it had been one of the most humiliating moments of her life when she looked down and saw that she was naked from the waist up.

Even worse, Barney had walked away from her with no difficulty. He hadn't even glanced back at her. How was she supposed to take that? It definitely hadn't been a compliment. And, hello, if he had stayed in the dining room, she would have had no regrets in the morning.

Chapter Fifteen

Over the next two weeks, Barney learned how it felt to exist in a constant state of physical frustration. Night after night, he took Taffeta out on the town and got so aroused that he could barely see straight, only to drive her back home and not touch her. He couldn't fall asleep. Cold showers didn't help. He wondered if Taffeta was experiencing the same ache of desire that he was. They cuddled and kissed in public, but at evening's end, it was strictly hands off. They circled each other like wary combatants expecting a surprise attack.

Barney reasoned that he would have breezed through this part of their bargain if he hadn't been required to act romantic for the benefit of onlookers. Only that was demanded of him, and his body didn't recognize the difference between pretend touching and the real thing. For him the public displays of affection seemed all too genuine.

Barney had kept company with several gorgeous women over the years, but he'd never felt desire this intense with any of them. He analyzed the reasons for that and decided it was Taffeta's sweet nature and genuine goodness that really got to him. He could see the pain in her eyes whenever she thought of her daughter, which happened often, but she somehow set that aside and never took it out on him. Some mornings he would awaken to find her outside with his animals, feeding the horses cookies, tossing scraps to the chickens, and having long conversations with his supposedly pregnant cow, Mary Lou.

She had laughed until she got tears in her eyes when Barney told her the tale of a bull named Romeo, who was rented out by many local farmers to provide stud services.

"I paid to have Mary Lou artificially inseminated two years ago," Barney had shared, "and it was a rodeo from start to finish. Mary Lou wanted no part of it. When I tried to herd her into the squeeze chute, she veered away and butted the inseminator. I swear, he flew ten feet. Then she ran me over. When a thousand-pound cow steps on you, it hurts like the dickens. I had to have my ribs wrapped and do light work duty for a month.

"So this last autumn, when I heard about Romeo, I decided that getting her pregnant the natural way was the easier way to go. It was only fifty bucks a month to rent him."

"And did he do his job?" Taffeta asked.

Barney had warmed to telling the story. "Don't get ahead of me. When the owner pulled in with the stock trailer and unloaded Romeo into the pasture, my heart soared with excitement. That bull literally ran toward Mary Lou! I thought, 'Way to go, Romeo!

Get the job done straightaway. I'll pay the fifty bucks and send you home.' But Romeo bypassed Mary Lou and went straight for my hay. The owner said Romeo was probably tired because he'd just spent a month out to pasture with nearly a hundred cows."

"That would make any bull tired, I guess," Taffeta mused.

Barney nodded. "Yep, and all indications were that Romeo had met his baby quota for the year. I never once saw him make a romantic overture. Mary Lou just stood around, looking downcast and rejected, chewing her cud."

That got another laugh from Taffeta. "Poor Mary Lou! The local rent-a-bull didn't want her!"

"My brothers nicknamed Romeo the midnight lover, and I could only hope they had it right, because he sure as heck didn't do any business during the day."

Taffeta had loved the story, and after that, she'd bonded with Mary Lou, fussing over her as if she were with calf even though Barney didn't know for sure if the cow was pregnant or not. Her belly had grown, but he didn't know if that was due to gestation or if she was just fat. Taffeta wasn't helping on that score with all the treats that she gave her. Kate had given Taffeta her horse cookie recipe, and one weekend Barney's whole house had been redolent with the scent of molasses as Taffeta baked batch after batch. Enjoying the sight of Taffeta working in his kitchen, Barney spent his Sunday off making sourdough bread, which led to some jousting between him and his wife for the use of the oven.

Barney's umpteenth attempt at turning out the

perfect loaf was once again a failure. That time, he'd tried to make a big baguette, and it was so hard and dense that he could have used it as a ball bat.

Hands gooey with cookie dough, Taffeta had asked, "Are you territorial about your bread-making endeavors?"

"Hell, no. If you can make sourdough, teach me!"

She'd placed two baking sheets in the oven and stepped to the sink to scrub her hands. How she managed to look so sexy in baggy clothes, Barney didn't know, but she did. It seemed she was starting to come into her own, even if she did still hide her figure. "Remember my telling you about Mrs. Brassfield, the old lady who taught me how to love? Well, she also taught me how to make fabulous sourdough bread. It's very tangy, rises beautifully, and tastes divine."

"So, what am I doing wrong?" Barney thumped his baguette on the granite. "That sounds like a drunk banging on drums."

She giggled. "I think it's your starter. In all the sourdough cookbooks I've seen, it says to create a starter with flour and water. Some recipes call for a dab of yeast as well. Others suggest potato water instead of plain water. But Mrs. Brassfield used pineapple juice and flour instead."

"Pineapple juice? I don't want sweet sourdough bread."

"It won't be sweet. It is a fabulous starter. And do you want to hear something really weird? I'm often online looking for different ways to use sourdough, and I recently stumbled across a scientific study done on sourdough starter. I can't remember the scientist's name now, but she studied all kinds of starters under a microscope and discovered that pineapple juice as a hydrator keeps the pH level of the starter lower, creating a perfect environment for yeast to grow. Somehow Mrs. Brassfield figured that out on her own by trial and error. People who love sourdough try all different things to make the perfect starter, and she stumbled upon pineapple juice long before a scientific study was done."

Barney headed straight for Flagg's Market to buy a pack of six-ounce cans of pineapple juice. When he got home, he dumped his old starter down the sink and watched over Taffeta's shoulder as she blended a new batch with pineapple juice. He realized that he enjoyed being in the kitchen with her. The faint scent of roses that clung to her blended sweetly with the smell of warm molasses. Standing behind her, Barney felt his mouth watering as he studied the sensitive indentation at the nape of her neck. He yearned to kiss her there and taste her skin.

"Some people say to never use metal utensils with sourdough," she said, "but Mrs. Brassfield never fussed over things like that." She grabbed Barney's large wire whisk from the utensil crock near the stove. "You want to work air into your starter," she said. "Yeast bacteria are present in the flour, but your starter will also capture yeast spores from the ambient air."

For Barney, creating a new starter with Taffeta was almost as arousing as engaging in sexual foreplay. He wanted her so badly that his groin throbbed, and he seriously considered picking her up, lying her on the table, tearing her clothes off, and enjoying her as a starving man might a smorgasbord.

One morning before they both left for work, they grabbed a quick breakfast together at the kitchen table. Taffeta took a banana from a bowl that also held apples, oranges, plums, and kiwis. Sitting across from him, she carefully drew down the peel and then skimmed her small white teeth over the flesh of the fruit. Mesmerized, Barney stopped chewing a mouthful of cereal to watch her. *It's a guy thing,* he told himself. *She isn't deliberately trying to make me come in my jeans.* And he knew he had that right. Taffeta wasn't a tease, and she never made a calculated attempt to turn him on. But, he realized dismally, she could arouse him without even trying.

Barney left for the department wondering when he'd gotten so damned horny that he could be jealous of a stupid banana. But he was. When he arrived at work, he nearly snapped Garrett's head off for wishing him good morning.

"What the hell's so good about it?"

Garrett gave Barney a wondering look. "Uh-oh. The honeymoon must be over."

Barney winced. Being a huge grump when he came on duty was no way to project to the world that he was head over heels in love with his wife. "The honeymoon is *not* over," he retorted. "I just didn't get much sleep last night, so I'm tired."

That was the absolute truth. Barney had tossed and turned all night, barely catching a wink because he couldn't stop thinking about Taffeta, sound asleep in her own room and oblivious of the torture he was going through.

Shuffling through a stack of papers, Barney took a deep breath and slowly exhaled.

"Well," Garrett said, "there are worse ways to get tired, man."

Barney gave the junior deputy a warning look. If Taffeta were actually his wife, he would never discuss their love life with a coworker, or with anyone else, for that matter, and he sure as hell didn't plan to now. The fact that they actually had no love life to discuss was a mere technicality. "Careful, Garrett. Don't step over that line."

The other deputy bent his head back over a report and said nothing more. Barney tried to focus on his own tasks, but his mind was filled with visions of Taffeta skimming her teeth across the length of a banana. *I'll live through this,* he assured himself. He just wasn't sure how.

Over the next few days as Barney came to know Taffeta better, he realized that there were so many beautiful facets to her personality that he'd never tire of discovering something new about her that he admired. It wasn't only her looks that wowed him; it was the soul-deep essence of who she was that he found overwhelming. Though his parents bore living testimony to the possibility of love at first sight, Barney had never believed that it would happen that way for him. He wanted to find the right lady—and maybe he had done so in Taffeta—but he was in no hurry to reach that conclusion. People who jumped into relationships usually ended up jumping back out of them just as quickly. He would have to know a woman as well as he knew himself before he ever told her that he loved her.

That said, Barney had to concede that Taffy—he'd fallen into the habit of using her nickname when he addressed her—was an extraordinary person. She loved her little girl so much that there was no sacrifice too great for her to make to ensure the child's happiness and well-being. As for his animals, she'd taken to farm life as if she'd been born with a pitchfork in her hand. Day by day, her timidity around the horses diminished. She had named all of his hens and was waiting until a perfect handle for the rooster came to her. Every day, she lured Mary Lou into the inexpensive head gate that Barney had purchased and attached to side panels to create a squeeze chute. As a reward for cooperating, Mary Lou got cookies. The cow that had once been terrified of the chute and had trampled Barney to avoid it now raced into the enclosure and willingly thrust her head through the V-shaped catch to get her goodies. At first, Taffeta hadn't used the manual squeeze mechanism, but now she did so as part of the practice routine. To Barney's amazement, Mary Lou eagerly thrust her head through the opening, showed no sign of panic when Taffeta dropped the squeeze bar, and happily munched on cookies until released.

"When her baby comes, she may need help," Taffeta mused aloud one evening. "It'll be easier to help her give birth if she'll just walk into the chute and let me catch her head. Right?"

Barney nodded, wondering why he'd never thought of using treats as a way to acclimate Mary Lou to the chute. "That's amazing," he said. "Now let's add a new element for her to get accustomed to."

He had fabricated a hock bar with his welder. He swung it across the rear end of the chute and locked it down. Taffeta watched with a bewildered expression. Mary Lou shifted nervously when she felt the steel against her back legs. "Can you give her a couple more cookies to distract her?" Barney asked. "Whisper sweet nothings in her ear, too. She needs to get used to this."

Taffeta fed the Hereford-Angus mix, cooed to her, and scratched her woolly white topknot. "She doesn't like that bar behind her legs. Is it really necessary?"

"If she has trouble dropping her baby, she may get frantic. The bar will stop her from kicking whoever comes in behind her to pull her calf." Barney wished he could afford a really nice squeeze chute instead of this jury-rigged one, but the important thing was that it worked. "A cow can be dangerous."

"Oh, he's so silly," Taffeta said to the cow. "You'd never kick anybody. Not my sweet Mary Lou."

Barney could have reminded Taffeta that sweet Mary Lou had once cracked two of his ribs, and maybe for safety reasons, he should have. But after watching his wife and the cow interact, he honestly didn't believe Mary Lou would go berserk around Taffeta. The two of them seemed to have forged a very special friendship, and the bovine obviously trusted Taffeta in a way that she had never trusted Barney.

"For a person who never had a pet, you sure have taken to my animals," he commented.

Taffeta circled the chute and unlatched the bar behind Mary Lou's hocks. "Let's not test her patience by keeping this behind her for too long," she said. "I'll do it every day from now on so she gets used to it." She smiled up at Barney. "As for the animals, I'm making up for lost time and learning how to be a farmer. When I get Sarah, I'm going to try my best to get a place similar to this so she can have a horse, raise baby calves, and collect eggs. What a wonderful way for a little girl to grow up!"

Barney had met so many women in Crystal Falls who pretended to like farm animals and horses, but in the end—usually about the time they stepped in a pile of shit—their true colors showed. Taffeta had manure on her running shoes right now, and she didn't seem to notice, let alone feel disgusted. Was she real, this lady? Or was he dreaming?

Chapter Sixteen

The next morning when Barney emerged from his bedroom, fully dressed in his uniform, Taffeta was nowhere to be seen. He checked the living room and the kitchen. Where the hell was she? As he passed the window over the sink, he caught a flash of movement out in the yard. He peered through the glass and saw Taffeta outside, coaxing Mary Lou into the squeeze chute. Hands resting at the edge of the sink, Barney made fists over the cold stainless steel as his wife walked around the narrow pen to fasten down the hock bar. Before getting it secured, she bent down, putting her head right in Mary Lou's line of fire. He nearly had a heart attack.

By the time he got outside, Taffeta was rewarding Mary Lou for her acquiescence with cookies. She saw Barney and beamed a proud smile. "She's getting used to that kick bar! When she has her baby, it'll all go smooth as soft butter."

"Don't *ever* put your head down behind her back legs like that again!" Barney's pulse was still racing. "Do you realize that cow could kill you?" He snapped his fingers. "One kick, just like that, and you'd be laid out."

Taffeta's eyes went round. "I didn't mean to give you a scare," she apologized. "You're right. I wasn't being careful. I won't do it again."

Barney's bones felt like candle wax gone soft in the sun. It hit him then how much he'd come to care for this lady. In the golden light of early morning, she looked too damned beautiful for words, and he knew she was just as sweet inside as she appeared to be on the outside. He wasn't ready to put a name to the way he felt about Taffeta, but he knew he had entered uncharted emotional territory. If something happened to her, he wasn't sure he'd ever get over it.

"When you're working with large animals, sweetheart, never for an instant forget how powerful they are. Mary Lou wouldn't mean to hurt you, but if she gets startled, kicking is instinctive. The same goes for my horses. They're gentle giants and have never tried to kick me, but that doesn't rule out the possibility. One time my brother Ben was leading a mare toward the stable and another horse, tethered to a hitching rail, kicked at the mare, accidentally nailing Ben on the thigh. The force of the blow cracked his femur. He was laid up for two months."

Barney wanted to keep going, telling her every scary story he could think of, but he needed to give her credit for having good sense. He'd made his point. Now he just wanted to find a quiet place to figure out exactly what was going on in his head about Taffeta. Was he falling for her? Or was he just reacting to hormonal spikes from nearly constant arousal?

* * *

Taffeta had once fantasized about Barney Sterling only at night in the solitude of her apartment, but now she found herself dreaming about him frequently throughout the day. When dealing with customers in her store, she sometimes went spacy and missed big chunks of a conversation, which forced her to ask people to repeat themselves. It was embarrassing, and more than once, she felt her cheeks grow hot. But though she tried, she couldn't stop thinking about her husband even when he wasn't around.

Oh, how she wished that he would make love to her. She had tried every seduction maneuver she could think of, and so far nothing had worked. Barney Sterling was a hard nut to crack, and as much as she resented the fact, she was coming to accept that he'd only ever make love to her at a time of his choosing and on his own terms.

Even so, she couldn't help being acutely aware of him when he was close to her. She yearned to run her hands over his sturdy shoulders and arms, to feel the play of his muscles when he moved. When they got home from town at night, everything within her rebelled as she hurriedly threw on unattractive clothing so he wouldn't be tempted to make a move on her. For the first time in her life, she'd met a man who strongly appealed to her on nearly every level, and she couldn't do a single thing to reel him in.

On Monday, three weeks and two days after their chapel wedding, Taffeta got a call from her private investigator in Erickson. Sarah's teacher was a friend of his, and he spoke with her weekly to get the inside scoop on how Sarah seemed to be doing. That morning, the teacher had called him with some concerning information. Sarah had bruises, one on her cheek and another on her arm. When the teacher asked Sarah what happened, the child had looked frightened and said that she fell down. The teacher said the bruises could have been due to a fall, but she thought she should mention it, all the same. Over the weekend, the child had stayed with a woman who danced at a strip club. She associated with some pretty rowdy fellows.

After the call, Taffeta trembled with a blend of anger and fear for her daughter. A stripper who hung out with rowdy men? What on earth was Phillip thinking? Taffeta wanted to drive to Erickson, find Phillip, and pummel him with her fists. Instead she struggled not to cry. What would she say if a customer came in and caught her on the verge of tears?

Just as Taffeta asked herself that, the entry bell jangled. Only it wasn't a customer who'd caught her at a bad moment. Barney stood in the doorway.

The instant Barney saw Taffeta's face, he knew something was wrong, and he suspected that it involved Sarah. He pushed the door closed and strode over to the counter. His wife looked up at him with tears sparkling in her eyes.

"What is it?" he asked.

"Sarah's teacher called my investigator in Erickson. She says Sarah came to school this morning with bruises. Sarah says she fell down, but the teacher fears otherwise. My little girl stayed last night with a woman who dances at a strip club, and she hangs out with some rowdy men. The teacher suspects that Sarah was struck by one of the boyfriends."

Barney could tell that Taffeta was barely managing to hold it together. Without hesitation, he retraced his steps to the entrance, locked the shop door, and flipped over the sign to read CLOSED. Taffeta didn't object, which spoke volumes. She clearly knew she was about to lose it and didn't want to have a meltdown in front of others.

He moved behind the counter and slipped an arm around her waist. "Come upstairs, honey. I'll make you a cup of tea. We'll hash this out. You'll feel better after we talk."

Barney felt her trembling as he guided her up the stairway. His heart ached for her. She loved that child so very much. It had to be unbearable for her to think that some guy had deliberately harmed the little girl. She probably wanted to rip somebody's head off, most likely her ex-husband's first.

Barney had every intention of doing precisely what he'd said he would. Sit her down at the tiny table. Make her some tea. Talk her down. Offer her whatever comfort he possibly could. But the minute Taffeta felt safe from prying eyes inside the flat, she burst into tears.

"My little girl is being mistreated by strangers!" she cried. "She needs me, and I'm not there. She needs help, and there's nothing I can do. *Nothing!*"

Barney drew out a kitchen chair and helped her sit down. Then he crouched beside her and took her into his arms. All his life, his father had taught him never to make promises he might not be able to keep, but he found himself vowing, "You'll soon have your daughter, Taffy. Please, don't cry. If it's the last thing I ever do, I'll make sure of that."

Apparently soothed by his words, Taffeta went limp in his arms. To Barney, it felt as if her body melted against his and was being absorbed through the pores of his skin. *Oh God.* She was such a sweet lady and didn't deserve to go through this shit. He brushed his lips lightly over her hair, pressed them to the pulse point in her temple, and then trailed kisses down her cheek.

She moaned—not with pain, but arousal. Unmistakable arousal. Barney wasn't sure how it happened, but the next thing he knew, he was devouring her mouth. He'd kissed her countless times in public, but he'd always had his guard up, silently telling himself, *This isn't real. Don't get carried away.* Only now they had no audience, and he had no grip on his self-control.

Neither did Taffeta. At the back of his mind, he knew she was running from the pain by trying to drown herself in desire, but his muddled brain couldn't hold on to that thought. She was like an ember coaxed into flame. Her tongue slipped past his lips. The kiss became deeper, hungrier, and wilder. He'd heard of spontaneous combustion between two people, but he'd never experienced it. In that distant part of his mind, he knew he should stop this before it even started, but she wasn't on the same wavelength.

With feverish urgency, she unbuttoned his uniform

shirt. Next, she untucked his T-shirt and thrust her hands under the hem to run her palms up over his belly to his chest. Somewhere between point A and point B, he lost it and plummeted right over the edge with her.

Trailing clothes behind them, they barely made it into the bedroom. He'd wanted her in his arms for so long. To him, it seemed that he'd been holding her at arm's length for a year, not just a few weeks. Now she was pressed full-length against him. He could feel the warmth of her silken skin, hear the jagged rhythm of her breathing, and feel her need almost as much as he could his own.

He fleetingly considered calling a halt, but desire overcame all his noble intentions. He was in, and there was no turning back.

Taffeta had dreamed of being with Barney like this countless times, and he didn't disappoint. When they were both naked, he grasped her shoulders and held her at arm's length to take in her body. She felt no trace of shyness. Instead she returned the favor, drinking in every line of him with her eyes.

He muttered something under his breath, short bursts of words that didn't link together to form a coherent sentence. Locking a hard arm around her, he tumbled onto her bed, taking her down with him. In all her fantasies, he'd been a lover with a slow hand, but he wasn't now. She'd once been on a roller coaster that seemed as tall in places as a skyscraper, and she felt the same way with him, as if her stomach had dropped to the floor and her heart was some-where above her head.

His mouth and hands seemed to be everywhere at once on her body. There was no slow buildup and no asking; he just took. It was a frantic joining, and Taf-feta rode the waves with him, peaking in wild pas-sion, digging in her nails on his back to hold on, lost in sensation as their desire mounted. She was des-perate to have him inside her. Her belly felt as if hot lava swirled low at its base. Her lungs ached for lack of air. Her nipples throbbed and sprang taut when his coarse chest hair abraded them.

He was heat. He was forged steel. She melted against him, glorying in the pleasure of making love to him. When his shaft thrust into her wet passage, she shrieked at the jolt of sensation and locked her legs around his waist as he drove himself deep into her, again and again. She couldn't breathe and didn't care. The need within her magnified. She felt as if her whole body might explode as the urgency mounted.

Then he slammed home one final time, his body locking into a sculpture of hard muscle above her. His facial muscles drew taut. His mouth twisted into a grimace. And then she felt the rush of liquid fire as he ejaculated. She felt each throb of release deep within her, and the pressure inside her suddenly exploded, sending her into the throes of orgasm with him. Dimly, even as she climaxed, she marveled at the feeling. She'd come close a couple of times with Phillip, but he'd always stopped too soon, leaving her hanging on the edge.

Barney collapsed onto her, catching most of his weight with one elbow. He was still inside her, and she didn't want him to leave until his hardness vanished and he slipped out of her.

She clung to him, so breathless she could barely speak. "Don't—go. Stay—with—me."

As their pulse rates slowed, they shifted, holding on to each other, skin against skin, limbs intertwined, too spent to actually move.

"Oh God, Taffy, I'm so sorry," he whispered, his voice ragged. "I didn't mean for that to happen."

Taffeta felt like a little girl whose fondest wish had just been granted by her fairy godmother. She giggled. "I'm very glad it did. I've never experienced anything so wonderful."

"I haven't, either," he said on an outward rush of breath. "If and when it ever happened between us, I meant to go slow. Instead I went after you like a crazy man. If there's a next time, I'll do better."

"If you do better, you'll kill me," she said, and she meant it. What he'd just given her was beyond all of her wildest fantasies about him.

He drew her closer and feathered kisses across her forehead. Oh, how she loved feeling his lips against her skin. Then he suddenly tensed.

"Shit!" He let go of her and jackknifed to a sitting position, naked as the day he'd been born and so gorgeous Taffeta wanted to study him for hours. Only he leaped off the bed in a flurry of motion. "I'm on duty! And, oh, shit, *fuck*! I didn't use a condom."

Taffeta had never heard him use the *F* word, which

conveyed just how upset he was. She grabbed the coverlet. They hadn't bothered with drawing back the bedding. She rolled off the mattress and tugged the chenille around her. "Condom?"

He fixed a sharp gaze on her, his chest still heaving. "Yeah, you know, those things every responsible man uses to keep from getting a woman pregnant or giving her a venereal disease." He snatched up his uniform pants and strode from the bedroom, muttering something about his shirt. "*Dammit*. Not that I've got a venereal disease," he said over his shoulder. "I've always practiced safe sex, until *now*. But I sure as hell have plenty of little swimmers standing ready to do their duty." He homed in on his uniform shirt. Then he found his T-shirt. "I can't believe I did something so irresponsible."

Taffeta clutched the bedspread closer. "Barney, it's going to be okay. I don't think it's my fertile time of month."

"Well, I pray to God not!"

The vehemence of that pronouncement thrust like a sword into her heart. Would it really be so unthinkable to him if he'd gotten her pregnant? As if he realized what he had just said and how it might have sounded, he froze and looked at her. "I didn't mean that. Well, I meant it, but not the way I said it. We're just learning about each other, you know? When I father a child, I want to be in an established, forever relationship. Don't you?"

Taffeta, taken off guard, couldn't think what to say and blurted, "I was a baby nobody wanted. No child of mine will ever be a piece of trash that I throw away."

Barney knotted his hand over the garments he held. "You're right. I didn't mean—well, I'm just upset and shooting off my mouth without thinking, Taffy. And just for the record, I feel the same way. If what just happened results in a baby, I'll step up to the plate, and we'll somehow make it work."

Taffeta already knew that. Before her stood one of the most wonderful men she'd ever known, a relentlessly responsible and serious guy in so many ways. It was almost a compliment that he'd lost control with her and engaged in unprotected sex. She had a feeling that he'd never been careless with any other woman. If that didn't send her a strong signal about how he felt about her, what would?

He sighed. "I'm messing this up nine ways to hell, aren't I? Saying all the wrong things. Hurting your feelings. This should be a special moment. We should have time to talk. Can you just pretend I haven't said anything until we talk tonight?"

"I'm good," she said. "Don't worry about me. You're on duty, and you need to get back to work."

"Of *course* I'm going to worry, Taffy. This happened because I brought you up here to comfort you about Sarah and calm you down. Instead we barely talked about her and fell into bed, and now I'm running out on you."

Oddly his murmured promise that he'd help her get Sarah back had been a huge comfort to Taffeta. Until Sarah was safe, Taffeta would worry and be upset, but she trusted Barney and believed in him. With only a few words, he had eased some of the pain in her heart.

He resumed searching for the rest of his clothes, and Taffeta helped him, feeling oddly shy about letting the bedspread slip. What was that about? His hands or mouth had just been on nearly every part of her body. What did she have left to hide?

Clinging to the bedspread, she raced around, finding a sock here and a boot there. She froze when she came across his gun and Taser belt. Wary of the weapons, she scooted the belt into plain sight and started crawling around on the floor, looking for his other sock.

"I am *so* screwed," he said. "I can't find one sock or my boxers!"

A fleeting image of Barney in boxer shorts shot through her brain. He was the most gorgeous man she'd ever seen.

Taffeta finally found his boxers. Somehow they'd worked their way under one of the pillows. *Along with his honor,* she guessed. "I found them!"

Barney raced in from the tiny living room, still naked and clutching his outer clothes, which he wouldn't put on without the basics. Taffeta held out the garments and took advantage of the opportunity to admire his body as he hopped around on one foot and then the other to dress.

"I'm still missing one sock," he observed as he put on his boots. "But that's fine. No one will notice."

As he strapped on his gun belt, she felt just a tiny

bit sorry for herself. He was leaving her. Raking a hand through his hair, he retrieved his Stetson from the kitchen table, planted it on his head, and strode toward the door. Hand on the knob, he hesitated. Then he swung back around, covered the distance between them, and caught her up in his arms.

Holding her close, he said, "*That* was the best. It really was, Taffy. But I have to go. No more tears. I mean it. Sarah will be okay until we can get custody. Kids live through worse. We're going to bring her home soon. I promise."

We? Taffeta hugged her waist as he drew away. If only that were a Freudian slip of the tongue. She loved Barney Sterling. There was no denying it. Maybe he'd break her heart. But she couldn't control her feelings for him and didn't want to try, especially not now. Making love with him had been the most incredible experience of her life. If she lived to be ninety, alone and unsatisfied, she would at least have the memory of experiencing wild, crazy, mindless sex with a wonderful man just once in her lifetime.

'Tis better to have loved and lost than never to have loved at all. She believed in that. Mrs. Brassfield had taught her that. So while she had the chance, she would love this man with every breath she took, even if it wasn't meant to last.

After leaving Taffeta's apartment, Barney nearly ran a stop sign because his thoughts were on her instead of his job. *Hot damn.* Over the years, Barney had enjoyed sex with some women more than he did with others, but he had never experienced anything close to what he just shared with Taffy. He remembered wondering while they danced at their wedding reception if they would move with the same perfect harmony while making love. Now he had his answer. It was as if their bodies were made for each other. And as he peeled the layers away to learn who she really was, he couldn't help feeling that their hearts came from the same mold as well. How could a guy keep his head on straight when everything between two people seemed so right?

Barney could barely wait for his shift to be over.

When Taffeta finally got herself tidied up, she hurried downstairs to reopen her shop for business. Her first customer entered minutes later, a petite young woman with cropped dark hair, gorgeous blue eyes, and a darling heart-shaped face. Taffeta instantly recognized her. Sissy Sue Bentley from the Cauldron. She looked like a pixie even though she wore a long-sleeve gray T-shirt and jeans. Taffeta adored old movies—one of her favorites was *Breakfast at Tiffany's*—and this young lady could have been Audrey Hepburn's double.

"Hi," she said. "I'm Sissy Sue Bentley. I own the Cauldron on West Main. I've been in lots of times to offer you my lunch specials, but I've never taken time to really introduce myself."

Taffeta and Barney had intended to do dinner at Sissy's restaurant and never had done so. Studying the younger woman, Taffeta tried to imagine having anything in common with her. In appearance, they were complete opposites, but when Taffeta searched

Sissy's eyes, she glimpsed sadness in their blue depths. Sadness and wisdom.

"It's a pleasure to meet you!" Taffeta shook her hand. "My husband and I are planning to have dinner at your place soon."

Sissy grinned. "Well, the menu isn't fancy, but I've finally learned how to grill a decent burger without charring the edges. My aunt Mable left me the place, and my only experience in a café was waiting tables for six months."

Taffeta thought she looked too young to take over a business, but looks could be deceiving, and she sensed in Sissy a quiet strength that had possibly been tempered by hardships. "I love hamburgers. But I'm sure you're not here to discuss that. How can I help you?"

Sissy wrinkled her nose. "I'm on my feet and at a dead run twelve hours a day. My arches are killing me. One of my patrons said you might carry shoe inserts that would help."

"Aha! I think I have just the thing!"

Taffeta was helping Sissy select shoe liners when the bell jangled again. She straightened to look over a top row of merchandise and saw Barney's brother Ben entering the shop. From the knees down, his jeans were dusty, but otherwise he looked freshly showered and sunshine clean.

"Hi, Ben. Barney isn't here, I'm afraid."

Ben grinned, reminding her so much of her husband that it was uncanny. He circled the shelving to stand at the end of the aisle. "Believe it or not, I dropped in to say hi to you, not Barney."

Ben's gaze dropped to the tiny woman crouched behind Taffeta. Taffeta saw his jaw muscle start to tic. He didn't look back up. It was as if his eyes had gotten stuck in their sockets.

Sissy pushed upright, holding a box of inserts. As she straightened, Ben's gaze followed her upward. "I think these will help!" she said. "And they won't demolish my bank account."

Taffeta remembered her manners. "Sissy, this is my brother-in-law Ben Sterling. Ben, this is Sissy Sue Bentley. She's fairly new in town, just like me. Her aunt passed away and left Sissy her café, the Cauldron over on West Main."

Ben said, "I think I have a sudden craving for a burger and fries."

Sissy's cheeks went pink. She flashed a startled look at Taffeta. Ben's grin broadened. Taffeta could almost feel the electricity that snapped in the air. She bit back a smile, wondering if the legend of Mystic Creek might be at work again. Sissy looked like a doe caught in the blinding glow of headlights.

When the pair left at the same time, Taffeta couldn't help smiling. She would have bet her last dollar that Ben would now become one of Sissy's most regular customers. He was a little older than Sissy, who looked to be in her early twenties. Taffeta wasn't sure how old Ben was, but he was Barney's senior and probably in his early thirties. That was a ten-year difference. Although Taffeta supposed age didn't really matter when two people struck sparks off each other. Maybe Ben was just what Sissy needed, someone older and more mature with a lot of experience under his belt. Or maybe Sissy's youthful outlook on life was exactly what Ben needed.

Taffeta needed to focus on her own love life, since she and Barney had just struck enough sparks to ignite an inferno. She glanced at the clock and nearly groaned aloud. She had five more hours to put in before she could call it a day and be with Barney again.

Chapter Seventeen

At the end of his shift, Barney got delayed at work with his report and briefing Erin De Laney, the female deputy who'd come on duty to relieve him. Once he left the building, he ran to his truck, hopped in, keyed the engine to life, and peeled from the parking lot. He exceeded the speed limit on the country roads to get home as fast as he could and only relaxed when he saw Taffeta's Honda parked in front of his house. He'd messed up so badly after having sex with her, saying all the wrong things and acting like a complete jerk, that he wouldn't have been surprised to find that she'd moved back to her shop apartment.

Heck, as far as he knew, she could be inside packing right now to do just that, and he wouldn't blame her.

He leaped from the Dodge and broke into another run. His boots echoed loudly on the wooden veranda as he scaled the steps and gained the welcome mat with two long strides. He pushed open the portal, rushed inside, and yelled, "Taffy?"

"I'm right here, Barney."

He blinked, searched, and saw her standing in the

archway to the dining room. She wore that silky blue slip thing that he'd glimpsed her in the night Paul Kutz filed a complaint against her. She looked so beautiful. Her dark hair lay in a satiny drape over her slender shoulders. Her eyes, large and uncertain, clung to his. His mouth went as dry as sunbaked dirt.

"Sweetheart, you don't have to—I didn't expect you to—holy hell."

Her mouth curved into a tremulous smile. "I closed up early and came home to fix you a special dinner, including a loaf of sourdough made with your new starter."

Barney didn't give a shit about food. She sidled closer, her smile turning impish. "But first, you have to enjoy the appetizer." She made a fist over the front of his uniform shirt and tugged. He followed her like a well-trained puppy to her bedroom. She let go of his shirt and turned to face him again. "At least, I *hope* you'll enjoy the appetizer. I'm the only choice on the menu."

Barney forced himself to speak with a throat that felt closed off and a tongue that felt like rubber. "Don't we need to talk first? I handled everything all wrong this afternoon."

She shook her head. "I want you, Barney. Will you please make love to me?"

Somewhere at the back of his mind, Barney knew an honorable guy would keep his pants zipped. But how could he say no to a request like that?

The first time with Barney had been wild, frenzied, and fast. Taffeta wouldn't have been disappointed if he had treated her to the same experience again, but Barney seemed determined to do things more slowly. He stepped closer to lightly trail his hands down her arms, his fingertips igniting her skin wherever they touched. Then he bent to trail kisses over her shoulder, tracing the narrow strap of her chemise.

"I don't think I've told you how special you are to me," he whispered. "Before we do this again, I think you need to know that I've never felt this way about another woman."

Taffeta noticed that he had carefully avoided saying the *L* word, but she didn't mind. She was coming to realize that Barney had to think everything through before he made a move, and he felt out of control when he did anything impulsive.

She tipped her head to nibble the side of his neck. "I've never felt this way about another man, so we're even."

She helped him unbutton his shirt. It was like unwrapping a fabulous birthday present for the second time, but knowing what was under the layers only increased her pleasure. When he was bare from the waist up, he unbuckled his trouser and holster belts. Then he toed off his boots. She almost giggled when she saw that one of his feet was bare, but he didn't give her a chance. He grabbed the hem of her chemise and swept it off over her head.

"You are so beautiful," he whispered.

"I have stretch marks on my hips, and my boobs sag from nursing Sarah." She thought of her other flaws. "My stomach isn't as flat as it used to be, either. And my right breast is slightly bigger than my left one."

He came to stand in front of her again. "Slightly is right." He cupped her breasts in his palms, making her breath catch. "I think you're perfect, and right at this moment, my opinion is the only one that counts."

He caught her up in his arms and gently lowered her to the bed. His gaze smoldered as he stripped off his pants, his boxers, and the one sock. She heard coins fall from a pocket and jangle on the floor. When he lay next to her, Taffeta rolled toward him, intoxicated by the scent of his cologne and the muskiness of his skin.

"You don't have to go slow," she whispered. "This morning was fabulous."

"This morning *was* fabulous," he said, his voice thick with desire, "but this time I want to explore every inch of you, taste every inch of you, and give you the best sex you've ever had."

"You already did."

"No. I gave you fast and hard. This time my aim is to go slow so you can have multiple orgasms."

Taffeta couldn't argue with a plan like that. For her, just attaining a climax once had been the experience of a lifetime.

His mouth closed over her nipple, and Taffeta forgot everything except the wonderful man who held her in his arms. Making love with him earlier had been like riding waves on a storm-tossed sea, but now he changed the tempo. The currents of desire within her eddied slowly. He suckled her breasts. He nibbled the sensitive skin at the bend of her arms. He even drew her fingertips into his hot, silken mouth. Every touch, every deep kiss, every shift of his body against hers increased her need.

She wanted to give him pleasure as well, but when she tried to run her hands over him, he whispered, "Don't, honey. I'm way too hungry for you. That'll push me over the edge. I want to do this right."

By the time he finished with her, Taffeta had climaxed so many times she'd lost count and was once again so aroused that her whole body throbbed with urgency. He'd left no part of her unattended. When he finally rose over her and thrust into her, she cried out, locking her legs around his hips and lifting her own to meet his thrusts. *Barney.* Darkness veiled her eyes, leaving her able to see only starbursts. She soared higher and higher, clinging to him as if he were her only anchor.

They climaxed together, their rhythm growing faster, the thrusts harder. He drove deep into her, the tempered, pulsating length of him connecting with pleasure points inside her that she hadn't known she possessed. They peaked together and spiraled over the edge into shared oblivion. When he groaned and lowered himself to lie beside her, Taffeta felt as if every bone in her body had dissolved.

Barney held her close in his arms, their legs intertwined, skin slick with sweat. He pressed his face to her hair, tightened his embrace, and murmured, "Where have you been all my life?"

"I was waiting for you," she replied. "And I'd nearly given up on ever finding you."

"You didn't. I found you. And I'm sure glad I did."

Taffeta was slowly coming back down to earth, and

she wanted—no, *needed*—Barney to know that she wasn't in bed with him out of a sense of obligation or gratitude. "I'm falling in love with you, Barney Sterling." In truth, Taffeta knew that she'd already taken the leap, but she sensed that Barney needed time to accept the sudden shift in their relationship. "Last time, you didn't believe me when I told you that I had a crush on you from the first time I saw you—or that I fantasized about being with you. But it's the truth. You can call it a lonely woman's solution to needs that couldn't be fulfilled, but you were the man I imagined dancing with—you and only you."

His embrace tightened. "I have feelings for you," he confessed. "But I'm not ready to put a name on them yet. Maybe I never will be."

"And that's fine. Feelings are very individual. I won't be the first woman to fall in love with a man who can't love her back. I'm an adult. I understand the risks. But no matter what your feelings are toward me, you shouldn't feel guilty about being with me. I *want* to make love with you, and that is my choice to make. Right?"

Barney's heart caught. *Love* was a word that a lot of people said without meaning it. He had never told a woman outside his family that he loved her, and he wasn't going to start with Taffeta. He cared for her. He enjoyed her company. She was a very special person, and he couldn't help wondering if he had finally found his one true love. But it was too soon for him to know that for certain.

He sensed that she was waiting for him to say

something, and he wasn't sure what. He fell back on the truth. "I care about you. As far as romantic relationships go, I care more about you than about any woman I've ever known. But I'm not sure it's love, at least not the real, forever kind."

"It's okay, Barney. Knowing you care for me is enough for now. I'm happy to wait and see where that leads us."

For the next week, Barney and Taffeta continued to be seen together in town, only now the romantic gestures were no longer an act, and when they got home, they hurried either to his room or to hers to tear off each other's clothes and fall into bed. For Barney, the sex was out of this world, the absolute best he'd ever had. Some nights they went for seconds or thirds, unable to get enough of each other. He'd never dated the same woman twice and had laughingly told his brothers that he was a love-'em-and-leave-'em kind of guy. But the truth was that, until meeting Taffeta, he'd never hungered for a woman after he'd been with her once. That first night, Taffeta had referred to herself as his appetizer, and she hadn't called it wrong. She was a delicious morsel that only whetted his appetite for more. Though each time with her left him totally sated and limp with exhaustion, the moment he recovered physically, he wanted her again.

One night in the throes of passion, Barney nearly blurted out that he loved her. He managed to bite back the words in the nick of time. This was a new experience for him. He had never felt compelled to say those words to a woman.

The next day during his lunch break, Barney dropped by his older brother Ben's place to say hello. Ben, a rodeo broker who leased out livestock that he raised and trained for competition, was on the road a lot, following the circuit to make sure his animals were kept safe and treated humanely. If any guy on earth had a heap of experience with women under his belt, it had to be Ben.

When Barney pulled up at Ben's place, he saw his brother exit an outdoor horse stall attached to the indoor riding arena. Ben closed the gate and jogged across the yard toward Barney's truck. Of late, Ben had looked worn-out every time Barney saw him, but today there was a new bounce in his step. Barney swung out of his truck.

"Hey, bro, you been overdosing on vitamins?" he asked with a laugh.

Ben grinned. Like all the Sterling men, he was tall and deceptively slender with a loose-jointed stride, but when he stripped off his shirt, he had a body on him that most weight lifters might envy. "Nah, just having a good day," he replied. "I'm sick-to-death tired of being on the road all the time, and this morning I decided to think about making some changes."

"What kind of changes?" Barney asked as he followed his brother toward the house, a one-story farm home much like his own, which Ben had renovated. "I figured you'd be stuck in the same rut until you retire because the money's so good."

Ben threw open the front door and led Barney to the kitchen. "Can you cheat for once and have a beer while you're on duty?" he asked as he opened the fridge. "I've got some nice brews."

Barney seldom drank anything alcoholic while working. "What the hell? Why not? My whistle needs wetting, and one beer won't hurt."

Straddling a stool at the bar, Barney watched Ben snap off the beer caps. Each of them took a long pull from their sighed in appreciation. "So why the sudden desire to make some changes in your life?" Barney asked.

"I'm tired," Ben admitted. "My horse trailer with living quarters is nice. Hell, with two slide-outs, who can complain? But it's not the same as being at home, not the same as having a wife and kids, not the same as having people besides parents and siblings who give a shit about me. I think I'm about ready to settle down and give Mom another grandchild."

Barney felt as if he'd just been blindsided. "You? I thought your motto was to stay footloose and fancy free."

"Has been," Ben agreed. "And I've enjoyed it. Buckle bunnies totally turn me off, but I've met some nice women with good heads on their shoulders during my travels." He shrugged. "One-night stands get old, though. I'm ready for something permanent."

Barney's radar alerts went off. "You've met someone."

Ben laughed. "Correction. I'm shopping. I have sighted in on an interesting prospect, but even when I try to be friendly with her, I can't get to first base."

"Who?"

Ben took another slug of beer. "Her name is Sissy Sue. God. It sounds like something from *Hee Haw*. Remember when Mom and Dad used to laugh themselves sick over those silly old reruns? But that's her name, Sissy Sue. She's prettier than the sunrise, the sunset, and everything in between."

"Sissy Sue Bentley over at the Cauldron?"

Ben arched his eyebrows. "You know her? Maybe you can give me another introduction. I met her in Taffeta's shop last week. But when I go into her place for dinner at night, she acts like I have head lice."

Barney had come here for some advice from Ben. Wasn't that just the way it went with brothers? When he needed a few words of wisdom whispered in his ear, his brothers upstaged him with problems of their own. "I think Sissy Sue has been through some really hard times, Ben. If you're interested in her, don't rush her and don't lose your patience."

"What kind of hard times?"

Barney sighed. "I can't say for sure. I only know that I'm a damned good judge of people after being in law enforcement, and Sissy Sue sends off signals to me that life hasn't treated her kindly. She reminds me a lot of Taffy. I think that if they ever got to know each other, they'd have a lot in common."

"I'm a little old for her," Ben mused aloud.

"Hello, you're barely dry behind the ears," Barney said with a laugh. "And I have a feeling that Sissy is one of those people who is older than she seems. Life can do that to some of us. Have you ever seen photos of starving children in some undeveloped country and looked deeply into their eyes? They have wisdom way beyond their years."

Ben nodded. "And you think Sissy is like that?"

Barney sighed. "Could be I'm wrong, but yes, that's how she comes across to me. Sometimes I stop at the Cauldron for a quick meal when I'm working. Eating alone, you have nothing better to do than watch people, and I always end up observing Sissy as she deals with customers. She's watchful and a little edgy with men, more relaxed with women."

Ben frowned as he assimilated that bit of information. "I'll bear that in mind." As his expression cleared, he focused on Barney. "What's up with you? You rarely show up here just to chitchat. You must have had a reason for dropping by."

Barney noted that his family members all seemed to think visits from him were rare. He needed to work on that. But for the moment, he just took another slug of beer. "I think I may be falling in love. Only how can a guy know if it's the real deal? Have you ever been in love?"

Ben grinned. "If I'd ever been truly in love, I'd be married. When I find the right lady, I sure as hell won't let her get away." Then his humor faded. "It sounds to me as if you're in one hell of a pickle, Barney. I know your marriage to Taffeta isn't permanent, but you're legally bound to her until she regains custody of her daughter. Have you told her that you've got your eye on another woman?"

Barney couldn't help laughing. "I haven't got my eye on another woman, Ben. I think I'm falling for Taffeta."

Ben blinked, peered into the mouth of his beer bottle as if all the answers to the mysteries of the universe might be found there, and then lifted his gaze. "What's so bad about falling for your wife? I'm sorry. I don't see the problem."

"How can I be *sure* I'm in love with her?" Barney asked. "She's wearing her heart on her sleeve. I don't want to hurt her. I need to be certain of my feelings and not lead her on."

Ben studied Barney as if he were a strange insect he'd never seen. "You remember when you decided to build that bookcase when you were seventeen? You took your own money and went into town to buy the wood. It had to be your own design. You sat out in the garage and stared at the boards for a whole damned week! You drew sketches and then you threw them away. Dad nearly went apeshit crazy, waiting for you to actually *start*. You think everything to death, Barney. You always have."

"Yep, and I still have that bookcase. It's awesome."

"I have to admit it's nice. And thinking about it paid off. When you finally committed to making a saw cut, you knew exactly what you wanted. But just remember one thing, okay? Women aren't boards. They have feelings that run deep. You think it to death for too long, and she may be gone before you finally make up your mind."

"I almost told her that I love her last night. But I want to be absolutely sure before I say those words."

"You ever almost say them to another woman?" Ben asked.

"No."

"Well, then," Ben replied. "I reckon that should tell you something, bro."

"For me, it isn't that simple, Ben. Taffeta is a truly sweet and special lady. I'd never hurt her for anything in the world. If I tell her I love her and then realize later that I don't, I could break her heart."

Ben laughed and shook his head. "Would you just listen to yourself? I've never heard you speak so highly of a woman. You need to stop analyzing it to death and just go with your gut."

Barney left Ben's feeling as if he were standing on the edge of a cliff and about to get pushed off. People didn't fall in love overnight. It took time to know a woman well enough to truly love her. Right? He thought of his parents, who had gotten married shortly after they met and had been happy together for years. Maybe Ben was right and Barney was trying to rationalize an emotion that was inexplicable.

Another week passed, and every night, Taffeta experienced intimacy with Barney that grew increasingly more mind-blowing. During the day, she could think of little else but the coming evening. Would it be as good again, or would he suddenly do the "wham, bam, thank you, ma'am" and leave her yearning for satisfaction? At the end of each shift, Barney continued to drive home, sweep her up into his arms, and make love to her as if he were on a mission to show her what *true* lovemaking should be like.

On the following Wednesday morning as Taffeta was opening her shop, she realized that it had been over a week since Bud Pierce, her private investigator, called her with an update on Sarah. He normally called every Monday without fail. Taffeta had been so focused on Barney that she'd lost track of time. What kind of mother was she?

During a lull in business, she skipped dusting shelves, which was a never-ending task, perched on the stool behind the counter where she sat to make out orders or do the books, and dialed the man's cell phone number. He answered on the fourth ring.

"Hey there, Ms. Brown. Sorry I'm late in calling, but things started popping over here."

"Popping?" Taffeta's heart leaped. "Is my daughter all right?"

The private eye chuckled. "She's absolutely fine. She spent last night with her grandparents. I had just gotten off the phone with Sarah's teacher when you called. According to her, Sarah says her daddy got tired of taking care of her, so she'll be staying with her grandma and grandpa from now on."

Relief washed through Taffeta. "That's wonderful news!"

"Excellent news. And this whole situation is finally starting to make sense to me."

"I'm not following," Taffeta said.

"On the surface, it appeared that Phillip took Sarah because his mother was too sick to care for her and his father was stretched too thin. But that never really added up for me. Phillip isn't exactly Daddy of the Year, and his father is a pretty wealthy man. If his wife got too sick to take care of their granddaughter, why didn't he just hire a sitter? Instead Phillip took the kid."

Taffeta frowned. She wasn't sure where the investigator was going with this, but he definitely had a point. Cameron Gentry could easily have afforded to hire a sitter for Sarah, and he loved the child so much that Taffeta couldn't imagine him hesitating.

"I know Phillip pretty well after tailing him for so long," Pierce continued. "I don't think he likes kids or wants anything to do with them. But suddenly he took the kid. Didn't that ever strike an off-key note with you?"

"It does now," Taffeta admitted. "At the time, I didn't think about *why* Phillip suddenly took Sarah. I was so worried about what might happen to her that I didn't think about much else."

"Well, it always struck me as being strange," the investigator replied. "I don't think Phillip got a sudden dose of paternal instinct, and I sure as hell don't believe that Cameron Gentry willingly dumped his granddaughter on his irresponsible son. I've thought about it and thought about it, and I'll bet you a hundred bucks that Phillip tried to use Sarah as a bargaining chip."

"A bargaining chip?"

"Yep. His father stopped giving him money. I think Phillip tried to put the squeeze on Cameron again, saying he would take the child if his dad didn't give him a nice, fat check. And for once, Cameron stood his ground and called Phillip's bluff for some reason. I'm sure he never dreamed that Phillip would follow through on the threat and take the kid. But that's what happened. Cameron could do nothing about it. Phillip has custody, and grandparents in Oregon have no legal rights."

Taffeta closed her eyes. There was no longer much of anything that she would put past Phillip, not even using his little girl to blackmail his father for money. "Oh God. You may be right, Mr. Pierce. Phillip probably took Sarah, believing that his father would grow frantic and change his mind about giving him more money."

"And I don't doubt for a second that Cameron did change his mind. But when he caved and decided to hand over the cash, Phillip realized that he had his father over a barrel and asked for even more. For reasons we may never know, Cameron couldn't or wouldn't pay him that much."

"So Phillip got stuck with Sarah," Taffeta concluded. "Knowing Phillip, he hit his father up for a couple of million or more. He would have known it would be his last chance to tap into his father's savings." Taffeta could almost picture it. Phillip was a selfish, greedy man. "What Phillip didn't count on was his father saying no. Cameron would do almost anything for Sarah. But maybe Grace's illness has him in a financial pinch. If he's hiring nurses for in-home care, the expenses would add up fast."

The PI chuckled. "So Phillip's power play boomeranged on him, and he got stuck with his kid. Even for a guy who doesn't give a rat's ass, a child is a lot of trouble. Phillip couldn't just leave her alone. He could have been arrested for neglect or child endangerment. When he realized that his dad wasn't going to pay his price, he tired of the power play and took Sarah back to his parents' last night."

"I just pray she's with her grandparents for good.

I plan to appeal my conviction and regain custody, but the wheels at my end aren't turning as quickly as I'd hoped."

"Well, now it won't matter how long it takes," he said. "I know you miss your little girl, but at least she'll be safe and happy with her grandparents. Like I said, I've been tailing Phillip. I was parked across the street last night when he took Sarah back to his folks' place. He dumped all her clothes and toys on the porch, pushed her inside the house, and peeled rubber as he drove away. All indications are that he's finished with fatherhood and all the inconveniences."

After ending the call, Taffeta remained on the stool with her head resting on the heels of her hands. *Safe, my little girl is safe.*

Almost giddy, Taffeta had to resist the urge to jump, clap her hands, and laugh. She wished she could call Barney, but he was working. Whether he was driving the roads today or had desk duty, she knew he would answer if she dialed his cell. But it didn't seem right to bother him. Telling him the wonderful news about Sarah could wait.

Business remained slow, so Taffeta began dusting the shelves and merchandise. Things collected a powdery film in only one day, so attacking one section of the shop at a time helped her stay on top of it. She was in the herbal supplement aisle when the bell over the door jangled. She pushed herself erect and saw Barney walking into her shop.

"Hey, gorgeous," he said with a grin. "I was on East Main, and I couldn't resist stopping for a kiss."

"Barney!" she cried. "I can't believe you're here! I have the most fabulous news!"

He took in her elated smile. "You just won the lottery, and we're billionaires."

Taffeta laughed. "Nope. It's even better than that! Sarah is back with her grandparents permanently! Phillip took her home last night, and Sarah told her teacher this morning that her daddy is tired of taking care of her. From now on, she'll be with her grandma and grandpa."

"Ah, Taffy, that's fabulous." Barney closed the distance between them and grabbed her around the waist to twirl her down the aisle. She dropped her dust rag and threw both arms around his neck. "I know you've been worrying a lot about her," Barney said. He stopped twirling to glance at the clock. "This calls for a celebration! A couple of deputies at the department owe me. I can get someone to cover for me and take the afternoon off. You can close the shop. Let's go somewhere special and whoop it up."

"I'd rather just go home," she murmured. "Being alone with you is celebration enough."

He searched her gaze. She felt a sudden hardness pressing against her. "That sounds wonderful," he agreed, his voice raspy with desire. "I'll stop by Flagg's Market to get some nice wine and cheese."

"I'll run over to the Jake 'n' Bake for a fresh loaf of bread."

He grinned. "Last one home is a monkey's uncle!"

Chapter Eighteen

Taffeta beat Barney home. She suspected that he might have had trouble finding someone to cover for him. But just in case he was on his way, she decided to feed his animals a little early so he'd have no farm chores to worry about when he got there. She wanted his complete and undivided attention for the entire evening.

While walking to the barn, Taffeta got another call from Bud Pierce. She was almost afraid to answer for fear he'd tell her that Phillip had taken Sarah away from his parents again. As it happened, the news was grim, but it was about Grace Gentry, not Sarah.

Sadness pressed heavily on Taffeta's heart as she fed the animals. While throwing hay to the horses, she heard Barney's truck pull into the front parking area. Minutes later he stepped out onto the back porch and watched her with a pensive frown. Not wishing to spoil their evening, she pasted on a smile and waved at him. Apparently she was a lousy actress, because the creases on his brow only deepened.

He strode slowly toward her, the well-oiled swing

of his lean hips making her pulse race even though she'd just gotten bad news.

"What is it?" he asked, joining her in petting the horses.

"You know me too well."

He smiled slightly. "I can read you like an open book. Don't leave me hanging. What happened?"

"My investigator called again. He just got the skinny on what's wrong with Grace. He has a contact who works at the hospital, and in exchange for money, she gives him information." She swallowed hard. "It's bad, Barney. Grace has breast cancer and is undergoing aggressive chemo treatments, which make her sicker than a dog. To make matters worse, she has heart blockages, and they need to do a triple bypass, but they must wait until she's off chemo and regains her strength."

"That'll make it difficult for her to watch Sarah, won't it?"

Taffeta nodded. "Cameron will hire someone to watch Sarah. They also have a full-time housekeeper who has living quarters on the property. I'm not worried about my daughter now. It's the news about Grace that makes me heartsick." She sent him a devastated look. "I know she's my ex-mother-in-law, but during my marriage, she was like my mom—the only mom I ever really had." Tears burned in her eyes. "What if she dies, Barney?"

He gathered her close in a tight hug. "You'll feel very sad, and it will take a long time for that to go away." He tucked in his chin to gaze down at her. "But let's hope that doesn't happen. Did she have her breast removed or only a lumpectomy?"

"A lumpectomy, and they think they got all the cancer. But the chemo is half killing her, which puts stress on her whole body. She's a massive heart attack waiting to happen."

Barney pressed his lips to her forehead. "It's great news that they got all the cancer, Taffy. And I'm sure she has a fabulous team of doctors watching over her, with medications on board to keep her heart stable. It's natural for you to worry, but let's not go shopping for a casket quite yet."

A laugh bubbled up her throat. "How is it that you can always manage to make me feel better?"

He trailed light kisses to her cheek and then to her ear. "I don't know, but go with it. I have plans for you tonight, and we have a lot to celebrate, not only the news about Sarah, but also your appeal."

Drawn into a swirling current of need by his kisses, she blinked and tried to focus. "My appeal?"

He straightened and smiled down at her. "You received some documents today from Bryan Vorch. He somehow lost your cell phone number and called me instead. He said you need to sign them right away and overnight them back to him. He's ready to file. Once it's sent in and on the appellate court dockets, you can go to see Sarah's grandparents. If they will agree to support you in an attempt to get the custody ruling reversed, a judge may look favorably on the fact that you're going back to trial to get your conviction overturned. It's not as if you're doing hard time and desperate to get out of prison. If you just bide your time, your period of parole will end, and the conviction will be behind you. Why would you bother to appeal the decision if you aren't actually innocent?"

The thought of facing another judge frightened Taffeta. She was still on probation. If the judge got ticked off, she could find herself behind bars again. She decided to say nothing to Barney of her fears. As Sarah's mother, she had to do what was right for the child, regardless of the possible consequences. As she moved forward, she didn't want to burden Barney with worry. He might get nervous and try to talk her out of going to Erickson at all.

Though Barney hadn't yet said the words, Taffeta knew that he loved her and would protect her with his life. She could see it in his eyes when he looked at her. She felt it in the way that he touched her. She wasn't sure why he was hesitant to tell her of his feelings. She suspected it was that honorable streak that ran so strongly through him. He couldn't say the words until he knew for certain he meant them.

Taffeta was okay with that. In fact, she admired Barney for it. When Phillip had courted her, he'd told her he loved her at the end of their second date. Older and much wiser now, Taffeta doubted that Phillip had ever loved anyone but himself. He'd only wanted to use her. Barney was so different.

Together, they made what Barney called a relish plate, with different fresh vegetables and dip, slices of cheese and bread, olives, and pickles. Taffeta carried the food out onto the front veranda. Barney brought out two goblets and a bottle of wine.

"I went wild and spent almost fifteen bucks on this vino," he said as he sat down next to her. "We can roll it over our tongues and lie like rugs about all the different flavors we detect."

Taffeta grinned. "Sounds like fun to me." Giving him a sidelong glance as he handed her a glass of ruby liquid, she added, "Remember that tannin and a hint of oak are always safe fibs."

"A sommelier I'm not," he confessed with a laugh.

"Where did you learn about sommeliers?"

"A movie I watched. And then after our dinner at Peck's Red Rooster, I looked it up online. Fascinating stuff. How can people taste a wine and know exactly where it originated, not to mention what year it was made? Blows my mind."

It was now early May. The afternoon felt almost balmy after the long, hard winter. They relaxed on the comfortable Adirondack chairs and chatted. An occasional vehicle passed by out on the road. Taffeta eyed a gnarly old oak that had long ago taken root among the pines. With limbs thick and sturdy, it would be a great tree to support a tire swing. She could almost see Sarah pumping her legs as she sailed back and forth, high into the air.

Barney didn't touch Taffeta. Their chairs sat a foot apart. But she still *felt* close to him, as if the sheer strength of his muscular body transcended space to embrace her in its warmth. When they had finished the bottle of wine and nibbled away nearly half of the relish plate, they both stood and walked languorously into the house. No words between them were necessary. They headed for his room and the king-size bed.

Gazes locked, they stood facing each other as they undressed. She knew their lovemaking would be incredible. Every time they were together, she marveled. It just kept getting better and better between them. Barney knew exactly where and how to touch her. She was learning his body as well. Every intimate encounter they had was magical and beautiful, a physical communion that surpassed anything Taffeta had ever imagined.

Later when they lay sated in each other's arms, Barney asked, "Do I think everything to death?"

The question made her smile against his shoulder. "Yes," she said softly. "And I'm glad you do. I know exactly where I stand with you. You don't play games or say anything you don't mean. It's one of the things I admire most about you."

He sighed, toying absently with a strand of her hair. "Do I frustrate you half to death?"

Taffeta giggled and playfully nipped his neck. "The very last thing I feel is frustration. Being with you, making love with you—well, I'm more content now than I've ever been in my life."

He ran his hand lightly over her arm, making all her nerve endings sing. "I think I'm in love with you," he whispered. "But what if I'm wrong?" He rolled onto his side to cup her face between his hands, his gaze solemn and searching. "We haven't known each other that long. Can people really fall in love so quickly?"

"I can only speak for myself, Barney. I think I fell in love with you the first time I ever saw you."

This time he didn't argue or act as if he didn't believe her. "Did it frighten you?"

Taffeta thought back. "At first, it didn't. I only fantasized about you, and I didn't see how I could get into very much trouble doing that."

"Until I saw you shadow dancing." He trailed a thumb over her cheekbone, touching her as if she were made of fragile glass. "Were you dancing with me that night? In your fantasy, I mean."

Taffeta felt as if she were stripping herself bare, but he'd asked the question, and she couldn't deny him an answer. "Yes. You startled me half out of my wits when you knocked on my door and told me it was you. It's kind of creepy when fantasy and reality collide."

He grinned. "You were so stinkin' cute, wearing that sexy slip and holding a frying pan high. When do you plan to make your fantasy become a reality?"

"What do you mean?"

His grin turned devilish. "When are you going to dance with me, wearing only that slip?"

Taffeta giggled. "For real? I guess anytime."

"Now?" he asked softly. His gaze heated on hers. "I can't imagine anything sexier than letting fantasy and reality collide in my living room."

Barney left her to pull on his boxers and turn on the stereo. Taffeta freshened up and slipped into the chemise. She felt a little silly when she reached the front of the house and started to dance with Barney. He seemed more interested in watching her than he was in moving his feet. This was the first time she'd ever purposely danced dirty for an audience, even if it was only one man.

She needn't have worried. Her performance didn't last long before Barney swept her up into his arms and carried her back to his bed.

The following Wednesday, Barney came home from work, and within minutes Bryan Vorch called on the house phone in order to speak to both of them on the speaker. He said that the Oregon Court of Appeals had reviewed her case, deemed it worthy of a hearing, and was going to schedule a date. Having just put a loaf of sourdough in the oven for its second rise, Taffeta straightened from closing the door and turned to look at her husband.

"When?" she asked Bryan as she moved closer to the phone. "Soon, I hope."

"I'm sorry, Taffeta. It'll be in late June, if we're lucky. But that's really quick, considering, and the date may be changed. You need to focus on the fact that the court will hear your case. Appeals are denied all the time."

After Bryan hung up, Barney looked so solemn that it alarmed her. "Isn't that great news?" She heard a shrill note in her voice. "My appeal wasn't denied. My hearing is going to be scheduled. We're finally moving forward."

Barney nodded. "Yes, we are, possibly a little faster than you're prepared for. It's time for you to contact Sarah's grandparents and request a meeting."

A jolt of fear shot through her. "Now?"

"Now."

Taffeta knew that the timing for that was perfect. Earlier that day, her investigator had called. He'd reported that Sarah was still with her grandparents and Phillip was avoiding his folks' house. He'd also told her that Grace Gentry was just ending a break between chemo treatments and would start the next round on Friday. She would still be feeling halfway good well into next week and possibly longer. The side effects of chemo didn't normally get bad with the first or second infusion.

Even so, she could feel herself trembling with a sudden rush of nerves. "Oh, Barney. I don't know if I have the guts to call them. They probably hate me."

"Or they still love you, as you do them, and they've come to realize that they did you a terrible disservice by believing Phillip's lies." He curled his arms around her. Taffeta always felt stronger—and safer—when she was in his embrace. "I'll be right here with you when you call. We'll give it thirty minutes so the dinner hour is over. If it gets nasty on the phone, I'll make love to you afterward until you're mindless and forget all about it."

Taffeta watched the clock, wishing she could just get it over with. But Barney was right about waiting. In the past, Grace had always insisted that dinner be served at six sharp. It would be impolite to call when they were eating, and Grace was a stickler on good manners.

When at last the clock read seven, Taffeta's palms went wet as she dialed the number.

Cameron answered, "Hello, Gentry residence." In the background, Taffeta could hear her daughter's sweet voice. The sound cut through her like a knife. "Hello?" Cameron repeated.

She collected herself and said, "Hi, Cameron. This is Taffeta."

Her ex-father-in-law said nothing for a second that seemed to last a small eternity. Taffeta half expected him to hang up. She groped wildly for Barney's hand, found it, and clung to his fingers as if they were a lifeline.

"Hello, Taffeta," Cameron finally said. "It's great to hear your voice. You are often in our thoughts."

"You're both often in mine as well." Taffeta swallowed to keep her voice steady. "I, um, was wondering if you and Grace would consider meeting with me for a conversation. I'm willing to visit your home if that will be easier for Grace, or we can meet somewhere on neutral ground."

"What's on your mind, Taffeta?"

That was Cameron, just as she remembered him, always direct and to the point. She needed to be just as candid with him. He was a barracuda in the courtroom and had no patience with people who beat around the bush. "I never harmed Sarah," she said, her voice quivering. "Phillip lied about me on the stand. I've filed for an appeal, and my case has been accepted. I should soon have a hearing date. I hope to get my conviction overturned and get custody of my daughter again."

"I wish you the best of luck with that," Cameron said. "And I'm sure Grace will feel the same way when I tell her. But how does that involve us?"

Taffeta clung tighter to Barney's hand. "I'm very concerned about my little girl. I've heard of Grace's health problems. I am so sorry about that, by the way. I know Grace is far too ill to care for Sarah right now. I also know that Phillip had Sarah for a while, took lousy care of her, and left her with unsavory individuals."

"Sarah is back with us now," Cameron said. "She's perfectly safe. You don't need to worry."

"I know that she's safe for now, Cameron, but will she remain safe? At any moment, Phillip could show up and demand that you hand her over to him. If that occurs, you'll be powerless. The law in Oregon gives you no rights as grandparents. I feel that Sarah would be safer from her father if I were the custodial parent."

Cameron said nothing for a moment. That told Taffeta that the man didn't believe Phillip was above coming back for the child.

"Let me speak with Grace, Taffeta, and call you back," he said.

Taffeta dug her nails into the phone, not wanting the connection to be broken. She could still hear Sarah's voice in the background. But the line went dead.

Lowering the phone from her ear, she buried her face against Barney's chest. His strong arms came around her. "He said he'll talk to Grace and call me back," she said. "Only what if he doesn't?"

"Hey, he heard you out. Your point about Phillip coming back for Sarah is valid. The man isn't stupid. I'm pretty sure he'll keep his word and call you, even if it's only to tell you to get lost."

* * *

All Barney could do was hold Taffeta tightly in his arms while they waited for the call. With every passing second, his heart hurt for her even more. Her love for her daughter was written all over her face. If Sarah's grandparents refused to meet with her, Barney knew it would tear her apart. He could only pray that didn't happen.

When the cell phone finally rang, Taffeta jerked as if someone had touched her with a red-hot brand. She clamped one hand over her mouth for a second and then answered on the third ring.

Barney leaned in close so he could hear Cameron's side of the conversation.

"I've talked with Grace," he said. "We're willing to meet with you. Can you be in Erickson by midmorning tomorrow? Both Grace and I feel that the conversation should take place in our home while Sarah is away at school."

"We can be there," Barney whispered. "Say ten o'clock?"

Taffeta said into the phone, "I can make it there by ten, if that works for you and Grace."

"Ten will be great."

"Will you mind if my husband accompanies me?" Taffeta asked.

"Of course not. Bring him along," Cameron said. "What is the man's name? I didn't know that you had remarried."

"His name is Barney Sterling. He's a county deputy in Mystic Creek."

"Please convey to him that he will be more than welcome."

After a brief farewell, Taffeta broke the connection. "He said yes!" she cried. "Yes, yes, *yes*! They must not hate me after all."

"Of course they don't." Barney couldn't see how anyone could hate Taffeta. She had a heart of pure gold. "This is fabulous, honey."

Taffeta was so preoccupied that she forgot the bread rising in the oven and proofed it for too long. Barney helped her finish fixing dinner and clean the kitchen. Then he took her to bed and made love to her, clearly trying his best to take her mind off everything but him. It worked—for as long as the sex lasted. But when he fell asleep next to her, Taffeta couldn't follow him into slumber.

Not wishing to disturb him with her tossing and turning, she slipped from bed and went to the living room. She stared out the window into the darkness, her mind racing with possibilities that filled her with dread.

She had no idea how long she'd been standing there, mere minutes or hours. But suddenly strong, warm arms came around her waist from behind.

"Oh, Barney!" she cried. "You startled me half out of my wits."

He didn't ask what was troubling her. Instead he said, "Taffy, you can only trust in God. It sounds to me as if Phillip's parents are good people. At least they agreed to talk with you, and they know in advance what the discussion will be about. That's a very positive sign."

Taffeta turned in his embrace to hug his neck. His arms tightened around her.

"No matter what happens," he whispered, "I want you to remember one thing. I love you with all my heart. If you can't regain custody of Sarah, at least you can count on always having me."

Tears streamed down Taffeta's cheeks. *Barney.* Trust him to choose the perfect moment to finally tell her that he loved her.

"And all won't be lost if Sarah's grandparents refuse to support you," he said. "Bryan Vorch feels confident that he can get your conviction overturned. Once that happens, you can fight for custody in court. I can't imagine any judge ruling against you. At that point, it'll be clear to everyone involved that Phillip lied on the stand. In fact, they may press charges against him for perjury."

Taffeta released a taut breath, and for the first time since she had been arrested and forcibly removed from her daughter's bedside at the hospital, she felt confident that she would one day get Sarah back. Maybe not immediately, but once she did, her daughter would be safe at her side. While she waited, she would love Barney Sterling with every fiber of her being.

Chapter Nineteen

Barney normally wore civilian clothes while off duty, but the following morning, he dressed in his uniform. After flashing a sheepish grin at Taffeta when he entered the kitchen, he said, "I want to put my best foot forward." He shrugged. "That isn't to say everyone respects lawmen or believes they are squeaky clean. Cameron Gentry has undoubtedly already done a background check on me, though, and I know he found nothing bad. At seventeen, I wrecked my pickup. I lost control on an icy curve and rolled it. The officer at the scene put it on record that I wasn't speeding, no alcohol or drugs were involved, and he deemed it to be an unavoidable accident. Other than that, I've had no blemishes on my record, not even a speeding ticket."

"I never for a moment thought otherwise," Taffeta assured him.

She'd chosen to wear gray slacks and a matching blazer over a black silk blouse. This was how she'd once dressed during her marriage to Phillip, and she hoped Grace would approve. Styles had surely changed since Taffeta's arrest, but the slacks and blazer sported a classic cut and didn't look too dated.

Taffeta was so nervous during the drive to Erickson that she squirmed on the seat. Barney tried to distract her with a sing-along, but she couldn't get into it, and he finally turned off the stereo.

Memories slapped her in the face at every turn after they entered Erickson. This was her hometown. She'd grown up here, moving from one foster home to another. She'd attended school here, lost her virginity here, and had also made the worst mistake of her life here by believing she was in love with Phillip and marrying him. *Correction*. Maybe she'd been stupid to hook up with Phillip, but she should never think of her marriage to him as a mistake. She'd gotten her daughter, Sarah, because of that union, and she would never think of her little girl as being anything but a precious gift.

Barney used his cell phone navigation app to find the Gentry home. It looked exactly as Taffeta remembered it, a stately residence with *old money* written all over it. The pillared front porch was massive, adorned with only sculptured miniature shrubs in marble pots. As a teenager, she'd been wide-eyed with awe when she first saw it, and she'd been even more incredulous that someone as important and well connected as Phillip had even given her a second look, let alone asked her to marry him. Now Taffeta understood that fancy trimming didn't make the man.

Barney held her hand as they ascended the curved

steps to rap the door knocker. Taffeta smiled when he removed his hat so he wouldn't forget to take it off after stepping inside.

Cameron answered the summons. He'd aged since Taffeta last saw him and grown thicker around the middle. His dark brown eyes seemed faded with time. His gray hair had gone thin. He had always looked bigger than life to her. Now he seemed diminished.

He guided them into the spacious living room, which was well appointed, as always, with rich tapestry curtains draped back over white sheers, a grand piano in one corner, and gorgeous, framed originals adorning the walls. But the other furnishings were now less grand. The antique horsehair settee that Taffeta remembered had been replaced with two well-cushioned, leather sectionals with reclining seats. Apparently, as they aged, Grace and Cameron had decided to forfeit grandeur for comfort.

Grace sat in a separate leather recliner much like Barney's by the fireplace at home. Taffeta was shocked by the older woman's appearance. Grace, who had at one time set the fashion gold standard in her upper-end social circles, now looked skeletal and frighteningly pale. Her hair, once a shimmery salt-and-pepper, had turned almost white. Still cropped short, it had no shape or life and lay over her head like a limp cap.

Before, Taffeta would have greeted Phillip's mother with an affectionate hug. Now she wasn't sure of her reception or how to behave. "Grace," she murmured softly.

Grace smiled sadly and extended a bony hand. "Taffeta. It's so lovely to see you again."

Even Grace's voice sounded fragile. Taffeta grasped her cool fingers and then couldn't resist hugging her. "I'm so sorry about the problems with your health, Grace."

"It's Mom to you," she said firmly. "And it always will be."

Taffeta felt her mouth start to tremble. "Mom," she repeated. "The best one I ever had."

"The only one you ever had," Grace said with a wan smile, "but I'll take it. You are the only daughter I'll ever have."

Behind her, Taffeta heard Cameron already questioning Barney about his job. Did he aspire to become the sheriff of Mystic Creek someday?

Barney replied, "Sheriff Adams is the man for the job right now, and I'd never consider unseating him. He has worked hard to get where he is today. But when he retires, I'll definitely run for the office. I was born in Mystic Creek and grew up there. It's my town, and I care about the people there."

Giving Grace's hand a gentle squeeze, Taffeta went to sit beside her husband. She could tell by her ex-father-in-law's expression that he was impressed by Barney's answer. Cameron appreciated a young man with ambition, but he frowned upon those who had no scruples about climbing over older men to reach a higher rung on the ladder.

The conversation moved forward. Cameron spoke briefly of Phillip. "We're very disappointed in him." He glanced at Grace. "We don't know where we went wrong in raising him, but we definitely made some serious mistakes somewhere along the way."

Taffeta hated knowing that these two wonderful people blamed themselves for how their son had turned out, but she could think of nothing she might say to ease their pain.

"Anyway . . ." Cameron looked straight at Taffeta. "Both Grace and I feel that we owe you an apology. We were wrong to support Phillip during your trial, wrong to believe the things he told us. I'm so sorry for the part I played in that."

"And so am I," Grace inserted, her voice so faint that everyone gave her undivided attention. "He's my son, and I'll always love him. But that doesn't mean I like him."

Cameron took over. "When your son tells you that his wife has viciously abused your granddaughter, you're inclined to believe him. It was inconceivable to us that Phillip would tell such a terrible lie. Please forgive us for being so blind."

"Over time," Grace put in, "it became more and more apparent to us how totally screwed up Phillip is. When I began to suspect that he'd lied about you, I gently questioned Sarah. The child has no recollection of a single time when you were mean to her. I believe she grew terrified of you only because Phillip told her awful things." Grace spread her hands. "And we helped him do that, I'm afraid. Not many kind words were spoken about you in this household for several months, and I'm sure Sarah overheard our diatribes sometimes. Three-year-olds are impressionable."

Taffeta couldn't think what to say and was relieved

when Barney broke in. "Everyone in this room probably has regrets, but it's more important now to focus on the future and Sarah's well-being."

Barney turned to Taffeta. "Sweetheart, I know it's hard for you to talk about it, but I think you should tell Grace and Cameron about Sarah going to school with bruises."

As Taffeta related her conversation with the private investigator, Cameron clenched his teeth and Grace closed her eyes. They both looked devastated.

Cameron said, "Grace and I are very aware that Phillip has been a complete jackass. You must have wondered why we didn't hire someone to care for Sarah in our home to keep her away from him."

Taffeta chose her words carefully. "I suspect that Phillip used Sarah as a bargaining chip to get more money from you."

Cameron nodded. "You guessed right. And I stupidly called his bluff. I knew Phillip wanted no part of being a parent and thought he'd back off when I told him no. Instead he grew furious and left with our granddaughter." Cameron bent his head to stare at the floor between his feet. "I panicked and called him. At that point, I was willing to give him the money. But he upped the ante." His eyes dark with shadows, he met Taffeta's gaze again. "I'm a successful man, and I've invested wisely, but the amount Phillip demanded would have drained all my accounts." He glanced at his wife. "We have great health insurance, but it doesn't cover everything. I couldn't give him what he wanted, not with so many medical bills rolling in, so he kept Sarah."

"Oh, Cameron, I'm so sorry." Taffeta meant that from the bottom of her heart. "How horrible that must have been."

"It was beyond horrible. We could do nothing without taking Phillip to court to get custody, and we were advised against it because of Grace's poor health. Even if we were both in excellent health, we aren't exactly prime candidates at our age to raise a little girl. We have Sarah now only because Phillip is tired of the responsibility. The child cramps his style. He can't always find someone to take care of her."

Grace straightened in her chair. "You aren't the only one who hired an investigator. We did as well, and we were notified a few times when Phillip left Sarah alone in his car at night while he partied in a bar. Cameron called the police twice, hoping to get him arrested for it, but by the time the cops got there, Phillip had already left."

Cameron lifted a shoulder and smiled sourly. "I think our son has a friend at the police department who tips him off. It's the only explanation for how he evaded arrest."

Taffeta winced. *Poor Sarah.* She was too young to be left alone in a car, even in broad daylight. The child must have been terrified.

Cameron gestured limply with his hands. "Grace and I understand and sympathize with your yearning to get your child back. The time that Sarah spent with her father has impacted her in many negative ways." He flapped his wrist again. "Grace has been so ill that she can't help me deal with that, so I've been winging it, and I'm afraid I've done a pathetic job of correcting Sarah's behavior. I'm an old man. I adore that little girl. It about kills me to criticize her. I'm her grandpa. It's supposed to be my job to love her, spoil her, and let her parents take care of the discipline. Unfortunately Phillip dumped her off with unsavory people and was apparently oblivious of the changes in Sarah.

"But all of that is beside the point. It's clear to both Grace and me now that Phillip lied, not only on the stand, but to us countless times. We're willing to support you in any way that we can if you decide to fight for custody. Sadly, that may take a while, possibly more than a year, because you must first get your conviction overturned in appellate court."

Taffeta reached for Barney's hand. "I can't allow my little girl to remain in her present situation for over a year. At any time, Phillip can come back for her."

"Sarah will be staying with us from now on. Phillip knows now that I can't or won't buy him off, and if there's no money in it for him, he's finished playing daddy. When Grace is too sick to take care of Sarah, we have a good friend who will come in to help out."

Taffeta battled tears. She had no idea how long it would be before her case would be heard in appellate court. Until her conviction was overturned, she couldn't hope to get custody unless both Cameron and Grace would vouch for her in front of a judge. She wasn't certain that they were willing to do that.

As if Cameron read Taffeta's mind, he said, "I've checked into your options. Family law is my specialty. Until a judgment in your favor is handed down by the appellate court, you don't have a prayer of getting custody. Even if Grace and I stand firmly behind you, it would be highly unlikely. What judge in his or her right mind would grant custody to a convicted abuser?"

Taffeta vised her fingers on Barney's. A tremor ran through her.

Cameron flashed her a sympathetic look. "I don't mean to sound harsh, Taffeta. I'm only stating the facts as I see them. What Grace and I can do is go before a judge in private chambers and request that you be allowed frequent and unsupervised visitation with your daughter. I know you want more than that, and I know you deserve more than that, but at least, if Grace and I are successful, you'll be able to see Sarah often while you wait for a ruling from the appellate court."

Barney spoke up. "If Taffeta wishes to ask a judge for a reversal of the custody ruling, would you and Grace be willing to vouch for her?"

"We'd be more than willing. But I honestly don't think it'd be worth the effort. The odds are stacked against her." Cameron glanced at his watch. "It's time for me to pick up Sarah from school." He met Taffeta's gaze. "Would you like to stay until we get back so you can see your daughter?"

"I'd love to, but during our last visitation, Sarah grew hysterical. I don't want to upset her like that again. I need to move slowly forward with her, I think."

In a weak, tremulous voice, Grace said, "I've been working with Sarah on that. She may still be hesitant, but she won't be terrified. She's coming around and asks about you often."

Taffeta sent Cameron a questioning look. He smiled and said, "I think you should stay, honey. When she gets here, don't rush her. I think she'll come around faster than you anticipate."

Chapter Twenty

The next forty minutes of waiting for Sarah seemed like the longest of Taffeta's life. Rigid with nerves, she clung to Barney's hand, wondering when she'd come to count on him so much. Grace nodded off in her chair. Taffeta leaned closer to her husband.

"I'm so scared," she whispered. "If she screams and shrinks away from me again, I think I'll die."

He untangled their fingers and slipped his arm around her. "I don't think Grace or Cameron would have said it will be all right unless they believe it will be. Take a deep breath and try to relax."

Taffeta did as he said, but her body remained taut with tension. She jerked when she heard the front door open. A second later, Sarah entered the room. At first glance, Taffeta thought the child looked adorable in a pink top and jeans. Her curly dark hair bounced on her shoulders with every step she took. But then, with mind-numbing shock, Taffeta noticed not only how much older Sarah was, but also that the little girl had a rhinestone stud in her nose and gaudy, dangling earrings in her pierced ears, and wore makeup, her eyelids smeared with dark liner, her cheeks slashed with too much blush, and her lips stained with bright red lipstick.

If not for Barney's firm hold on Taffeta, she might have toppled off the sofa. Pain lanced into her heart. She had anticipated that this first meeting with her daughter would hurt. She had missed out on two years of Sarah's life. There were storybooks that she would never be able to read to Sarah because they were no longer age-appropriate for her. Taffeta had missed out on watching the child learn to draw her first letters, listening to her bedtime prayers, taking her to the zoo and the park, and—well, the sense of loss that Taffeta felt was indescribable. But never in her wildest imaginings had Taffeta expected to see her child wearing garish makeup, earrings, and a nose stud.

She sent Cameron a horrified look. He lifted his hands in that helpless gesture again. Now Taffeta understood what he'd meant when he said that Sarah's exposure to unsavory individuals had impacted her in a negative way.

Sarah ran straight to Grace, who had awakened. The frail older woman opened her arms, and the child gave her grandmother a careful hug. Even so, Grace winced.

"Shit, Grammy. I'm sorry." Sarah drew back. "No matter how hard I try not to hurt you, I always fuck it up."

Again, Taffeta wobbled on the sofa cushion and was grateful for Barney's grasp on her arm. Where had Sarah learned words like that? She was only five. And why, oh, why were Grace and Cameron pretending she hadn't said them?

"You have some very special visitors," Grace said to the child. "Did your grandpa tell you about them?"

"Yes." Sarah turned toward Taffeta, but her gaze halted on Barney. She stared at him for what seemed like an endless moment. Then her face went pale, the only color left because of the heavily applied cosmetics. Beginning to tremble, she cried, "A cop! What's he doing here? Make him go! Now! I don't like cops! They take daddies and mommies away to jail and leave little girls all alone with no food!"

Taffeta felt Barney stiffen. Then he pushed to his feet. Taffeta grabbed hold of his shirtsleeve. "Barney, no." Only even as Taffeta uttered the words, she could see by her daughter's reaction that his leaving might be the only option, at least for now. "I'm sorry. I'm so sorry."

Barney gave her hand a squeeze. "I'll take a drive. Don't shorten your visit on my account. I'll be fine. Call me when you're ready to leave, and I'll pick you up."

Sarah ran to her grandfather and cowered behind his legs as Barney crossed the room toward the archway into the foyer. "I can see myself out," he said over his shoulder. "Cameron, Grace, it was a pleasure to meet both of you."

The sound of the front door closing echoed through the large house, yet Sarah still trembled like an aspen leaf in a brisk breeze. Cameron scooped the child up into his arms and sat on the sofa with her.

"Cops aren't bad people," he gently assured his

granddaughter. "In fact, they're our friends. When we need help, we can call for them, and they always come."

Sarah shook her head. "*No.* They're *mean.* My daddy said. He told me to hide under a blanket on the floorboard if I ever saw a cop. He said the cops would take him away to jail and leave me all alone in the car forever and ever without any food or water."

Taffeta's stomach dropped. *Of course.* Sarah's terror of lawmen suddenly made perfect sense. Phillip had frequently left the child unattended in vehicles. In order to avoid any legal ramifications for endangering his child, he'd told her wild stories to make her so terrified of the police that she would hide from them.

In a faint voice, Grace said, "We'll have plenty of time later to discuss whether policemen are our friends or our enemies, Sarah, but for now, Deputy Sterling is gone, you have nothing to be afraid of, and someone who loves you very much is here to see you."

Sarah finally looked at Taffeta. "Hi," the child said.

"Hi." Taffeta tried to smile. She wanted to leap up and scoop her daughter into her arms. Instead she just drank in the sight of her. *Beautiful, so beautiful.* How long had it been since she touched her little girl? Her fingertips ached to feel her silken curls and satiny skin. And, oh, how she yearned to take her to the bathroom and scrub all that goop off her face. "That's a very pretty outfit."

"Thank you. Grammy says the color pops on me." Sarah shifted on her grandfather's knee. "She wouldn't buy me the outfits I really wanted, though. She said they were sneezy."

"Sleazy," Grace gently corrected. "Getups like those are worn by women with no taste in fashion and are inappropriate for little girls."

Sarah shrugged and cast her grandmother a snide glance. "Whatever, Grammy. You're an old lady and don't know what looks sexy."

"Sarah!" Taffeta wanted to bite her tongue the instant she spoke. Scolding the child now, when Sarah barely remembered Taffeta, if she even remembered her at all, might get the two of them off on the wrong foot. Nevertheless, Cameron and Grace apparently weren't giving the little girl guidance, and Taffeta couldn't let such rudeness go unaddressed. "Your grammy loves you very much, and she deserves to be spoken to with respect."

"You aren't my boss," Sarah popped back.

"No, I'm not," Taffeta agreed. "But I do want to be your good friend, and a good friend always speaks up when somebody is making a mistake. I think you may have hurt Grammy's feelings."

Sarah gazed thoughtfully at Grace. "I'm sorry, Grammy. Did I hurt your feelings?"

Grace nodded. "No lady likes to be told that she's old. And I'm actually not. I'm a pretty young lady trapped in an old woman's body. I'm also very good at choosing clothing that enhances one's appearance."

Taffeta noted that Grace didn't talk down to Sarah or avoid the use of big words. Just as the speech of Phillip's friends had rubbed off on Sarah, so had some of Grace Gentry's sophistication. Sarah didn't talk like any five-year-old that Taffeta had ever met—not that she'd known all that many.

"It's true, Sarah," Taffeta inserted. "When I first met your daddy, I had no idea how to dress properly. Your grandmother took me shopping, and every time I reached for something that wouldn't look good on me, she'd slap my hand."

Sarah giggled. "Nuh-uh." She flashed a questioning glance at Grace. "Did you really slap my mommy's hand?"

Grace smiled. "Maybe a time or two, and only in a joking way. Her taste in clothing was abysmally poor."

Sarah dimpled a cheek at Taffeta. "How come you hang out with cops?"

Taffeta wasn't certain how to answer. She definitely felt it would be unwise to mention that she was married to Barney, at least for right now. She chose to reply, "I don't normally keep company with cops. But that particular law officer is a wonderful person, and he's my very close friend."

Sarah wrinkled her nose. "Well, don't bring the asshole around me again. I don't like him."

Taffeta had to clench her teeth to stop herself from scolding Sarah for using bad language. On the one hand, she understood that children parroted the adults around them and couldn't be blamed for using foul words if they had heard them constantly. But it was still difficult to hear her little girl talk that way.

In that moment, Taffeta wished she had Phillip's dick clenched in a Vise-Grip. *He* was the guilty one. *He* had allowed people with filthy mouths to be around their daughter. What had he been thinking to allow the child to get her nose pierced? As the sole custodial parent, he'd surely had to grant permission in writing for the procedure to be done. Taffeta didn't mind the pierced ears so much. The gaudy silver fans that swung from Sarah's earlobes could be replaced with tasteful gold studs.

A wave of sadness washed over Taffeta. Oh, how she missed Barney. He'd been so instrumental in making this visit today possible; it didn't seem right that he couldn't be here, and without witnessing Sarah's behavior himself, he wouldn't be able to give Taffeta any advice on how to deal with the situation.

It struck Taffeta then that she'd come to count on Barney in ways that she'd never thought she might. He had become far more than merely her lover; he was the best friend she'd ever had.

Cameron quirked an eyebrow and gave Grace a meaningful look. Grace nodded slightly and said, "Sarah, come over here and tell me about your day at school. I think your grandfather would like a private moment with your mother."

Taffeta stood and followed her former father-in-law from the living room and across the foyer to his office. The room, opulently appointed with built-in cherry bookcases that surrounded a desk nearly as large as a tumbling mat, hadn't changed since she saw it last. Cameron sat in a leather chair behind the desk. Taffeta sat across from him.

She had no idea what Cameron wished to talk with her about, but judging by his expression, she knew it would be a serious conversation about Sarah.

He folded his arms on the desk and leaned toward her. "Now you know what we're up against with our granddaughter. She has a filthy mouth. When Phillip dumped her off here, the clothing she had with her—well, it was downright shocking. He allowed his girlfriends to dress her, and she looked like a five-year-old hooker. Her belly button was infected from wearing a navel ring that she didn't clean properly. I had to take her in to a doctor. He removed the ring, told Sarah it would make her sick if she wore it, and tossed it in the trash."

Taffeta sat back in her chair. "I'm shocked, too, Cameron." She paused. "Please don't take this as criticism, but I haven't heard either you or Grace correct Sarah when she speaks or behaves inappropriately."

He sighed and briefly closed his eyes before meeting Taffeta's gaze again. "It's hard for us. Sarah was exposed to things no child should ever see. She saw me giving myself an insulin shot, and she asked if I was shooting up. I was so upset to have her think that I do drugs. You just can't imagine."

Taffeta's stomach lurched. "I didn't know that you're diabetic."

"Recently diagnosed. Grace isn't the only one with health problems. Hers are just worse than mine. But that's beside the point. Sarah flinches if we gesture with our hands. She jumps if we startle her by speaking too loudly." His eyes filled with indescribable sadness. "God forgive me. I want to strangle my son. And I'm not just mouthing off, Taffeta. If I could get my hands around his throat, I don't think I could stop squeezing.

When Sarah left us, she was a sweet, precious little angel. Now she's defiant. She smears makeup on her face even though we've both told her not to. Her friends at school want nothing to do with her now."

Taffeta reached across the desk to lay her hand over one of his. "I know Sarah has been through hell, Cameron, but if you ignore her bad behavior, it will only grow worse. She attends a private Christian school. The mothers of the other little girls don't allow them to wear makeup or use foul language. Most of them are only *five*!"

"What am I supposed to do, spank her? I think she's been pounded on enough."

Taffeta tightened her grip on his fingers. "There are other forms of punishment. Take things away from her. Don't let her watch TV for an evening. Remove her favorite storybooks from her room."

"She has moved way beyond storybooks. Phillip bought her an iPad, and she surfs the Net or plays games to entertain herself."

"*What?* Sarah is too young to be surfing the Net, Cameron. Have you set up parental controls on the device?"

He gave her a hopeless look. "I didn't even know I could. I use computers all the time, but for me, they're a tool, not things I know how to fiddle with." With a shake of his head, he added, "One night I caught her watching male strippers."

"Dear God." Taffeta surged to her feet and paced in half circles around the chair. "I know how to fix the settings on her device. If you'll let me, I'll install parental controls and protect them with a password so Sarah can't figure out how to turn them off."

"She'll throw a fit."

"Let her." Anger turned Taffeta's blood hot. If Cameron ever got his hands on Phillip's throat, she would happily help strangle her ex-husband. "You've got to get her under control. Phillip has done immeasurable damage, and you and Grace are the only adults in Sarah's life who can help her get back on the right track."

"We don't want to be mean and make her hate us. She has been through enough."

Taffeta stopped pacing and met Cameron's gaze dead-on. "I understand that Phillip has put you in an intolerable position. Grandparents are supposed to be able to spoil their grandchildren. It shouldn't be your job to mete out discipline. I would take over if I could, but that isn't possible just yet. You and Grace are my daughter's only hope."

Cameron rested his forehead on the heels of his hands. "Maybe Phillip is such a mess because Grace and I were horrible parents."

Unable to swallow back the sound, Taffeta groaned. "You and Grace were *not* horrible parents. You were loving and attentive and fully engaged with your son. If you guys had a fault, it was being too generous. But that isn't what made Phillip what he is today."

Sighing, Cameron stood and left the room. He returned moments later with Sarah's iPad. Without hesitation, Taffeta set up parental controls on the device. Then she began closing all the site tabs, which told her that her daughter had been visiting pages that no little girl should ever see. The knowledge nearly broke Taffeta's heart.

When Cameron had returned the device to Sarah's room, they went back to the living area. Sarah had squeezed in beside Grace on the recliner. Taffeta lowered herself onto a cushion of the sofa, and Cameron resumed his seat on the other sectional. He said nothing and just settled back to watch.

Sarah was telling her grandmother about her spelling bee that morning. "I didn't do very good. Chantelle won."

Grace glanced at Taffeta. "Chantelle was once Sarah's good friend. The two of them were the best spellers in the class. They're learning only short words, but it's good for them, I think."

"I don't care if I can spell good now," Sarah inserted. "When I grow up, I'm gonna be a stripper like Daddy's friend Caitlin and make lots of bucks." Sarah looked pointedly at Taffeta's chest. "I sure hope I have bigger boobs than you do, or I'll have to get a boob-enticement operation."

"Enhancement," Taffeta corrected, feeling incredulous that her daughter spoke mostly like an adult with only occasional mistakes tossed in. "And I believe the proper term is breast augmentation."

Grace softly said, "You're far too smart a girl to be only a dancer, Sarah. You should go to college and choose a challenging and interesting career."

"Smart ladies use their looks to get rich." Sarah gave Taffeta an inquiring look. "Do you have a job?"

"I run my own business, a shop that sells health supplements."

"That sounds boring."

"Oh, but it isn't. Every day, I help someone, and that makes me feel good."

Sarah wrinkled her nose. "I still remember you. Do you remember me?"

Tears burned Taffeta's eyes. "Of course. How could I ever forget my little girl? I keep your picture beside my bed so I can look at you as I fall asleep each night, and I think of you every single day."

"Why didn't you ever come see me, then?"

"You cried the last time I came," Taffeta explained. "I didn't want to upset you like that again."

Sarah nodded. "I'm not afraid of you anymore. My grammy says that my daddy told me fibs about you."

Looking on, Grace said, "Sarah, I think your mommy would really, *really* like to get a big hug. It has been a very long time since she's seen you."

Being careful not to hurt her grandmother, Sarah climbed off the recliner, stretched her little arms wide, and scurried across the room. For the first time in nearly two years, Taffeta got to hold her daughter close again. The feeling was indescribable. Taffeta pressed her face against the child's hair and breathed in her sweet scent.

"I hope you'll consider staying for lunch," Grace said to Taffeta. "Tessa takes care of all that for me now, so it won't be an imposition. She's serving home-made beef ravioli."

Sarah clapped her hands. "Yummy! That's my *favorite*!"

Taffeta hadn't expected to see her daughter, let alone share a meal with her. For her, it was a dream come true. A few minutes later, Tessa came into the living room to announce that lunch was served. A plump woman with merry blue eyes and short silver-gray hair, she gave Taffeta a warm and welcoming smile.

"It's fabulous to see you again, Taffeta."

Taffeta pushed to her feet and crossed the room to give the housekeeper a hug. "You are a sight for sore eyes." As they broke apart, Taffeta asked, "How have you been? Do you still make the best apple pie this side of the Mississippi?"

Tessa laughed. "I don't know if it's quite that good, but I get no complaints."

Grace excused herself by saying, "I'll have my meal here in my chair, Tessa, if you wouldn't mind the bother."

Tessa flapped her hand. "You're never a bother, and I made you a special stew that should settle nicely on your stomach. I was afraid the ravioli might disagree with you."

Grace smiled. "You're a gem. Thank you so much."

As they adjourned to the dining room, leaving Grace behind, Taffeta noticed for the first time that Cameron seemed to experience pain as he walked. At her concerned look, he waved his hand.

"Diabetes. My circulation in my lower legs and feet isn't what it should be. Hopefully it'll improve now that I'm keeping my blood glucose levels in the normal range."

Over the meal, Cameron focused on eating, which allowed Taffeta to be the center of Sarah's attention. The child chattered almost nonstop, telling Taffeta about her school, her teacher, and the difficulties she was having with her former friends.

"They don't like me as much as they used to," the little girl confessed. "But my grammy is helping me to understand what I've been doing wrong."

Taffeta felt a strong urge to run back to the living room and give Grace a grateful hug. "So, what have you been doing wrong?" Taffeta asked.

"Just not being nice all the time," Sarah replied. "I was unhappy with my daddy. He doesn't like little girls. So I felt cross when I was at school." Flashing a bright grin, she added, "I'm not cross now, though, and I'm trying real hard not to use naughty words at school. Grammy says honey draws more flies than vinegar."

Sarah went on to tell Taffeta about her drawings and took her to the kitchen to show off those that Tessa had displayed on the refrigerator. "Oh my, you're very talented, Sarah." Taffeta tipped her head, trying to figure out what, exactly, she was looking at. "Tell me about this one."

"It's a dog. He lives next door. His name is Mac. He's old and doesn't want to play, but Grandpa says maybe I can have my own dog when I'm a little older."

Taffeta yearned to stop time from passing, but the minutes sped by. She put off leaving by helping Tessa clean up the kitchen. By then it was two in the afternoon. She and Barney needed to hit the road to get back to Mystic Creek. Barney had livestock to feed and water. She dreaded having to go home and fix dinner. It would be a collision with reality, and she wanted to hold on to this dream.

"So, what is the story behind this drawing?" She

pointed to a stick figure with long hair on a piece of paper. "Is it a picture of your grandmother?"

"No!" Sarah giggled. "It's of Caitlin." She stretched up to press a finger to a star shape. "She wears sparkles on her boobs when she dances naked. She danced at her house for me one night. You know what?"

"No, what?" Taffeta asked.

"Caitlin can make her boobs go in circles. She says she gets more money stuffed in her G-string than any other girl because she can do it so good. And she gets even more easy bucks if she sits on men's laps and lets them cop feels."

An icy sensation crept up Taffeta's spine. Would Sarah ever overcome what her father had done to her? When Taffeta got custody—and she was more determined now than ever before to achieve that goal—would she have the wisdom and parenting skills to help her daughter put all this behind her?

"Can you make your boobs go in circles?" Sarah asked.

Taffeta heard Tessa make a disgruntled noise low in her throat. In response to her child, Taffeta replied, "Boob swinging has never been one of my aspirations."

"What's a aspiration?"

"An aspiration is a talent or accomplishment that someone tries to achieve." Taffeta crouched beside Sarah. "I hate to bring this visit to an end, sweet one, but Barney and I have a long drive home, and he needs to get there in time to feed his livestock before dark." Drawing her cell phone from her pocket, she quickly texted her husband to ask him to come pick her up. Then, refocusing on Sarah, she forced herself to smile. "But I promise to come back as soon as I can to see you again."

"Are you shacking up with him?" Sarah asked.

Taffeta decided that the time had come for her to be honest with the child. "No. Barney and I are married, Sarah. He's my husband."

Sarah's eyes grew as round as coat buttons. "You married a *cop*? Why'd you do something so dumb?"

"It wasn't dumb. Barney is the most wonderful man I've ever met. If you'd only get to know him, I think you would like him very much."

Sarah shuddered. "You can have him."

Heavy of heart, Taffeta hugged her daughter and kissed her on the forehead. Then Sarah went with Taffeta while she bade Grace a tearful farewell.

Grace smiled wanly. "You tell that handsome young man of yours that I'm sorry he couldn't stay for the whole visit. I'd love to get to know him better."

In the entry hall, Taffeta embraced her ex-father-in-law, who had been the closest thing to a dad that she'd ever known. "Thank you so much for everything, Cameron." She lowered her voice to a whisper. "Be strong. Okay? A firm hand needn't be a hurtful one."

With tears in his eyes, he nodded and then left the foyer so Taffeta could have a last private moment with Sarah.

"Can you call me sometimes?" Sarah asked.

"If your grammy and grandpa don't mind, I'd love to!"

"They won't mind," Sarah assured her.

"Well, then, I'll call often. You can tell me more

about your drawings and how you're doing with your friends at school."

Leaving was one of the most difficult things Taffeta had ever done. When she stood alone on the front porch to wait for her husband, she finally allowed the tears to come. Silent tears. She wept with a sense of loss that ran so deep it made her bones ache. She'd missed out on so much of Sarah's life, and she could never get those years back.

They were lost to both of them forever.

Chapter Twenty-one

As Taffeta hoisted herself up onto the passenger seat of Barney's truck, he cast her a worried look. "How did it go with Sarah?"

Fastening her seat belt and closing the door with more force than was necessary, Taffeta replied, "It was wonderful in ways and awful in others."

Barney reached over to thumb a tear from her cheek. "You've been crying."

Taffeta nodded. "My heart is breaking. Sarah says words that a little girl shouldn't even know. She wears makeup, Barney! Not just to play dress-up, but all the time, even when she attends school. Her behavior and appearance have turned her into a pariah in the classroom."

"I saw the makeup," he said, his voice pitched low. "One good thing about it is that her face is washable. And her behavior can be modified over time."

He pulled away from the curb, and moments later, they merged with traffic on the highway that led to Mystic Creek. Taffeta tried to control her emotions, but she lost the battle and began to sob. It embarrassed her to lose control like that in front of someone, but she couldn't hold it all in. Her chest felt as if it might explode.

As Barney drove, he listened to her jerky account of the visit. Then he listed all the positive things that Taffeta had accomplished with her daughter. "Sarah warmed right up and seemed very relaxed with you. And it's awesome that she asked you to call her."

Taffeta knew it was a huge step forward, but the mother inside her wanted to scream and pound her fists on the dash. That little girl was her *daughter.* "I have no—idea when—I'll get to—see her again."

"Cameron says he will try to get you the right to have unsupervised visitations. The man went against a court ruling today by allowing you to be with Sarah without a court-assigned caseworker present. Both he and Grace are clearly on your side."

Taffeta clung to Barney's words, but the bottom line was that she still couldn't get custody of Sarah. "I won't be able to have her for visits in Mystic Creek. She's terrified of you."

Barney sighed. "While you were visiting with her, I drove around and had a lot of time to think. Sarah has to come first, Taffy. Your relationship with her has to come first. In order to rebuild a strong relationship, she needs to be with you in your home environment as often as possible. I know that our being married may increase your odds of regaining custody, but that doesn't mean we have to live together."

His words struck such dread into Taffeta's heart that she stopped sobbing. *"What?"*

"I'm moving out. I'll find a rental. Until Sarah

gets over being afraid of cops, it's important for me to stay out of the picture."

"No." Taffeta shook her head. "We're married. We love each other. Over time, Sarah will come to accept that."

"Yes, maybe over time. But you need to see her as often as possible *now*."

"But I'm not even getting unsupervised visitations with her yet. Isn't this plan a little premature?"

"No. We want Sarah to start feeling eager to come see you at your house. If she thinks I'm there, she'll dread it instead. I considered leaving when she visits and just staying with my folks or something. But that would essentially be putting a false face on our relationship and lying to your kid. You need to be able to tell Sarah, in all honesty, that we're not together anymore and won't be until she likes me and wants me around." Taking his eyes off the road for an instant, he stabbed Taffeta in the heart with a solemn and indescribably sad look. "Her father never once put her first, Taffy. Don't you see how important it may be to Sarah to know that you will? That nobody is more important to you than she is?"

Taffeta stared at his profile as he focused on driving again. She'd come to love this man with her whole heart. But did she love him so much that she would rather be with him than make her child happy? *Don't make me choose!* She wanted to scream those words at him. Only she knew it would be pointless. Barney had already made the choice for her.

It was so like him, she thought in silent misery.

Honorable to the core, a man who always tried to do the right thing.

"We don't want her to be afraid to come visit you," he said. "If she knows I still live there, she'll fear that I might show up at any minute even if I leave during the visits. I can't do that to her. She needs one-on-one time with her mother, with no outside interference or stress. You see that, don't you?"

Taffeta nodded, her throat so tight that she couldn't speak.

"It won't be forever. I'll think of a way to at least try to win her over. But until then, her father has poisoned her mind so badly against law officers that she actually trembled when she saw my uniform."

She swallowed hard to regain her voice. "But it's your house, not mine. If anyone is going to leave, it'll be me. I can go back to my flat above the shop."

"No," he argued gently. "Your living in a real home will be important when you go to court to regain custody."

"But it'll go against me if the judge discovers we aren't living together!"

"No," he said again. "You can just explain the situation, namely that Phillip told Sarah horrible stories about policemen so he could abandon her in his car without worrying that she might call out to a cop for help. When the judge learns that you and I have temporarily separated for the sake of the child, it will go in your favor, not against you."

Taffeta realized she was shaking. "What if it takes her years to get over her fear of cops?"

His burnished features drew into grim lines. "Then we'll be apart for a lot longer than we hope. We'll deal with it somehow. You can get a sitter for Sarah sometimes, maybe, and meet me somewhere." He flashed her a forced grin. "It'll be like dating. We never really got to do that. The sex will be mind-blowing."

"That isn't a marriage, Barney."

"No, but we'll sure as hell be putting our best effort into being good parents. The important thing is that Sarah isn't fearful that I might show up when she's with you in Mystic Creek or anywhere else. Judging from what you've said about her behavior and worldview, you're going to have enough issues to overcome without tossing in a stepdad she's terrified of."

Taffeta couldn't argue the point, and it nearly broke her heart.

Once they got home, Barney swept Taffeta up in his arms and carried her to his bedroom. She was so upset that she didn't think she could enjoy lovemaking right then, but Barney proved her wrong. She could feel his love for her in every touch of his hands on her body.

"Maybe," he whispered, "we should start trying to give Sarah a baby brother or sister."

The suggestion told Taffeta what she had instinctively known about Barney almost from the start; once he made a commitment, he was totally committed.

"Maybe so," she whispered. "Only that could be problematic if we aren't living together."

He kissed her so deeply that her head swam. "It

won't be forever. I'll make friends with her some-how. Trust me."

And then she forgot everything but this man who so gently made love to her.

Afterward, Barney threw on sweatpants and a shirt to go feed his animals. When he returned to the house, he stripped back down to his boxers, helped Taffeta into her chemise, and led her by the hand into the kitchen. "I'm starving!" he proclaimed. "Let's make grilled cheese sandwiches and tomato soup. That'll be quick, and I know it's a favorite of yours."

"Is this our last supper?" she asked.

"Don't think of it that way."

He opened a bottle of wine and filled two glasses, which they sipped from as they cooked. Taffeta found it difficult to feel down in the dumps with Barney teasing her, nibbling on her neck, and telling her how much he loved her.

"I have a confession to make," he said as they sat down to eat. "Remember that night when I knocked on your door because your music was too loud?" A gleam entered his eyes. "I asked you to put on a robe so you could open the door and talk to me."

"I remember every detail," she replied.

"Good. Then you recall asking me not to look while you ran to your bedroom for a robe."

Taffeta nodded. "And you said you wouldn't."

His lips quivered at the corners. "I lied."

Taffeta touched her napkin to her lips. "You peeked?"

"I more than peeked," he admitted. "Looking back, I don't know why it took me so long to realize I was in love with you. From that moment on, I couldn't get you off my mind, and I couldn't resist going back to your shop. I had it bad and just wouldn't accept it."

"Do you feel uncomfortable about loving me?"

He shook his head. "I feel as if everything in my life is suddenly right. Before meeting you, I never felt unhappy, but I did know something was missing. I also wanted to find the right lady and settle down, but I was in no hurry. Now, when I think about going back to that, I feel a little panicky. I've gotten a taste of perfection, and I don't think I can ever settle for less again."

"But now you *are* going to settle for less."

"Only for a while, and only for Sarah. If I'm going to be her stepfather, I've got to be the best one I can be. Putting her needs above my own is at the top of my list."

Tears burned in Taffeta's eyes, but she blinked them away, refusing to let them fall. "I have a confession to make as well," she pushed out. "When you were so determined not to make love to me, I did everything I could think of to seduce you."

His expression sharpened. "The bourbon sauce." He didn't phrase it as a question. "You little minx."

Taffeta nodded. "Yes, the sauce. And also the spider night. I didn't really see one, but I'm afraid of them, and it was easy for me to imagine one was on me."

Barney's mouth quirked at the corners. "And then I said I saw it in your bra."

"And I *really* panicked. Just for the record, I never intended to strip naked from the waist up. I just lost it."

He studied her for a moment, his expression revealing nothing. "And the banana?"

Taffeta drew a blank. "What banana?"

Barney nearly grinned again. "Nothing. Forget I mentioned it."

"You're not angry?"

"I don't get angry; I get even. I'm sentencing you to an undetermined amount of time taking ice-cold showers and not having sex."

Taffeta giggled. She couldn't help herself. "You mean my seduction attempts worked?"

"Oh yeah, they worked."

"I thought I totally bombed and gave up on trying."

"You didn't bomb, and you didn't need to try. Just being near you seduces me."

Taffeta searched his gaze. "Are you serious about having a baby with me?"

"Dead serious. We already have a child. Why not have another one when we have the situation with Sarah straightened out? I think it would be good for her to have a little brother or sister, and we don't want the age difference between them to be too great. I grew up in a big family. I'm not saying we should have a whole passel of kids, but a couple more sounds nice."

"I've always wanted to be part of a big family."

"And now you are. You've got mine."

"But making our own large family would be fun."

He chuckled. "Let's start with one more and see where that leads us."

"I hope our first baby is a boy," Taffeta said. "I already know the perfect name for him."

"What?"

"Barnabas Asher."

His eyebrows snapped together in a scowl. "Over my dead body." He leaped up from his chair as if to grab her. "You're going to pay for teasing me about my name."

Taffeta shrieked and jumped up so the table was between them. Then she darted from the kitchen and ran to the living room. Barney caught her near the sofa, fell onto the cushions with her in his arms, and kissed her. Electricity arced between them. She felt the jolt all through her body.

"What about my sentence to cold showers and no sex?" she asked breathlessly.

"That'll have to wait until tomorrow," he replied. "I'll start looking for a rental in the morning. Until I find one, I'll stay at Ben's. He has plenty of room."

He kissed her again, and Taffeta slipped over the edge into a vortex of burning need and pleasure. After making love, they lay exhausted in each other's arms.

"Why are you in such a hurry to get out of here?"

"So you can call Sarah tomorrow and tell her you've kicked me to the curb."

"I don't know what I'll say."

"Just tell her the truth, that she is the most important person in the world to you, and we've agreed that I should leave so she can feel comfortable and unafraid when she comes to visit you."

Taffeta tightened her arms around him, wishing she would never have to let him go.

* * *

The next morning, Taffeta awakened to find herself alone on the couch. She drew an afghan around her and wandered through the house, searching for Barney. Instead of her husband, she found a note from him on the kitchen table.

> *Ben says I can stay in the loft above his garage.*
> *I'm all packed up and ready to go, and I don't*
> *want to wake you. I'll call on the house phone to*
> *get you up before it's time for you to open the*
> *store. I'll come over, morning and night, to care*
> *for my critters, but I won't come in. When Sarah*
> *is here visiting, you may have to tend to them*
> *yourself if you think my presence on the*
> *property will send her into a tailspin. I love you,*
> *Taffy girl. Thank God for cell phones. Sext me*
> *whenever you can.*

Taffeta smiled through a rush of tears. She went to find her cell phone and typed, *I'm naked in the kitchen and dancing with my fantasy man.* She hit SEND. Within seconds, he texted back. *Your fantasy man better be me, or I'll kill him.* She grinned and typed *You are my one and only fantasy man, and I already miss you so badly that it hurts.*

After getting ready for work, Taffeta called Cameron Gentry to explain that she and Barney were temporarily separating for Sarah's sake. "Barney thinks it is very important for Sarah to feel comfortable and unafraid if and when she comes here to see me. I was wondering if you'd mind my calling Sarah tonight so I can tell her that he's gone."

"Not at all, and that husband of yours must be one fine man if he's willing to make sacrifices like that for a child who isn't even his."

Cameron had no idea just how wonderful Barney was. "Yes, he is a fine man," she agreed. "It wasn't my idea for him to do this. It was his, and he insisted upon it."

Minutes later as Taffeta drove to the shop, her thoughts remained centered on Barney. He loved his farmhouse, and he'd put so much of himself into every nook and cranny, working to restore it even on vacations. Now he'd be living in a barn loft. It didn't seem right that he'd been the one to move out. But Taffeta couldn't afford to rent a house on her meager income from the store, so she had no alternative plan.

She knew it was silly that she missed him so badly already. They'd made passionate love last night, but she felt as if she hadn't been with him for a month. An ache had taken up residence in her chest. How could she survive without him? With both of them working, they'd been apart far longer than this many times, but somehow not being with him now seemed different—so *final*.

Please, God, reach down and heal Sarah's battered little heart so Barney and I can be together again. Don't let this separation become final because my daughter won't accept him. Please work a little miracle.

Barney was cruising the roads of Mystic Creek when his personal cell phone rang. Glancing at the screen, he noted the number of the caller, which he didn't recognize. Sighing, he pulled the county pickup over onto the shoulder of the byway, shifted into park, and answered.

"This is Barney."

"Hello, Barney. It's Cameron Gentry."

Barney was surprised to hear from the man and wondered how he'd gotten his cell number. "Hi, Cameron. What's up?"

Gentry chuckled. "Taffeta called me this morning. She tells me that you've moved out of the house so Sarah won't dread going to see her mother."

"That's right. You saw how Sarah reacted. Seeing a man in uniform scared the bejesus out of her. She'll never want to visit her mother in Mystic Creek if she thinks a big, mean cop will be in the house."

"You're undoubtedly right," Cameron agreed, "and that's why I'm calling. I have a plan. Well, sort of a plan. A way for you to get to know Sarah on neutral ground."

Barney's interest was piqued. "Oh yeah? I'm all ears."

"On Tuesdays at her school, they have parent day. The mothers and fathers bring sack lunches and eat with their kids. During the winter, the meal is shared in the cafeteria. At this time of year, everyone eats at picnic tables on a big lawn behind the building." Cameron cleared his throat. "Anyway, Grace and I used to go together every Tuesday to have lunch with Sarah. Because of my wife's illness, I've been going either alone or not at all, depending on how Grace is doing.

"Bottom line, Sarah needs to spend some time

with you, and I'm thinking that would be the perfect place for that to happen, short visits with her in a place she feels safe. Teachers are there. Other parents are there. And, of course, I would be there if you can get time off from work to come. I know it's a long drive, and I'll understand if—"

"It's not that long a drive," Barney cut in. "And I think it's a great idea. What time do these shindigs take place?"

"Noon, and please don't show up wearing a uniform."

Barney laughed. "I normally don't when I'm off duty. I wore it to your home, hoping my badge would impress you."

It was Cameron's turn to chuckle. "Well, you were right. It did. Actually the background check I ran on you was what impressed me, but the uniform didn't hurt."

Staring at the dash, Barney frowned. "Is it necessary for Taffeta to know about these visits?"

"She doesn't have to know, but why would you want to keep them secret?"

"Because I may strike out with the kid. I don't want to get Taffy's hopes up and then disappoint her."

"Ah. I see your point. But I'm really hopeful about this, Barney. I called the school principal to get permission to bring you to the school and explained the situation with Sarah. The first thing the woman asked me was if you would be interested in coming early one morning to talk to the kids in the auditorium about your work. I think it would be good for Sarah to see that even her principal and teachers admire and respect lawmen. You'd be the hero of the day, and Sarah would have some bragging rights because you're her stepfather. It may be a great thing, all around."

"My job in Mystic Creek isn't all that exciting, nothing like the cops on TV who risk their lives at every turn. Every once in a while, I have to break up a bar fight or kick in a front door to stop some jerk from beating his wife, but mostly I just drive the roads. If a little old lady grows frightened, I walk through her house and then all around it to settle her nerves. And I do a lot of tree climbing."

"Tree climbing?"

"Yep. I rescue cats."

Cameron chortled with mirth. "It's a grade school, Barney. The kids will love hearing about cat rescue missions. If you could bring photographs that they can project onto a screen, it'll even give the kids visuals. That will entertain them and may even appeal to Sarah. She's begging for a kitten right now, and I can't give her one because Grace is allergic. When Grace gets well—if she gets well—she says she'll take allergy medications so Sarah can have a kitten, but right now her doctors want no additional stress on her body."

"Understandable. Taffeta told me that Sarah yearns to have a dog, not a cat."

"Yes, that's true. I told her she's not old enough yet to housebreak a dog and that we're too old to do it for her. A kitten will go in a litter box, no training necessary."

Barney made a mental note to get Sarah a puppy

and a kitten. Hell, he'd resort to bribery. A man had
to do what a man had to do.

Taffeta was absurdly nervous when she called her
daughter that night. Sarah's voice sounded so sweet
over the phone. Taffeta let the child talk about what
mattered to her for a while, the main topic of her
choice being the disappearance of all the cosmetics
that Caitlin, the stripper, had purchased for her.

"I think Grandpa stole my makeup and threw it
away," she said with an edge of anger in her voice.
"He and Grammy don't like for me to wear it."

Taffeta wished she could commiserate with Sarah,
but Cameron and Grace needed her support when
they made parenting decisions that displeased their
granddaughter. "I am glad it's gone. I don't like for
you to wear it, either."

"Why? You wear it."

"I'm an adult, and you are not. Five-year-old girls
don't need to wear cosmetics. They're beautiful without them. *You* are beautiful without them. Have you
considered that your wearing makeup may be one of
the reasons your friends don't like you very much
anymore? It makes you look different from them."
In truth, Sarah looked like a miniature clown. She
wore far too much blusher, she couldn't stay inside
the lines while applying lipstick, and she smeared
her mascara. Taffeta was delighted to hear that
Cameron had thrown the cosmetics away. "I can't
wait to see you without makeup. I'll bet you're a real
knockout."

"I've got no sippazz without it."

Taffeta smiled. "Do you mean pizzazz?"

"Yes, pizzazz. Caitlin says us girls gotta go for the glitz so the guys will like us."

Oh, how Taffeta was coming to dislike Caitlin. She settled for saying, "Well, I think you have plenty of pizzazz just the way you are."

Sarah went on to complain about her iPad being broken. She couldn't use it to visit Internet sites that she liked anymore. "I think Grandpa did something to it."

Taffeta couldn't let Cameron take the heat for that. "Actually I set up some parental controls on your iPad when I visited your house."

"Why the hell did you do *that*?"

"Because I'm your parent, and children your age shouldn't be allowed to visit inappropriate sites. There are some evil people on the Net, Sarah, and it's my job to protect you from them."

"You're not *really* my mommy now. I don't live with you."

It broke Taffeta's heart to hear her daughter say that. "I'm still your real mommy anyway, Sarah, and I hope to have you come live with me very soon."

"I ain't gonna live with no cop. That ain't the way I roll, cupcake."

Taffeta assumed that Caitlin had taught Sarah that expression. She knew for certain that Grace and Cameron never used the word *ain't*.

"That's actually the reason I called, Sarah. Barney has moved out of the house, so when you come to visit me soon, he won't be here."

"Are you getting a deport?"

Taffeta smiled sadly. "No, we aren't getting a divorce. We just aren't going to live together until you feel comfortable with having Barney in your life."

"Well, I'm not ever gonna want him in my life. Cops are assholes."

"If you never want Barney in your life, then he won't be. You are my little girl, and you are the most important person in the world to me. With me, you'll always come first."

Those words were the most difficult that Taffeta had ever uttered. She could almost hear the door slamming closed on her relationship with Barney.

Chapter Twenty-two

After ending her conversation with Sarah, Taffeta wandered through the empty house, feeling as if something vital and necessary inside her had withered away to nothing. *Barney.* She had just tossed him out of her life, and now she saw him everywhere she looked, standing in front of the stove, dancing with her in the living room, eating with her at the table, and making love to her in the king-size bed. How could something so perfect between two people possibly end? She missed him so much that every part of her body ached.

She drew her cell phone from her pocket to text him. *Do I really love Sarah more than anyone else in the world? There are different kinds of love, Barney. Mine for you has nothing to do with my love for Sarah, and the two kinds of love are totally different. I can't do this! I need you here to hold me tonight.*

In moments, he wrote back. *Be strong, sweetheart. I know how much you love me. I love you just as much. But sometimes a man and woman have to do what's best for their kid. Sarah needs time to accept me before I thrust myself into her life.*

On one level, Taffeta knew Barney was right, but there was a huge corner of her heart that belonged to only Barney, and without him she felt hollowed out and fragile, like one of those decorative eggs, shell left intact but drained empty on the inside.

She forced herself to eat, choosing her old standby, a grilled cheese sandwich and tomato soup. As she sat down to her meal, she recalled telling Barney over exactly the same fare that it might be their last supper. The thought made tears rush to her eyes, and she felt as if a giant, steel claw were crushing her heart.

She stumbled to bed, curled into a ball, and held his pillow close with her nose pressed against the linen. Faint traces of his scent lingered to tantalize her senses and deepen her pain. Barney. How could she live without him?

Saturday morning, the overcast skies reflected Taffeta's glum and hopeless mood as she opened her shop and prepared for the business day. As she set up her till, she thought of Barney. When she went upstairs to the flat to make a cup of coffee, she recalled all the good times that they had shared over more delicious brews from the Jake 'n' Bake.

Somehow she made it through the day, but her feet felt leaden and there seemed to be not a second that she wasn't thinking of him. He was, beyond a doubt, the one and only love of her life. What if Sarah never accepted him? What if Taffeta and Barney could never live together again as man and wife? Taffeta couldn't settle for occasional dates with him for sex in a loft or a cheap motel room. That wasn't a marriage. Husbands and wives were supposed to fall asleep in each other's arms every night. They were supposed to face the trials of life holding hands and supporting each other.

At day's end, Taffeta closed up her store and went out back to start her car and drive home. Only it wasn't *her* home. Barney had resurrected the old farmhouse from ruins and brought it back to life. Instead of going directly inside, she sat on one of the two Adirondack chairs, gazed at the tree where she'd once envisioned Sarah playing on a tire swing, and burst into tears.

She cried until she was exhausted. Her puffy face ached. She could no longer breathe through her nose. But the pain within her hadn't eased a bit. He was gone, not because he didn't love her, but because he loved her so much. Somehow she had to live without him, at least for now, and possibly for months or years.

She wasn't sure she could do that. Everything within her rebelled. Surely there had to be another way for them to get Sarah past her fear of cops.

Whether Sarah understood it or not, Barney would be the best father in the world to her. He would love her and support her. He'd play with her and laugh with her. When she misbehaved, he would intervene with a firm but gentle hand.

The three of them were a family. It was important

for Sarah to have a real family, with at least one sibling. If anyone on earth understood how important being part of a family was, it was Taffeta, who'd grown up without one. She wanted her daughter to have everything that she had yearned for as a kid.

Not only a mother, but also a father.

Barney's personal cell phone hummed a tune, notifying him that he had an incoming message. He'd taken the night shift and had desk duty, so he was able to draw the phone from his pocket and thumb the screen to read: *I've cried until I have no more tears to shed. I miss you so much that all I do is wander from room to room, remembering the good times between us. Is this separation really the only solution, Barney? I love you so much. It just doesn't seem right not to be with you.*

Barney sighed. Reading Taffeta's words tore at his heart because loving her as he did meant that he never wanted her to cry unless they were happy tears. He shared all her emotions, sometimes feeling as if he could endure losing his right arm more easily than losing her. He lay awake at night, yearning to have her tucked snugly against him. His body ached with unsatisfied need of her. And hell, maybe separating for a while *wasn't* the only alternative, but for now it was all he could think of.

He had hope, though. By attending Sarah's parent-day lunches, maybe he could make headway with the little girl. He'd chosen not to tell Taffeta about Cameron's plan so he wouldn't get her hopes up and then dash them. Knowing he would see Sarah on Tuesday, only three days away, was helping to keep his spirits up. Taffeta didn't have anything to lift hers and give her hope.

Barney considered telling her about the lunch visits. At least that would give Taffeta something to hold on to that might sustain her as they went through this difficult time. But no. Barney didn't kid himself. Sarah might be a difficult nut to crack, and his giving Taffeta false hope would be cruel.

He wrote back to her. *I'm feeling lost without you, too. I love you so very much. I lie awake at night, missing you, wanting you, needing to hold you. But this isn't about us, Taffy. Sarah comes first. I can't make choices that are better for me, knowing that she may suffer because I've been selfish.*

Within seconds, she texted back. *Then just come see me, not to stay all night, but just so we can be with each other for a while. Please?*

Barney was on duty and couldn't leave the department. He replied, *Then we'll be lying to the kid. Do we want her to grow up thinking it's okay to do one thing and tell us that she's doing something else? Parents teach by example. It's our job to teach Sarah to always be completely honest.*

Barney received no response. His gut clenched. He could almost see Taffeta curled up into a miserable ball on his bed, sobbing her heart out. She wasn't a woman who easily cried. He had always admired that she wasn't the whiny type who could turn on the tear spigot whenever life gave her a hard knock. Knowing that she'd cried tonight made his heart hurt for her. It also made him feel guilty as hell for not being there to comfort her.

Taffeta lay on Barney's bed, facing the nightstand where she had placed the dated photograph of Sarah. Barney was right, she decided. She wanted her daughter to mature into a straight-shooting and honest young woman, and no one could ingrain those qualities into her character but her parents. Or in this case, her mother. If Sarah clung to her terror of cops, Barney might never be a father figure in the child's life.

Taffeta squeezed her eyes closed, determined not to cry anymore. Blubbering about every little thing wasn't her way. Growing up in countless foster homes, she'd learned that tears accomplished nothing. In order to survive, she'd had to be strong. In order to make something of herself, she'd had to be driven. Going to college and carrying a full load of credits while she worked long shifts at night hadn't been easy. She'd made do with very little sleep so she could spend hours studying. Money had been tight. She'd wanted lots of things she hadn't been able to afford. But she had persevered.

She would be just as strong now, she promised herself. All crying did was give her a headache the next day. If Barney couldn't be a part of her and Sarah's life, she would have to accept that and move forward. Not so long ago, her only dream had been to have custody of Sarah again. No man had factored into her plans, and she hadn't felt the lack.

Now, though, she'd fallen in love with Barney, and he wasn't just any man. He was her one and only.

Her phone jingled. She lifted it from the nightstand and, bleary-eyed from weeping, tried to read Barney's message. It took her a moment to make out the words.

Law enforcement isn't my only career choice, Taffy. If Sarah doesn't come around, I'll quit this damned job in a heartbeat. I can find something else to do. Hell, maybe I'll even make more money. Wearing a badge isn't the be-all of my existence. You are. Please don't cry and feel sad. I'll fix this. One way or another, we'll be a family. You've got my word on it.

Taffeta closed her eyes and clutched the phone to her chest. *Barney.* He loved being in law enforcement. She'd never actually asked him if he liked his job. It hadn't been necessary. He had been born to be a cop. Knowing that he would give up his career in order to be with her was both exhilarating and devastating. It thrilled her to know that he loved her so much that he would alter his whole life for her. It tore her apart to imagine him making that kind of sacrifice.

She fell asleep with the phone still pressed over her heart. It was all she had of Barney to hang on to.

Barney eagerly awaited the following Tuesday. Since his marriage to Taffeta, he'd been using his seniority at the department to avoid taking night shifts so he could spend his evenings with his wife. But now that he couldn't be with her, he'd covered two night shifts already to build up some comp time to get Tuesdays off.

On Tuesday morning, he left Mystic Creek at eight sharp. He wore jeans, a long-sleeved civilian shirt, riding boots, and a ball cap. At a private school, some of the fathers might show up wearing suits, but Barney wasn't a suit man except at funerals and weddings, and even then he wore western-cut apparel. During the drive, he must have rubbed his jaw a dozen times to make sure he'd gotten a good shave. He kept tossing aside his hat to finger-comb his hair. *Damn.* He'd dated some really hot babes and never felt this worried about how he looked. It was just so important that his appearance would appeal to Sarah and not frighten her.

Cameron Gentry was standing in front of the school waiting for Barney when he showed up. Barney parked his truck and loped through the lot, hit the sidewalk, and didn't slow down until he reached Cameron's side.

"Am I late?" Barney asked.

"No," the older man assured him. "I just showed up early in case you did."

Barney noted that Cameron wore lightweight khaki slacks and a short-sleeved plaid shirt. That made Barney feel better. His own attire was a notch down on the dressy scale, but he wasn't so far off target with his selection of attire that people would stare.

Cameron gave Barney an understanding smile. "You look fine, Barney. Stop worrying."

"Am I that obvious?"

The older man laughed and clapped a hand over Barney's shoulder. "Come on. Let's get this lunch started." He lifted a metal lunch pail with colorful butterflies all over it. "Tessa fixed us peanut butter and jelly sandwiches, sliced apples, and juice packets. Sarah is a PB and J girl."

The interior of the school looked different from what Barney was accustomed to, with no student lockers lining the hallway.

As if reading Barney's mind, Cameron said, "This place is leased and wasn't built to be a school. Each class has a cloakroom where the kids stow their outerwear and backpacks. The price is right for the church that runs the school, and the kids get a quality education from grades K through six. Then they graduate to a combination middle school and high school building a few blocks away."

Cameron led Barney to a set of double doors at the end of the corridor that opened onto a fenced playground bordered by a spacious parklike area peppered with picnic tables and shade trees. No other adults had arrived yet, so the two men had the place to themselves. They sat near a large maple already leafy with spring growth. In Mystic Creek, the trees were only now just starting to bud.

Cameron set aside the lunch box. "Just so you know, Grace and I have been trying to prepare Sarah for this visit. Grace got her first treatment Friday in this round of chemo, but she isn't feeling too bad yet. She helped me select online videos of policemen doing good deeds, and we sat with Sarah to watch them on my laptop last night."

"And?"

Cameron shrugged. "Sarah still detests cops. I tried to find snippets of footage with cops rescuing animals, but I came up empty. I undoubtedly used poor search terms. I'm a whiz on a computer when I'm working with our office software, but I'm not good at much else."

Barney heard chattering as children burst from the building. He glanced toward the doors and saw kids swarming out of them like ants from a nest. Adults followed, calling to their kids and pointing to tables. Some of the fathers wore suits, but others wore jeans and work boots, or casual clothing, which made Barney feel less conspicuous.

Sarah, with her glossy dark hair and enormous brown cycs, was easy to spot, not because Barney saw no other darling little girls, but because Sarah froze in her tracks when she noticed him. Stiff-legged, with her tiny fists knotted at her sides, she moved into a slow walk toward Barney and Cameron.

"Hi, sweetheart," Cameron called. "I brought a friend to have lunch with us."

Sarah came just close enough to their table for her voice to be heard. To her grandfather, she said, "You tried to trick me!" And to Barney, she said, "My mommy lied to me. She told me you were gone and I'm the most important person in the world to her. I *hate* her now." She jabbed a tiny finger at Barney. "You tell her don't ever call me again! She lies, just like my daddy!"

Sarah spun away and ran back into the building. Barney felt as if he'd just gone several rounds in the ring with Mike Tyson. His diaphragm felt as if it had been punched by an iron fist. His jaw ached from clenching his teeth. His eyes burned with what he feared might be tears.

"Well, hell," Cameron murmured. "That went well."

Barney struggled to collect his composure. He never should have come here. Not only had he cemented in Sarah's mind that he was a sneaky bastard, but he'd also turned the child against her mother again. Would Taffeta ever forgive him?

When he finally found his voice, he said, "My wife is going to hate me for this. It was a crazy idea, and I shouldn't have come here."

"Nonsense." Cameron opened the lunch pail, placing a bagged sandwich and apple slices in front of Barney before serving himself. "I've already talked with Sarah's teacher. Trust me when I say she is no fan of Phillip's, and your willingness to make yourself scarce for a while to mollify Sarah totally impresses her. She told me that, if this visit didn't go well, she is going to launch a policeman awareness week, starting this afternoon. She would like you to culminate her campaign by coming an hour before lunch next Tuesday to give a lecture in the auditorium to all the children about your job as a deputy sheriff. She believes that her efforts, combined with yours, may bring Sarah around."

"And if it doesn't?" Barney asked, his voice gruff with emotion.

Cameron toyed with his still-packaged apple slices. "Then we'll try plan B."

"Which is?"

The older man shrugged. "Damned if I know, but we'll think of something."

Barney felt like a robot as he drove back to Mystic Creek. He kept hearing Sarah's voice, commanding him to tell her mother never to call her again. *What have I done?* The question circled endlessly in his mind. Sarah had accepted her mommy back, and things had been going great between them until Barney had interfered and screwed everything up.

He felt so sick at heart that he finally pulled over into a rest area, parked away from the restrooms where travelers flocked back and forth, folded his arms over the steering wheel, and battled tears. His father had taught him at a young age that it was perfectly fine for a man to cry, and Barney believed it to be true. Real men could shed tears and still be masculine. But for some reason, his losing control now over the lunch-hour debacle in Erickson, which had been his fault, seemed more like a self-pity party than a real reason for grief. What he needed to do was get out of the truck and give himself a good ass kicking.

Taffy. She loved her little girl with every ounce of her being, and now Sarah might never trust her again.

Barney groaned and relaxed on the seat, letting his head loll on the padded rest as he stared through a blur at the cab ceiling. There was no way around it. Sarah had been taught to detest and fear law officers, and those feelings might remain deeply ingrained within her for years. Barney knew people who feared doctors, dentists, snakes, spiders, and even dogs. There never seemed to be any rational reason behind those phobias.

The individuals who suffered with them just went through life hoping they never ran into the person or thing that terrified them.

He loved his Taffy girl. He'd lived all his adult life searching for her without even realizing that he was looking—or what he was yearning for. Now, at long last, he'd found her, and for a short time they'd been so happy, the kind of happy that made marriages last forever. He didn't want to lose her. A part of him felt as if he might die if he did.

But he had to walk away. Even if he changed careers, Sarah might never trust him. In her young mind, the adults in her life had tried to trick her. And in a way, Barney knew he was guilty as charged. That little girl had been to hell and back. Under ideal circumstances, gaining her trust wouldn't be easy.

No question about it, he had to remove himself from the picture.

After a long Tuesday at her shop, Taffeta was in the kitchen—Barney's beautiful kitchen—when her cell phone rang. She knew Barney's ringtone and nearly tripped over her own feet racing to the table to answer the call before it went to voice mail.

"Barney? Oh, I'm so glad you called."

"Hey," was all he said in response.

"I miss you so much," she said. "How did your work-day go?"

"I didn't work today. Instead I drove to Erickson and totally destroyed any chance you may have had to rebuild a relationship with your daughter."

Taffeta sank onto a kitchen chair. "You what?"

"Cameron had this brilliant idea of how I could slowly get to know Sarah on neutral ground where she would feel safe and less likely to be afraid of me." He quickly told her about the parent-day lunches at the school and how he'd been invited to attend with Cameron. "Even though I wore civilian clothes, she took one look at me and went ballistic. She said her grandpa had tried to trick her. She said you had lied to her about me being out of your life, and she said for me to tell you never to call her again."

Taffeta pressed her free hand over her heart. "Oh God."

Barney's voice went thick. "I love you, honey. I'd never deliberately do anything to hurt you, but I've managed to anyway. I'm so sorry. We need to call it curtains, you and me. From this point forward, you have to focus on nothing but your daughter. It kills me to say it, but we're done."

Taffeta sensed that he was about to hang up. "Wait, Barney. Don't hang up. Please don't."

"Why? So you can blast me with your anger? Okay, fair enough. Let me have it, and then I'll hang up."

"I'm not angry." As Taffeta pushed out those words, she knew she truly meant them. "Not angry with you, anyway. Angry at Phillip, yes."

"Phillip didn't sneak off to see your child behind your back. That was me."

"But you had nothing but good intentions."

"The road to hell is paved with them, Taffy, and I've just reached that destination."

Her heart twisted, and tears filled her eyes. "You promised me forever at the chapel."

"And I didn't mean a word of it. Remember that, our fake wedding? Those vows meant nothing."

Taffeta realized that he was doing his damnedest to hurt her and make her hate him. Without even needing to ponder on it, she knew why. If she was hurt and hated him, she'd get over losing him faster. His honorable streak was rearing its ugly head again. Barney seldom allowed anything to be about him. He always wanted to look out for everyone else, especially those he loved. Maybe that was what made him such a great cop. He really cared about people.

"Bullshit," she shot back. "Maybe our vows meant nothing when we made them, but they mean something now. Do you really think I'll allow you to chicken out and run the first time we hit a rough spot, Barnabas Asher Sterling? Well, think again, because we're life partners, and we don't run to hide our heads in a hole when life throws us rotten hands of cards!"

She heard him swear under his breath. "I may have destroyed your chances to get your daughter back, Taffy. Do you *get* that?"

"Yes, I get it, and I'm also very upset about it. But it isn't your fault, I don't blame you at all, and I'm not going to let Phillip Gentry's sick lifestyle and total lack of responsibility toward my daughter destroy what you and I have." She took a deep breath. "I'm going to call Cameron and ask him to explain to Sarah that I've changed my mind about kicking you to the curb. It's absurd to allow an abused little girl to run our adult lives!"

He cursed again. Before he could say more, she broke in. "We're going to tackle this problem together,

Barney. I won't accept no for an answer because I need you beside me for strength. I need your arms around me when my heart is breaking. I need your advice when I'm not sure how the hell to deal with Sarah." She heard her voice going shriller with every word, but she couldn't stop herself. "I need you to hold me at night! I need to make love with you until all the pain goes away! I—need—my—husband! Do *you* get *that*?"

Long silence. For a full second, she thought that he'd hung up on her. Then he said, "Yes, I get that. I'll be there in thirty. But just for the record, I think you're out of your mind to choose me over your kid."

"I'm not choosing you over my kid!" Now she was mad. "I'm choosing to be with the one person in the world who stands beside me, the one person I can trust to advise me, the *only* person I can trust to lay down his life for me, and the only man I know who's wonderful enough to be a wonderful dad to my daughter! Without you, I may never get Sarah back. You make me a better person, a stronger person, and a wiser parent. Come home. That's an order. If you aren't here in thirty, I'll hunt you down and drag you home by your ear."

With a slam of her thumb on the END button, she hung up on him.

Chapter Twenty-three

Barney stared at his phone, not quite able to believe that the woman who'd just been screaming at him over the airwaves had been his sweet, tolerant wife. Then his mouth quirked in a suppressed grin. Maybe she was right about them solving this problem with Sarah together. His parents had faced many fierce storms during their marriage, nearly going bankrupt once, almost losing their Sarah to pneumonia once, and God knew what else. They'd always stood shoulder to shoulder to face problems, and they had always prevailed in the end, even if all they could do was pray together for God's help.

He grabbed his satchel and started stuffing his clothes and toiletries back into it. As he started down the exterior stairway that led from the loft, Ben emerged from his house and stood on the side porch, arms folded, feet spread, a bewildered expression moving over his sun-darkened face.

"You leaving already? I thought the honeymoon period in the landlord-tenant relationship would last for at least a week."

Barney stopped at the bottom of the steps to face his brother. "Taffy is screaming at me to come home. I've messed everything up, Ben, absolutely *everything*, but she still wants me there."

Ben lifted one hand to stroke his jaw, his hazel gaze moving slowly over Barney's face. "What the hell did you do?"

Barney glanced at his watch. "I don't have time to tell you. She gave me thirty minutes to get there before she comes to find me and drag me home by my ear."

Ben threw back his head and guffawed. When his mirth subsided, he shook his head. "Go, then. But I want to hear the details of this story when you've got a minute to fill me in."

Barney made good time getting home without taking the curves of the windy road on two wheels. When he pulled up in front of his house, Taffeta stepped out onto the porch. He cut the engine to stare at her for a moment, realizing that she had been the final, missing touch needed to complete his restoration of the old farm dwelling. *Taffy.* With her dark hair spilling over her shoulders, her lovely figure outlined against the smoke-blue siding, and the toe of one shoe tapping the plank veranda with impatience, she epitomized what every man with brains dreamed of when he pictured home, the place that would wrap around him like an embrace after a long day and warm him from the marrow of his bones out, the place where he could turn loose of all his worries, the place where he would always find love.

He climbed out of the truck. His wife bounded

down the steps to run toward him. He broke into a sprint and met her halfway.

"Don't you *ever* leave me again!" she cried as he caught her in his arms. "Never, never, *never.*"

"I won't." He pressed his face against her hair. "It was a stupid idea. It just—well, never mind. I won't do it again. We have to stand together and solve our problems."

"Yes." She breathed the word out on a sigh. "I can't face the hard things without you, Barney. And as much as I love her, Sarah is a tangled-up mess. It's going to take both of us to straighten her out."

He led her into the house, ignoring his urge to take her to the bedroom. Something far more important than his physical needs required attention and had to be discussed.

They sat at the table and talked about Sarah's fear of lawmen. Taffeta summed it up with "When a person is afraid of snakes, allowing him to avoid snakes will never cure his fear. By removing you from the picture, we were doing the same thing, Barney. We're essentially telling Sarah that she has good reasons to be afraid of you."

Barney mulled that over and nodded. "So, where do we go from here? Aside from going there together, what's your plan?"

She stretched her arm across the table to place her hand over his. "I think your idea to visit her school for parent-day lunches is fabulous."

"Actually it was Cameron's idea, not mine, and it backfired, big-time."

"But you saw the wisdom in it. I think you need to

accept the invitation to lecture at Sarah's school in the auditorium. It'll make a strong statement to Sarah. She'll see the principal, the teachers, and all the other students hanging on every word you say. She'll see their admiration and respect. Even if she doesn't immediately come around, she's a smart child, and I think she'll eventually come to realize that maybe her father had good reasons to be afraid of cops, but she has none."

Barney sighed. "I've never talked to a group of kids. Adults, no problem, but what'll I say to a slew of children?"

"Tell them about your job. Do you have any pictures of yourself while you were rescuing a cat?"

Barney tried to recall. "I made the front page of the newspaper a few times. They may have photos on file. Once, I had to go up in a boom lift to rescue a kitten at the top of a tree."

Taffeta's eyes shimmered with fascination. "What's a boom lift?"

"It's a box that can be raised up high. It's a piece of aerial equipment that will lift a man—well, I don't know—thirty to fifty feet up."

Her mouth quivered into a smile. "Tell me about it."

"Well, by the time we got a boom lift into Mrs. Dominique's backyard, which meant removing part of her privacy fence, a local reporter was on the scene. I was the officer on call, so it was my job to get into the box and go up. It was icy that night, and the fire department had its hands full with wrecks and couldn't be bothered with a cat. The sound of the equipment and the box itself terrified the kitten, and it kept climbing higher to get beyond my reach. To gain some height, I climbed up on the edge of the boom box and held on to the spindly treetop to keep my balance."

Taffeta's eyes went wide. "Dear God, at possibly fifty feet up? To save a kitten?"

Barney couldn't help grinning. "This was a very special kitten to Mrs. Dominique. I'm pretty sure she would have had a coronary if I had left Hercules up there to freeze to death—or she would have tried to climb the damned tree herself. So I stood on the edge of the box, holding on to spindly branches for balance. Did I mention that it was icy out?"

"Oh God, you fell."

He chuckled. "No, but I did slip off the boom box and wound up clinging for dear life to a wobbly treetop."

Taffeta's face paled.

"I'm agile. The operator moved the box closer to me, and I was able to swing a leg back into it. The kitten, terrified by all the swaying, decided I was a safer bet than the tree and leaped at me, digging all its claws into my shirt to hold on. I was a hero who wasn't. I'm pretty sure the newspaper office has heaps of pictures of that, not that any of them are very flattering to me as a deputy."

"You risked your life for a kitten. That's pretty awesome."

"That's my job, Taffy. I climb trees and risk breaking my neck to save kittens. One time some kids lifted the lid off a gutter drain, and a dog fell into the hole." He laughed at her horrified expression. "Lucky for me, the department pays for my dry-cleaning bills, because another deputy had to lower me into the manhole to get the dog and bring it back up. It had broken a leg, and before transporting it to the vet, we had to splint the bone. Not much excitement happens in Mystic Creek, so that made it into the newspaper, too."

"Barney, that's perfect. Kids will love to hear those stories and see pictures of things like that."

He shook his head. "They think cops or deputies are like the ones on TV, facing dangerous criminals who are shooting bullets at them. In larger cities, it can be like that on a bad shift. Other times, a cop deals with slightly less exciting stuff. But in Mystic Creek? My job gets so boring sometimes that I'm glad to get a kitten, cat, or dog call. It even relieves the boredom to play referee when two geriatric neighbors get into a dispute over whose garbage can is whose."

"Do you enjoy your job?" she asked. "I assumed that you do, but I never thought to ask."

"I love my job. Well, sometimes I get frustrated, but mostly I enjoy dealing with people and crazy situations. You remember Crystal, the natural redhead who runs Silver Beach Salon?"

"Yes."

"Well, just to show you how nutty my job is, one night she called in about a tarantula loose in her kitchen. Given that we don't have indigenous tarantulas here, I was dubious. When I got upstairs to her flat, she wouldn't get off the table to answer the door, so I had to shoulder my way in. There she stood on the kitchen table, clinging to her cell phone, wearing nothing but one of those slip things that you like to fantasy-dance in. She swore to me on her mother's grave—though I doubt that her mother is dead yet, because she isn't that old—that a huge tarantula had scurried across her kitchen floor and hidden under her stove.

"Now, *that* was a lot of work. I moved her stove. No tarantula. I moved her refrigerator. Before I finally found the spider, a little guy that resembled a daddy longlegs, I'd also moved every stick of furniture in her house."

"She's *gorgeous*," Taffeta whispered. "I mean, I bet she makes every man within a mile of her drool. Did she reward you with sex?"

Barney jerked back to the moment, studied his wife's sweet face, and realized she had the green monster called jealousy digging its claws into her heart. *Shit.* "Hell, no. Sex? With Crystal? She isn't my type."

"What is your type?"

Barney felt on solid ground again. "A man doesn't really know what his type is until he finds her. I searched and searched until I found *you*."

She tipped her head, gazing dubiously at him. "So you didn't try Crystal on for size?"

"Nope." Barney tried never to lie to this woman. She was the heart of his heart. "I tried a lot of women on for size, Taffy, but never Crystal. And just so you know, I never spent the night with any of those women. I engaged in intimacy, yes, always taking safety precautions, but as soon as it was over, I left. No morning wake-up coffee. Few second dates. I never found anyone who called to me the way that you did and still do. Please don't be jealous of Crystal. She's a nice lady, and she might be a great friend for you."

Taffeta finally smiled. "Okay, I felt a stab of jealousy for a second. Crystal is so—" She waved a hand. "Well, she's everything I'm not, beautiful, smart, friendly, self-confident, fashionable, and—"

"You're all of those things, too," Barney inserted. "But you have one other feature that really whammed me."

"What is it?"

Barney tried to describe it in his mind and came up blank. "I don't know. It's a special feeling I get when I look at you or see you smile or hear your voice. It's what made me fall in love with you."

She studied his face and nodded. "I understand. That's how I feel about you, too. So finish the spider story."

"Well, I found the spider and showed it to her on a paper towel. She screamed and almost fell off the table, telling me to smash it. I couldn't do it. It wasn't a dangerous spider, not even one that would bite and leave an itchy spot. So I opened one of her windows and set it outside on the sill."

"Was she happy with that resolution?"

"As long as the *tarantula* was out of her apartment, she cared about nothing else. Not even how much it might cost her to repair her door."

Taffeta sighed and rested her chin on her folded hands to gaze at him. "The kids will love to hear about your job, and I think the reality of being a small-town cop is a better slant for your presentation. Like you said, on TV, cops have shoot-outs with bad guys. The videos seldom feature lawmen like you, who know people personally and help them when they're scared, or angry, or in trouble. Children need to realize that most cops are their friends, people they can trust. Sarah needs to know that, and maybe, by listening to you talk about your job, she can learn that."

Barney sighed. "It's a long shot, sweetheart. That kid is terrified of me."

"All we can do is try, pray, and be patient." She toyed with the saltshaker. "Bottom line, we're husband and wife. We're committed to each other. It may take time for Sarah to accept that, but in the end, she has to, because you're a permanent fixture in my life."

"And if she never accepts it? She's your daughter. I know how much you love her. I'll never expect you to put me first, Taffy. It's your God-given duty to put her first, always."

"And I am." Taffeta straightened on the chair. "There are some bad cops out there. We hear about them all the time on the news. But they are the exception, not the rule. They make the news because they either did something bad or are accused of doing something bad. Officers like you don't make the news because good cops, the real heroes, are too mundane for the sensationalism required to keep news channel ratings high. What kind of life will Sarah have if she grows up and becomes a stripper or a drug user, or both? I need to get her on the right path, and I can only do that with your help. She needs a good mother and a good father—who just happens to be a law officer."

Barney loved her too much to argue the point, especially since he wasn't sure his leaving had been the right decision in the first place. "All right. We're in this together, for better or worse. Now will you dance for me naked?"

Taffeta burst out laughing. She was already pulling that pink top that he loved off over her head as she rose from the chair. Barney wanted her so badly that he scooped her up in his arms before she could ask him to turn on the music. The stereo wasn't part of his plan anyway. The tango he wanted to engage in would occur on his king-size bed.

Barney had no clue how to prepare photographs for a slide projector show. He kept saying he needed transparent photos. Taffeta, who had learned how to do slide shows in college, took it upon herself to drive around Mystic Creek, asking people whom Barney had helped if they had any photographs of the events. Amazingly Mrs. Dominique had taken heartwarming photos of Barney with the half-frozen kitten long after the news crew had left her property. Barney, wrapping the kitten in a heating pad. Barney, dripping thin, warm mush into the kitten's mouth. Barney, holding the kitten close to his neck with his chin tucked in to form a cocoon of warmth with his body heat to save the kitten.

When Taffeta looked at all the photographs that

she'd collected from people all over town, including the newspaper office, she came to understand things about Barney Sterling that she'd never imagined. He was a big, strapping man, yet he could gently lift a dog with a broken leg without being bitten. Even more important, if the dog had bitten him, she could tell by the determined expression on his face that he wouldn't have cared. He was a true hero, helping the injured, or needy, or frightened, and he didn't do it for the glory. She came to love him even more as she organized the pictures that showed so clearly what a dear person he truly was. She had not made a mistake by trusting in him.

On her laptop at work, she created the story of Barney's life as a deputy in Mystic Creek with pictures that she had scanned into her computer. She contacted the school to be sure they had the electronic equipment needed to project the slide show onto a large screen, and she was told that not only did the school have the equipment but an experienced operator would be on hand to play the show for the children.

She expected Barney's objections when she told him, "I think you need to prepare your opening speech and nothing more. I don't want you to see the images in the slide show beforehand, Barney. I want you to watch the photographs come up with the kids and be spontaneous with them. You're so warm and natural with everyone. If you go in prepared, you may sound like a recording."

He had just poured each of them a glass of wine

before dinner. Holding his glass halfway to his mouth, he gaped at her. "You want me to fly by the seat of my pants?"

Taffeta wanted to hug him. "That's how you do your job, by the seat of your pants. I want you to just talk to the children, as if they are your friends. I'll admit, I have a stake in this, but I don't think I'm making a bad call. I've listened to too many well-rehearsed lectures, and they are often boring. It'll be more fun for you and the kids if you're searching for me in the crowd, asking where I found that picture. And then you can tell the kids about it. They'll love it." She paused to swallow. "Sarah will love it."

The following Tuesday, Barney was as nervous as a long-tailed cat in a roomful of Irish line dancers. Taffeta accompanied him during the long drive, chattering excitedly about his presentation, saying the kids would absolutely love it. Barney hadn't seen any of the pictures that she'd scanned into her computer and organized into a slide show. He kept glancing with growing dread at her laptop case, which rested on the floorboard at her feet. Most of the time, he enjoyed being spontaneous, but he felt out of his element stepping onto a stage without any of his lines rehearsed. He could only hope that he didn't blow the whole thing.

Taffeta chose to sit with her ex-father-in-law in the front row. The school janitor had set up what looked like hundreds of chairs in divided rows where the audience could sit to watch Barney on the stage.

The podium, sporting a microphone, sat off to the right so that Barney could make eye contact with the kids as he talked and also see the huge projection screen.

Today he wore his uniform, and he was worried about that. The whole idea behind this performance was for him to win over Sarah, and she started to hyperventilate when she saw any man wearing a badge. Offstage, Barney watched through a crack in the back curtains as the auditorium began to fill with kids. The kindergartners came first and filled the front rows. He had eyes only for Sarah, who made a point of glaring at her grandfather and mother before choosing a chair as far away from them as she could possibly get. She clearly hadn't yet forgiven Cameron or her mom for what she believed had been a betrayal.

The principal, an attractive, well-dressed blonde in her forties, stepped up to the podium first to introduce Barney. "Today we have a very special guest who is going to speak to you about what it's like to be a law officer. His name is Deputy Barney Sterling. He is a peace officer in Mystic Creek, a small town on the other side of the Cascade Mountains. Over the last week, all of you have learned a lot about policemen. Today you are going to hear a real lawman speak to you about what his job is like." She stepped away from the stand and turned toward the curtains. "I proudly welcome Deputy Barney Sterling."

When the principal began to clap to invite Barney onto the stage, all the kids followed suit. Barney's knees turned to water. He'd never experienced stage fright. Normally he felt at ease when he spoke to large crowds. But he'd never had so much at stake all those other times.

He stepped out and somehow remembered to shake hands with the principal before he moved behind the podium. *Showtime.* Only his well-practiced, introductory speech fled from his mind. He drew a complete blank. All he could think of to say was "Hi. My name is Barney."

Great start, Sterling. He swallowed. His throat felt like sandpaper. Stickiness clung to his tongue. When he moved his lips, they stuck to his teeth. His hands trembled. Sweat beaded on his brow. He looked at Taffeta. She smiled and gave him a thumbs-up. That didn't help him out at all. He slid his gaze to Sarah, who sat in the second row, her thin arms hugging her waist, her expression contorting her sweet little face into a grimace of hatred. He locked gazes with her, and instead of trying to remember his speech, he said all the things that he'd wished a hundred times that he could tell this little girl.

"A lot of kids are afraid of cops. To me, being a cop who wants to help kids when they're in trouble, that's really sad. I know your parents have told you never to talk to strangers, and if you're smart, you never should. There are a lot of really nice people in our world, but there are also a few bad ones, and terrible things can happen to children who trust them.

"As a deputy, I see all the reports that come in about missing children, and there are so many across our country that it breaks my heart. Most of the time, those kids have been kidnapped, and a huge percentage of them are never found. When I see pictures of those missing kids, I wonder if they were afraid to approach a cop to ask for help right before they were kidnapped.

"Most cops are on the streets to help people. Yes, we arrest people sometimes for committing crimes. Yes, we stop cars and give the drivers tickets for speeding. A lot of kids hear their parents complaining about some cop who stopped them and fined them a lot of money just for the heck of it. But the truth is, when people drive too fast or run red lights, they are putting other people in danger. Your principal introduced me as a peace officer. I like to think that I'm more a safety officer."

Sarah glared at him. Barney held her burning gaze.

"On television, you'll see movies about cops in big cities. They shoot guns at criminals. They slam offenders against walls. They act all mean and tough. But most real cops never have to use their guns. Where I live, the town is pretty small. I know most of the people in Mystic Creek, and they are my friends. When they call for help, they usually need me to do little things for them. I've never had to fire my gun. I've never had to hit someone, not even if they tried to hit me first. Instead I use my training to block the blow, and then I get that person under control, using moves that will cause no physical injury.

"But mostly, my job is pretty boring. I drive the roads to make sure someone hasn't driven off into a ditch. I look at the houses I pass to make sure the people inside are safe." Barney smiled at Sarah. "And I eat a lot of really fabulous donuts."

Barney cleared his throat and directed his gaze at Taffeta. "My wife has prepared a slide show for you. I haven't seen any of the pictures, so I'll be winging it as I tell you about each of them. Be prepared. Being a cop isn't as exciting as you probably think."

Taffeta rose from her seat and went backstage. An instant later, a picture of Barney in civilian clothes popped up on the huge screen. At first, he couldn't remember what he'd been doing. He was bent over at the corner of a sidewalk, and hidden behind his legs was an old lady, half sitting up with her feet spread and the tops of her thigh-high support hose showing.

"Ah. That lady's name is Esther. She lives alone in a tiny, old house. She's very old and she fell down one afternoon as she started to cross the street in town. I was off duty, so I wasn't in uniform, but as a deputy, I'm always on duty to help people." Barney glanced out at the kids. "How many of you are always on duty to help people if they fall down?" Countless hands shot up. Barney grinned and nodded. "So you see? All of us are safety officers, even if we aren't cops. The biggest difference between all of you and me is that I get paid to help people. So I spend all my shifts looking for trouble and stop to help if someone needs me."

The next photo came up. Again, Barney wore jeans, riding boots, and a ball cap. He was crouched in front of Percy Holden, one of the town drunks, an older man who dressed like a homeless person and spent far too many nights passed out on a sidewalk in town.

"To protect his privacy, I can't tell you this man's name. He is one of the town drunks in Mystic Creek. I probably shouldn't call him a drunk. It's more appropriate to say that he has a drinking problem or is an alcoholic." Barney looked out at the kids again. "How many of you know people who drink too much alcohol?"

Way too many hands went up to suit Barney. He hoped those kids weren't dealing with alcohol abuse at home. But what really broke his heart was to see Sarah raise her hand.

Chapter Twenty-four

It took Barney a moment to collect himself and remember what he'd been saying. *Sarah*. He knew for a fact that the child had been exposed to far more than mere alcohol abuse, and it sickened him to think that she thought such behaviors were normal.

He glanced at the projector to recall the story he'd been telling. "Anyway, this old fellow spends all his money on booze, and that morning, he asked me for a few dollars to get some food." Barney shrugged. "You can see in that picture that I'm handing him money. I knew he'd probably spend it on liquor instead of nourishment. But when people are in a jam, I feel an obligation to help if I can. What that man did with the money was up to him. At least I knew that I'd given it to him in case he was really hungry."

One little boy in the audience shouted, "My dad buys homeless people food and takes it to 'em. That way he knows the money goes for food and nothing else."

A little girl cried, "My mommy says that we always

need to ask ourselves, 'What would Jesus do?' So she always gives people at least a dollar!"

Barney remembered that this was a Christian school where the children were taught faith values. He also realized that Taffeta had been right. These kids weren't bored. They couldn't wait for the next picture to come up.

When it came, Barney grinned. It was a photo of him, clinging to the spindly top of a pine tree with a huge blue boom box high in the air behind him.

"Uh-oh. I'm not at my best in this picture," he told the kids.

A boy yelled, "How'd you get so high in the tree?"

Barney explained how an equipment operator had lifted him up into the air in the big box. "A little kitten had climbed nearly to the top of the tree. It was my job to go up there to save it for her owner, Mrs. Dominique, who is an old lady and lives all alone. The kitten was all the family she had, and she loved it very much. You can't really see the kitten yet." He winked at Sarah. "But I have a feeling you'll see her in the next few shots."

The next photo came up, showing Barney with one leg hooked over the edge of the boom box. "It was really icy that night, and the sound of the equipment and seeing me in that big boom box frightened the kitten, making her climb even higher to get beyond my reach. I climbed onto the edge of the box to gain height, holding on to branches to keep my balance. But my boots slipped. In this picture, I'm trying very hard to get back inside the box so I won't fall."

The next photograph showed Barney safely back inside the box. The children clapped and cheered.

Barney said, "I don't remember losing my hat. The branches of the tree must have knocked it off. At this point, I still couldn't reach that poor kitten. She was wet and shivering. I was afraid she would get so cold that she might die."

The picture changed. The newspaper photographer had caught the kitten in midair as she jumped from the tree toward Barney. "In this picture, the kitten must have decided the loud noise and big box were a lot less scary than being trapped in the tree was. She jumped at me without warning."

The next shot showed Barney with a bedraggled kitten clinging to his shirt. "She was so scared when she hit my chest that she dug her claws clear through my shirt."

"Were you mad at her?" a little girl asked.

"Heck, no. I was so glad to have her safe that I barely felt the scratches."

In the next slide, Barney held on to the box with one hand and held the kitten safely against him with the cup of his palm and fingers. "The operator is taking us down now. Mrs. Dominique, the kitten's owner, was crying because she was so happy that her kitten was safe."

The next few slides showed the old woman holding the wet kitten to her tear-streaked cheek. Then there were pictures that Mrs. Dominique must have taken in the privacy of her home of Barney trying to warm the kitten in a heating pad and then dribbling runny mush into her tiny mouth.

He explained, "I had to get the kitten's body temperature up quickly. Kittens are mostly fur and bone, without much fat to protect them from the cold. I thought the warm food would help bring her temp up from the inside out."

"Did you save her, Mr. Barney?" a girl asked.

"Well, she lived, but I can't take all the credit. Mrs. Dominique said a lot of prayers that the kitten would be okay."

The next picture was of Barney standing several feet below a street manhole in knee-deep water. He had a dog tucked under one arm and a rope tied around his waist, which he gripped with his free hand.

"I think all of you have seen those big, round grates on streets in your town. They are called manholes. The lids can be lifted with a crowbar, and some kids had uncovered this manhole. We'll never know the names of the kids who did it, but showing you this picture is a good lesson to all of you. A dog was running along the street and didn't notice that the hole wasn't covered. He fell through it and broke his front leg. In this picture, I'm waiting for two other deputies to pull me and the dog up out of the hole."

By this time, Barney had set aside his concerns about Sarah and had slipped into lawman mode. He was here to inform all of these kids, not only one little girl. And dammit, what he had to say was important. Maybe his job wasn't as adventurous as it was portrayed in films, but what he did, day to day, served a good purpose.

The next image on the screen showed Barney, his

uniform smeared with muck, crouching over the injured dog with the two other deputies, as he tried to splint the dog's fractured leg.

"We had to transport this poor dog to the vet for emergency treatment. We're trying to stabilize the broken bone so sharp edges of the ulna wouldn't cut him up inside or sever a main artery. He was a really nice dog. I know it had to hurt really bad when I straightened his leg to splint it, but he never even growled or offered to bite me."

In the next frame, Barney was carrying the dog toward a county truck for transport. "We made him a soft bed with our deputy jackets on the backseat of the truck. We got him safely to the vet's office, and he went home the next day with his leg in a cast. I still see him sometimes when I'm driving the roads of Mystic Creek. One time, I stopped just to say hi and see if he remembered me. I think he did, because he whined and licked my hand."

More photographs flashed on the screen. It was the longest hour of Barney's life. When the slide show was over, the children were allowed to ask him questions. Barney patiently replied to each query, acutely aware that Sarah hadn't raised her hand and didn't appear to have any intention of doing so. *Okay.* He'd given this his best shot.

Then, from the corner of his eye, he saw her shyly push up her arm. *Awesome.* He nodded toward her. "Yes, Sarah? What is your question?"

"What do you do if you find a little girl alone in her daddy's car late at night?"

Barney chose his words carefully. "Well, it is dangerous for young children to be left alone in cars whether it's daytime or nighttime, so it's my job to make sure the child is safe, and that would be my first concern. How I did that would depend upon the situation."

"Do you take the daddy away in handcuffs to throw him in jail and leave the little girl to be cold, all alone, and hungry until her daddy can come back?"

Careful, he warned himself. "No law officer would *ever* leave the little girl alone in the car. I would call in for another deputy to come help me handle the situation. When possible, a female officer is sent to the scene." He winked at Sarah. "Little kids seem to trust lady cops more than they do men cops. I'm not sure why that is, because I'm a good guy and I really like kids. But a child can't know that about me until she gets to know me.

"If available, a lady deputy would approach the car, talk to the little girl until she felt unafraid, and then would take her to a safe place where she would be warm, get food, and wait for a responsible adult in her family to come pick her up. Most kids ask for hot cocoa. Do you like hot cocoa?"

Sarah nodded. "With marshmallows."

"Of course, marshmallows. All cocoa needs marshmallows to be really good. So the little girl would be safe and happy until her mommy or grandma or grandpa came to take her home."

"What would happen to the daddy?"

Barney really, *really* wished that Sarah hadn't

asked that question. "Well, it is against the law for an adult to leave a young child alone in a car. The police didn't make that law. Very smart people at a higher level of law enforcement made that a law. Lots of car windows roll up and down by pushing a button. Too many children have been badly hurt by poking their head out a window opening when the window is sliding up. Kids also tend to play with the gadgets inside cars, so bad things can happen. The car can roll, sometimes out into traffic. Or, if it's cold outside, the child may freeze to death. Or if it's hot weather, a child can suffocate.

"So there are many very good reasons that it is against the law to leave a young child unattended inside a car. A parent—or any adult, for that matter—who leaves a young child alone in a car is cited by an officer for what we call Child Endangerment and sometimes also Neglect. That means that an adult who deliberately left a little girl unattended in a car did a very bad thing. If it's a first offense, meaning that the daddy has never been caught doing it before, he'll probably receive only a warning. The second time he's caught, he'll receive a fine, which means he'll have to pay money to the court in that area. If it's the third time, his punishment may be harsher. He might be fined even more money and be put in jail for a short period of time."

Sarah pinned her gaze on Barney, her brown eyes wide with wariness. Though Barney yearned to talk with her longer, he hadn't come here for a one-on-one, so he pointed to the next child with a question.

* * *

Barney chose to sit alone at a picnic table for lunch outdoors rather than with Taffeta and Cameron. He hoped that Sarah would join her mother for lunch, and he felt fairly sure his presence at Taffeta's table would prevent the child from approaching. Cameron had brought sandwiches, sliced fruit, and juice in brown sacks today because Sarah's small pail couldn't hold enough food for three adults and a child.

Barney, keeping his eye on Taffeta's table and hoping to see Sarah join her mother, had just removed his food from the bag and was about to unwrap his sandwich when he glimpsed Sarah from the corner of his eye. He froze and turned to look at her. She stood about three feet from his table.

"Well, hello, Sarah." Barney didn't have to feign the tone of surprise in his voice. He'd never expected Sarah to approach him. "Would you like to share my lunch?"

She glanced at the bagged food. "I have my own. My grandpa has it."

"Oh, that's right." Barney opened the zipper closure of his sandwich bag. "Well, I hope you enjoy eating with your mom and grandpa."

She watched him take a bite of his PB and J. "I could bring my sack to your table and eat with you, I guess."

Barney quickly swallowed. "I'd like that. It's kind of lonesome sitting by myself."

"Why aren't you sitting with my mommy, then?"

Honesty was always the best policy. "I know you

don't like me," he replied. "I was afraid you wouldn't sit with your mommy if I was eating with her."

"I like you better now." She tugged on her red T-shirt. "Not a whole lot better, not enough to sit next to you. But I could sit far away." She pointed to the farthest edge of the opposite bench. "Right there, maybe."

Barney smiled. "I'd like that."

Sarah scampered away to collect her lunch bag from her grandfather. When she returned, she perched on the other bench, as far away from Barney as she could get without falling off onto the ground. He noticed Taffeta gazing in their direction. He wouldn't allow himself to look her way.

Sarah took a bite of an orange slice. "How often do you save tiny kittens?"

"Now and then. I'm called to get grown-up cats out of trees a lot more often than kittens."

"Do you like climbing trees to save them?"

Barney grinned. "I used to love climbing trees. Now that I'm older, not so much, so I only do it when I have to. And not all the things I save are kittens and cats."

"Nope. I know you saved a dog." She drew half of her sandwich from the unzipped plastic bag. "You were brave to go in that deep hole. It was dark and scary down there."

"The other deputies kept their flashlight beams on me, so I wasn't really brave. I had plenty of light. I just didn't like standing in all that icky water."

"Why was it icky?"

Barney sighed. "Well, I'm not really sure how our city sanitation works in Mystic Creek, but judging from the stink, I think there was some sewer water in the mix."

"What is sewer water?"

"I don't want to ruin your lunch by telling you."

"You won't ruin my lunch."

"Well, when you flush your toilets at home, the water and everything else in the bowl goes into sewer lines."

Sarah wrinkled her nose. "Yuck. Was there a lot of shit down there?"

Barney decided then and there that he wasn't going to pull his punches with this child. "That's a word I will try never to say in your presence, Sarah, and I would appreciate it if you wouldn't say it around me."

"Shit, you mean?"

Barney nodded.

He half expected her to tell him to stuff it and leave, but instead she shrugged. "My grandpa and grandma don't like that word, either. I'm trying to talk nicer, but sometimes I forget and say bad words anyway."

"Well, I'm glad you're trying so hard. Is it okay if I remind you when you forget?"

"I guess. I won't be talking to you very much, though."

Roll with it. "That's true," he agreed.

Cheek bulging with a bite of sandwich, Sarah asked, "Do you ever save other kinds of animals?"

Barney took a sip of juice to clear the food from his mouth. "Well, sure. Horses get loose a lot, sometimes cows. When I'm out cruising, I can't just leave them on the roads to cause car accidents. So I find out who they belong to, call the owner, and help get them herded back into their fences."

"Aren't you scared?"

"No. I have horses and a cow. I'm used to them."

"What other things do you save?"

Barney sorely wished that he could save one very cute little girl who was wrapping his heart around her little finger. "Have you ever seen baby chickens?"

She nodded and frowned with a distant expression on her small face. "Mommy took me to a store once that had baby chicks in a big, long bucket."

"A trough," Barney clarified. "At feed stores where they sell chicks, they keep the babies warm in deep troughs with a heat lamp. When people buy chicks, they bring them home and do something similar, but they don't always have a box or trough that's deep enough, and sometimes the baby chicks escape."

Sarah had stopped eating, her gaze fixed on him. "Uh-oh."

"Uh-oh is right," Barney agreed. "One night I got a call from a lady who was keeping baby chicks in her bathtub. One of them got loose and climbed into the cupboard under her vanity."

"What's a vanity?"

"In bathrooms, a vanity is a cabinet, normally with a sink, that has a mirror or medicine cabinet above it. This lady's vanity had a sink, which meant that she had water pipes inside her vanity cabinet. Plumbers cut holes in the wall to fit pipes through for sinks, and they often leave a larger hole than the diameter of the pipe. The lady's escaped chick somehow climbed through the hole around the pipe and ended up inside the wall.

"The lady didn't know what to do. She could hear the chick peeping inside her wall, but she had no way to get the baby back out. So she called the sheriff's department, and I just happened to be on duty."

"Did you save the baby chick?"

"I did. But I had to listen with my ear against the Sheetrock to figure out where the chick was, and then I had to saw a great big hole in the lady's wall to reach inside and catch the chick. I put it back in the tub with all the other chicks and told the lady she needed a big trough and that she should put wire over the top of it to keep her chicks from escaping again."

"Was she mad about the hole in her wall?"

Barney laughed. "Well, fixing holes in walls doesn't fall under my job description, so she had to hire someone to come out and do the repairs. I'm sure she wasn't happy when she got the bill."

Sarah wiped her mouth with a section of paper towel that had been in her sack. "Well, what the hell did she expect? You had to make a big hole to reach in and get the baby."

"There's another word you should try not to say," Barney observed. "Hell, I mean. Have you heard me say it?"

"No, but I've heard lots of other people say it."

"Well, I'm sorry to hear that, because five-year-old girls shouldn't use that word."

Sarah shrugged. "I know. Grammy says she'll never wash my mouth out with soap, but sometimes she wants to." She cocked her head to give Barney a questioning look. "If I come to see my mommy at her house someday, maybe I can go with you sometime to rescue a kitten."

For that privilege, Barney would be willing to deposit a kitten at the top of a tree so Sarah could watch him risk breaking his neck to save it. "It's a date, little lady. I'd love to have company on a kitten-rescue mission."

Sarah put her half-eaten lunch back in the bag. "I'm going to sit with my mommy and grandpa for a while. I like you better than I did, but I still don't like you lots."

Barney was glad to have made some progress, even if only a little. "Do you think you could come to like me better if I came for lunch on Tuesdays? You could still sit far away from me. All we'd do is talk."

Sarah considered him with a solemn gaze. "What if I don't always want to sit with you?"

"I'll understand. You don't have to sit with me. I'd just like to be available to visit with you in case you'd like to sit with me."

"Why?"

Barney replied, "I love your mommy. Your mommy loves you. I think it would make her very happy if you and I could be friends. Maybe not best friends, or anything like that. Just friend friends."

Sarah mulled that over. "Okay. You can come on Tuesdays." She raised a tiny finger. "But if you're an asshole even one single time, I'll never sit with you again."

Barney watched his stepdaughter flounce away, swinging her lunch sack at her side. "Oh, Taffy," he whispered, "you've got your work cut out for you with that little twerp, and so have I."

Chapter Twenty-five

After the lecture in the auditorium, Barney made the long drive to and from Erickson every Tuesday. Taffeta wished she could accompany him, but she drove over by herself for visitations with her daughter in order to allow Barney and Sarah to grow acquainted on their own terms. Sometimes Barney came home looking deflated because Sarah had chosen to sit with her teacher to eat lunch. Other times, he walked into the house beaming from ear to ear and regaled Taffeta with accounts of his talks with Sarah.

She still cussed like a sailor, he told Taffeta one night, but the nose stud had finally vanished. Another night, he related that Sarah hadn't uttered one bad word during the entire meal. Another night he walked in with tears in his eyes. As Taffeta waited for him to speak, believing that something horrible had happened, she watched his Adam's apple bob as he struggled to talk.

His mouth contorted. His strong features twisted.

The tears he battled not to shed spilled over his lower lashes onto his sun-weathered cheeks. "Today she asked me if we could be best friends," he pushed out. And then he grabbed Taffeta into his arms, bent his head to press his face against her hair, and started to sob. "Jesus, Taffy, those w-were the most beau-beautiful words I e-ever heard. Sh-she wants m-me to be h-her best fr-friend. Do you underst-stand how m-much that m-means to me?"

One of the most beautiful gifts in Taffeta's life was to know just exactly how much Sarah's offer of friendship, the best-friend kind, mattered to this big, skilled law officer who could take down a grown man lickety-split and pin him to the floor. That kind of war was a matter of course for him in his line of work. Overcoming the hatred and fear of a little girl was, in his opinion, the greatest victory of his life.

Knowing how much Barney loved her—knowing that somehow that love he felt had extended to her daughter—meant everything to Taffeta. She wept with him. They sobbed, clenched in each other's embrace, and swayed like two intertwined saplings being buffeted by a strong wind.

When both of them finally recovered from the storm of emotion, Barney cradled Taffeta in his arms, still swaying slightly, and said, "What does being best friends with a little girl mean? Will I have to wear pink ribbons in my hair and nail polish with polka dots?"

Taffeta started to laugh, and then so did he. They finally collapsed onto chairs at the table and held their sides until their mirth subsided. Barney held up a big, broad hand. "I think clear polish might work. I could live with that."

Taffeta's mouth started to tremble. "You will not be required to wear nail polish of any kind, Barney. You're a man, and being a strong male role model in her life is the most important thing that she needs. No ribbons, no sparkles. She only needs for you to be *you*. She'll love you just for who you are. Trust me on this."

He held her gaze with tears still swimming in his eyes. "I'll even wear lipstick for her, I swear to God. You cannot imagine how it felt when she looked up at me with those huge brown eyes and asked if I'd be her best friend. Not just friend friends, but best friends. She stressed the difference."

During one of her visits to the Gentry home in Erickson, Taffeta was told by Cameron that he had petitioned the court right after her first visit to grant her unsupervised visitations with her daughter. He cautioned her not to expect a swift ruling. The month of May slipped away into June, and June sped by until it was July. Taffeta worked in her shop every day and went home to be with her wonderful husband at night, except for when he pulled a double shift so he could always have Tuesdays off. It seemed to her that she would never have her daughter for a visitation in her own home, let alone regain custody. That saddened her.

But life went on, demanding that she run her business, pay the bills, shop for groceries, clean the house, and cook. Barney always helped with the household chores, just as she went out to help him with the chickens and livestock. Sometimes depression threatened to bog her down, but she always managed to shrug it off. She had so many blessings to be thankful for, the most wonderful one being Barney. He loved her so much. Being with him was such a gift. Whenever she saw him, her heart blossomed with joy, and judging from the way he looked at her, he felt the same way.

It was good. No, it was wonderful.

But until she got her daughter back, it would never be perfect.

Her visits with Sarah were fun, and Taffeta looked forward to them. But there were also hurdles to jump whenever she kept company with her daughter. Sarah seldom used bad language now, but she still slipped sometimes and shocked Taffeta with a filthy word. Sarah also still grew sassy with adults and didn't show them proper respect. Slowly Taffeta assumed more and more parental responsibility, calling Sarah onto the carpet for a scold to correct her behavior instead of leaving the entire burden of discipline on Cameron's shoulders. Grace, weakened and sick from chemo, no longer had the strength to deal with Sarah at all, and the friend who came daily to be a grandmother substitute felt uncomfortable about correcting Sarah's manners.

Taffeta had come to accept that she wouldn't soon be awarded custody. Before that could happen, the appellate court had to overturn her child abuse conviction, and at that level in the judicial hierarchy, things seemed to move slowly. When—and if—Taffeta was pronounced innocent, she could file for a hearing with the court in Erickson to regain custody.

One evening, she told Barney, "I'm afraid Sarah will be eighteen and graduating from high school before I can have her come live with me."

Barney hugged her close. "I know all this waiting is very hard. I also know being patient has to be really difficult. Maybe it will be easier when the Erickson court finally grants you the right to have unsupervised visitations with Sarah. At least then, you'll be able to have her here, in our home environment."

Taffeta yearned with all her heart for that day to arrive, but after waiting for so long, she feared that the Erickson court might never grant her that privilege.

The following week, Taffeta was behind the counter at her shop, making a list of supplements that she needed to order, when Barney walked in with Sarah in tow.

"Surprise!" he said. "Cameron pulled strings to hurry things up, got you unsupervised visitation, and came to the department with a very special present. He wanted me to deliver her here so we can celebrate as a family."

"Hi, Mommy!" Sarah, wearing a blaze of bright yellow, dashed behind the counter. "I get to stay with you for a whole *week*! Even longer if I want! Grammy says my grandpa will come and get me if I get homesick, but I don't think I will."

Taffeta dropped to her knees and wrapped both arms around her little girl. This had to be a dream. In a moment, she'd wake up.

"How come you are crying?" Sarah asked. "Aren't you glad I'm here?"

Taffeta gave a wet laugh. "I'm crying because I'm so happy! You're the very best present anyone ever gave me!"

Over the top of the child's head, Barney said, "Cameron says that she's missing vacation Bible school, but that's just fine because she attends a private Christian school nine months a year. When he got the word that you'd been granted unsupervised visitation, he packed her a suitcase, yanked her out of Bible school, and drove her here. Until regular school reconvenes, you can have her for as long as you like as long as she doesn't get homesick."

A lump had taken up residence at the base of Taffeta's throat, making it difficult for her to speak. She silently scolded herself for acting like a ninny, collected her composure, and hurriedly prepared to close her shop for the day, maybe for the entire week. She could scarcely believe Grace and Cameron's generosity and made a mental note to call them later to say thank you.

But for now she could focus on only Sarah.

As she collected her purse and fished for her car keys, Barney said, "No way am I letting you drive home, honey. You're shaking like a leaf."

Taffeta realized that she actually was trembling from head to toe. "You're right. I probably shouldn't drive."

"Besides," Barney said, tousling Sarah's dark curls, "how often do I get to chauffeur two gorgeous ladies?"

Sarah giggled. "I'm not a lady yet."

"Oh well, a beautiful lady and a gorgeous little girl, then."

Once outside, Barney took Sarah's hand as they walked along the sidewalk to his truck. Taffeta noticed that he shortened his steps to accommodate the child's shorter stride. She bit back a smile, thinking what a wonderful father he would be.

Instead of heading straight home, Barney treated them to lunch at Dizzy's Roundtable Restaurant. Sarah was fascinated by the revolving dining area, which Taffeta knew had been Barney's intent.

"Do people really get dizzy on this damned thing?" Sarah asked him.

"Watch your language, missy," Barney said firmly. "As for your question, I don't know. But I don't think so. It goes too slow. Do you feel dizzy?"

Sarah's curls bounced as she shook her head. "Nope. I only feel hungry."

Once they got to Barney's house, Sarah was equally fascinated by Barney's farm animals. She chortled over the chickens and tried to get the rooster to crow. Barney let her help feed the horses and Mary Lou. Sarah noticed the cow's huge stomach and asked why it was so fat.

"We think she's about to have a baby calf," Barney said.

"And it's in her tummy?" Sarah asked.

Barney sent Taffeta a look that begged her to take over.

Taffeta bit back a grin. "All female mammals carry their babies inside them," Taffeta told her daughter.

"They have a special place called a womb where the babies are safe, warm, and fed until they grow big enough to be born."

As children will, Sarah accepted that explanation without further comment and moved on to ask questions about the horses. Why did they have elbows on their back legs and not on their front ones? Why were their manes and tales so long, and the rest of their hair was short? How could they eat cookies that were so hard that they cracked people's teeth?

The child scampered around the farm with what seemed like boundless energy and protested when Taffeta said it was time to go inside and make dinner.

"But this is so fun, and I'm not hungry!"

Taffeta was sorely tempted to give in and spoil her daughter rotten. But in the end, she knew that would be a disservice to Sarah. "You can help me and Barney cook," she offered instead.

Sarah peered up at Barney as the three of them walked to the house. "Do you and my mommy live together? My mommy said once that you moved out."

"We decided that it was a mistake for me to move out," Barney replied.

"How come?"

"We're married, and we love each other very much. Married people are supposed to be together. We missed each other too much to stay apart."

Sarah peered up at Taffeta. "You said I was most important! So how come did you let him come back when I still didn't like him?"

Taffeta chose her words carefully. "Right after your father took you back to your grandparents, you were doing and saying things that little girls shouldn't. I needed Barney's advice on how to be the best mommy I can be, and since he's legally your stepfather, I also wanted his help to raise you. So he and I talked, and we decided that we needed to offer you a *real* family, with both a daddy and a mommy."

Taffeta expected Sarah to protest or feel that she'd been hoodwinked. Instead she gave Barney an inquisitive look. "Does that mean you're my new daddy?"

Barney shrugged. "Do you need a new daddy?"

Sarah nodded. "The one I've got doesn't like me."

"Well, then, I'll apply for the job," Barney said. "I like you. I like you a lot."

Sarah bounced ahead of them up the porch steps. "Do you have a dog?"

"No," Barney confessed.

Sarah struggled to open the door. Barney lent a hand, and the three of them spilled into the kitchen.

"How come don't you have a dog?" Sarah demanded.

Barney leaned down to her eye level. "I was waiting for you to help me pick one out."

Sarah clapped her hands and jumped in place. "Yay! I want a great big one with long hair!"

"Will you be happy with a puppy that will grow to be a big dog with long hair?" Barney asked.

"I'll be very happy with a puppy," Sarah assured him. "We'll have to clean up after it and be very 'sponsible, though. My grandpa says puppies pee and poop on the floor. That's how come he's making me wait until I'm older to get a dog."

Barney grinned. "Well, you strike me as being a

pretty responsible little girl, and your mommy and I can help you train our puppy to go potty outside."

Sarah bounced up and down again as if she had springs on the soles of her shoes.

After a simple dinner of macaroni and cheese with a side of broccoli, Taffeta gave Sarah a bath and helped her put on the pajamas that Cameron had put in the child's suitcase. For Taffeta, fulfilling the role of mother again felt incredible. God had sent her a miracle. *No,* she corrected herself. *God sent me two miracles, my daughter and the most wonderful man on earth.* She cuddled with Sarah in the guest room bed to tell her stories. It was sheer heaven to be with her daughter again. Sarah began to yawn and blink her heavy eyelids. Taffeta found herself stifling yawns as well and wondered if it was true that yawning was contagious.

"I love you, Mommy," Sarah murmured. "I 'member you. When I was little, you put ribbons in my hair."

Tears swam in Taffeta's eyes. Another miracle. Her daughter remembered some of the special times they'd shared. Maybe she would never recall everything, but they had a starting point upon which to build a relationship.

When Barney stepped to the guest room doorway to check on his wife and daughter—yes, he meant to take Sarah's invitation to be her new daddy very seriously— he found the two of them wound around each other like yarn in a skein. Both of them were sound asleep. He rested his shoulder against the doorframe, smiling to himself.

Even in her sleep, Taffeta had her arms locked around her little girl. She apparently feared that the child might be snatched away from her again while she drifted in dreamland. *Well, old man, it looks like you'll be sleeping alone tonight.* Barney didn't mind. He was elated for Taffeta and would happily forgo having a bed partner for the entire week, if that was how it went. *All for a good cause.* It wasn't every day that a mother and child were reunited after nearly two years.

Sighing, he walked through the house to turn off the lights, locked all the exterior doors to keep his wife feeling safe, and then made his way to his room. Stripping down to only his boxers, he climbed into bed, rolling onto his back with his arms folded under his head. He was still grinning when his eyes fell closed.

Sometime later, Barney awakened to the light touch of feminine hands on his belly. He rolled to gather his wife into his arms.

"You don't need to worry about me, honey. I'm fine. Go back and enjoy being with Sarah."

Her response was a deep kiss that would have blown his socks off if he had been wearing any. He felt tears on her cheeks and cupped her face between his hands.

"What's wrong, sweetheart?"

"Nothing," she whispered. "Everything is absolutely right. That's why I'm crying."

Barney kissed away the wet trails on her skin. "Well, that's just plain silly."

"No. You made this possible, Barney. If not for you, Sarah wouldn't be here tonight. I never would have had the courage to face Cameron and Grace without you beside me."

"I'll be beside you as long as I have breath left in my body. I love you, Taffy. With everything I've got, I love you."

As they made love, being careful not to make too much noise, Taffeta asked, "Are you still interested in giving Sarah a baby brother or sister?"

Barney whispered, "Damn straight. Are we on?"

"Absolutely. If we make a baby together tonight, it'll be born next spring, probably in mid-April."

"No protection, then. Watch out for swimmers because here they come."

She sighed as he buried the length of himself into her warm, moist depths. "Oh, Barney, I love you so much. If I live to be a hundred, I don't think I'll ever find the words to tell you just how much."

"You'll never love me more than I love you," he whispered.

He quickened the tempo, and neither of them spoke again as they sank together into a current of pleasure and gratified needs. Just before he went over the edge with her, Barney fleetingly thought that they didn't need to express their feelings for each other with words.

Not when they had *this*.

Epilogue

Taffeta detested courtrooms. The faint scents of disinfectant and furniture wax always floated on the air, and the people who sat in the spectator area behind her fidgeted, coughed, and whispered, creating a constant drone of noise. This was the day that she'd dreamed of for nearly three years and would hopefully end with her being granted sole custody of her daughter. Only what if it didn't turn out that way? As dearly as she loved Barney and as happy as he'd made her, she knew he had no magic wand to make all her wishes come true.

A dull pain throbbed in her temple. Her lower back ached. Her ankles, formerly a normal size, now felt like melons ballooning over the tops of her shoes. She sighed and placed a protective hand over her swollen middle. The baby kicked just then, bumping some part of his body against her cupped palm. Barney said their boy was fated to be a soccer champion— or maybe a famous football player. Taffeta didn't care

what sport the child wanted to play; she just wished
he'd stop practicing until after he was born.

The judge entered the room just then, and the
court deputy boomed, "All rise."

Easy for you to say, buster, Taffeta thought crossly
as she struggled up from her chair. *You aren't almost
nine months along.* Her distended belly bumped the
edge of the table, and she knew Barney was grinning
even though he sat out of her sight on the other side of
the railing behind her. He loved everything about her
pregnancy, even his late-night drives into Mystic Creek
for the crazy foods she craved. Taffeta felt like a fat
water buffalo and was pretty sure she looked like one,
but Barney insisted that she'd never been more beautiful. The thought made her smile slightly as she watched
the judge, an older man with gray hair and wire-frame
glasses, take his seat at the bench.

Before examining the documents awaiting his
perusal, he scanned the packed room. Taffeta knew
what caused his puzzled frown. Barney's whole family, Phillip's parents, and a remarkable percentage of
the population of Mystic Creek were present. This
evening, Barney's parents, Kate and Jeremiah, were
throwing a huge celebration party in their backyard.
Other men were bringing their barbecues to help
feed the multitudes, and their wives were bringing
side dishes. Taffeta only hoped that a ruling against
her didn't rain on their parade.

To the deputy, the judge muttered, "I thought this
was a routine custody hearing, Rip. Do I have my
wires crossed?"

The officer turned toward the bench. "There are just a lot of family and friends present, Your Honor."

The judge harrumphed, snapped his gaze back to the spectator gallery, and said, "Please be seated."

Taffeta could no longer sit; she plopped. *I'm not really nervous,* she assured herself. *Nothing can go wrong.* Months ago, her child abuse conviction had been overturned by the Oregon Court of Appeals. Phillip had been arrested last month for perjury and drug dealing, and a week ago he had signed away all his rights as Sarah's father in exchange for a million dollars from his dad to cover his forthcoming legal expenses. There was no way that the judge would deny Taffeta custody of her daughter today. As Barney kept saying, this hearing was a mere formality and the outcome was a slam dunk.

Even so, Taffeta's pulse raced. Unlike Barney, she'd once been victimized by the justice system. Granted, Phillip had orchestrated that by lying through his teeth, but it was still difficult for Taffeta to trust that she would receive fair treatment.

The judge leafed through the paperwork. A buzzing sound filled Taffeta's ears, and little spots danced in front of her eyes. For an awful moment, she thought she might faint. Instead she missed most of what the judge said, and her first indication that she'd been granted custody was when Barney came forward to curl an arm around her shoulders, bent low, and said, "Congratulations, Taffy. Didn't I tell you it'd be a slam dunk?"

He helped her stand up and led her to the public seating area to be hugged and congratulated by Kate and Jeremiah, Jeb and Amanda, Ben, Jonas, and both of his sisters. Townspeople hung back to give the Sterling family time to rejoice. Then a sea of smiling faces moved past Taffeta, and she shook countless hands. She felt like a bride in a receiving line.

The Sterlings left immediately to make the long drive back home to prepare for the bonfire party and barbecue. They planned three large fires to ward off the chill of April's evening air, and everyone would have to wear coats, but there would be a celebration no matter what the weather was like. People in Mystic Creek were accustomed to braving the elements.

Weary beyond description, Taffeta leaned against Barney for support as she greeted even more people, many who had become good friends, others who were still total strangers. Barney knew everyone by name, of course.

When the courtroom finally emptied, Taffeta blearily focused on two individuals who had never left their seats in the very back row, Grace and Cameron Gentry. They beamed happy smiles at her, but Taffeta wondered if their expressions concealed pain. Unless Phillip's expensive defense attorney pulled off the impossible, Grace and Cameron's only son would soon be doing prison time. In addition to that, they had essentially just lost their granddaughter.

"I need to speak with them," Taffeta said to Barney.

Lending her the support of his strong arm, Barney guided her into the row just ahead of her ex-parents-in-law. Taffeta tried to lower herself gracefully onto the bench seat, but her tailbone panged as her posterior connected with the wood anyway. She hooked her arm over the back, bringing up one knee to brace herself as she met Grace's and Cameron's gazes.

"You look worse than I feel," Grace said with a weak laugh. She had undergone triple-bypass surgery two weeks earlier, and according to what she'd told Taffeta over the phone, she still wasn't allowed to do much of anything. "And I feel pretty awful."

"I'm exhausted," Taffeta confessed. "Mostly from nerves, I think. I was so afraid that the judge would deem me unfit to be Sarah's mother."

"Not a chance," Cameron said. "I would have raised hell."

"And been charged with contempt of court," Grace reminded him.

Barney sat beside Taffeta, also turned sideways on the bench. "I would have gone to jail with you, Cameron," he said with a laugh.

Taffeta loved Phillip's parents. When Phillip had married her, she was terrified of them. What if they didn't like her? What if they felt that she was unworthy to be Phillip's wife? But never once had these people treated her with anything but kindness.

"I want you to know that I'll accommodate you in every way I can so that you can maintain a strong relationship with Sarah," Taffeta said to them. "Barney feels the same way I do about that. You are her grandparents, and she should spend lots of time with you."

Grace smiled through sudden tears. "We both know that you'll make sure we see a lot of Sarah. And we're looking forward to that. Cameron is dying to take her to Disneyland. But I'm afraid that will have to wait until midsummer. I should be recovered enough by then to keep up with her again."

It was now mid-April, a little over a year since Taffeta's shadow dance had brought Barney to knock on her apartment door. "That isn't so long to wait," Taffeta mused. "After the baby is born, maybe we can come back to Erickson for a visit."

"What are you going to name him?" Cameron asked.

Barney injected, "I'm leaving it up to Taffy, my only stipulation being that he won't be named after me."

Taffeta felt less weary now that she was starting to relax, and she gave a genuine laugh. "I think Barnabas Asher Sterling is a fabulous name."

Her husband gave her a long look. *"No,"* he said. "I wouldn't curse a kid with that handle for a million dollars." He grinned at Cameron. "I'd love to chat longer, but she's tired, and I need to get her home. By the time we run by your place to collect our daughter and attend the celebration barbecue at my parents' house, it'll be late, and she'll be dead on her feet. And," he added, "she's close to our due date, so getting her back home to be near her doctor is important."

Cameron arched an eyebrow. "I understand that you're going to adopt Sarah," he said to Barney.

"God willing, yes. Taffy and I both think she should bear the same surname as all her siblings as she's growing up. I hope you don't mind that she'll no longer go by Gentry."

With a shake of his head, Cameron replied, "She'll always be our granddaughter, no matter what name she goes by. And before we know it, she'll get married and might change it anyway."

"Not until she's thirty," Barney informed him. "I don't plan to let her date until she's twenty-nine."

Grace chortled and then flattened her hand over her recently opened breastbone, grimacing at the pain. "Oh my. You caught me by surprise with that one."

Just then, Taffeta caught movement from the corner of her eye and turned to see Tessa, the Gentrys' housekeeper, enter the courtroom. Sarah stood beside her, grinning broadly.

"Hi, Mommy! Hi, Daddy! Tessa brought me here so I can go straight home with you!"

Cameron winked at Taffeta. "Her things are packed and in the trunk of our car. We thought it would be easier on you to take her home from here."

Taffeta reached over the seat to squeeze Cameron's hand. "You're the best, Dad."

Cameron blushed but smiled. "Music to my ears. I've lost a son, but apparently I've gained a daughter."

Barney pushed erect and met Taffeta's gaze. "I'll go out with Tessa to get all Sarah's stuff into my truck. Until I get back, you can chat with Cameron and Grace."

"Can I go help?" Sarah asked.

"Sure." Barney exited the row and took hold of Sarah's small hand. "You have to stand on the sidewalk while I carry stuff, though. No running out into the street."

Smiling, Taffeta drew her gaze back to Cameron and Grace. "I grew up in foster homes. I've never clapped eyes on my mother or my father. I know that both of you have endured a great deal of pain over Phillip's behavior, and I'll understand if you're not quite ready for this, but I'd love to be granted permission to call you Mom and Dad. I'd also like to think of you as my parents. As Sarah and our other children grow up, that will make things more normal for all of them. They'll have grandparents on Barney's side and grandparents on my side." Taffeta paused, trying to read their expressions. "That doesn't mean that Barney or I will expect you to treat our other kids as if they're your actual grandchildren. He and I talked about it, and we'll explain to our younger kids that Sarah is your real granddaughter, and they're only grandchildren by marriage."

Grace closed her eyes, and tears streamed down her cheeks. Cameron looked as if he was about to pucker up and cry, too. "Sweetheart, the instant Phillip brought you home, you became the daughter Grace and I were never able to have. We're so sorry now that we turned our backs on you during your trial, or that we ever believed, even for a short time, that you had harmed Sarah." He swallowed, making his larynx bob. "We didn't expect your forgiveness.

And we certainly never expected you to still love us. Having you as our daughter now—well, we'd both be honored. Right, Grace?"

Grace lifted her tear-soaked lashes. "Absolutely right. But I have to correct you on one point, Taffeta. Cameron and I would never dream of treating your other children differently than we do Sarah! No matter how many kids you have, we'll never take her somewhere and leave them behind. *Never.* We'll love them all and feel privileged to have the chance!"

"We wanted a half dozen kids," Cameron said. "But after Grace had Phillip, she couldn't conceive again. We considered adoption, but—" He sighed and lifted his hands. "Phillip was a handful, even when he was little. Difficult beyond belief. We decided it wouldn't be fair to bring other children into the mix."

Taffeta wanted to lean over the back of the bench to hug both of them, but her belly was too large. "I love you guys, and I think all my children are going to be very lucky to have you in their lives. You need to come for the Fourth of July. Barney's family does it up big. And you absolutely *can't* miss Christmas! Sarah will love having you there, and little Barney will love it, too. He'll be old enough to interact with you a little by then. There is nothing sweeter than a baby's smile."

Grace drew her eyebrows together in a frown. "You aren't *really* going to name that baby Barnabas, are you? What if he grows up and goes into local law enforcement like his father?"

Taffeta laughed. "If I named this child Barnabas, my husband would never forgive me. They do have a biblical theme for names in his family, though. Maybe I'll name this little guy Moses."

Caught off guard, Cameron snorted with laughter. Grace only smiled. "I sincerely hope you're joking. Whether you're my daughter or not, I'll help Barney torture you if you name my grandson Moses."

Taffeta feigned surprise. "You don't *like* that name? I think it's absolutely grand." Then she relented. "It may be the wrong century for it, though. That said, old-fashioned names are in right now, and I think Moses is pretty cute."

Just then Barney and Sarah returned. "I've got all her stuff loaded into the truck. We need to make tracks for home and get your legs elevated for a while before the party. Your ankles are twice their normal size."

Taffeta struggled to her feet, made her way to the center aisle, and met Grace and Cameron there for farewell hugs. Sarah gently embraced her grandmother, careful not to hurt her, but she latched onto Cameron's neck and refused to let go for a few seconds.

"We'll see you again very soon," Cameron assured the little girl. "And we'll see you on video calls often. Those are always fun."

Sarah finally let go of her grandfather. "I'll show you our new puppy. Now that I'm going to live with Mommy, my new daddy says we're going to the Mystic Creek No-Kill Shelter to pick out a dog. He'll be little at first, but someday he'll be great big with long hair."

Moments later, Taffeta and Barney left the courthouse, each of them holding Sarah's hand. April had gifted them with sunshine instead of showers, and to Taffeta, it was like stepping outside into a shimmer of gold as they walked down the steps.

"Ready to go home?" Barney asked Taffeta over the top of Sarah's head. "I've been told that mysterious things can happen there. People who stand along Mystic Creek are destined to fall in love and live happily ever after."

Taffeta smiled, but she refused to laugh. She now believed in the legend of Mystic Creek. Barney had confessed that he did as well.

"I love you, Taffy," Barney said.

"I love you, too, Barney."

"I love you, Mommy," Sarah chimed in, following it with "I love you, Daddy!"

"I love you, too, Sarah," Taffeta replied. "More than you'll ever know."

Barney reached down with his free hand to tickle Sarah's ribs. "I love you, Sarah," he said. "I always wanted my own little girl, and now I've got you."

As he stood tall again, he said, "We sound like the Waltons saying good night to each other. Did you ever watch those reruns?"

Taffeta grinned. "I adored them."

"We're going to be like that," Barney said. "A large family in a house that's filled to the brim with love."

Taffeta nodded. No matter what challenges might lie ahead of them, she would love Barney Sterling with every breath she took, and she knew that he would love her just as deeply.

She was ready to go *home*. Home to Mystic Creek where miracles happened. Today was the first day of the rest of their lives, and she meant to enjoy every second of it.

Don't miss the first book in bestselling author
Catherine Anderson's Mystic Creek series,

SILVER THAW

Available now!
Read on for a preview.

Jeb Sterling swore under his breath as he trudged across
his steer pasture, snatching up litter. Small pieces of pink
paper decorated the grass, looking like overblown clover
blossoms. They were everywhere. Why had someone chosen to toss trash from a car window in front of *his* place?
Jeb took pride in his property and spent hours each summer at the business end of a Weedwacker. His fencing,
made of metal pipe that he'd welded together, always
sported immaculate white paint. The landscaping he'd
done around his house could be featured in *Better Homes
and Gardens*. He did *not* appreciate some jerk using his
land as a garbage dump.

Stalking around the enclosure, Jeb grumbled aloud as
he picked up the pink slips and crushed them in one
hand. As he captured the sixth before it fluttered away,
his anger changed to bewilderment. *What the hell?* Somebody had written a note on this one. Smoothing the
damp, wrinkled strip, Jeb read aloud, "'I wonder how

much money I need to buy a decent used car. I don't care if it looks awful as long as it runs. Walking back and forth to work in this cold weather is the pits.'"

Frowning, Jeb collected more pink strips from the pasture, then found a few more on his front lawn, and another in his driveway. He took the lot inside and sat at his custom-made dining room table, which he'd designed to seat twelve, twenty with inserts, similar to tables once common among large farm families.

Pushing a hank of blondish brown hair off his forehead, he smoothed the notes flat. *I wish I could find secondhand winter boots for my little girl. I can't afford new ones, and my boss says we'll soon have deep snow.* Jeb shook his head. Winter boots for a kid didn't cost all that much. Or did they? Thirty years old and determined to stop counting birthdays, Jeb remained a bachelor and had no kids. He was not an expert on the cost of children's apparel. Maybe one of his younger brothers or sisters would get married and start reproducing soon. Then Jeb's parents might stop bugging him about settling down and providing them with a grandchild.

Judging by the handwriting, delicate and flowing, Jeb decided the notes had to be from a woman. Most guys he knew did a print-write thing.

The next note made him grin. *I wish I could meet a man as kind and wonderful as the hero in one of the romances I love to read, someone who'd be a fabulous father to my little girl and make both of us feel safe.* Jeb guessed this lady liked to read sappy love stories. His smile faded. Why did this woman and her child feel unsafe? And, hello, was he being targeted? He found it difficult to believe these messages had landed on his property by accident. Maybe this gal had seen him working outside and decided he looked like promising husband material.

No way, sister. Jeb wasn't that desperate. His mother kept telling him the lady of his dreams would cross paths with him right when he least expected it. But so far that hadn't happened, and Jeb was coming to accept that it probably never would.

Just then his dog farted. Jeb groaned and glanced over his shoulder. "Damn, Bozo, turn the air blue, why don't you?"

A brindle Fila Brasileiro mastiff, Bozo had a dark brown muzzle and ears, with a gold body that looked as if it had been splattered with different shades of mud. The dog woke from his nap, yawned, and then shook his head, sending strings of drool flying from his flapping jowls to decorate everything within a three-foot radius. When Bozo was younger, Jeb had raced around to clean up the drool immediately, but then he'd read online that once dried, it could be wiped easily from surfaces or vacuumed up.

"If I ever meet the right woman, she'll take one look at you and run screaming in the other direction. You know that, right?"

Bozo growled—his way of talking. Grinning, Jeb resumed reading the notes. *My only weapons are a cast-iron skillet and a butcher knife hidden under my mattress so my daughter won't find it. If my husband tracks us down, I pray that God will give me the strength to knock him out with the frying pan. I will die before I let him hurt my baby again.*

Bozo let loose with another fart. Flatulence was a trait of the mastiff that Jeb had overlooked when deciding on a breed. Waving a hand in front of his face, he wished he could lend this poor lady his dog, not to torture her with the less-than-aromatic delights, but for security. With Bozo on guard, she wouldn't need a heavy skillet for protection.

Jeb turned his attention to the next note. *Damn,* he thought. *This could become addictive.* He felt as if he were peering into someone's heart. This lady clearly had an abusive bastard for a husband, was as close to flat broke as a person could get, and, to top it all off, had a little girl she could barely support.

Jeb wondered once again if she was targeting his land with her notes. He thought of his cantankerous old neighbor across the road. Tony Bradley, who farmed full-time for a living, had a heart of gold that he tried hard to hide. *Time to take a stroll.* If Tony had found pink slips of paper on his land, then Jeb could relax. Jeb didn't like the idea that some desperate female had set her sights on him. Even if she had no car, she could walk by his land if she lived nearby.

Bozo went with Jeb to Tony's place. Mastiffs needed plenty of exercise, at least a thirty-minute walk each day, which Bozo got by following Jeb around as he tended to his livestock. Extra walking never hurt—although he tried to make sure his mastiff seldom ran. That was bad for the joints and hips of a dog that weighed two hundred and thirty pounds; also, mastiffs could easily become overheated, even in cold weather.

With the crops all harvested, old Tony was in "winter" mode, when he repaired his equipment, fed his animals, watched TV, and worked crossword puzzles. Jeb found him tinkering with his tractor, an ancient John Deere that had lost nearly all its identifying green and yellow paint and was probably worth more as an antique than Tony's whole farm was.

"Hey, Tony!" Jeb called out. "Got tractor problems?"

The old man resembled a stout stump with a two-day growth of whiskers and was dressed in tan Carhartt outerwear smudged with grease. He cast a cranky glare at Jeb. "Betsy never has problems. Kind of like a woman, son. All she needs is a little lovin' to keep her motor tuned."

Jeb drew to a stop near a front tire that was taller than his hip. Bozo chose that moment to shake his head and send drool flying. Just then, Mike, Tony's red tri Australian shepherd, bounded out from under the tractor. The two canines sauntered off to take turns pissing on every bush in sight.

"What brings you over?" Tony wiped his hands on a rag so greasy that it only smeared more oil onto his fingers. "If you haven't found a new cleaning lady and you're wantin' to hire my wife, you're out of luck. Mike sheds like a son bitch and I'm sloppy, so we keep Myrna pretty busy."

Jeb hadn't started looking for a new cleaning person since his last one had quit. "I'm between jobs right now." Jeb saw no need to elaborate. He and Tony had been neighbors long enough that the old man understood his on-and-off-again work schedule. Jeb had just finished a furniture order from a man who'd wanted a special Christmas gift for his wife, but otherwise it had been a slow season. "I figure I can muck out the house myself for a while. When the building market picks back up in February or March, I'll send out some feelers." He winked. "And I promise not to steal Myrna."

Tony, a tobacco chewer, leaned sideways to spit. "Good thing. She's got a hip goin' out on her, I'm afraid. Hurtin' her off and on."

Jeb hated to hear that. Myrna was a sweet gal and only sixty-three, a bit young to need a hip replacement. "I hope she gets to feeling better soon. A couple of months back, my mom hobbled around from pain in her hip." Kate Sterling's version of hobbling was to limp at a fast pace. "She was about to see Doc Hamilton when the discomfort went away."

"I see his partner, Dr. Payne." Tony chuckled. "Signed on with him out of curiosity. If I was a young doctor with a last name that sounds like *pain*, I'd get it changed."

"He may be young, but I've heard he's good," Jeb observed. "Maybe you should take Myrna to see him."

"Damned woman won't go. She's too stubborn by half, my Myrna."

Not sure what to say, Jeb whacked the frozen ground with the heel of his boot. Tony worshiped his wife and didn't share personal stuff unless he was truly troubled.

"So what brings you over?" Tony asked.

Jeb fished a handful of pink strips from his coat pocket and extended the crinkled lump. "Just wondering if you've found any of these on your land."

Tony squinted. "Son bitch. You gettin' those, too? Got my Myrna in a tailspin, I'll tell ya. She drives me half nuts tryin' to figure out who's writin' 'em. Has me lickin' my finger to test the wind direction."

Jeb stuffed the notes back in his pocket. "I didn't consider the possibility that they floated into my place on the wind. How many have you and Myrna found?"

"A good twenty." Tony spat again, narrowly missing

Bozo, who'd come to lie at Jeb's feet. "I got my theories on it, if you don't mind me sharin'. The writer is a female, and she's lonely. Has no friends. Works as a cook somewhere and makes barely enough to scrape by. Also yearnin' to find herself a man. In one message, she wished for Prince Charming to carry her and her child away on a white steed to live happily ever after."

"Really." Jeb recalled the note about the woman's wish to find a hero. "She must be having a hard time of it."

"And she's probably uglier than a fence post if she's that desperate."

Jeb thought about it and decided Tony might be right. A beautiful woman didn't normally have to search for a man to rescue her. Men stood in line to apply for the job. Not that Jeb cared if this gal was homely. She clearly needed a friend. He tried and failed to imagine having nobody to talk to. He'd grown up in Mystic Creek and couldn't go into town without seeing someone he knew. He also had heaps of family here.

"Well," he said, "I'm glad to hear the notes aren't landing only on my property."

Tony laughed. "You're safe. I haven't asked our neighbors if they've found any, but you can rest assured, as many as we've gotten, you aren't bein' singled out."

Jeb studied the clouds. "Looks like snow tonight."

Tony nodded. "Myrna says there's a bastard storm front moving toward us."

Jeb ended the conversation the way he and Tony always did, by walking away. He and Tony said only what needed to be said. Polite farewells weren't part of their repertoire.